The Penguin Book

of the

International

Short Story

The Penguin Book *of the* International Short Story

Edited by

RABIH ALAMEDDINE
and JOHN FREEMAN

PENGUIN PRESS | NEW YORK | 2026

PENGUIN PRESS
An imprint of Penguin Random House LLC
1745 Broadway, New York, NY 10019
penguinrandomhouse.com

The editors wish to thank Desi Isaacson for his help with this book.

Designed by Amanda Dewey

LIBRARY OF CONGRESS CATALOGING-IN-PUBLICATION DATA
Names: Alameddine, Rabih, editor | Freeman, John, 1974– editor.
Title: The Penguin book of the international short story / edited by Rabih Alameddine and John Freeman.
Description: New York : Penguin Press, [2026]
Identifiers: LCCN 2025032723 (print) | LCCN 2025032724 (ebook) | ISBN 9780593834138 (hardcover) | ISBN 9780593834145 (ebook)
Subjects: LCSH: Short stories
Classification: LCC PN6120.2 .P46 2026 (print) | LCC PN6120.2 (ebook)
LC record available at https://lccn.loc.gov/2025032723
LC ebook record available at https://lccn.loc.gov/2025032724

Printed in the United States of America
1st Printing

The authorized representative in the EU for product safety and compliance is Penguin Random House Ireland, Morrison Chambers, 32 Nassau Street, Dublin D02 YH68, Ireland, https://eu-contact.penguin.ie.

The stars had only one task: they taught me how to read.
They taught me I had a language in heaven
and another language on earth.

—Mahmoud Darwish, from "Poetic Regulations,"
translated by Amira El-Zein

CONTENTS

INTRODUCTION

Rabih Alameddine and John Freeman

As Americans, we tend to think that how we see the world is how everybody else does. We believe the United States, like the pre-Copernican earth, is the center of the universe and everything revolves around us. Do writers from other countries have different concerns? What can stories from around the world tell us about who we are, about humanity, about the world in general? While researching stories for this book, we were astounded that there were many amazing stories that we had never heard of. We realized that for a long time it was the norm for 75 percent of the stories in international anthologies to be American or English. If the book needs to be more "internationalized," the editors add Irish stories. If the book needs to feel even more foreign, an Australian story. To make sure that the book is seen as completely international, perhaps a sprinkling of the ubiquitously anthologized Borges, Kafka, and García Márquez (three of our favorite writers, but come on!). Not too many, mind you, otherwise the anthology might turn out to be too salty.

In this volume, we are hoping to expand this restrictive paradigm just a tad.

We set conditions for the number of stories we looked at, as well as what we ended up selecting. From the beginning, we imagined this book being a selection of wonderful stories and not an exhaustive account or textbook of the international short story. Just as important, we wanted to look at contemporary stories, a glance at what is happening around this world of ours. We decided to look at writers who are still living. Of course, since neither of us likes rules, not even ours, we broke it once (for Pedro Lemebel's story). Sadly, Zoë Wicomb died in the final months of our preparing this book. Her story was the first we chose, and not for a second would we drop it on a technicality. And the last condition: Imitating Phileas Fogg, we decided to travel the globe in eighty days—thirty-four stories, in this case—and not necessarily stop in every port.

In order to travel the world well, one needs great guides. Ours were the amazing translators working today, who pointed us in so many directions. We are lucky to be living at a time when the art of translation has improved drastically and the stories appear seamless. Without the ear and craft of these immensely talented readers, none of us could hear this music from elsewhere.

It should be mentioned that we also wished to enlarge a sense of how the story delivers pleasure—that complex form of contentment which only a short story can provide. This readerly joy can derive from narrative, from page-turning energy; it can also come from setting, that sense of place, or familiarity, or unfamiliarity made real. A good story can do much to situate us in the world. Joy can also come from the orality of a story's language, or a rhythm to its prose, a sense of mischief, or a spike of absurdity, a well-made character portrait.

There are so many ways a story can be great. We wanted, in making this book, to reflect as many ways as we could.

Long before it was printed in magazines or literary journals, the short story was essentially a tale told briefly. In its earliest days, it came from fables and oral stories, and as we read around the world, we found that this very old form has begun to return to its original roots.

Fables, tall tales, strange happenings are all back at the center of the international short story; they seem to us to be where the most interesting writing is happening. Very few of the best stories we came across could be called realistic in the conventional sense. Perhaps this is because in the past few decades, an agreed-upon sense of what is real has broken down. Writers in the past fifty years have become better and better at structuring extraordinary loops within small spaces. Many of the stories in this book achieve these effects by straddling the genre boundary between flash fiction, prose poem, vignette, and feuilleton. We loved being free to enter and exit stories with a sense of arrival or departure, rather than beginning and end. We found we turned to definitions of what "real" is, what "society" is, that were unstable, often thrillingly so. That sense of engagement, the rapture it can produce, is best described by the word *love*—that feeling you have upon encountering a thing made so uniquely, only that writer could have produced it.

Both of us read in search of that feeling. We also read stories because we are restless, life is finite, and to read a tale is still the swiftest, cheapest, most extravagantly immersive form of travel. In a world of ever-stricter boundaries, this freedom of movement—of becoming or transforming or simply disappearing—that any great short story promises is second to none. These are radical freedoms, and they are under the greatest threat we have witnessed in our lifetimes. Perhaps here is the core of their subversiveness: Great stories are inherently anti-nationalist. They do not give us a glimpse of another national character; they give us the opportunity to leave our own behind. For their ability to do that, among many other things, we love them.

Of course, we chose these stories because we loved them. We would die on their hills. Yet we also liked quite a few others, which we ended up not selecting because they did not fit the collection, be it in length or the fact that they did not fit with the collection as a whole, with the anthology as a book. Just as an example, we could have picked two or three stories each from Samanta Schweblin and Mariana Enriquez, or from Zoë Wicomb or from Can Xue. Their stories are that good. But doing so would have been a mistake, because we were also interested in what we call the tuning-fork theory. An anthology has to work as a book, where reading one story will hopefully make another shine. It has to layer discrete, exquisite stories into a whole that resonates and sings.

We hope you can sing with us.

The Penguin Book

of the

International

Short Story

Super-Frog Saves Tokyo

Haruki Murakami

Translated from Japanese by Jay Rubin

Katagiri found a giant frog waiting for him in his apartment. It was powerfully built, standing over six feet tall on its hind legs. A skinny little man no more than five-foot-three, Katagiri was overwhelmed by the frog's imposing bulk.

"Call me 'Frog,'" said the frog in a clear, strong voice.

Katagiri stood rooted in the doorway, unable to speak.

"Don't be afraid, I'm not here to hurt you. Just come in and close the door. Please."

Briefcase in his right hand, grocery bag with fresh vegetables and canned salmon cradled in his left arm, Katagiri didn't dare move.

"Please, Mr. Katagiri, hurry and close the door, and take off your shoes."

The sound of his own name helped Katagiri snap out of it. He closed the door as ordered, set the grocery bag on the raised wooden floor, pinned the briefcase under one arm, and unlaced his shoes. Frog gestured for him to take a seat at the kitchen table, which he did.

"I must apologize, Mr. Katagiri, for having barged in while you were out," Frog said. "I knew it would be a shock for you to find me here. But I had no choice. How about a cup of tea? I thought you would be coming home soon, so I boiled some water."

Katagiri still had his briefcase jammed under his arm. Somebody's playing a joke on me, he thought. Somebody's rigged himself up in this huge frog costume just to have fun with me. But he knew, as he watched Frog pour boiling water into the teapot, humming all the while, that these had to be the limbs and movements of a real frog. Frog set a cup of green tea in front of Katagiri, and poured another one for himself.

Sipping his tea, Frog asked, "Calming down?"

But still Katagiri could not speak.

"I know I should have made an appointment to visit you, Mr. Katagiri. I am fully aware of the proprieties. Anyone would be shocked to find a big frog waiting for him at home. But an urgent matter brings me here. Please forgive me."

"Urgent matter?" Katagiri managed to produce words at last.

"Yes, indeed," Frog said. "Why else would I take the liberty of barging into a person's home? Such discourtesy is not my customary style."

"Does this 'matter' have something to do with me?"

"Yes and no," said Frog with a tilt of the head. "No and yes."

I've got to get a grip on myself, thought Katagiri. "Do you mind if I smoke?"

"Not at all, not at all," Frog said with a smile. "It's your home. You don't have to ask my permission. Smoke and drink as much as you like. I myself am not a smoker, but I can hardly impose my distaste for tobacco on others in their own homes."

Katagiri pulled a pack of cigarettes from his coat pocket and struck a match. He saw his hand trembling as he lit up. Seated opposite him, Frog seemed to be studying his every movement.

"You don't happen to be connected with some kind of *gang* by any chance?" Katagiri found the courage to ask.

"Ha ha ha ha ha ha! What a wonderful sense of humor you have, Mr. Katagiri!" he said, slapping his webbed hand against his thigh. "There may be a shortage of skilled labor, but what gang is going to hire a frog to do their dirty work? They'd be made a laughingstock."

"Well, if you're here to negotiate a repayment, you're wasting your time. I have no authority to make such decisions. Only my superiors can do that. I just follow orders. I can't do a thing for you."

"Please, Mr. Katagiri," Frog said, raising one webbed finger. "I have not come here on such petty business. I am fully aware that you are assistant chief of the Lending Division of the Shinjuku branch of the Tokyo Security Trust Bank. But my visit has nothing to do with the repayment of loans. I have come here to save Tokyo from destruction."

Katagiri scanned the room for a hidden TV camera in case he was being made the butt of some huge, terrible joke. But there was no camera. It was a small apartment. There was no place for anyone to hide.

"No," Frog said, "we are the only ones here. I know you are thinking that I must be mad, or that you are having some kind of dream, but I am not crazy and you are not dreaming. This is absolutely, positively serious."

"To tell you the truth, Mr. Frog—"

"Please," Frog said, raising one finger again. "Call me 'Frog.'"

"To tell you the truth, Frog," Katagiri said, "I can't quite understand what is going on here. It's not that I don't trust you, but I don't seem to be able to grasp the situation exactly. Do you mind if I ask you a question or two?"

"Not at all, not at all," Frog said. "Mutual understanding is of critical importance. There are those who say that 'understanding' is merely the sum total of our misunderstandings, and while I do find this view interesting in its own way, I am afraid that we have no time to spare on pleasant digressions. The best thing would be for us to achieve mutual understanding via the shortest possible route. Therefore, by all means, ask as many questions as you wish."

"Now, you *are* a real frog, am I right?"

"Yes, of course, as you can see. A real frog is exactly what I am. A product neither of metaphor nor allusion nor deconstruction nor sampling nor any other such complex process, I am a genuine frog. Shall I croak for you?"

Frog tilted back his head and flexed the muscles of his huge throat. *Ribit! Ri-i-i-bit! Ribit-ribit-ribit! Ribit! Ribit! Ri-i-i-bit!* His gigantic croaks rattled the pictures hanging on the walls.

"Fine, I see, I see!" Katagiri said, worried about the thin walls of the cheap apartment house in which he lived. "That's great. You are, without question, a real frog."

"One might also say that I am the sum total of all frogs. Nonetheless, this does nothing to change the fact that I am a frog. Anyone claiming that I am not a frog would be a dirty liar. I would smash such a person to bits!"

Katagiri nodded. Hoping to calm himself, he picked up his cup and swallowed a mouthful of tea. "You said before that you have come here to save Tokyo from destruction?"

"That is what I said."

"What kind of destruction?"

"Earthquake," Frog said with the utmost gravity.

Mouth dropping open, Katagiri looked at Frog. And Frog, saying nothing, looked at Katagiri. They went on staring at each other like this for some time. Next it was Frog's turn to open his mouth.

"A very, very big earthquake. It is set to strike Tokyo at eight-thirty a.m. on February 18. Three days from now. A much bigger earthquake than the one that struck Kobe last month. The number of dead from such a quake would probably exceed a hundred and fifty thousand—mostly from accidents involving the commuter system: derailments, falling vehicles, crashes, the collapse of elevated expressways and rail lines, the crushing of subways, the explosion of tanker trucks. Buildings will be transformed into piles of rubble, their inhabitants crushed to death. Fires everywhere, the road system in a state of collapse, ambulances and fire trucks useless, people just lying there, dying. A hundred and fifty thousand of them! Pure hell. People will be made to realize what a fragile condition the intensive collectivity known as 'city' really is." Frog said this with a gentle shake of the head. "The epicenter will be close to the Shinjuku ward office."

"Close to the Shinjuku ward office?"

"To be precise, it will hit directly beneath the Shinjuku branch of the Tokyo Security Trust Bank."

A heavy silence followed.

"And you," Katagiri said, "are planning to stop this earthquake?"

"Exactly," Frog said, nodding. "That is exactly what I propose to do. You and I will go underground beneath the Shinjuku branch of the Tokyo Security Trust Bank to do mortal combat with Worm."

AS A MEMBER OF the Trust Bank Lending Division, Katagiri had fought his way through many a battle. He had weathered sixteen years of daily combat since the day he graduated from the university and joined the bank's staff. He was, in a word, a collection officer—a post that carried little popularity. Everyone in his division preferred to make loans, especially at the time of the bubble. They had so much money in those days that almost any likely piece of collateral—be it land or stock—was enough to convince loan officers to give away whatever they were asked for, the bigger the loan the better their reputations in the company. Some loans, though, never made it back to the bank: they got "stuck to the bottom of the pan." It was Katagiri's job to take care of those. And when the bubble burst, the work piled on. First stock prices fell, and then land values, and collateral lost all significance. "Get out there," his boss commanded him, "and squeeze whatever you can out of them."

The Kabukicho neighborhood of Shinjuku was a labyrinth of violence: old-time gangsters, Korean mobsters, Chinese mafia, guns and drugs, money flowing beneath the surface from one murky den to another, people vanishing every now and then like a puff of smoke. Plunging into Kabukicho to collect a bad debt, Katagiri had been surrounded more than once by mobsters threatening to kill him, but he had never been frightened. What good would it have done them to kill one man running around for the bank? They could stab him if they wanted to. They could beat him up. He was perfect for the job: no wife, no kids, both parents dead, brother and sister he had put through college married off. So what if they killed him? It wouldn't change anything for anybody—least of all for Katagiri himself.

It was not Katagiri but the thugs surrounding him who got nervous when they saw him so calm and cool. He soon earned a kind of reputation in their world as a tough guy. Now, though, the tough Katagiri was at a total loss. What the hell was this frog talking about? Worm?

"Who is Worm?" he asked with some hesitation.

"Worm lives underground. He is a gigantic worm. When he gets angry, he causes earthquakes," Frog said. "And right now he is very, very angry."

"What is he angry *about*?" Katagiri asked.

"I have no idea," Frog said. "Nobody knows what Worm is thinking inside that murky head of his. Few have ever seen him. He is usually asleep. That's what he really likes to do: take long, long naps. He goes on sleeping for years—decades—in the warmth and darkness underground. His eyes, as you might imagine, have atrophied, his brain has turned to jelly as he sleeps. If you ask me, I'd guess he probably isn't thinking anything at all, just lying there and feeling every little rumble and reverberation that comes his way, absorbing them into his body, and storing them up. And then, through some kind of chemical process, he replaces most of them with rage. Why this happens I have no idea. I could never explain it."

Frog fell silent, watching Katagiri and waiting until his words had sunk in. Then he went on:

"Please don't misunderstand me, though. I feel no personal animosity toward Worm. I don't see him as the embodiment of evil. Not that I would want to be his friend, either: I just think that, as far as the world is concerned, it is in a sense *all right* for a being like him to exist. The world is like a great big overcoat, and it needs pockets of various shapes and sizes. But right at the moment Worm has reached the point where he is too dangerous to ignore. With all the different kinds of hatred he has absorbed and stored inside himself over the years, his heart and body have swollen to gargantuan proportions—bigger than ever before. And to make matters worse, last month's Kobe earthquake shook him out of the deep sleep he was enjoying. He experienced a revelation inspired by his profound rage: it was time now for him, too, to cause a massive earthquake, and he'd do it here, in Tokyo. I know what I'm talking about, Mr. Katagiri: I have received reliable information on the timing and scale of the earthquake from some of my best bug friends."

Frog snapped his mouth shut and closed his round eyes in apparent fatigue.

"So what you're saying is," Katagiri said, "that you and I have to go underground together and fight Worm to stop the earthquake."

"Exactly."

Katagiri reached for his cup of tea, picked it up, and put it back. "I still don't get it," he said. "Why did you choose me to go with you?"

Frog looked straight into Katagiri's eyes and said, "I have always had the profoundest respect for you, Mr. Katagiri. For sixteen long years, you have silently accepted the most dangerous, least glamorous assignments—the jobs that others have avoided—and you have carried them off beautifully. I know full well how difficult this has been for you, and I believe that neither your superiors nor your colleagues properly appreciate your accomplishments. They are blind, the whole lot of them. But you, unappreciated and unpromoted, have never once complained.

"Nor is it simply a matter of your work. After your parents died, you raised your teenage brother and sister single-handedly, put them through college, and even arranged for them to marry, all at great sacrifice of your time and income, and at the expense of your own marriage prospects. In spite of this, your brother and sister have never once expressed gratitude for your efforts on their behalf. Far from it: they have shown you no respect and acted with the most callous disregard for your loving-kindness. In my opinion, their behavior is unconscionable. I almost wish I could beat them to a pulp on your behalf. But you, meanwhile, show no trace of anger.

"To be quite honest, Mr. Katagiri, you are nothing much to look at, and you are far from eloquent, so you tend to be looked down upon by those around you. *I*, however, can see what a sensible and courageous man you are. In all of Tokyo, with its teeming millions, there is no one else I could trust as much as you to fight by my side."

"Tell me, Mr. Frog—" Katagiri said.

"Please," Frog said, raising one finger again. "Call me 'Frog.'"

"Tell me, Frog," Katagiri said, "how do you know so much about me?"

"Well, Mr. Katagiri, I have not been frogging all these years for nothing. I keep my eye on the important things in life."

"But still, Frog," Katagiri said, "I'm not particularly strong, and I don't know anything about what's happening underground. I don't have the kind of muscle it will take to fight Worm in the darkness. I'm sure you can find somebody a lot stronger than me—a man who does karate, say, or a Self-Defense Force commando."

Frog rolled his large eyes. "To tell you the truth, Mr. Katagiri," he said, "*I'm* the one who will do all the fighting. But I can't do it alone. This is the key thing: I need your courage and your passion for justice. I need you to stand behind me and say, 'Way to go, Frog! You're doing great! I know you can win! You're fighting the good fight!'"

Frog opened his arms wide, then slapped his webbed hands down on his knees again.

"In all honesty, Mr. Katagiri, the thought of fighting Worm in the dark frightens me, too. For many years I lived as a pacifist, loving art, living with nature. Fighting is not something I like to do. I do it because I have to. And this particular fight will be a fierce one, that is certain. I may not return from it alive. I may lose a limb or two in the process. But I cannot—I *will* not—run away. As Nietzsche said, the highest wisdom is to have no fear. What I want from you, Mr. Katagiri, is for you to share your simple courage with me, to support me with your whole heart as a true friend. Do you understand what I am trying to tell you?"

None of this made any sense to Katagiri, but still he felt that—unreal as it sounded—he could believe whatever Frog said to him. Something about Frog—the look on his face, the way he spoke—had a simple honesty to it that appealed directly to the heart. After years of work in the toughest division of the Security Trust Bank, Katagiri possessed the ability to sense such things. It was all but second nature to him.

"I know this must be difficult for you, Mr. Katagiri. A huge frog comes barging into your place and asks you to believe all these outlandish things. Your reaction is perfectly natural. And so I intend to provide you with proof that I exist. Tell me, Mr. Katagiri, you have been having a great deal of trouble recovering a loan the bank made to Big Bear Trading, have you not?"

"That's true," Katagiri said.

"Well, they have a number of extortionists working behind the scenes, and those individuals are mixed up with the mobsters. They're scheming to make the company go bankrupt and get out of its debts. Your bank's loan officer shoved a pile of cash at them without a decent background check, and, as usual, the one who's left to clean up after him is you, Mr. Katagiri. But you're having a hard time sinking your teeth into these fellows: they're no pushovers. And there may be a powerful politician backing them up. They're into you for seven hundred million yen. That is the situation you are dealing with, am I right?"

"You certainly are."

Frog stretched his arms out wide, his big green webs opening like pale wings. "Don't worry, Mr. Katagiri. Leave everything to me. By tomorrow morning, old Frog will have your problems solved. Relax and have a good night's sleep."

With a big smile on his face, Frog stood up. Then, flattening himself like a dried squid, he slipped out through the gap at the side of the closed door, leaving Katagiri all alone. The two teacups on the kitchen table were the only indication that Frog had ever been in Katagiri's apartment.

THE MOMENT KATAGIRI ARRIVED at work the next morning at nine, the phone on his desk rang.

"Mr. Katagiri," said a man's voice. It was cold and businesslike. "My name is Shiraoka. I am an attorney with the Big Bear case. I received a call from my client this morning with regard to the pending loan matter. He wants you to know that he will take full responsibility for returning the entire amount requested by the due date. He will also give you a signed memorandum to that effect. His only request is that you do not send Frog to his home again. I repeat: he wants you to ask Frog never to visit his home again. I myself am not entirely sure what this is supposed to mean, but I believe it should be clear to you, Mr. Katagiri. Am I correct?"

"You are indeed," Katagiri said.

"You will be kind enough to convey my message to Frog, I trust."

"That I will do. Your client will never see Frog again."

"Thank you very much. I will prepare the memorandum for you by tomorrow."

"I appreciate it," Katagiri said.

The connection was cut.

Frog visited Katagiri in his Trust Bank office at lunchtime. "That Big Bear case is working out well for you, I presume?"

Katagiri glanced around uneasily.

"Don't worry," Frog said. "You are the only one who can see me. But now I am sure you realize that I actually exist. I am not a product of your imagination. I can take action and produce results. I am a real, living being."

"Tell me, Mr. Frog—"

"Please," Frog said, raising one finger. "Call me 'Frog.'"

"Tell me, Frog," Katagiri said, "what did you do to them?"

"Oh, nothing much," Frog said. "Nothing much more complicated than boiling Brussels sprouts. I just gave them a little scare. A touch of psychological terror. As Joseph Conrad once wrote, true terror is the kind that men feel toward their imagination. But never mind that, Mr. Katagiri. Tell me about the Big Bear case. It's going well?"

Katagiri nodded and lit a cigarette. "Seems to be."

"So, then, have I succeeded in gaining your trust with regard to the matter I broached to you last night? Will you join me to fight against Worm?"

Sighing, Katagiri removed his glasses and wiped them. "To tell you the truth, I'm not too crazy about the idea, but I don't suppose that's enough to get me out of it."

"No," Frog said. "It is a matter of responsibility and honor. You may not be too 'crazy' about the idea, but we have no choice: you and I must go underground and face Worm. If we should happen to lose our lives in the process, we will gain no one's sympathy. And even if we manage to defeat Worm, no one will praise us. No one will ever know that such a battle even raged far beneath their feet. Only you and I will know, Mr. Katagiri. However it turns out, ours will be a lonely battle."

Katagiri looked at his own hand for a while, then watched the smoke rising from his cigarette. Finally, he spoke. "You know, Mr. Frog, I'm just an ordinary person."

"Make that 'Frog,' please," Frog said, but Katagiri let it go.

"I'm an absolutely ordinary guy. Less than ordinary. I'm going bald, I'm getting a potbelly, I turned forty last month. My feet are flat. The doctor told me recently that I have diabetic tendencies. It's been three months or more since I last slept with a woman—and I had to pay for it. I do get some recognition within the division for my ability to collect on loans, but no real respect. I don't have a single person who likes me, either at work or in my private life. I don't know how to talk to people, and I'm bad with strangers, so I never make friends. I have no athletic ability, I'm tone-deaf, short, phimotic, nearsighted—*and* astigmatic. I live a horrible life. All I do is eat, sleep, and shit. I don't know why I'm even living. Why should a person like me have to be the one to save Tokyo?"

"Because, Mr. Katagiri, Tokyo can *only* be saved by a person like you. And it's *for* people like you that I am trying to save Tokyo."

Katagiri sighed again, more deeply this time. "All right then, what do you want me to do?"

FROG TOLD KATAGIRI HIS PLAN. They would go underground on the night of February 17 (one day before the earthquake was scheduled to happen). Their way in would be through the basement boiler room of the Shinjuku branch of the Tokyo Security Trust Bank. They would meet there late at night (Katagiri would stay in the building on the pretext of working overtime). Behind a section of wall was a vertical shaft, and they would find Worm at the bottom by climbing down a 150-foot rope ladder.

"Do you have a battle plan in mind?" Katagiri asked.

"Of course I do. We would have no hope of defeating an enemy like Worm without a battle plan. He is a slimy creature: you can't tell his mouth from his anus. And he's as big as a commuter train."

"What *is* your battle plan?"

After a thoughtful pause, Frog answered, "Hmm, what is it they say—'Silence is golden'?"

"You mean I shouldn't ask?"

"That's one way of putting it."

"What if I get scared at the last minute and run away? What would you do then, Mr. Frog?"

"'Frog.'"

"Frog. What would you do then?"

Frog thought about this a while and answered, "I would fight on alone. My chances of beating him by myself are perhaps just slightly better than Anna Karenina's chances of beating that speeding locomotive. Have you read *Anna Karenina*, Mr. Katagiri?"

When he heard that Katagiri had not read the novel, Frog gave him a look as if to say, What a shame. Apparently Frog was very fond of *Anna Karenina*.

"Still, Mr. Katagiri, I do not believe that you will leave me to fight alone. I can tell. It's a question of balls—which, unfortunately, I do not happen to possess. Ha ha ha ha!" Frog laughed with his mouth wide open. Balls were not all that Frog lacked. He had no teeth, either.

UNEXPECTED THINGS DO HAPPEN, however.

Katagiri was shot on the evening of February 17. He had finished his rounds for the day and was walking down the street in Shinjuku on his way back to the Trust Bank when a young man in a leather jacket leaped in front of him. The man's face was a blank, and he gripped a small black gun in one hand. The gun was *so* small and *so* black it hardly looked real. Katagiri stared at the object in the man's hand, not registering the fact that it was aimed at him and that the man was pulling the trigger. It all happened too quickly: it didn't make sense to him. But the gun in fact went off.

Katagiri saw the barrel jerk in the air and, at the same moment, felt an impact as though someone had struck his right shoulder with a sledgehammer. He felt no pain, but the blow sent him sprawling on the sidewalk. The leather briefcase in his right hand went flying in the other direction. The man aimed the gun at him again. A second shot rang out. A small eatery's sidewalk signboard exploded before his eyes. He heard people screaming. His eyeglasses had flown off, and everything was a blur. He was vaguely aware that the man was approaching with the pistol pointed at him. I'm going to die, he thought. Frog had said that true terror is the kind that men feel toward their imagination. Katagiri cut the switch of his imagination and sank into a weightless silence.

WHEN HE WOKE UP, he was in bed. He opened one eye, took a moment to survey his surroundings, and then opened the other eye. The first thing that entered his field of vision was a metal stand by the head of the bed and an intravenous feeding tube that stretched from the stand to where he lay. Next he saw a nurse dressed in white. He realized that he was lying on his back on a hard bed and wearing some strange piece of clothing, under which he seemed to be naked.

Oh yeah, he thought, I was walking along the sidewalk when some guy shot me. Probably in the shoulder. The right one. He relived the scene in his mind. When he remembered the small black gun in the young man's hand, his heart made a disturbing thump. The sons of bitches were trying to kill me! he thought. But it looks as if I made it through OK. My memory is fine. I don't have any pain. And not just pain: I don't have any feeling at all. I can't lift my arm . . .

The hospital room had no windows. He could not tell whether it was day or night. He had been shot just before five in the evening. How much time had passed since then? Had the hour of his nighttime rendezvous with Frog gone by? Katagiri searched the room for a clock, but without his glasses he could see nothing at a distance.

"Excuse me," he called to the nurse.

"Oh, good, you're finally awake," the nurse said.

"What time is it?"

She looked at her watch.

"Nine-fifteen."

"P.M.?"

"Don't be silly, it's morning!"

"Nine-fifteen a.m.?" Katagiri groaned, barely managing to lift his head from the pillow. The ragged noise that emerged from his throat sounded like someone else's voice. "Nine-fifteen a.m. on February 18?"

"Right," the nurse said, lifting her arm once more to check the date on her digital watch. "Today is February 18, 1995."

"Wasn't there a big earthquake in Tokyo this morning?"

"In Tokyo?"

"In Tokyo."

The nurse shook her head. "Not as far as I know."

He breathed a sigh of relief. Whatever had happened, the earthquake at least had been averted.

"How's my wound doing?"

"Your wound?" she asked. "What wound?"

"Where I was shot."

"Shot?"

"Yeah, near the entrance to the Trust Bank. Some young guy shot me. In the right shoulder, I think."

The nurse flashed a nervous smile in his direction. "I'm sorry, Mr. Katagiri, but you haven't been shot."

"I haven't? Are you sure?"

"As sure as I am that there was no earthquake this morning."

Katagiri was stunned. "Then what the hell am I doing in a hospital?"

"Somebody found you lying in the street, unconscious. In the Kabukicho neighborhood of Shinjuku. You didn't have any external wounds.

You were just out cold. And we still haven't found out why. The doctor's going to be here soon. You'd better talk to him."

Lying in the street unconscious? Katagiri was sure he had seen the pistol go off aimed at him. He took a deep breath and tried to get his head straight. He would start by putting all the facts in order.

"What you're telling me is, I've been lying in this hospital bed, unconscious, since early evening yesterday, is that right?"

"Right," the nurse said. "And you had a really bad night, Mr. Katagiri. You must have had some awful nightmares. I heard you yelling, 'Frog! Hey, Frog!' You did it a lot. You have a friend nicknamed 'Frog'?"

Katagiri closed his eyes and listened to the slow, rhythmic beating of his heart as it ticked off the minutes of his life. How much of what he remembered had actually happened, and how much was hallucination? Did Frog really exist, and had Frog fought with Worm to put a stop to the earthquake? Or had that just been part of a long dream? Katagiri had no idea what was true anymore.

Frog came to his hospital room that night. Katagiri awoke to find him in the dim light, sitting on a steel folding chair, his back against the wall. Frog's big, bulging green eyelids were closed in a straight slit.

"Frog!" Katagiri called out to him.

Frog slowly opened his eyes. His big white stomach swelled and shrank with his breathing.

"I meant to meet you in the boiler room at night the way I promised," Katagiri said, "but I had an accident in the evening—something totally unexpected—and they brought me here."

Frog gave his head a slight shake. "I know. It's OK. Don't worry. You were a great help to me in my fight, Mr. Katagiri."

"I was?"

"Yes, you were. You did a great job in your dreams. That's what made it possible for me to fight Worm to the finish. I have you to thank for my victory."

"I don't get it," Katagiri said. "I was unconscious the whole time.

They were feeding me intravenously. I don't remember doing anything in my dreams."

"That's fine, Mr. Katagiri. It's better that you don't remember. The whole terrible fight occurred in the area of imagination. That is the precise location of our battlefield. It is there that we experience our victories and our defeats. Each and every one of us is a being of limited duration: all of us eventually go down to defeat. But as Ernest Hemingway saw so clearly, the ultimate value of our lives is decided not by how we win but by how we lose. You and I together, Mr. Katagiri, were able to prevent the annihilation of Tokyo. We saved a hundred and fifty thousand people from the jaws of death. No one realizes it, but that is what we accomplished."

"How did you manage to defeat Worm? And what did *I* do?"

"We gave everything we had in a fight to the bitter end. We—" Frog snapped his mouth shut and took one great breath, "—we used every weapon we could get our hands on, Mr. Katagiri. We used all the courage we could muster. Darkness was our enemy's ally. You brought in a foot-powered generator and used every ounce of your strength to fill the place with light. Worm tried to frighten you away with phantoms of the darkness, but you stood your ground. Darkness vied with light in a horrific battle, and in the light I grappled with the monstrous Worm. He coiled himself around me, and bathed me in his horrid slime. I tore him to shreds, but still he refused to die. All he did was divide into smaller pieces. And then—"

Frog fell silent, but soon, as if dredging up his last ounce of strength, he began to speak again. "Fyodor Dostoevsky, with unparalleled tenderness, depicted those who have been forsaken by God. He discovered the precious quality of human existence in the ghastly paradox whereby men who had invented God were forsaken by that very God. Fighting with Worm in the darkness, I found myself thinking of Dostoevsky's 'White Nights.' I . . ." Frog's words seemed to founder. "Mr. Katagiri, do you mind if I take a brief nap? I am utterly exhausted."

"Please," Katagiri said. "Take a good, deep sleep."

"I was finally unable to defeat Worm," Frog said, closing his eyes. "I did manage to stop the earthquake, but I was only able to carry our battle to a draw. I inflicted injury on him, and he on me. But to tell you the truth, Mr. Katagiri . . ."

"What is it, Frog?"

"I am, indeed, pure Frog, but at the same time I am a thing that stands for a world of un-Frog."

"Hmm, I don't get that at all."

"Neither do I," Frog said, his eyes still closed. "It's just a feeling I have. What you see with your eyes is not necessarily real. My enemy is, among other things, the me inside me. Inside me is the un-me. My brain is growing muddy. The locomotive is coming. But I really want you to understand what I'm saying, Mr. Katagiri."

"You're tired, Frog. Go to sleep. You'll get better."

"I am slowly, slowly returning to the mud, Mr. Katagiri. And yet . . . I . . ."

Frog lost his grasp on words and slipped into a coma. His arms hung down almost to the floor, and his big wide mouth drooped open. Straining to focus his eyes, Katagiri was able to make out deep cuts covering Frog's entire body. Discolored streaks ran through his skin, and there was a sunken spot on his head where the flesh had been torn away.

Katagiri stared long and hard at Frog, who sat there now wrapped in the thick cloak of sleep. As soon as I get out of this hospital, he thought, I'll buy *Anna Karenina* and "White Nights" and read them both. Then I'll have a nice long literary discussion about them with Frog.

Before long, Frog began to twitch all over. Katagiri assumed at first that these were just normal involuntary movements in sleep, but he soon realized his mistake. There was something unnatural about the way Frog's body went on jerking, like a big doll being shaken by someone from behind. Katagiri held his breath and watched. He wanted to run over to Frog, but his own body remained paralyzed.

After a while, a big lump formed over Frog's right eye. The same kind of huge, ugly boil broke out on Frog's shoulder and side, and then over his whole body. Katagiri could not imagine what was happening to Frog. He stared at the spectacle, barely breathing.

Then, all of a sudden, one of the boils burst with a loud pop. The skin flew off, and a sticky liquid oozed out, sending a horrible smell across the room. The rest of the boils started popping, one after another, twenty or thirty in all, flinging skin and fluid onto the walls. The sickening, unbearable smell filled the hospital room. Big black holes were left on Frog's body where the boils had burst, and wriggling, maggotlike worms of all shapes and sizes came crawling out. Puffy white maggots. After them emerged some kind of small centipedelike creatures, whose hundreds of legs made a creepy rustling sound. An endless stream of these things came crawling out of the holes. Frog's body—or the thing that must once have been Frog's body—was totally covered with these creatures of the night. His two big eyeballs fell from their sockets onto the floor, where they were devoured by black bugs with strong jaws. Crowds of slimy worms raced each other up the walls to the ceiling, where they covered the fluorescent lights and burrowed into the smoke alarm.

The floor, too, was covered with worms and bugs. They climbed up the lamp and blocked the light and, of course, they crept onto Katagiri's bed. Hundreds of them came burrowing under the covers. They crawled up his legs, under his bedgown, between his thighs. The smallest worms and maggots crawled inside his anus and ears and nostrils. Centipedes pried his mouth open and crawled inside one after another. Filled with an intense despair, Katagiri screamed.

Someone snapped a switch and light filled the room.

"Mr. Katagiri!" called the nurse. Katagiri opened his eyes to the light. His body was soaked in sweat. The bugs were gone. All they had left behind in him was a horrible slimy sensation.

"Another bad dream, eh? Poor dear." With quick, efficient movements the nurse readied an injection and stabbed the needle into his arm.

He took a long, deep breath and let it out. His heart was expanding and contracting violently.

"What were you dreaming about?"

Katagiri was having trouble differentiating dream from reality. "What you see with your eyes is not necessarily real," he told himself aloud.

"That's so true," said the nurse with a smile. "Especially where dreams are concerned."

"Frog," he murmured.

"Did something happen to Frog?" she asked.

"He saved Tokyo from being destroyed by an earthquake. All by himself."

"That's nice," the nurse said, replacing his near-empty intravenous feeding bottle with a new one. "We don't need any more awful things happening in Tokyo. We have plenty already."

"But it cost him his life. He's gone. I think he went back to the mud. He'll never come here again."

Smiling, the nurse toweled the sweat from his forehead. "You were very fond of Frog, weren't you, Mr. Katagiri?"

"Locomotive," Katagiri mumbled. "More than anybody." Then he closed his eyes and sank into a restful, dreamless sleep.

The Illumination of Santiago

Nona Fernández

Translated from Spanish by Idra Novey

It was a German company, she said. One that had arrived to install the light. There were many workers and technicians who disembarked with cables, light bulbs, and pliers in the Plaza de Armas, the first in all of Santiago to be illuminated. She said the work went on throughout the city for some years. She didn't specify how many, but I guess it was long enough for one of those German electricians to meet a woman and have four Chilean children with her. Two dark-skinned kids with blue eyes, a girl with straight blond hair, and, finally, a redhead.

One night, the mother of the children told them that they were going to the city center. The father had completed a section of his city-wide project and they were going to celebrate with a special ceremony in the plaza. The two dark-skinned children, the blond girl, and the redhead set out, walking along the half-dark streets lined with gas lamps, which were lit each day at dusk. The blond girl was holding her mother's hand, she told me. Their shadows lengthened up the walls and across the ground, extending their backs without disconnecting from their feet. Her mother's shadow was small and thin. Her redheaded brother's shadow was in constant motion, darting in front of the others. Hers, tiny with skinny legs, was a shadow so dark that she got scared just looking at it, she told me. It didn't matter how much they hurried or how fast they turned the corners, the shadows were always there behind them, following the same route they followed, stepping on their steps, swallowing each moment as it ended.

After a long walk, the girl arrived with her mother and siblings at the Plaza de Armas, where they met up with other women, men, and children waiting to see the spectacle of electric lights. The place was packed. Grandparents sat on the benches and used the cathedral stairs for extra seats. Perched on their fathers' shoulders, kids peered out, straining to see. There were animals, too. Dogs, chickens, and a few mules, she told me. Nobody wanted to be left out. Hundreds of heads and bodies with their respective shadows stood together, expectant, waiting in the public square for illumination.

I don't know how things started. I don't remember if she told me. Maybe there was a ceremony, like her mother said there would be. Somebody gave a speech, standing on a dais made for the occasion or on top of the existing cathedral stands. Maybe they talked about progress, a new era, the future about to arrive and present itself that very night, in the penumbra at the center of the city, the belly button of the country. Or maybe there was nothing ceremonial at all and a white-haired German man just counted out loud to three:

eins, zwei, drei.

Maybe he hit the switch then, and swiftly, to prevent anyone from seeing how it happened, each of the streetlights installed in the plaza clicking on at once, an act of magic unlike any trick the public had ever witnessed.

THE PEOPLE WENT SILENT.

We stood with our mouths open, she told me.

Not even a fly moved, everything was quiet while we stared up at the lit bulbs.

THE LIGHT WAS MUCH brighter than the flames in the gas lamps. It was all-encompassing and didn't leave anyone out. Intrusive and surprising, it made people's faces appear in the darkness. People in Santiago had never seen each other this way. Under the electric lights, the redheaded brother looked even more redheaded. His hair glowed like an ember in the wood-fed heater they lighted in the winter. The light moved between people's bodies, intensifying colors, shapes, and designs. It grasped onto people's waists, tangled their hair, narrowed their hands, shoulders, torsos, backs. It brought out a new dimension of each one. People drew closer to the lights and smiled under the bulbs, looking at their own illuminated bodies, turning around to show others, like a person showing off a new suit.

The blond girl was very small, and she told me she took it all in without letting go of her mother's hand because she didn't understand what was going on. The brightness of the light bulbs was so potent it caused all the shadows in the plaza to disappear. Wherever they looked, not a single shadow remained, she told me, the light had swallowed them all. The blond child, in her childishness, thought that the night had abruptly ended and that sunrise had arrived. She thought the hours that were normally dark for sleeping had been dissipated under the lights, that those hours were gone, and at any moment she would have to head to school again. The light resuscitated the day, making it appear from complete darkness with the flick of the switch. She told me she got scared. She told me the first thing she thought was that the electric light must be dangerous, given how fast it got rid of the shadows. She told me the electric light played tricks with time and that no one, not even someone with an illuminated mind, could do that.

After a few minutes somebody applauded, and the applause caught on. Others joined in, and then everyone began to clap their palms, stunned and incredulous at what they were seeing. What happened after that she never told me, but I can guess that there was a party, a drunken spree with guitars and dancing, and the festivities lasted all night in the plaza, where time no longer passed, where the new lights halted it to allow the parties to continue.

The German company continued spreading light through the city. In the following years, they put thick cement poles along the rest of the streets, poles that carried the new streetlights and cables. A whole block would switch on in some central neighborhood. The next month another one, and then another, and another. The city began appearing gradually, its darkest corners, once shadowed even in daylight, exposed, revealing the design that still emerges now, each day and night.

Through windows, the light entered houses, rooms, lit first the pillows of the most fortunate, who from then on began to imagine in their twisted dreams a city that had become limitless. With its neon lights—little brightly colored ones, and security spotlights. An alert city, always switched on, an insomniac city. The streetlight poles, the first ones, bore the name of the German company that had erected them. It was a circular logo with an acronym inside. Three or four indecipherable letters JTR, or GSBM, or CETA. I think it was CETA. These poles lasted in Santiago for many years. On a walk for a kilo of bread, or a quart of oil, holding hands with the blond girl, who with time had transformed into my grandmother, I saw this acronym imprinted on the poles of the street where I was born. That's the company where my father used to work, she told me, and she showed me the logo with her wrinkled, pale hand, like a testimony of the night when, according to her, we began cheating with time.

Apples

Gunnhild Øyehaug

Translated from Norwegian by Kari Dickson

1

The dog came pelting towards me. Mouth half-closed around a stick, coat rippling. *Freeze time*, I thought, so we stay like this forever, me here on the field, open and white, and the dog with the snow glittering and swirling around it in midflight.

It was afternoon by the time we turned home. The dog ran in front of me, behind me, beside me. Completely untroubled. When we got to the cabin, dusk was falling. I brushed the snow from us, gave the dog some food, water, lit the fire.

Later in the evening there was a knock at the door. It was Sonja, who owned the dog. The dog leapt to its feet, ran to its owner and jumped up, Sonja laughed and said doggy things to the dog, Sonja looked at me with a questioning and slightly dumbfounded smile, as though she was saying to me, without saying, you could just have rung and told me. *Freeze time*, I thought, as I stood watching the dog jumping up at Sonja and Sonja looking at me with her gently quizzical smile, as though she wondered who I was, who could just take the dog like that and not say anything, again. You like the dog, Sonja said, and I nodded. You can come and visit, you know, Sonja said. I nodded again, would you like something to eat, I asked, I've just baked some rolls. Sonja looked at me, as though taken aback, either because I'd baked the rolls or because she wasn't sure what to do, OK, she said.

I put the rolls and a pot of tea on the table. Sonja looked around the cabin; the dog was lying on a blanket on the sofa, asleep. I hoped that I wasn't dreaming, that I wouldn't wake up and it would all be a romantic dream, that a person and a dog had come to visit me, that I'd made them food, that I'd put cheese on the table, that I saw a person standing there looking at my family pictures hanging on the wall, as though she was genuinely interested, and the dog lay sleeping on the sofa, and felt cared for and safe. And I liked the way I had written this, intimate and honest, and I liked the fact that Sonja was named after a variety of apple.

2

The class clapped. The author showed a page from a fruit encyclopaedia on the digital blackboard, with an illustration of a round, red apple, and the text underneath said that Sonja was an autumn apple, resistant to apple scab, sweet in flavour, with a rich red colour and good keeping quality. Well, the author said, that was something I wrote yesterday to show you a way to turn everything upside down at the last moment, first: a realistic story without any meta levels, where "I" has a dog and is happy and looking for moments to freeze, and then at the very end destroys everything by saying "I liked the way I had written this," so everyone falls out of the story, and knows that what they have just read is fiction. Obviously, it's not a style I would use for anything I was going to publish, said the author who was the lecturer that day. The creative writing class at the creative studies college looked at the author. They didn't actually chorus "oh", but might well have done by the look on their faces. The author was tall, had dark hair and a long, pointed nose that gave him a distinctive profile, his slim hands holding a pen as he spoke. He looked at the class. His name was Aksel, after his farmer father's favourite potato. Aksel caught young Signe's look of scepticism—or was she irritated or annoyed? She had a slightly protruding upper lip, and a very sweet mouth, and when she didn't believe something, the pout became even more pronounced. Her eyes were big and serious, and it was clear she was thinking something. Her hair was light brown and cut in a bob that framed her face. Aksel waited, he waited for a critical comment, or at least a question, from Signe. Does anyone have any strong objections to the text? Aksel said. A hand went up, we don't know very much about his background, the student said, we aren't told much about why it's so important to him that someone comes to visit, what it is that he finds difficult with other people. Aksel nodded. True, he said. Perhaps there could be something in the room that gives a clue, he could have an aquarium or something like that, the aquarium could represent the confined, introverted space, keeping all the fish at a distance from him, another student said, which made Aksel smile, good idea, he said. An aquarium in a cabin? a third student said, that's not very realistic. No, that's true, the second student said. And what would the aquarium symbolise, would the aquarium symbolise him, that he was an aquarium with fish in it, with a glass wall to keep the world out, or would the fish represent the world he couldn't connect with because he was outside the aquarium? a fourth student wondered. Let's forget the aquarium! the second student said. Everyone laughed, and the corners of Signe's mouth turned up, but barely. Why does he want to freeze time? another student asked. Signe turned to the student, but *that*'s obvious, Signe said, who usually corrected everyone, he wants to freeze time because it's much easier to live in a happy moment than with all the difficult stuff before and after, and in any case, it's a device to illustrate writing, writing is an attempt to stop the constant flow of all that is difficult, to hold it still, to observe it. Signe glanced at Aksel, just long enough for him to realise that she wondered if he was impressed by what she'd said, before she looked at the floor. Her objection didn't come until the day was over and he was out on the street that ran like a long sentence past the creative studies college which lay more or less in the heart of Oslo, not far from the fjord. Signe came out with her bag through the glass doors, and stepped onto the pavement where Aksel was standing lighting a cigarette. She looked at him with the same sceptical expression, pout and eyes. Let's continue in the present tense. It's easier, when it comes to dramatic experience: I know, Aksel says, I know I shouldn't. By this, he means smoking. There was something, Signe says, something I thought about that text you read out today. I could tell, Aksel says. Signe looks surprised. Oh, she says, because she doesn't really like the author's overconfidence. What I thought was this: I liked the story without the meta sentence at the end, which just ruined the whole thing. I liked it when he was out in the snow with the dog, and he was happy, and that then he went back to the cabin and baked rolls and had a visitor. End of. What you're saying is that you like a realistic narrative, Aksel says. What I'm saying is that I like stories that are genuine, Signe says. That are not clever and pretending to be something they're not. But it was only an example, the author says. I don't believe you, Signe says. I think you liked it when you were writing it. I think you were into it. I think you were in the landscape in your head, I think you pictured the snow, and the dog, and I think you liked that there was something about the dog that the protagonist longed for, and I think you thought that if you named a person after an apple, the meta device you used to leave your own story would somehow feel less obvious because of the symbolism of the person growing out of the soil, which we all do really, in a way. AND: I don't for a second believe that you actually wanted to deconstruct it at the end, I think it's exactly what you're looking for, but you're trying to camouflage it. Aksel: I don't mean that all stories should finish with "I liked the way I had written this." Signe: And I don't mean that that's what you meant. I think you have a longing, and that's alright. Aksel: I've never said that it's not alright to long for something. Signe: But that's precisely what you do when you undermine your own story about it. Aksel: I don't agree. Signe: What's your argument? Aksel: I'll have to think first before I can answer that. Signe: Have you read Inger Christensen's poem about dreams? Aksel looks at her. Every time she opens her mouth she makes him a little more like a snowy field inside—empty, he has nothing to say. It's something about her eyes, they're so incredibly big and see right through him, he can't hide anywhere, he feels nervous, or is it anxious? I can't remember, he says. It's in

Alphabet, Signe says, and it, or rather she, compares an apricot tree in bloom with someone who's dreaming, when the tree is flowering, it's full of dreams, apricot blossom is the dream, you understand? And then she says she finally understood that "A dreamer / must dream like trees / be a dreamer / of fruit to the last." That's utterly wonderful, Aksel says. And it is wonderfully true. But you know, he says and looks at Signe, in the same collection of poems there's another apricot tree in a dream that someone dreams, and did you notice what that apricot tree does? Signe's eyes flicker with uncertainty. The apricot tree scrutinises the dreamer, the "I" that is, before turning around and leaving suddenly. What do you think about that? Aksel says and takes a drag on his cigarette before dropping it to the ground and stepping on it with the toe of his shoe. Signe looks at the stubbed-out cigarette. The stubbed-out cigarette grows into a symbol. She looks at him with a stubbed-out cigarette in her eyes. I think I need to think about it again, Signe says, because she's actually never thought about it, the fact that this collection of poems that she loves for its tangible content (apricot trees exist, etc.) and strong morals (take care of the planet), also uses meta devices. She, who normally catches everything, has failed to catch something so fundamental. What we are witnessing is an intellectual turning point for Signe. And Signe would no doubt wish that this entire conversation had a different outcome from the one it did, that she had not become the apricot that she naturally became for him, in fact, it took her several years to get over it, that she had gone home with him, this and that happened, in short, that in the course of a few months they went through the whole tiresome young woman/older man relationship that inevitably follows its necessary dramaturgy based on the young woman's need to be seen and her essentially mature mind that finds no resonance in her male peers, and the older man's attraction to youth and constant longing to be seen, a longing that for some men is voracious and never satisfied, so constantly seeks out new, fantastic girls, but time and again these girls' lack of life experience seems to ruin the relationship for the older man, whereas the man's lack of listening ears appears to ruin the relationship for the young woman, not least, that he almost exactingly uncovers great flaws in her not yet fully developed sense of self (which is exactly what provokes the need in him to carry on searching for the perfect woman who does *not* have this flaw), but the most frustrating thing of all, says Signe, and surveys her students at the University of Bergen, who are sitting listening to her story, which she has slipped into so unexpectedly, was that it ended just as I had wanted his story about the cabin and the dog to end, with fruit, that's to say, my bare arse, to put it humorously, and normally that would have been the kind of irony that I appreciate, but now I'm so old, and this is my last day as professor at this institute, and this story is what started it all for me, the reason I became a literary scholar in the first place, and I feel, actually . . . nothing. Nothing at all. The students clap uncertainly. Signe smiles at them, she is sixty-eight years old and a rather large lady, and she has to bend over slowly to pick up her bag from the floor. She takes her coat from the chair and leaves Auditorium A for the last time.

3

Outside, the sky is blue, it's late May, and Signe walks to the bus that will take her home. She passes a flower shop, which is blooming with bouquets of tulips and roses and anemones, and bushes she does not know the name of, which are temptingly green in their own way standing there in their pots, but at the back, right against the flower shop window, on a small table, is a little tree that catches her eye, and she stops. And this is what the scene looks like from the outside: a stout, older woman stands looking at a tree. She holds her bag with both hands in front of her girth, resting the bag on her stomach, as older women with bags often do. And what is happening inside her is this, she is asking the question: What kind of tree is that? She leans over to look at the label where the name of tree is written. And it says: Sonja.

Next scene: Signe takes the apple tree to the counter, she pays, the apple tree is given to her in a plastic bag, but that doesn't work, Signe has to carry the apple tree in her hands. Thankfully the tree is small and thin, and it's not far to the bus.

For the entire bus journey home, Signe is in a strange mood. Another line from Inger Christensen's book pops into her mind, perhaps because she is carrying an apple tree: right at the end of the collection, there's a poem about some children sitting by a road after a war, and they have lost everything. And then the poem says: *there is no one to carry them anymore.* She sits with the apple tree on her lap and looks out at the sky. It's blue, with wispy white clouds. When she eventually gets home, she lets herself into the small, red house in a garden that is so well-suited to an older woman of girth, and puts down the apple tree in the hall. Sonja? Signe calls. The story crackles with surprise. Sonja answers from one of the rooms, but Signe can't make out if it's the kitchen or the living room. Mum! Sonja shouts. Sonja comes hopping out into the hall—Sonja is Signe's forty-five-year-old daughter. She has Down syndrome and works in a sheltered workplace, where, in her own words, she makes "everything" and always finishes for the day half an hour before Signe comes home from university. Sonja is the result of the months when Signe and Aksel went through the relationship dramaturgy of young woman/older man, and Signe has been alone in her responsibility for Sonja, from the time even before she discovered she was pregnant, as Aksel disappeared in a way that no one can really hold against him: he drowned in the Mediterranean, he dove in too deep, down to a coral reef, and he should perhaps have remembered the discussion in class about the aquarium as a possible symbol, he might perhaps have seen that it was in fact a foreshadowing, but he didn't, he dove down and there he drowned, in all that blue, with fish of all colours swimming cheerfully around him. Signe hugs Sonja. Let's make dinner now, Signe says. Signe feels a lump in her throat a number of times through dinner, it must be because it was her last day as a professional, now she's a pensioner, all that's missing is the big farewell party, and so she embarks on the final stage of her life. How will Sonja get on without her is a question that has cropped up more than once, even though she's not ill, she's just old, there's no doubt about that. She tries to keep the chitchat going, asks in a thick voice: So how was it at work today? Just like normal, Sonja says. I love you, Signe wants to say. And was Andrea nice today? Signe asks. Andrea Liliane *Hamar*, Sonja corrects her. Signe smiles. Was Andrea Liliane *Hamar* nice today? Signe asks, it's easier now, she will be able to eat without crying. She is always nice, Sonja says. Oh, Signe says, I had the impression that Andrea could be a little naughty at times. Yes, Sonja says. But not today. She's learnt to behave herself. That's good, Signe says.

Sonja and Signe do the washing up. Signe washes and Sonja dries. Signe looks at her, looks at her daughter who is standing there drying the plates with such care, the tears well up in her eyes, *freeze time*, Signe thinks, freeze time as I stand here looking at her! But time does not freeze, Signe hands her an already dried plate. There! Sonja says. Now we'll have coffee! Yes, Signe says, and swallows. But first, I've got a surprise for you, Signe says, wait a moment. Signe goes out into the hall, and comes back into the kitchen with the small apple tree. Oh! Sonja cries. A tree! It's an apple tree, Signe says, and it's called the same as you. Sonja Olsen? Sonja says. Just Sonja, Signe says. I thought we could plant it in the garden. Let's plant it now, Sonja says. OK, Signe says.

4

Signe and Sonja kneel in the garden and pat down the soil around the trunk of the small tree. They are both wearing gardening gloves. The story is unsure as to where it should end. If it should end here, or if it should end with Signe's young fingers that once leafed through a book and found a poem by Inger Christensen where it said that "A dreamer / must dream like trees / of fruit to the last," and she felt that this was so true that it couldn't be truer, that it was a truth that was radiant and luminous—or if it should stop with an open, white landscape where Aksel is throwing a stick to a dog that's not his, that he has borrowed, or if it should stop when the dog picks up the stick and comes running back in a way that is ridiculously happy, as though the dog is smiling (but it's actually because it has a stick in its mouth) and its long black-and-white fur ripples around the dog's body as it jumps through the circus director's hoola-hoop-like hoop, stretched with thin greaseproof paper. Sonja, the small tree, has no answer, just a thin trunk and a few branches, and some budding leaves. And in this moment, she stands there in the garden, a tree in waiting, something that will grow, blossom, bear fruit, lose fruit, lose her leaves, be covered in snow, etc. with an astonishing patience and the peace that is particular to apple trees.

My Sad Dead

Mariana Enriquez

Translated from Spanish by Megan McDowell

But now it's time for you to come back.
You have been away long enough.

—LYDIA DAVIS, *Can't and Won't*

First, I think, I should describe the neighborhood. Because the neighborhood is where my house is, and my house is where my mother is. You can't understand one thing without the other. You can't understand why I don't leave. Because I *could* leave. I could leave tomorrow.

The neighborhood has changed since I was little. These houses, originally for workers, were built along these narrow streets back in the '30s: stone houses with lovely little gardens and tall windows with iron shutters. One could say that it was the residents themselves who gradually ruined the houses with all their innovating: the air-conditioning units, the tiled roofs, a tacked-on upper story made of different materials, exterior facings and paint jobs in ridiculous colors, cheaper knockoffs replacing the original wooden doors. But aside from the residents' poor taste, the neighborhood suffered because it became an island. On one side we're bordered by the avenue: it's like an ugly river we have to ford, and there's nothing much along its shores. To the south we have the housing projects, which have grown ever more dangerous, with kids selling crack on the stairways and sometimes pulling guns on one another when they fight, or firing into the air if they're mad after their team loses a match. To the north is a tract of land that was supposed to be developed into some kind of sports field, but that never happened, and now the area is occupied by very poor shanties, the best ones made of concrete blocks, the more precarious ones of tin and cardboard. The housing project and this slum merge to the east of our neighborhood.

I understand how things go: if misery is stalking you the way it does everyone in my country and my city and you have to resort to crime in order to survive, then that's what you do. There's more money in crime than in lawful work. In any case, there isn't much lawful work available, not for anyone. And if living a better life entails risk, well, it's a risk many people are willing to take.

Few of my neighbors—the inhabitants of this island of little houses built when the world was different—think the way I do. I want to be clear: I get scared sometimes, too. I don't want a stray bullet to hit me, either, or my daughter when she (rarely) comes to visit. I don't want to be regularly robbed at the bus stop or whenever I'm in a car waiting at a red light on the corner by the projects. I, too, go home crying when a teenager pulls a knife on me and snatches my phone. But I don't want to kill them all. I don't think they're a bunch of freeloaders and immigrants and miscreants and deadbeats, all expendable and unsalvageable. My ex-husband, who works for an oil company and lives in Patagonia, tells me that the neighbors are just afraid. I tell him that fascism generally starts with fear and then turns into hatred. He tells me I should sell the house and move to the south to be closer to him. We're divorced, but we're friends. We've always been friends. His new wife is delightful. I tend to use our daughter, Carolina, as an excuse for staying here, but it's just an excuse. Carolina lives far away from me and from this house, and she works as a fashion editor at a glossy magazine. She doesn't need me.

I stay because my mother lives here. Can I say that about a dead woman? She's *present*, then. Ever since she first appeared to me, I've understood that word better. She was here, she occupied a physical space, and I sensed her presence before I could see her.

My mother was a happy woman until she got cancer and came home to die. Her agony was long, painful, and undignified. It's not always like that. The wise patient with bald head and yellowed skin who sits in bed imparting life lessons is a ridiculous romanticization, but it's true that there are people who suffer less. It has to do with physiology, and also temperament. My mother was allergic to morphine. She couldn't use it, and we had to resort to other, impotent painkillers. She died screaming. A nurse and I did what we could for her. We couldn't do much. I'm a doctor, but I haven't worked with patients in a long time; instead, I do administrative work at a private medical company. At sixty, I don't have the energy, patience, or passion for hospital work anymore. Also, it's true, for a long time I denied (denial is a powerful drug) a fact that I finally had to come to terms with when my mother appeared. Namely, that ghosts exist, and I can see them. Though they seek me out, I'm not the only one who sees them: in the hospital, the nurses used to go running. I tried to reassure them, saying, "Come now, you're imagining things."

It was morning when I first heard my mother scream. Not the wee morning hours under the cover of night, but in the glaring daylight, so ill-suited to haunting. I went outside to see if there was someone in the street. It was a stupid, knee-jerk reaction driven by my own panic: I couldn't believe that I was hearing my dead mother's cries, and I thought maybe they were coming from outside. An accident, a fight.

The houses in the area, though very pretty, are built close together in a semidetached style, and noise carries. My next-door neighbor, Mari, hardly ever leaves her house, because she's terrified she'll be robbed or murdered or who knows what other phobic fantasies. Just as I went outside, she came to lean wide-eyed out her window that looks into my little front yard. Mari remembered my mother's real screams, too, and she was shocked and dumbfounded.

"It's the TV, Mari. It's okay," I told her.

"It's just—you realize what it sounds like, Doctor?"

"It really does. I can't believe it."

And I went back inside.

Since I didn't know what to do, I started looking around the house for the source of the cries, and asking my mother, as if I were praying, to be quieter. I didn't urge her to stop wailing entirely—just a little discretion, that was all I asked. I'd made the same request of other ghosts, first at the hospital and later on at a clinic. Sometimes that pleading worked. My mother always did have a sense of humor, and my appeal to turn down the volume made her laugh. I didn't find her that day—which I took off from work—but I did that night. She was sitting on the floor of the room where she'd died, which is now a storage room for furniture I never take the time to toss or give away. She was thin, but thin like she'd been at the beginning of her cancer, not the brittle and feverish wraith of her final months. I didn't dare approach; leaning in the doorway, my knees shaking, I sang to her. And as I sang I sank down until we were seated face-to-face, me with my legs crossed, her kneeling. I sang the song I used to sing when her pain had been unbearable, the song that used to soothe her, or so I chose to think. That night, she didn't scream.

But ghosts, I've learned, get upset. I don't know what they think, if they think at all, because it's more like they repeat themselves and the repetitions seem like thoughtless reflexes, but some of them do talk and have opinions and bad moods. My mother wanders the house. Sometimes she seems to know I'm there, and other times she doesn't. Sometimes it seems that the fury returns to her, the fury of her degraded body, the colostomy bag, the humiliation; she used to be so elegant, and I remember how she cried, "The smell, the smell!" Sometimes it was worse than the physical suffering. So she screams, and her screams can be pure rage. I have several ways of calming her down, but there's no reason to go into them here.

The interesting thing is what started to happen around the neighborhood. It made me realize that I wasn't crazy—I'd considered the possibility, as anyone would after seeing her dead mother climbing the stairs—and also that my mother wasn't the only ghost around.

MY NEIGHBORS HAVE "SAFETY" MEETINGS. They don't accomplish much. There have been break-ins around the neighborhood, some violent muggings, an old lady beaten. It's awful, the stuff that happens here. But the neighbors are even worse. They go to those meetings and yell about how they pay their taxes (which is only partly true: they evade everything they can, like most middle-class Argentines) and how they've bought guns and are taking classes on how to use them. And they describe exactly what they think the police should do to criminals: the suggestion of murder always comes up, or humiliation, medieval torture, an eye for an eye, that sort of thing. There's one man I don't know, a little older than me, who declares that the police should display the heads of these "illegals" on stakes, like in colonial days. No one opposes him, or even rolls their eyes. All the meetings end with the neighbors invoking their grandparents, such good people, all those European immigrants who arrived with nothing but the shirts on their backs, who came to find honest work, who were poor but dignified, who were white. Just another myth. The immigrants of that era were, in many cases, poor and thieving; others were anarchists running from the police, and most of them became dishonest merchants who prioritized earning money over assuming any kind of ethical responsibility. But I don't argue anymore, if I ever did. I'm resigned to that worldview they all share. It's a lie, but arguing against a credible lie is a task for titans.

I go to the meetings because I want to know what they're planning. I want to know in advance if they're going to close off the street, for example. One time, they installed an alarm system unbeknownst to me, and I accidentally set it off when I leaned against a door to check my phone messages. They also mounted a camera at my house without my permission, but I have to admit the thing has been helpful. At least it lets me see if someone tries to pick the lock, which has already happened, in fact, a couple of times. The camera is broken now, and I haven't found the time to fix it. I can just hear my daughter: "Mom, your stubbornness is going to get you killed and I'll be the one to find you lying here dead and I hope you've got money put away for my therapy because I'm not spending mine."

The emergency meeting they called in mid-July was a real shitshow. A horrible thing had happened, and the neighborhood was full of

TV cameras, from the regular stations and from cable and every other kind of media. Three teenage girls had been coming back from a party in the early morning. They had to cross our neighborhood to reach the projects, and someone shot them from a car. They didn't even have time to run. They died in the street. They were young, all three of them fifteen years old, and they'd been walking along holding hands and huddling over a phone to look at messages. And that's how they appear in the photo: huddled together but fallen, one on top of another, with their cropped shirts showing their flat stomachs, their leggings bloodied, and their sneakers brand-new. One girl's face was destroyed by the bullets, and she stared up at the treetops with what remained of her eyes. The others, beneath her, bled to death right there. The identities of the murderers were still unknown when the neighborhood meeting was called, but it was clear enough to us what had happened: one of the girls must have been the daughter or relative of a more or less important criminal—an asphalt pirate, a mini-narco, a pimp. That person had offended someone or owed them money: it was revenge. As the days passed, this theory was confirmed. A yellow police cordon blocked off the corner where the girls had been killed, but all around it people left bouquets of flowers, cardboard hearts, and teddy bears—a street-side grave with offerings more appropriate to little girls than teenagers.

I saw them one day at dusk as I was returning home from work. My taxi dropped me off right at the corner with the police cordon and the tributes to the girls. "Lu, we love you always!!!!!!!" "Justice for Natalia." "My little angel, you were gone too soon." They were taking photos as they walked: the three heads squeezed into the frame, pierced tongues sticking out (why do girls like to stick out their tongues so much?); a second round of pictures with duck-bill lips, that premature, phony sensuality. It had seemed especially grotesque in the real photographs of the girls that had appeared in the newspaper articles, pictures that had been posted on Instagram or TikTok, as my daughter explained to me: I didn't understand those images with dog noses or bunny ears, and then I found out they were "filters."

The ghost girls were laughing as they walked. At that hour, nearly nighttime, my neighborhood is deserted. "The night is dark and full of terrors," says a priestess in the epic series that my daughter watches with true fanatic zeal, and that I can't get into because it has too many characters (though its violence, which other people find disturbing, doesn't bother me). The ghost girls couldn't get the flash to work, and that made them laugh harder. They were incredibly compact—there's no other way to put it. They seemed like living girls doing the things that fifteen-year-olds do: oblivious to what's happening around them, wearing clothes a size or two too small for their bodies, their hair dyed and colorful, a jostling whirlwind of blue, green, black streaks. The neighborhood's windows opened timidly, and the silence rang out like a gunshot. Then someone in the house closest to the girls screamed. They were still about half a block away from me but I could already see them clearly, and I understood. One of them was bleeding from the neck. The blood flowed slowly down, and she wiped it away distractedly as if it were rainwater, or beer that some clumsy boy had spilled on her at the party. Another girl, the one whose face was destroyed, was taking photos unconcernedly, and the smallest one, skinny to the point of illness, had three red holes in her abdomen. I didn't want to look anymore; they reminded me of my mother and her cancer, her moribund thinness.

Then the girls started to look at the photos they had taken, and what they saw made them cry. "No, no, no," they said, and they shook their heads and looked at one another, looked at the photos, and saw the purplish green of putrefaction, and the blood, dried and fresh, the bullet wounds baring white bone, the blind eyes. The photos broke the spell of friendship and teenage immortality. Then they started to run. The ghost girls ran in desperate circles, and their wailing was truly terrifying. Their confused desperation. Had they only just realized that they were dead? How unfair: usually the dead have the good fortune not to see themselves decompose, even when they return as ghosts. My mother, for example: her image doesn't decay. But ghosts take different forms. I wonder if the shapes they take are determined by the dead people themselves or by those of us who see them—maybe those images are a collective construction.

The neighbors started to scream, too. It was madness. I heard a voice shout that someone had fainted and needed an ambulance, but who was going to call it with the girls right there, rotting in the lovely golden twilight? One of them, the one with blood running down her neck—the bullet had hit an artery—reminded me of Carolina. I don't know why. It wasn't her clothes: this girl wore the kind of cheap shirt and leggings you can buy in the neighborhood, maybe even at the supermarket. But there was something in the way she wore all that cheapness that reminded me of my daughter's unexpected flair (I say "unexpected" because I certainly don't have the gift of knowing which color goes with which, or what pants can make my legs look longer). Yes, the girl's leggings were cheap, made of black Lycra, but her white shirt draped prettily over her buttocks, just so, and, with some bulky sneakers that were possibly men's, the outfit gave her a style—an "urban chic," as my daughter would say—that was very particular. Her shoes were a brash royal blue, and around her bloody neck hung a little chain with a Victorian pendant that broke the street style with an ironic touch. As I describe her, I believe I'm imitating my daughter, who always adds a brief explanatory note to her fashion layouts. In any case, maybe because that girl made me think of Carolina, she was the one I approached.

Of course I was scared, my heart reverberating in the pit of my stomach as if it had relocated there. And I'm no longer of the age for that kind of fright: I'm already at risk for an arrhythmia, or even angina. Also, the neighbors were watching. But I couldn't just leave those girls like that. Did I know I would be able to calm them? I knew. One just knows these things. In the hospital, when I pacified my first ghosts more than ten years ago now—I knew then, too. But at the hospital they didn't calm down much. There were too many of them, and they fed off each other. Hysteria is contagious among spirits as well as humans. The phenomenon will never be studied, of course, because no one would believe it. I'm embarrassed myself. I think about this thing I do and I'm reminded of those cable series, disgraceful, false productions about Hollywood mediums and ghost hunters. TV programs spawned by the crisis of ideas and the economic crisis, made with bad actors and worse scripts, all identical, all ignorant, not even entertaining. That's not what I am, I tell myself; but I am also that, in a way.

I called the girls by their names, which was enough to get them to look at me, but not enough to stop them from screaming. For that, I had to talk to them. Ask them to delete the photos. They had trouble obeying; that's how it always is. And then I had to ask them to move on. Make them laugh a little. Talk to them about clothes. Ask them about the party they were coming from. Never mention the murder. They wailed a little more at the sight of the memorial and the police tape, but soon the moans faded to whimpers and hugs, self-pitying tears, until finally the girls, too, disappeared, or more like dissolved. Their images vaporized like watercolor paint or alcohol.

I had to sit down by the cordon for a second, and soon my neighbor Julio came out and joined me. Julio is very friendly, and he used to have a lovely corner bar in the neighborhood, but he couldn't keep up with the rent on the place. The drinks and food were too expensive and the customers too few, and, in sum, it was the same old story of restaurants and bars that go broke. I find it all deeply sad, and that's why I felt a greater affection for Julio than he perhaps deserved.

"What did you do, Doctor?"

"It's Emma, Julio. Call me Emma, please."

"What did you do, Emma?"

The question was repeated over the following weeks. There were semi-secret meetings among those who had seen what happened. Then the gatherings broadened to include those who hadn't been there. Needless to say, there was a whole lot of distrust and incredulity. They wore me down. I told them about my mother. My neighbor Mari vouched for my story but scolded me for lying to her that time I'd said the screams were coming from the TV.

"Mari, what did you want me to say? I was scared, too. I thought I was crazy."

That's not true, not entirely. A person knows when she's going crazy; it doesn't happen overnight, not even after a trauma. Everything, everything in the body is a process. Including death.

. . .

THE NEIGHBORS STARTED TO come see me in secret. Ashamed. The ghost epidemic—because that's what it was—coincided with the neighborhood's worst period. Whoever had ordered the hit on the three teenagers had now taken over the business in the housing projects. They were terrorizing people, with the muggings escalating to kidnappings: a particular kind of kidnapping called "express." The kidnappers pull their victims into a car and take them around to ATMs until they've withdrawn an amount the thieves deem acceptable. Sometimes these express kidnappings end in violence—beatings, rapes, the odd shooting—owing to an incredible misunderstanding. The thieves—who are, for the most part, very young men—don't have jobs, so they don't have bank accounts. They don't know that banks in Argentina let you withdraw only small amounts from ATMs, maybe twenty-five thousand pesos a day, or double that if you're a customer of the bank. If you have two accounts, you can get more cash by withdrawing from two different banks. But if not, well, you can't get much. And the thieves, those frightened and agitated boys, want more. And they think they're being lied to. That their victims are looking down on them and trying to cheat them. "You think I'm some kind of dumbass, huh? I'll show you." And then the punch, the gun butt to the face, the panic. They haven't done it to me yet but it happens a lot, and it happens to people who live in the projects, too. I mention that because I don't want to be unfair—not everyone in the projects is a criminal, of course. A lot of people have an apartment there the same way I have a house here, and no one can or wants to move, and that's it.

When the first neighbor came, I was chatting with Mom. Sometimes I talk to her. She's there, after all, and although she doesn't talk, she looks at me, and sometimes she nods. If she's not in a rage, she laughs. It's a shame she doesn't talk; we'd have more fun if she did. I don't invite my girlfriends over anymore because Mom might appear to them. My daughter comes less and less, but that's not her fault—she has a lot of work. In this country, she has to make the most of it: you never know how long a job will last, whether you're about to be fired or not—

the order to cut back on personnel can come suddenly, and it can take years to find another job. Best to prepare for that wait with a good nest egg. She and I talk on the phone and chat online. She doesn't know about her grandmother. I could tell her, but why? For now, there's no need.

Paulo was the first of the neighbors to visit me. He has two little girls, both in grade school. His wife "suffers from nerves"—that is, she has panic attacks. Paulo has a brother in the United States, and at the neighborhood meetings he goes on and on about how well people live there, what a safe country it is. I don't correct him. As I said, I don't like to argue. Paulo beat around the bush a lot before finally telling me his problem. He even asked if he could smoke, and seemed surprised when I said yes. To ease the tension I told him, "You know, most doctors smoke. Too much stress."

Paulo's problem, then: three months ago, a burglar tried to break into his house. From the roof. He knew it was a thief because the guy was carrying a small handgun, a .22. When they saw the intruder, Paulo locked his wife and daughters in a room and got a hammer—he wasn't one of the people who'd bought a gun for self-defense—and started to dial the police. Then, through the second-floor window, he saw the thief slip and fall from the roof to the patio below. When he told me that, I remembered the incident. It had been a subject of conversation at one of the neighborhood meetings, the one when they'd decided to request more of a police presence from the Ninth Precinct. The thief had died from the fall. I didn't ask Paulo if he'd let him die, but I think that's what happened. It's possible the man could have survived if the ambulance had arrived in time. I can imagine Paulo, hammer in hand, watching that death from the window, feeling like a small-time god with the power to decide another man's fate. Would I have done the same thing if my family had been threatened? Maybe. It's easy to have ethics when what you love is not in danger. I like to think I wouldn't have done it, though. I'm an idealist—I prefer naivete and paternalism to hatred.

However it happened, the thief came back. Paulo's wife heard him walking on the roof but Paulo didn't believe her. After all, she suffered from nerves, poor thing. Until he heard the footsteps himself. And he saw the burglar fall to the patio again. Soundlessly. That's what his ghost thief does, walks and falls, walks and falls. Paulo told me that once the thief is on the ground, "he laughs his ass off at us."

I agreed to go over there one night. The wife took the opportunity to show me the medication she'd been prescribed. On the whole, it seemed like too much, but I know doctors nowadays would rather over-prescribe than do a more comprehensive treatment. Paulo and his wife invited me to have dinner with them—hot dogs with mashed potatoes ("For the girls," the mother told me, "since they won't eat anything else")—but I'd already eaten at home. I waited. The footsteps came after the kids were in bed, fortunately. I decided that my work would begin after the ghost had fallen—once he'd finished his nightly rounds.

It took only a few minutes to dissuade him. It doesn't matter what I said or what I did: there's a moment when it all becomes very mechanical. This was my third encounter with uneasy neighborhood ghosts, but really I'd calmed some of them, my mother and the murdered girls, many times. I don't send the ghosts anywhere, nowhere good or bad. There's no peace or closure. No reconciliation. No passage to the other side. All of that is fiction. I just soothe them and keep them from reoffending so often that they make life unbearable for the living. But they do come back eventually; it's as if they forget, and we have to start all over again. Why is that? I remember how, when my husband and I were newlyweds, we had a beautiful cat, all white with a black nose, who always seemed surprised on weekends when we spoiled her with a special can of tuna. When I wondered if maybe she had some kind of memory problem, my husband said, "No, it's just that she has a tiny brain. Don't you see how small her head is?" But her face was so intelligent! And ghosts are a little like that. They seem human, they seem smart, but they're really just a sliver of a person that is compelled to repeat itself. They don't have brains, but they do have something that thinks, so to speak. It's just that it's as small as that of my cat, whose name was Florencia and who used to purr every night between my husband and me before we went to sleep. I miss my husband, but not as a husband. I miss his friendship, his conversation, his food (he's an excellent cook). But he needs to fall in love and care for someone, and I need to be alone.

After the ghost thief, others came. "Why this invasion?" I asked my mother once, and she seemed to be listening attentively. She didn't reply, she can't, but I already knew the answer: It wasn't the neighborhood that was being invaded. It was me. I was attracting them. That's why it didn't make sense for me to leave, not unless I learned how to rid myself of that magnetism. In truth, though, it didn't bother me. The fear very soon became adrenaline. When many days passed without a neighbor knocking at my door, I'd start to get impatient.

But this story only matters because of one ghost in particular, one with whom I behaved differently. One I couldn't or didn't want to help. Or is it the neighbors I help? The two things are intertwined.

My daughter's birthday is December 23. That year, maybe because we hadn't seen each other much, she invited me to her smaller "inner circle" party. (She'd had another, with friends and acquaintances, the weekend before: she isn't superstitious and doesn't mind celebrating in advance.) She also invited me to stay and spend Christmas and even New Year's with her, if I wanted, at her house in Palermo. I knew I would be invited to New Year's parties, so I said no to that, but I agreed to stay for Christmas and a few days more. I left my house carrying a bag, and I went by taxi, because I'd long since sold my car. I'm not that old, but neither am I young enough to drive as attentively as a city like Buenos Aires requires.

The days I spent with my daughter were good. We fought very little and laughed a lot. We watched her epic series and I half fell in love with Ned Stark, the kind of man I've never had, with a square jaw and an animal back. Plus, the actor wasn't all that much younger than me—maybe ten years, I figured. One night, I almost told Carolina about the spiritualist talent I'd acquired in old age—we had opened a bottle of champagne and were drinking it very cold, with lemon ice cream, ideal for the city's humid heat and stifling air. But I was afraid of ruining a visit that was nearly perfect. She'd have every right to think me demented. So I went home the afternoon of the twenty-ninth, crossing the city by subway this time, because going aboveground would have been an absurd proposition. In addition to the usual end-of-year protests, there were several others: state workers striking for raises; picketers blocking off streets, clamoring for bags of food; laid-off workers demonstrating in front of the Labor Ministry, demanding to be rehired; and a very large march in front of Congress, calling for stronger public safety measures.

A youth had been murdered: sixteen years old, a kid called Matías with an Italian last name. He'd been kidnapped. An express kidnapping, but the boy was a minor and didn't have an ATM card, so his captors had changed their plan and decided to ask his family for ransom. The family didn't have any ransom money. That night, the kidnappers still had him in the car—they must not have known where to take him and the boy escaped. He didn't get far. His captors shot him in the slum that borders our neighborhood to the north, the one that had been planned as a sports field, then became a vacant lot, and is now a neighborhood of squatters that the authorities are constantly threatening to evict, but probably never will. Where would they send all those people? Plus, some of the houses are now being built with good bricks and have a second story. Not long ago, on my way to buy food, I saw that a news kiosk and an ice cream shop had opened there. The police arrested a few suspects from the slum, but apparently the kidnappers weren't from around there. People on TV were calling for the death penalty, as they always do in my country when a terrible murder is committed.

Strangely, and in spite of the fact that the crime had happened so close by, my neighbors didn't call an emergency meeting. I waited for it for a few days—a phone message, or sometimes a piece of paper stuck to the door with Scotch tape—but there was only silence, eyes lowered in the grocery shop, a certain haste when buying cigarettes at the kiosk. I attributed it to nerves, though this tense reticence was not how my neighbors usually reacted; they tended more toward exaggerated anxiety shouted at the top of their lungs.

The knocks at my door woke me up. It was late, I knew before I looked at the clock: I've gone to bed in the early morning since I was young, a habit from being on call that I could never shake. It was a gentle knocking: someone was outside. I decided to ignore it. But the sound continued, rhythmic, insistent, growing in urgency, until I realized that now the person was pounding with both fists, as if to break down the door. I was scared. I thought about locking my bedroom door, but, oh right, I didn't have the key. What could I put between me and whoever it was who wanted to get in? Should I call Mari? The police? I sat up in bed, and when I heard the whispering, the sweat on my hands went cold, but at the same time I felt calmer: it wasn't a real person pounding. His low voice, his pleading, wouldn't have reached me from the front door. "Please, open up," he was saying. He spoke politely. "Please, they're after me. I don't want to rob you, I'm not a thief. They kidnapped me! Please let me in or they'll kill me, they'll kill me!"

I ran downstairs and looked out the window. The boy was on the sidewalk. A tall teenager, very visible under the streetlight. He was pale like all dead people, but I couldn't see his wounds, even though he was dressed for summer in a white T-shirt, soccer shorts, running shoes. Where had he been shot? I couldn't remember. During the days I'd spent with my daughter, I'd been happily disconnected from the news and TV. So here was Matías with the Italian last name, murdered just blocks away from my house, and I didn't know exactly how he had died or why he was knocking at my door.

Although I could guess. Was my neighbors' silence related to this apparition? Of course it was, I told myself. And in more ways than one.

Matías stopped beating on the door when he saw me. He approached the window, and his eyes—alive, totally alive, insect-like, with the buzzing shine of beetles—held vengeance and rage. I wasn't afraid of him, because I knew he couldn't take his revenge in the material world, but the frustration of being unable to act added layers to his fury, endless layers. He was going to spend what time he had—and I suspected that

Matías with the Italian last name had all the time in the world—running up and down this street. Until the street no longer existed, if necessary. These people had helped kill him, and he was never going to let them sleep. Never.

"You're not going to open up?" he asked. His voice was clear, not very different from a living person's. He no longer sounded so polite.

I went to the door, turned the key, and opened it. Matías stayed in the doorway. Then I saw the hole in his temple. It was subtle, like a mole. It wasn't bleeding. It reminded me of the suicides I used to get at the hospital. Most of them male, most his age, not all so precise with the gunshot; they often destroyed their faces or put the gun barrel in their mouths.

"It's too late now," Matías told me. I knew I couldn't calm him, not this one, and in a very loud voice I said, "I wasn't home that night! You know that. I would have let you in."

"Yeah? I don't believe you," he said.

A conversation! Not just replying to questions with a shake of the head. Matías with the Italian last name could have conversations. How was he different from the others? I stayed on the threshold with the door open and the light on and I watched him leave. He ran from one house to another, knocking; he knocked on every door. First lightly, then with fists, and finally kicking. He started by politely entreating people to open up, and he ended with insults; he was terrified in his anger, his desperation, but he was also astonished. My neighbors turned on their lights, but no one opened their door. I heard one man moan.

Matías with the Italian last name kept pounding on doors until the sun came up. Only then did I go back inside. He didn't miss a single house. They all got what they deserved.

I looked up his last name online. Cremonesi. Matías Cremonesi. Sixteen years old, he was in high school, played basketball—of course, with that height—and they'd shot him on a small soccer field in the slum. One of the murderers had been caught. Naturally, he said the other man had wielded the gun and pulled the trigger, and he'd done it only because Matías had seen their faces when he escaped. And he knew them. This confessed murderer was from the housing projects, and Matías was, too. Why kill a neighbor? The kidnapper, who was nineteen, said again that it hadn't been their intention, that they'd only wanted him to take some money from an ATM. "But he said he didn't have a card. He lied to us and we got mad. We weren't in our right minds."

THAT DAY AT NOON, my neighbor Julio, the one with the failed bar, paid me a visit. The neighbors had sent Julio because they knew I liked him. He didn't hem and haw like Paulo, the one who'd watched the burglar die. He was direct. He claimed not to feel guilty. Yes, they had all heard the boy that night. Yes, they all thought it was a trick, a lie by a cunning thief who wanted to pass himself off as a victim so he could get into someone's house. Yes, when they looked out the window and saw a teenager, their suspicion had been confirmed—weren't thieves always teenage boys? "And don't give me that shit about how they're victims, too," he said. "You may think that. All of them victims of society. Stop fucking around, Emma." I hadn't opened my mouth. "You can think that way because they've never really gotten you. But they're not victims of anything." I still hadn't said a word. I understood he was trying to deal with his guilt.

"How long did he knock on people's doors?" I wanted to know. "How long did he ask to be let in?"

Beneath the hatred, Matías's ghostly eyes had been imbued with fear, the adrenaline of his final night, when he realized that he was going to die alone. He'd had to comprehend that no one was going to help him, not even by making a phone call, and that he was surrounded by hoodless executioners hiding behind the facade of a middle-class, respectable neighborhood.

Julio didn't want to answer. He said he didn't know. "A while. Does it matter?"

"It matters," I told him. "Because the boy is furious. And what can I tell him to convince him to leave us alone? That we were wrong? It's not enough."

"You have to try."

"No," I replied. "I don't know how."

"You don't want to. You think you're better than us. You wouldn't have let him in, either!"

"That's what Matías told me last night."

"Don't use his name."

"Why not? He does have a name."

"And how are we going to sleep? What about the children?"

"Julio, you all should have thought of that sooner. Buy some sleeping pills. I can give you a prescription. It's a very fine medicine, no side effects."

Confounded, Julio pounded the table. "Do you think I'm stupid?"

"Not at all. But I'm no one's servant. I'm willing to deal with this presence until it changes on its own. Though as you know, they aren't prone to change. And you can stop yelling at me in my own house—it's not the best way to convince me."

Julio left, and I felt disappointment. I had thought him a better person. Other people came to plead with me. Several of them. I told them to go and cry in church. They were angry at me, but it would pass. Maybe they'd go crazy. None of them took me up on my offer of a prescription for sleeping pills. It never ceases to amaze me how much suffering a person will put up with because they're prejudiced against psychiatric drugs. Or maybe they just didn't want to accept something like that from me, at least for the time being.

Matías came back every night to carry out his routine. Some of the neighbors shouted more than he did. When I woke up—rarely, because I did take sleeping pills—I chatted online with my ex-husband, who, down south, was also awake. "It's age," he told me. "I don't sleep well anymore."

With the passing days, one of my neighbors—the owner of the car service—broke. He gave a statement to the police saying that Matías Cremonesi had knocked at the door of his business begging for a ride home, pleading to be a passenger. But Matías Cremonesi didn't have any money on him, and my neighbor had refused to take him. A ten-block drive, at most. Plus, he added, the boy didn't look trustworthy. He seemed high. What if he was lying, what if he was a thief?

What could he steal? I thought. The man had nothing; no one ever used that car service. My neighbor the driver spent all his time drinking mate and listening to soccer games. He had two customers a week, maybe three. He got by because he owned his building—he couldn't have paid rent. He regretted his mistake, he said. "Poor kid, but you just don't know what kind of insecurity we live with in this neighborhood."

I told my husband how on the night the whole neighborhood had left Matías in the street and in danger, the night he died, I had been staying at Carolina's house. "But," I wrote to him in our chat, "what if I had been there? Would I have opened the door? Or would I have acted like all the others?"

"Maybe you wouldn't have opened," he answered. "But you would have at least called the police. They didn't even do that?"

"They didn't even do that," I replied.

I didn't tell him that the boy's ghost came every night to remind us of our meanness and our cowardice. It was a secret among the neighbors. My family was so far away! Except for Mom, of course. My ex-husband asked me, again, to go live with him and his wife down south. "She's pregnant," he told me.

"You're crazy," I said. "Sixty is too old to have a baby."

"Why do you think I can't sleep?" he asked.

"I'll think about moving," I lied.

It turns out that my ex-husband's wife has a high-risk pregnancy, and I think he'd like to have me close by to help if there's an emergency or complication. But I'm no longer on the side of the living. I can't leave my mother alone; she spends more and more nights sitting in the kitchen, just as she did when she was sick and couldn't sleep for the pain. Nor can I leave the rotting girls who laugh hand in hand on the street, though they appear less and less often. Where will they go, if someday they leave for good? Where are they during those long periods when I don't see them? The other day, one of them, the one who reminds me of my daughter, took a picture of me with her ghost Samsung. Where is my image? To whom does she show it? Nor do I want to abandon the drunken thief who died alone on the patio under Paulo's gaze: sometimes I see him perched on the roof, expectant as an owl. Is he planning something? And I can't leave the relentless Matías, though he hates me: his knocking is my lullaby. I don't know if I could sleep without his visits. All of them, my sad dead, are my responsibility. I asked my mother if Matías would let me soothe him someday, and she did something incredible: she stuck out her tongue at me. My mother wears a very pretty blue dress printed with anchors, and she looks like a seasoned old sailor. I returned her salute by sticking out my tongue, too, and we laughed together, and I wondered if I was going to grow old with her in this house, until the two of us, mother and daughter, were the same age, going up and down the stairs, sitting in the kitchen, anchors on her dress, coffee stains on my white shirt, and, outside, a future of dead boys and a city that just doesn't know what to do anymore.

War of the Clowns

Mia Couto

Translated from Portuguese by Eric M. B. Becker

One time two clowns set to arguing. The people would stop, amused, to watch them.

—What's that? they asked.

—Why, it's only two clowns arguing.

Who could take them seriously? Ridiculous, the two comedians reparteed. The arguments were common nonsense, the theme was a ninnery. And an entire day passed.

The following morning, the two remained, obnoxious and outdoing each other. It seemed as though, between them, even yucca soured. In the street, meanwhile, those present were exhilarated with the masquerade. The buffoons began sharpening their insults with fine-edged and fine-tuned barbs. Believing it to be a show, the passersby left coins along the roadside.

On the third day, however, the clowns resorted to violence. Their blows were clumsy, their counterkicks zinged more across air than across bodies. The children rollicked, imitating each jester's blows. And they laughed at the two fools, their bodies tripping upon their own selves. And the boys wanted to repay the delightful goodness of the clowns.

—Dad, give me some coins to leave on the sidewalk.

On the fourth day, the jabs and blows grew worse. Beneath their makeup, the faces of the clowns began to bleed. Some kids became scared. Was that real blood?

—It's not serious, don't fret, their parents soothed them.

Missed aims resulted in some being struck by blows. But it was light fare, only serving to add to the laughs. More and more people joined the gallery.

—What's going on?

Nothing. A friendly unsettling of accounts. It's not worth separating them. They'll tire themselves out, it's nothing more than a bit of clowning around.

On the fifth day, however, one of the clowns armed himself with a stick. Advancing on his adversary, he discharged a blow that tore off his wig. The other, furious, equipped himself with an identical truncheon and responded with the same lack of proportion. The wooden rods whistled through the air in somersaults and deliriums. One of the spectators, unexpectedly, was struck. The man fell, deadspread.

A certain confusion arose; the supporters divided into two camps. Little by little, two battlefields began to form. Various groups traded drubbings. Still more lay fallen.

The quarrel entered a second week and in the surrounding neighborhoods it was heard said that a dizzied pandemonium had set in around the two clowns. And the thing embroiled the entire plaza. And the neighbors found it funny. Some went to the plaza to verify the reports. They returned with contradicting and inflamed versions of their own. The neighborhood continued to divide itself, in opposing opinions. Conflicts spread to other neighborhoods.

On the twentieth day, shots could be heard. No one knew exactly where they came from. It could have been from any point in the city. Full of terror, the inhabitants armed themselves. The tiniest movement seemed suspect. The gunshots spread. Dead bodies began to pile up in the streets. Terror reigned over the whole city. Soon, massacres ensued.

At the beginning of the month, all the city's inhabitants had died. All except the two clowns. That morning, the comics sat, each one in his corner, and cast off their ridiculous dress. They looked at each other, worn out. Later, they rose to their feet and embraced, laughing at the flags dispersed along the ground. Arm in arm, they gathered the coins from the roadsides. Together they crossed the ravaged city, careful not to tread on the corpses. And they went in search of another city.

One Minus One

Colm Tóibín

The moon hangs low over Texas. The moon is my mother. She is full tonight, and brighter than the brightest neon; there are folds of red in her vast amber. Maybe she is a harvest moon, a Comanche moon. I have never seen a moon so low and so full of her own deep brightness. My mother is six years dead tonight, and Ireland is six hours away and you are asleep.

I am walking. No one else is walking. It is hard to cross Guadalupe; the cars come fast. In the Community Whole Foods Store, where all are welcome, the girl at the checkout asks me if I would like to join the store's club. If I pay seventy dollars, my membership, she says, will never expire, and I will get a 7 per cent discount on my purchases.

Six years. Six hours. Seventy dollars. Seven per cent. I tell her I am here for a few months only, and she smiles and says that I am welcome. I smile back. The atmosphere is easy, casual, gracious.

If I called you now, it would be half two in the morning; I could wake you up. If I called, I could go over everything that happened six years ago. Because that is what is on my mind tonight, as though no time had elapsed, as though the strength of the moonlight had by some fierce magic chosen tonight to carry me back to the last real thing that happened to me. On the phone to you across the Atlantic, I could go over the days surrounding my mother's funeral. I could go over the details as though I were in danger of forgetting them. I could remind you, for example, that you wore a suit and a tie at the funeral. I remember that I could see you when I spoke about her from the altar, that you were over in the side aisle, on the right. I remember that you, or someone, said that you had to get a taxi from Dublin because you missed the train or the bus. I know that I looked for you among the crowd and could not see you as the hearse came after Mass to take my mother's coffin to the graveyard, as all of us began to walk behind it. You came to the hotel once she was in the ground, and you stayed for a meal with me and Sinead, my sister. Jim, her husband, must have been near, and Cathal, my brother, but I don't remember what they did when the meal had finished and the crowd had dispersed. I know that as the meal came to an end a friend of my mother's, who noticed everything, came over and looked at you and whispered to me that it was nice that my friend had come. She used the word "friend" with a sweet, insinuating emphasis. I did not tell her that what she had noticed was no longer there, was part of the past. I just said yes, it was nice that you had come.

You know that you are the only person who shakes his head in exasperation when I insist on making jokes and small talk, when I refuse to be direct. No one else has ever minded this as you do. You are alone in wanting me always to say something that is true. I know now, as I walk towards the house I have rented here, that if I called and told you that the bitter past has come back to me tonight in these alien streets with a force that feels like violence, you would say that you are not surprised. You would wonder only why it has taken six years.

I was living in New York then, the city about to enter its last year of innocence. I had a rented apartment there, just as I had a rented apartment everywhere I went. It was on 90th and Columbus. You never saw it. It was a mistake. I think it was a mistake. I didn't stay there long—six or seven months—but it was the longest I stayed anywhere in those years or the years that followed. The apartment needed to be furnished, and I spent two or three days taking pleasure in the sharp bite of buying things: two easy chairs that I later sent back to Ireland; a leather sofa from Bloomingdale's, which I eventually gave to one of my students; a big bed from 1-800-Mattress; a table and some chairs from a place downtown; a cheap desk from the thrift shop.

And all those days—a Friday, a Saturday and a Sunday at the beginning of September—as I was busy with delivery times, credit cards and the whiz of taxis from store to store, my mother was dying and no one could find me. I had no mobile phone, and the phone line in the apartment had not been connected. I used the pay phone on the corner if I needed to make calls. I gave the delivery companies a friend's phone number, in case they had to let me know when they would come with my furniture. I phoned my friend a few times a day, and she came shopping with me sometimes and she was fun and I enjoyed those days. The days when no one in Ireland could find me to tell me that my mother was dying.

Eventually, late on the Sunday night, I slipped into a Kinko's and went online and found that Sinead had sent me email after email, starting three days before, marked "Urgent" or "Are you there" or "Please reply" or "Please acknowledge receipt" and then just "Please!!!" I read one of them, and I replied to say that I would call as soon as I could find a phone, and then I read the rest of them one by one. My mother was in the hospital. She might have to have an operation. Sinead wanted to talk to me. She was staying at my mother's house. There was nothing more in any of them, the urgency being not so much in their tone as in their frequency and the different titles she gave to each email that she sent.

I woke her in the night in Ireland. I imagined her standing in the hall at the bottom of the stairs. I would love to say that Sinead told me my mother was asking for me, but she said nothing like that. She spoke instead about the medical details and how she herself had been told the news that our mother was in the hospital and how she had despaired of ever finding me. I told her that I would call again in the morning, and she said that she would know more then. My mother was not in pain now, she said, although she had been. I did not tell her that my classes would begin in three days, because I did not need to. That night, it sounded as though she wanted just to talk to me, to tell me. Nothing more.

But in the morning when I called I realized that she had put quick thought into it as soon as she heard my voice on the phone, that she had known I could not make arrangements to leave for Dublin late on a Sunday night, that there would be no flights until the next evening. She had decided to say nothing until the morning; she had wanted me to have an easy night's sleep. And I did, and in the morning when I phoned she said simply that there would come a moment very soon when the family would have to decide. She spoke about the family as though it were as distant as the urban district council or the government or the United Nations, but she knew and I knew that there were just the three of us. We were the family, and there is only one thing that a family is ever asked to decide in a hospital. I told her that I would come home; I would get the next flight. I would not be in my new apartment for some of the furniture deliverers, and I would not be at the university for my first classes. Instead, I would find a flight to Dublin, and I would see her as soon as I could. My friend phoned Aer Lingus and discovered that a few seats were kept free for eventualities like this. I could fly out that evening.

YOU KNOW THAT I do not believe in God. I do not care much about the mysteries of the universe, unless they come to me in words, or in music maybe, or in a set of colours, and then I entertain them merely for their beauty and only briefly. I do not even believe in Ireland. But you know, too, that in these years of being away there are times when Ireland comes to me in a sudden guise, when I see a hint of something familiar that I want and need. I see someone coming towards me with a soft way of smiling, or a stubborn uneasy face, or a way of moving warily through a public place, or a raw, almost resentful stare into the middle distance. In any case, I went to JFK that evening and I saw them as soon as I got out of the taxi: a middle-aged couple pushing a trolley that had too much luggage on it, the man looking fearful and mild, as though he might be questioned by someone at any moment and not know how to defend himself, and the woman harassed and weary, her clothes too colourful, her heels too high, her mouth set in pure, blind determination, but her eyes humbly watchful, undefiant.

I could without any difficulty have spoken to them and told them why I was going home and they both would have stopped and asked me where I was from, and they would have nodded with understanding when I spoke. Even the young men in the queue to check in, going home for a quick respite—just looking at their tentative stance and standing in their company saying nothing, that brought ease with it. I could breathe for a while without worry, without having to think. I, too, could look like them, as though I owned nothing, or nothing much, and were ready to smile softly or keep my distance without any arrogance if someone said, "Excuse me," or if an official approached.

When I picked up my ticket and went to the check-in desk, I was told to go to the other desk, which looked after business class. It occurred to me, as I took my bag over, that it might be airline policy to comfort those who were going home for reasons such as mine with an upgrade, to cosset them through the night with quiet sympathy and an extra blanket or something. But when I got to the desk I knew why I had been sent there, and I wondered about God and Ireland, because the woman at the desk had seen my name being added to the list and had told the others that she knew me and would like to help me now that I needed help.

Her name was Joan Carey, and she had lived next door to my aunt's house, where myself and Cathal were left when my father got sick. I was eight years old then. Joan must have been ten years older, but I remember her well, as I do her sister and her two brothers, one of whom was close to me in age. Their family owned the house that my aunt lived in, the aunt who took us in. They were grander than she was and much richer, but she had become friendly with them. Since the houses shared a large back garden and some outhouses, there was a lot of traffic between the two establishments.

Cathal was four then, but in his mind he was older. He was learning to read already, he was clever and had a prodigious memory, and was treated as a young boy in our house rather than as a baby; he could decide which clothes to wear each day and what television he wanted to watch and which room he would sit in and what food he would eat. When his friends called at the house, he could freely ask them in, or go out with them.

In all the years that followed, Cathal and I never once spoke about our time in this new house with this new family. And my memory, usually so good, is not always clear. I cannot recall, for example, how we got to the house, who drove us there, or what this person said. I know that I was eight years old only because I remember what class I was in at school when I left and who the teacher was. It is possible that this period lasted just two or three months. Maybe it was more. It was not summer, I am sure of that, because Sinead, who remained unscathed by all of this (or so she said when once, years ago, I asked her about it), was back at boarding school. I have no memory of cold weather in that house in which we were deposited, although I do think that the evenings were dark early. Maybe it was from September to December. Or the first months after Christmas. I am not sure.

What I remember clearly is the rooms themselves, the parlour and dining room almost never used and the kitchen, larger than ours at home, and the smell and taste of fried bread. I hated the hot thick slices, fresh from the pan, soaked in lard or dripping. I remember that our cousins were younger than we were and had to sleep during the day, or at least one of them did, and we had to be quiet for hours on end, even though we had nothing to do; we had none of our toys or books. I remember that nobody listened to us or smiled when they saw us, either of us, not even Cathal, who, before and after this event, was greatly loved and wanted by people who came across him.

We slept in my aunt's house and ate her food as best we could, and we must have played or done something, although we never went to school. Nobody did us any harm in that house; nobody came near us in the night, or hit either of us, or threatened us, or made us afraid. The time we were left by our mother in our aunt's house has no drama attached to it. It was all greyness, strangeness. Our aunt dealt with us in her own distracted way. Her husband was often away or busy; when he was in the house he was mild-mannered, almost good-humoured.

And all I know is that our mother did not get in touch with us once, not once, during this time. There was no letter or phone call or visit. Our father was in the hospital. We did not know how long we were going to be left there. In the years that followed, our mother never explained her absence, and we never asked her if she had wondered how we were, or how we felt, during those months.

This should be nothing, because it resembled nothing, just as one minus one resembles zero. It should be barely worth recounting to you as I walk the empty streets of this city in the desert so far away from where I belong. It seems as though Cathal and I spent that time in the shadow world, as though we were quietly lowered into the dark, everything familiar missing, and nothing we did or said could change this. Because no one harmed us or made us afraid, it did not strike us that we were in a world where no one loved us, or that such a thing might be of any significance. We did not complain. We were emptied of everything, and in the vacuum came something like silence—almost no sound at all, just some sad echoes and dim feelings.

I PROMISE YOU THAT I will not call. I have called you enough, and woken you enough times, in the years when we were together and in the years since then. But there are nights now in this strange, flat and forsaken place when those sad echoes and dim feelings come to me slightly more intensely than before. They are like whispers, or trapped whimpering sounds. And I wish that I had you here, and I wish that I had not called you all those other times when I did not need to as much as I do now.

My brother and I learned not to trust anyone. We learned then not to talk about things that mattered to us, and we stuck to this as much as we could with a sort of grim stubborn pride all of our lives, as though it were a skill. But you know that, don't you? I don't need to call you to tell you that.

. . .

At JFK that night, Joan Carey smiled warmly and asked me how bad things were. When I told her that my mother was dying, she said that she was shocked. She remembered my mother so well, she said. She said she was sorry. She explained that I could use the first-class lounge, making it clear, however, in the most pleasant way, that I would be crossing the Atlantic in coach, which was what I had paid for. If I needed her, she said, she could come up in a while and talk, but she had told the people in the lounge and on the plane that she knew me, and they would look after me.

As we spoke and she tagged my luggage and gave me my boarding pass, I guessed that I had not met her for more than thirty years. But in her face I could see the person I had known, as well as traces of her mother and one of her brothers. In her presence I could feel that this going home to my mother's bedside would not be simple, that some of our loves and attachments are elemental and beyond our choosing, and for that very reason they come spiced with pain and regret and need and hollowness and a feeling as close to anger as I will ever be able to manage.

Sometime during the night in that plane, as we crossed part of the western hemisphere, quietly and, I hope, unnoticed, I began to cry. I was back then in the simple world before I had seen Joan Carey, a world in which someone whose heartbeat had once been mine, and whose blood became my blood, and inside whose body I once lay curled, herself lay stricken in a hospital bed. The idea of losing her made me desperately sad. And then I tried to sleep. I pushed back my seat as the night wore on and kept my eyes averted from the film being shown, whatever it was, and let the terrible business of what I was flying towards hit me.

I hired a car at the airport, and I drove across Dublin in the washed light of that early September morning. I drove through Drumcondra, Dorset Street, by Mountjoy Square, down Gardiner Street and through the streets across the river that led south, as though they were a skin that I had shed. I did not stop for two hours or more, until I reached the house, fearing that if I pulled up somewhere to have breakfast the numbness that the driving with no sleep had brought might lift.

Sinead was just out of bed when I arrived but Jim was still asleep. Cathal had gone back to Dublin the night before, she said, but would be down later. She sighed and looked at me. The hospital had phoned, she went on, and things were worse. Your mother, she said, had a stroke during the night, on top of everything else. It was an old joke between us: never "our mother" or "my mother" or "Mammy" or "Mummy," but "your mother."

The doctors did not know how bad the stroke had been, she said, and they were still ready to operate if they thought they could. But they needed to talk to us. It was a pity, she added, that your mother's specialist, the man who looked after her heart, and whom she saw regularly and liked, was away. I realized then why Cathal had gone back to Dublin—he did not want to be a part of the conversation that we would have with the doctors. Two of us would be enough. He had told Sinead to tell me that whatever we decided would be fine with him.

Neither of us blamed him. He was the one who had become close to her. He was the one she loved most. Or maybe he was the only one she loved. In those years, anyway. Or maybe that is unfair. Maybe she loved us all, just as we loved her as she lay dying.

And I moved, in those days—that Tuesday morning to the Friday night when she died—from feeling at times a great remoteness from her to wanting, almost in the same moment, my mother back where she had always been, in witty command of her world, full of odd dreams and perspectives, difficult, ready for life. She loved, as I did, books and music and hot weather. As she grew older she had managed, with her friends and with us, a pure charm, a lightness of tone and touch. But I knew not to trust it, not to come close, and I never did. I managed, in turn, to exude my own lightness and charm, but you know that too. You don't need me to tell you that either, do you?

I regretted nonetheless, as I sat by her bed or left so that others might see her, I regretted how far I had moved away from her, how far away from her I had stayed. I regretted how much I had let those months apart from her in the limbo of my aunt's house, and the years afterwards back in our own house, as my father slowly died, eat away at my soul. I regretted how little she knew about me, as she, too, must have regretted that, although she never complained or mentioned it, except perhaps to Cathal, and he told no one anything. Maybe she regretted nothing. But nights are long in winter, when darkness comes down at four o'clock and people have time to think of everything.

Maybe that is why I am here now, away from Irish darkness, away from the long, deep winter that settles so menacingly on the place where I was born. I am away from the east wind. I am in a place where so much is empty because it was never full, where things are forgotten and swept away, if there ever were things. I am in a place where there is nothing. Flatness, a blue sky, a soft, unhaunted night. A place where no one walks. Maybe I am happier here than I would be anywhere else, and it is only the poisonous innocence of the moon tonight that has made me want to dial your number and see if you are awake.

As we drove to see my mother that morning, I could not ask Sinead a question that was on my mind. My mother had been sick for four days now and was lying there maybe frightened, and I wondered if she had reached out her hand to Cathal and if they had held hands in the hospital, if they had actually grown close enough for that. Or if she had made some gesture to Sinead. And if she might do the same to me. It was a stupid, selfish thing I wondered about, and, like everything else that came into my mind in those days, it allowed me to avoid the fact that there would be no time any more for anything to be explained or said. We had used up all our time. And I wondered if that made any difference to my mother then, as she lay awake in the hospital those last few nights of her life: we had used up all our time.

She was in intensive care. We had to ring the bell and wait to be admitted. There was a hush over the place. We had discussed what I would say to her so as not to alarm her, how I would explain why I had come back. I told Sinead I would say that I'd heard she was in the hospital and I'd had a few days free before classes began and had decided to come back to make sure that she was OK.

"Are you feeling better?" I asked her.

She could not speak. Nonetheless, she let us know that she was thirsty and they would not allow her to drink anything. She had a drip in her arm. We told the nurses that her mouth was dry, and they said that there was nothing much we could do, except perhaps take tiny drops of cold water and put them on her lips using those special little sticks with sponge tips that women use to put on eye make-up.

I sat by her bed and spent a while wetting her lips. I was at home with her now. I knew how much she hated physical discomfort; her appetite for these drops of water was so overwhelming and so desperate that nothing else mattered.

And then word came that the doctors would see us. When we stood up and told her that we would be back, she hardly responded. We were ushered by a nurse with an English accent down some corridors to a room. There were two doctors there; the nurse stayed in the room with us. The doctor who seemed to be in charge, who said that he would have been the one to perform the operation, told us that he had just spoken to the anaesthetist, who had insisted that my mother's heart would not survive an operation. Her having had a stroke, he said, did not help.

"I could have a go," he said, and then immediately apologized for speaking like that. He corrected himself: "I could operate, but she could die on the operating table."

There was a blockage somewhere, he said. There was no blood getting to her kidneys and maybe elsewhere as well—the operation would tell us for certain, but it might end by being exploratory, it might do nothing to solve the problem. It was her circulation, he said. The heart was not beating strongly enough to send blood into every part of her body.

He knew to leave silence then, and the other doctor did too. The nurse looked at the floor.

"There's nothing you can do then, is there?" I said.

"We can make her comfortable," he replied.

"How long can she survive like this?" I asked.

"Not long," he said.

"I mean, hours or days?"

"Days. Some days."

"We can make her very comfortable," the nurse said.

There was nothing more to say. Afterwards, I wondered if we should have spoken to the anaesthetist personally, or tried to contact our mother's specialist, or asked that she be moved to a bigger hospital for another opinion. But I don't think any of this would have made a difference. For years, we had been given warnings that this moment would come, as she fainted in public places and lost her balance and declined. It had been clear that her heart was giving out, but not clear enough for me to have come to see her more than once or twice in the summer—and then when I did come I was protected from what might have been said, or not said, by the presence of Sinead and Jim and Cathal. Maybe I should have phoned a few times a week, or written her letters like a good son. But despite all the warning signals, or perhaps even because of them, I had kept my distance. And as soon as I entertained this thought, with all the regret that it carried, I imagined how coldly or nonchalantly a decision to spend the summer close by, seeing her often, might have been greeted by her, and how difficult and enervating for her, as much as for me, some of those visits or phone calls might have been. And how curtly efficient and brief her letters in reply to mine would have seemed.

And, as we walked back down to see her, the nurse coming with us, there was this double regret—the simple one that I had kept away, and the other one, much harder to fathom, that I had been given no choice, that she had never wanted me very much, and that she was not going to be able to rectify that in the few days she had left in the world. She would be distracted by her own pain and discomfort, and by the great effort she was making to be dignified and calm. She was wonderful, as she always had been. I touched her hand a few times in case she might open it and seek my hand, but she never did this. She did not respond to being touched.

Some of her friends came. Cathal came and stayed with her. Sinead and I remained close by. On Friday morning, when the nurse asked me if I thought she was in distress, I said that I did. I was sure that, if I insisted now, I could get her morphine and a private room. I did not consult the others; I presumed that they would agree. I did not mention morphine to the nurse, but I knew that she was wise, and I saw by the way she looked at me as I spoke that she knew that I knew what morphine would do. It would ease my mother into sleep and ease her out of the world. Her breathing would come and go, shallow and deep, her pulse would become faint, her breathing would stop, and then come and go again.

It would come and go until, in that private room late in the evening, it seemed to stop altogether, as, horrified and helpless, we sat and watched her, then sat up straight as the breathing started again, but not for long. Not for long at all. It stopped one last time, and it stayed stopped. It did not start again.

She lay still. She was gone. We sat with her until a nurse came in and quietly checked her pulse and shook her head sadly and left the room.

We stayed with her for a while more; then, when they asked us to leave, we touched her on the forehead one by one, and we left the room, closing the door. We walked down the corridor as though for the rest of our lives our own breathing would bear traces of the end of hers, of her final struggle, as though our own way of being in the world had just been halved or quartered by what we had seen.

We buried her beside my father, who had been in the grave waiting for her for thirty-three years. The next morning I flew back to New York, to my half-furnished apartment on 90th and Columbus, and I began my teaching a day later. I understood that I had over all the years postponed too much. As I settled down to sleep in that new bed in the dark city, I saw that it was too late now, too late for everything. I would not be given a second chance. In the hours when I woke, I have to tell you that this struck me almost with relief.

The Flower Garden

Mieko Kawakami

Translated from Japanese by Hitomi Yoshio

It happened at three o'clock in the afternoon on a sunny spring day, three months ago exactly.

There she was, standing on the terra-cotta tiles of the entryway to my house, next to my collection of colorful Repetto ballerina flats and my husband's polished shoes. I had carefully chosen those tiles considering the balance of colors and the overall nuanced effect.

Just then, I heard a voice.

The woman's lips remained still as she stared into my face. I heard the voice again. I listened, but couldn't decipher the words. I knew, intuitively, that they were directed toward me. I held my breath and focused on the voice. It was solid, a distinct alto. What was it saying? I couldn't tell. All I knew was that it was speaking to me. I stood there, staring silently at the woman who had appeared before me.

She was petite and demure looking, not the type of beauty that immediately attracted attention. But her long eyelashes, especially when she averted her gaze, left an impression that they were meant to attract the opposite sex. I felt strangely irritated by her plump lips and perfectly straight teeth. Her parents must have paid a fortune to fix them when she was young. Everything about her seemed calculated, from the way she moved her eyes to the way she held her head, from her perfect posture to the tone of her voice. You could see the marks of effort that you often see in women who are neither beautiful nor unattractive. These women surround themselves with cheerful colors and objects of the finest quality, pretending to enjoy them. They perfect the charade for so long that they convince themselves, and those around them, that their cheerfulness is the natural result of their inner confidence. That was the kind of woman that appeared before me. She was accompanied by the real estate agent whose voice I could barely stand to hear, who, for several months now, had brought strangers to my house, day in and day out, to leave their ugly footprints in every corner. In short, the woman was a potential buyer.

"THIS IS IT. I had a vague sense of what I wanted, but I didn't know exactly. Oh, this front porch! It's perfect."

Bowing her head slightly, the woman looked into my eyes with a smile. The real estate agent was nodding vigorously next to her. "I'm glad the house pleases you. It's quite different from what you had requested, but I see you rather like these *charming* types of homes. Well, this really expands our choices." With a smile flashing across his face, he introduced me as the owner's wife. I bowed in return and, offering each a pair of slippers, walked toward the living room.

I never volunteered any information unless they asked me a specific question. You can learn all you need to know about a house by walking around. If I were eager to sell, I would have said all kinds of things—for instance, how the house was designed by the British architectural firm that undertook the famous restaurant and garden in Gaienmae, or how we used the finest stucco for the walls and ceilings, even inside the closets. I could have told them how the light filled the rooms according to the season, how serene the neighborhood was, or how the dishwasher was top of the line, made by the German manufacturer Miele. But I said nothing. I didn't have the slightest desire to tell a random stranger how I had groomed and loved the house, or how much time and care I had devoted to perfecting it. The fact was that I was being driven away from my own home.

"Just look at the door, the color of the walls, these bay windows . . . everything is perfect. And with such a spacious dining room, you could put a sizable table there. It's always been my dream to have a solid wood dining table." Peering into the dining room and the kitchen, the woman sighed and exclaimed in an exaggerated fashion. *Of course everything is perfect. What could you possibly know about it?* I scoffed inwardly, trailing a few steps behind her.

Who was this woman anyway? Her bag and shoes were not expensive looking—it was hard to gauge how old she was. Plus, it was rare for a woman to come to a viewing alone. Since it was a Saturday, her husband should have come with her if she were married, and if not, she would have been accompanied by a parent or some other relative. (I gained all sorts of useless knowledge like this in the past few months.) Yes, it was indeed unusual that a woman would come to a viewing alone. She didn't seem like the type that would buy a house all on her own, and was definitely too young to buy one worth well over a hundred million yen, even with a mortgage. Who knows, perhaps her husband was buying the house for her, and he happened to be busy. That's how it was for me after all. Or could it be a gift from her parents? Yes, that must be it. But if so, wouldn't they want to come see the house for themselves?

Under normal circumstances, the seller has the right to choose the buyer, and to even inquire about his or her background to the extent that the information is not confidential. All parties are more or less equal between the seller, the buyer, and the agent who works on commission. But this was not so in our case. We had no right to ask questions or to make decisions. They would have laughed in our faces if we had insisted. When my husband's company filed for bankruptcy, we had no choice but to let go of our house, which was still under mortgage. "Voluntary liquidation," they had called it. Neither my husband nor I—who had designed the house and grew to love it over the years—was to decide on the value and its future occupant. No, it was to be handled by a random stranger who had never seen or set foot in the house.

Everything happened so quickly. It was worse than a situation defined by the common expression "downward spiral"—I may have felt some kind of pain or fear then. Instead, with no end in sight, I felt like a tiny grain floating amid a giant blank space where I could see and touch nothing. Everyone was laughing at me behind my back, though people never voiced their scorn—those who called or came to see me, neighbors who greeted us on the street, anonymous passersby, friends I hadn't seen in years were all laughing because the ostentatious house had caused our downfall.

Quiet by nature, my husband rarely spoke to me about his work. The accounting was processed internally by his employees, and I had no interest in that sort of thing to begin with. I knew he was involved in asset management and stocks, but those were handled at work and had nothing to do with me or my house. My role was simply to manage the household with the money left over after the monthly mortgage and insurance payments had been made. One day would pass, followed by another, and before long a whole year had passed without significance.

I couldn't recall a single occasion when I felt we were financially lacking, even when my husband was an ordinary salaryman before he started his own business. He was never concerned with how I spent our money, since we had neither children nor extravagant taste to speak of. From his demeanor, I always assumed that business was going well, and had no cause for worry. When we built our present house six years ago after getting rid of the house his father had left behind (how I had detested that traditional Japanese house with its gloomy gray tiled roof), the paperwork was taken care of by my husband and his company. All I had to do was sit down over tea with the architect my husband had chosen, discuss the layout of the house that I had drawn up, and confront the challenge of turning my vision into a reality.

So, like a child under parental care, I was completely oblivious as to what was happening to my husband's company and to my own home. Perhaps my husband had wanted it that way. I was kept in the dark until the very end, until the day he announced out of the blue that we would have to sell the house. I was aware that our nation was facing a financial crisis, and had even expressed concern when the topic came up among the neighborhood wives, but I never dreamed that the recession could affect us personally.

My life until then was made up of a series of numerical repetitions. The familiar numbers that appeared in the bank statement every month. The bill from my favorite antique furniture shop. House fixtures and furnishings would arrive carefully packaged. New fabric of the season. The bill from the farm in Kyushu prefecture that delivered fresh vegetables and meat. These appeared simply as numbers on the credit card bill, and I never imagined that they would come to an end. Those things happened to other people, living in other parts of the world. It was like politics—we understand that political issues are real and important, but still imagine that they exist in another realm separate from our everyday lives. I couldn't imagine that words like "bankruptcy" and "foreclosure" would have any relevance to my own life. It never occurred to me that the two realms might come together.

"YOU HAVE SUCH GIRLISH TASTE."

"Pardon me?" I said, startled, with a smile frozen on my face.

"Oh it's just that everything feels so *delicate*," the woman said. "And so *deliberate* too, from the wallpaper to the windows to the overall look of the house. We women never grow out of it, do we? I'm the same—I've always loved this kind of aesthetic. Take what you're wearing—it's so girlish in the most tasteful way. Straight out of a childhood dream."

"Thank you," I uttered, and said no more.

The woman proceeded to praise every item in the room in an exaggerated manner. "How lovely the wallpaper is. Oh, the colors, the patterns. The height of the sink is just right. The tiles give such a foreign feel. Everything is just *lovely*." Couldn't this woman keep her mouth shut for a second? Why must she babble on and on? She must believe that people like to be flattered—perhaps she was in that line of work. There are those who believe that as long as you flatter, people will like you and help you get on in the world. Or, was there disdain behind all her flattery? Perhaps it was both. In any event, the woman's exaggerated behavior annoyed me, leaving discomfort as if something was stuck between my teeth.

"Could I take a look at the bathroom?"

"Of course."

She opened the cabinet where the toilet papers were stored, checking the width and the door. She made sure the water ran properly. Buyers always inspect every corner of the house—the layout of the closets, the shelving unit in the powder room, the inside of the dishwasher, the position of the showerhead, the depth of the bathtub, the grout of the tiles—everywhere from the storage room to behind the shelves. The only things they refrain from opening are the wardrobe drawers. The woman went around the house nodding approvingly and making mental notes, while the real estate agent followed closely behind her. After inspecting the kitchen, she opened the back door and asked about the garbage collection schedule. I answered.

"Do you get a nice breeze? It must come in from here and go out over there. Could I see the second floor? Do you mind?"

In silence, we ascended the small spiral staircase made of solid natural wood, designed to perfection. I always took special care to polish the handrail, but as I placed my hand on it, I noticed that it was already growing dull. My heart ached. The woman walked briskly down the hallway. "May I see the bedroom?"

"Please."

"What's that over there?"

"A walk-in closet. You can also enter from the other side."

"What's on the other side?"

"A room I use as an atelier."

"An atelier? Oh, is that a sewing machine I see?"

"Yes, I use it to sew clothes."

"My goodness," the woman exclaimed in a high-pitched voice. "Are you a designer? Or do you make patterns?"

"No, it's just a hobby of mine." I noticed that my voice was faint.

"What a fairy-tale room," the woman burbled on. "I love the way the triangular roof frames the walls against the high ceilings. So charming. The wallpaper echoes the living room, yes? And look at all this lace. You make clothes, you said? What a refined hobby."

The woman seemed to smirk at me. As she turned and walked back toward the bedroom, I noticed that her footsteps and mannerisms had changed. Now, it was as if she were showing a visitor around her own house, proud of every little detail. "Oh, that tiny door over there?" She scurried back into the bedroom.

"It leads to a kind of dressing room," I answered.

"Oh, so this is the 'boudoir' in the layout. What a lovely dresser. This room has such a *foreign* feeling."

I WATCHED AS THE WOMAN walked across the carpet in my little room and stood next to the window with its delicate, ornamental shutters. The room would fill with gentle light in the morning and cool air in the evening. The woman was about to have it all. *She's standing where I should be.* When she reached for the curtain, I almost cried out, "Keep your hands off!" But I didn't. Then, looking through the window, the woman let out a short gasp. "Oh, the garden! Those flowers!"

I remained silent. Out of everything I was proud of in the house, what was most precious to me, what I had most invested my time and energy in, was the flower garden. The ground was covered in different varieties of thyme, so that from afar, it gave the impression of green waves. And floating among the waves were anemones, forget-me-nots, violets, ranunculus, and tulips, all of which had just begun to deepen their color. In the shaded parts of the garden, there bloomed spring starflowers, ajuga, and impatiens. Flowers also filled the front porch, which was custom designed. How carefully I had chosen the front gate! The fence with the angel relief would soon be covered with climbing roses. Every year, when the weather got warm, the Lady Banks' roses bloomed in clusters. Next to them were the Dorothy Perkins, and on the other side were the Japanese roses. And let's not forget the Iceberg roses. The Uncle Walters drew attention with their stubborn faces, the only red you saw in the garden. Their petals felt smooth and rich, like velvet. How many hours had I spent choosing the perfect pot for each type of flower, considering the overall balance? I searched for weeks for a shade of brick for the flower bed that would match the outer walls. I buried the bricks—just the right tint between beige and pink—one by one, creating a gentle curve along which I carefully interwove the conifers and dead nettles. It was an utterly unique garden that I had created with immeasurable care. The mailbox, the curve of the exterior walls, the lamppost, the signature Juneberry tree—I labored to find perfection in every detail. In Tokyo, where houses resemble large gray tombstones straight out of a generic architectural catalogue, I had created a fanciful haven overflowing with blooming flowers that dazzled the mind and momentarily transported one to the Cotswolds. I had created the house that I had dreamed of since childhood.

"I love it. I really do. Should I go ahead and buy it?"

Having inspected the house, the woman sighed deeply and contentedly. Then, with the words, "May I?" she made herself comfortable on the living room sofa. "Isn't it cozy?" she said to the real estate agent in an eager tone.

"We're so pleased the house is to your liking," he answered with a look of satisfaction, as if he had just given her a gift. *We*, he had said.

The woman glanced at the decorative shelf near her and noticed the photograph of my husband and me smiling happily. It was taken on our wedding anniversary last year at our favorite steak restaurant. Last year . . . we were smiling then. I felt a sting in my throat and leaned against the wall. All I could do was press my fingers against my temples and wait for the lump in my throat to go away. "Should I go ahead and buy it?" she had said. I repeated the words in my head. *Should I go ahead and buy it?* I almost laughed out loud. I wanted to burst out laughing to her face. But instead, I leaned against the wall in silence.

"I love it. A charming little house with a garden—I bet life would be pretty cozy here. And so many flowers—it's like living in a fantasy manga world of Yumiko Ōshima."

The woman kept rattling on to herself with a contented look on her face. I kept my eyes firmly closed and my arms crossed over my chest. *Should I go ahead and buy it?* How dare she? How could that be possible? And who was this Ōshima? You might be filthy rich, but you were a stranger to this house until today. You found it by chance through a real estate agent. You know nothing about what it takes to maintain a place like this—all the work that goes into getting the roses to bloom every year, to keep the garden lush and green. You couldn't care less about the Kohler enameled cast-iron sink, William Morris textiles, Laura Ashley fabrics, or James Jackson's Jacpol antique wax polish. You think the house looks like a *fairy tale*? You were irrelevant to my house, my life, my past until now . . . how could you possibly *buy* all of this? What does that even mean? To make it all yours? I don't understand. Who are you anyway?

THE WOMAN THANKED ME and the real estate agent informed me that I would be contacted at a later date. They drove away.

I went back into the house and glanced at the clock. It had just turned five. At this time of day in spring, the flowers are engulfed in the mysterious aura of the evening mist, making you feel as if you've wandered into a Monet painting. How I loved gazing at the garden from the left-hand window of the living room. I would imagine myself from the outside, looking out through the small window of the house with its triangle roof, surrounded by modest yet well-groomed flowers amid the deep green. I never tired of gazing out as the garden faded in twilight, as the green leaves, the white petals, and the house melted into the darkness that fell soundlessly, the gentle fragrance of the evening accumulating.

And just like that, the house became hers.

The cutting board is all dried up. The edges of the cardboard boxes are frayed and black. The mattress is as hard as the bottom of a shoe. I imagined an empty toilet paper roll as I lay listlessly looking out at the electric wires hanging limp outside the window. *I am like an empty toilet paper roll*, I thought to myself as I looked around the cheaply furnished weekly apartment that was managed by someone my husband knew.

We had been able to take most of our dishes and clothing. Yet, for the past several days, I had been wearing a tattered old summer sweater that was covered in lint. It was almost three weeks since we moved into this apartment.

We left all of our furniture behind. We had no say in the matter. The realtor and the woman had agreed on the buying price, but apparently it was not sufficient according to whoever managed our debt. They ended up raising the price quite a bit, which resulted in renegotiations that delayed the closing date. We were allowed to continue living in the house until the deal was closed, so for a while, I imagined that we could live there indefinitely as if nothing had happened. But of course, that came to an end.

The woman settled on a price that was thirteen million yen above the initial asking price, but with the condition that she would have the right to buy all of our furniture for a price to be negotiated. This was convenient for both parties involved, so a price was agreed upon. The house was sold, as it was—only the inhabitants changed.

The same doors, the same tables, the same walls, the same garden, the same ornamental shelves, the same chairs. In my house, the woman became me. When I heard of the arrangement, I became so upset that I reproached my husband for the first time in twenty years. He responded with a look of fatigue. "We had to sell the furniture anyway to pay back the debt. If we hired a middleman, we would have had to bring money to the table." He was not trying to explain, or to convince or console me—he was simply stating the fact.

"Couldn't we have put everything in storage until we sorted things out and found a proper place?" I asked with tears in my eyes.

My husband answered in a low voice, "It was hard enough to take the clothes, the dishes, and all the little things with us. Plus, when we stepped out of the house, the furniture was no longer ours." Still unconvinced, I continued to question him for over an hour after we turned off the lights. "It's not going to be easy from now on—you know that, right?" was all he would say. Though he had stopped responding, I felt strangely excited and was unable to calm down. I buried my head under the thin summer futon in the stifling heat and cried until morning.

I CAN NO LONGER recall the events that took place after the contract was signed—how we were driven out of our house and ended up here. What did we say to the neighbors? Did we slip away in haste or make up some elaborate lie? When did we pack our belongings? What did we eat? What time did we wake up and go to bed? Everything was a blur.

My husband was now driving a secondhand domestic car. I seem to recall him saying that it belonged to an acquaintance of his. Where was he during those hectic few days—or was it weeks? How did it all end? Was it really over? Come to think of it, it must have been my husband who took care of everything, but I had no recollection of discussing anything or even exchanging words with him. How did we get through it all? Surely, I was there, awake, and moving my body. Yet my memory was vague, as if something were pouring out of me despite my efforts to contain it. It was the same when I tried to remember my childhood. How did I spend those last days? How did I end up here?

Then I remembered something the woman had said. "Don't worry, I won't be keeping the bed." We were standing at the entryway before the house was handed over to her. We happened to run into each other just for a moment.

The woman said those words to me after a polite greeting. The real estate agent had assured us that he would keep our misfortune confidential, but I knew then that he had lied. The expression on the woman's face, the way she looked at me—she knew everything and was enraptured by her own benevolence and sympathy. She knew it all—that I had lost everything and had no choice but to lead a miserable life with my old, bankrupt husband. She was laughing at us both, who had never questioned our values and life choices until now. She was filled with a sense of superiority over the fact that she, who could be our daughter in age, was doing us a favor by taking on the girlish fantasy house that nobody else would want to buy.

With a wide-brimmed hat covering my face, grasping the straps of my purse, I set out to visit the house, which was now an hour away and required three trains. This was already the fourth time I was going there. Fortunately, there was no one on the street in the middle of the day. It was so hot that sweat seemed to pour out when you just tried to keep your eyes open.

The house shone in the summer light. The neighborhood was dead silent, as if all the people had been annihilated, leaving the houses empty. On this summer afternoon, I sat on a bench in a small park down the street from the house. Under the bare branches of the wisteria no longer in bloom, I sat staring intently at the house. Hearing the rustle of branches in the wind, I watched a Juneberry tree—one I had planted—gently sway by the entrance gate. The color of the walls behind the tree was exquisite—a color that I loved, a color I had helped paint. The triangular roof. The tiny square windows. An abundance of green. Flowers blooming. Everything was as I had left it.

When I became thirsty, I would walk to a convenience store twenty minutes away and buy something to drink. Back on the bench, I saw no one save a few cars and an old woman with a bent back walking down the street very slowly.

THE WOMAN HAD BOUGHT the house on her own. I found out only two weeks ago, when the topic came up with my husband. I was lying on the futon when he told me, and propped myself up upon hearing the news. How long had it been since I looked into my husband's eyes? His face had a dark hue, having aged ten or twenty years.

"On her own? You mean, she lives there all by herself?" I asked in surprise.

"It seems that way," he answered.

"What does she do?"

"Apparently, she's a lyricist."

"A lyricist? You mean, someone who writes song lyrics?"

"Yes, that's what I heard."

"Is she famous?" My heart was beating fast.

"I don't know the details, but it seems that way." My husband replied in an uninterested manner with his head turned toward the TV screen.

"Do lyricists make so much money?" I continued in disbelief.

"It depends, I guess. You know that popular band, the Phantom Thief, is it? You've heard of them. I hear she writes for that band."

"So she must be very rich. And at her young age . . ."

"Only thirty-one apparently. Well, I suppose age has nothing to do with talent or royalties for that matter."

Our conversation ended there.

AS I AWOKE FROM my reverie, the air was reverberating with the sound of the cicadas. Clenching a plastic bottle, I imagined the woman sitting at my desk inside the atelier. You could see a small forest off in the distance through the right-hand window, and at this time of year, the pale green of the trees would stretch vertically, coolly swaying in the wind. When evening came, I used to listen to the church bells. I would stop what I was doing and go downstairs to prepare dinner while listening to Mozart on low volume, played by the beautiful pianist Irina Mejoueva.

I had no idea what kind of life a lyricist led. I never saw the woman once during the past two weeks. I noticed what looked like a red Alfa Romeo, rounded and toylike, where my husband's white Mercedes-Benz used to be. The only person I saw from the bench approaching the house was the mailman driving up in a scooter to deliver the mail. On all three previous occasions, not a single person had come in or out.

Did the woman spend all of her time inside? The house was far from the train station and the supermarket, so she would have to drive to go anywhere. There was no bicycle on the porch. Well, it was so hot these days, perhaps the woman ran all her errands in the morning and spent the rest of the day inside the house. Or perhaps her days and nights were reversed. Come to think of it, it wouldn't be surprising if a writer slept during the day and worked at night.

But the woman was a lyricist, not a writer. There was a big difference. A lyricist simply plugged words into songs, which were much shorter than books. It couldn't possibly be a meaningful occupation. Writing lyrics was simple—unlike writing the songs themselves. You just repeated the same words over and over, and all those popular songs had the same lyrics anyway. They had nothing to do with a song's success. All she had to do was string together cliché words like "dream" or "love" or "hope" to delight those teenage girls whose heads were stuffed with cotton candy. Who paid attention to lyrics anyway? If you exchanged one set for another, no one would notice, not even the singers themselves. You might miss them if they were gone altogether, but they held no value in themselves. The woman had surely manipulated her way into the industry. What a cheap, silly business. It wasn't because she was accomplished or talented that she managed to buy my house. The only talent she had was to suck up to the producers or some powerful man in the industry. She was nothing but a selfish single woman concerned only with herself. I saw right through her the first time we met. And it was through her manipulative ways that she succeeded in acquiring my house.

When I looked down, I saw fresh dirt on the ground where I had apparently dug my heels in. I took a sip from the water bottle. Glancing at my watch, I saw that it was just turning four o'clock. The sun was still high in the sky with no sign of relief. I was surprised that only two hours had passed. I felt I had been sitting on the bench for many hours, if not days, looking at the house for a long, long time. My handkerchief was soaked from the sweat trickling down my forehead and neck. Even in the shade, it was insufferable—but where else could I go? I thought of the flimsy futon in the weekly rental. I thought of the low ceilings, the cheap magnets on the cabinets, that atrocious vinyl that covered the floor, the dirty windowsill, the stained bathtub, the wrinkled tablecloth. Everything lacked imagination. I thought of the empty toilet paper roll. That was no place for me. It had nothing to do with me whatsoever.

I could see the Iceberg roses blooming so profusely that they covered the ground. They seemed so gallant, blooming just as they had last year, even though I was no longer there to take care of them. *It's okay, everything will be all right*, they seemed to be saying to me. I felt my chest tighten. I wondered how the dayflowers and the jasmines were doing. That corner of the garden lacked steady sunlight, so you had to be particularly careful how you watered them. Were they still blooming? Did that woman take care of them? I was worried, since I saw no sign of her watering the garden during my three visits. She probably did so only when she felt like it, if at all—that's the kind of person she was. I could tell just by looking. She had no idea you needed to give them plenty of water every morning and evening.

My roses. My darling little flowers. It's not easy to live with flowers. When you think about it, it's far more work than keeping pets. My lovely flower garden. *Are you in pain? Are you lonely? If you could speak, if you could walk, I know you would be by my side. You would have followed me. Who would want to stay with that woman? You had no choice.* What could I do? Oh, my house. My flower garden. What could I do?

It was then that I saw the front door open, without warning. I had been staring at the house with handkerchief in hand, and the house, silent until then, seemed to rouse itself. Involuntarily, I lowered my head as if to hide. The woman emerged in a navy dress and was carrying a red purse. She locked the door, made sure that it was locked, and started walking. I could feel my heart beating so loudly that my ears hurt. I couldn't move. Without noticing me, the woman came out of the gate and walked down the street toward the train station. When she was out of sight, I stood up with some hesitation and walked briskly to the edge of the park and watched, obscured by a tree, from behind the low fence. She was just about to turn the corner and disappear from sight.

I returned to my bench and took a breath, staying still for a while. I wiped the back of my neck with a handkerchief, then pressed it against my eyes. I exhaled deeply and looked straight at the house. *It's time.* My heart started to pound, so strongly that when I put my hand to my chest, I could feel it moving.

It's time. Yes, but time for what? I didn't know. All I knew was that the woman was no longer in the house. The woman was no longer in *my* house. That much I understood, but what was I to do? What *could* I do? No . . . what did I *want* to do? What I wanted was to get my house back. But what did that mean, to get it back? To live there again? How would I do that? I had no idea. But if someone asked me what I wanted, I would wish for things to go back to the way they were. The way they used to be when that house belonged to me.

Just look at it—the garden I cultivated, the flowers I cherished, the house I designed. It wasn't about money or property. That house was *mine*, period. Putting aside rigid ideas like ownership and legal rights, what I saw before me was simply . . . mine. It stood there, just as it used to. Think about it this way. If your child were taken from you, never to return again, the child would still be yours no matter what. Whatever changed on the surface, the core remained the same. The truth would withstand any change in circumstance. It didn't matter what people thought—even if no one understood, that house was *mine.* I could say so proudly. Look. There it was, *my house.*

I EMERGED FROM THE PARK, slowly crossed the street, and stood in front of the house. I walked up to the gate and turned the doorknob. The ground looked dry, as I had expected. The varieties of thyme, which normally grew abundantly this time of year, looked deflated. They felt limp to the touch, and the green waves were now shallow and murky. There was not enough water. I walked along the side of the house to the back. The bellflowers hung their little heads as if their energy was sucked out of them, and the larkspurs were all huddled together barely withstanding the heat. The only plants that managed to hang on were the wild strawberries and the ivies.

Finding the hose abandoned in the corner, I connected it to the water spigot, turned the faucet, and let the water flow. It flowed and flowed. The ground instantaneously turned dark and began to emit that earthy smell. I closed my eyes and inhaled deeply. It was a smell I knew so well—the smell of summer, of vegetation, of flowers. I breathed in the humid air through my nostrils and into my lungs, savoring the smell and the flow. I took it all in, filling myself up, then releasing it slowly. With the hose in hand, I walked up and down the garden, giving water to everything in sight.

The earth drank greedily. When I had watered enough, I picked the wilted flowers and the discolored grass and leaves inside the flowerpots, and placed them all in the compost by the shed. I took a bag of fertilizer and buried the pieces one by one in the soil. With slight hesitation, I returned to the shed and filled a large watering pot with diluted Hyponex plant food, and sprinkled it over the flowers and the leaves and the grass.

When all that was done, the garden seemed to come back to life.

I sat on the small terrace, and gazed contentedly at my flower garden that glistened in the summer light. Relishing the smell and the colors to my heart's content, I put away the hose, washed my hands, and sat on the terrace once more to enjoy the garden. The terrace was perfectly calculated to take in the undulating green landscape. Caressing the soft wood with my fingertips, I released a sigh from the bottom of my heart. The water drops on the leaves and flowers shimmered in the sunlight, which seemed gentler now. I could have sat there forever. *But the church bells will be ringing soon.* I took off my sandals to go to the kitchen, reaching for the knob behind me. I stood up unhurriedly and turned around toward the sliding glass door. I saw the woman's face.

THE WOMAN WAS LOOKING at me through the glass. Our faces were so close that our noses would have touched if it hadn't been for the glass door separating us.

It was as if we were looking in a mirror. How long had we stood looking at each other like that? I didn't know what she was thinking or whether she was breathing. All I was aware of was the absolute silence as the woman stood immobile before me. She never took her eyes off mine. Then, the glass door slid open and we were now facing each other directly. Her eyes and nose and mouth were at the same level as mine. I had never looked at another person's face so closely and extensively. I no longer knew what I was looking at. When I shifted my gaze to her mouth, I could see that the edges were slanted slightly upward, as if she were smiling.

"Come in."

She said this in a low voice, her gaze still fixed on mine. Her voice was much deeper than I remembered, but it sounded like a voice I knew. Then it occurred to me. It was the voice that sounded in my head when I saw the woman for the first time. Yes, that was it. Breathing through my nose quietly, I walked into the living room as if drawn by some mysterious force.

"How is everything? Living here, I mean . . ." I blurted out awkwardly, standing by the ornamental shelf and toying with my fingernails. The woman had a curious smile on her lips as she looked at me, and didn't answer my question.

"What do you want?" she said.

Oh, I was in the area and happened to pass by. I rang the doorbell but there was no answer, so I went around to the back to see if you were there, and noticed that the garden looked a little dry. So I thought, why not go ahead and water it? I was about to say all this, but the woman continued before I could utter a word.

"You've been hanging around the house since last week. It's creepy. What do you want?"

I glanced down, at a loss for words. The woman's toes were painted dark pink, but her little toe had barely any nail.

"How can you stand being out in this heat for hours?"

"There's a wisteria . . ." My voice sounded strangely raspy. I coughed. I was going to say, "It provides a bit of shade," but the woman cut me off by sighing loudly through her nostrils.

"Look, I can imagine how you must be feeling," she said.

I continued to stare at her little toe with no nail.

"You're having trouble accepting reality. It's normal. I could tell at a glance that this house meant everything to you. You still can't accept it, can you? You can't accept what happened?"

I nodded, as if to agree with everything she said.

"You can't let go of your former life, so you come back to the house. And you don't even know why."

I nodded again, as if to agree with everything she said.

"But did it never cross your mind that when you're kept by someone, this sort of thing could happen at any time?"

"Kept by someone?" I repeated.

"Exactly," she said. "You're like someone's pet. If something happens to the owner, the pet shares his fate. That's what's happening now, isn't it? I suppose a dog or a child can't help being kept, but you're a woman in your prime . . . well, you may be past your prime now, but you were at some point. What would you say if someone asked you, What have you done with your life?"

I couldn't answer right away as the word "kept" was still ringing in my ears. *What have I done with my life?* After a while, I came up with an answer. "I managed the house."

"You managed the house . . . yes, there's something in that," she nodded. "Listen, I understand how you must feel, but that doesn't make it okay to barge into a house that belongs to someone else. That's called trespassing. It's a crime."

She threw a piercing glance at me. Tension built behind my ears, and I nodded several times in silence.

"What about the keys?" the woman demanded, as if the thought suddenly occurred to her.

"The keys?"

"Yes, the keys. You must still have keys to the house. Did you make copies before handing over the set?"

"Oh no, I didn't," I answered. The woman peered at me suspiciously, then sat down on the sofa and leaned against the cushions.

"You love the house, don't you?" She said in a tone that was half mockery and half pity, her arms folded across her chest. I wasn't sure if my feelings toward the house could be summarized in the single word "love," but nodded nonetheless.

"Yes, well . . . I do have a strong attachment to the house. I designed and furnished it myself, so I feel deep inside that it belongs to me somehow . . . and as you said, I've lived here for a long time so it's hard to let go of that feeling. Perhaps . . . I think you might understand better if you thought of the house as a child . . . the tie between a mother and child is inseparable, right? That's how I feel about my house, like a mother and child . . ."

I felt something warm surge in my chest as I voiced the words that I had repeated over and over in my mind while sitting on the park bench, or lying under the covers of the coarse futon in the dark of the night when I felt so alone despite my husband who lay next to me. It was all I could do to keep the tears from spilling out.

"But even when you lived here, the house wasn't yours, really. It belonged to your husband." The woman looked confused. "Or was it purchased under your name?"

"No, not technically . . ." I answered in a weak voice. "It was my husband who bought the house, but we're proper husband and wife . . . and I was the one who made the decisions, down to every detail. So in that sense . . . for me, it's my own house. Of course, it's my husband's house too, but fundamentally, finances aside, I feel that it's mine."

"*Finances aside*?" The woman looked surprised. "*Proper husband and wife*? Everything you have, someone bought for you. The house, the furniture, the dishes, the silverware, the bed, all the knickknacks that struck your fancy . . . the flower beds, the gate, every piece of clothing you own . . . your husband bought them all for you, didn't he? How could you say so confidently, without a hint of hesitation, that those things are *yours*? Is there a switch that goes off when you're married that makes it okay to think in that way?" The woman continued, as if she truly didn't understand. "You said before, *managed the house*. Is it because of this that you gained a sense of entitlement? You never thought of getting a job?"

I shook my head. I had never seriously given a thought to working since I got married, nor had I ever discussed it with my husband. I felt uneasy and my head was foggy. It was all I could do to keep up with what the woman was saying.

"I'm not saying this to upset you," she continued. "Believe me. It's just that I'm intrigued. How could you put yourself in such a precarious situation? That's the part I don't understand. How can you trust someone so naively? How can you put your whole life into someone else's hands? Weren't you scared? Or anxious?"

I couldn't keep up with her deluge of questions, nor could I figure out how to convey my thoughts in words. All I knew, however vaguely, was that she was wrong. I wasn't sure which part exactly, but I knew it instinctively and abstractly. That's not what it meant to be husband and wife. I couldn't express it well, but that's not what marriage was either. All this woman was concerned about was money. She was missing what was truly important. I felt this in my gut, but how could I make her understand?

"Anyway, all of this is beside the point," the woman said, seeing that I wasn't going to explain myself. "I don't really care what you think or how you choose to live your life. People do whatever they want—it has nothing to do with me."

I kept silent, staring at her toes.

"It's just that I feel strange sometimes, living here, surrounded by all the furniture you left behind . . . or rather, that I bought from you. It's that strange feeling that bothers me. I've stayed in hotels for extended periods, but it's not the same. Plus, this is one hundred percent my house—I'm not a guest or a tenant—I have nowhere else to live but here. But something strange is going on. It's not that I feel guilty or pity or think you deserved what you got—in fact, I don't think of you at all. Emotions don't interest me. It's just that . . . there's something strange about the house itself. Maybe because I'm still new to the place, but I've grown used to living here. Surprisingly so. The furniture, the doors—I feel I've known them for years. It's almost uncanny how *natural* everything feels. When I moved in and slept in the bedroom for the first time, I woke up feeling as if I'd spent countless nights here before. As if my body already knew the house and everything was connected to my memory. It was really uncanny."

I didn't know how to respond. I continued to stare at the woman's toes in silence.

"I'm not talking about ghosts or anything like that," the woman laughed. "I'm even less interested in that kind of thing than in feelings."

"It's just that . . ." the woman held her breath and looked at me. "There's this scent. It's overwhelming. Do you know what I'm talking about?"

"A scent?" I asked.

"That's right. It's not that it smells bad. It's a peculiar sort of scent that's neither bad nor good. It's the scent itself that bothers me. When I catch a whiff, I . . ." The woman fell silent.

"Do you mean . . . the scent gives you a headache?"

"No, that's not it," the woman answered after a slight pause. "It just bothers me. The scent creeps in every day from out of nowhere, at random hours. Every single day. When I catch a whiff I become . . . confused. About what, I don't know, but it makes me feel shaken at my core somehow. I escape into the bedroom, into the closet even, but the scent comes after me. I light an aroma candle, take a shower, cook, all to no avail. I was so desperate once that I asked an acquaintance to come over and check it out, but she couldn't smell anything. I was at my wit's end—then one day, I noticed you sitting over there in the park, looking over here. Do you have any idea where the scent is coming from? I'm not talking about flowers or plants."

"No, I don't," I answered.

"Then . . . perhaps you're the cause of it after all," the woman snapped coldly. "It doesn't make sense logically, but I can't think of any other reason. It's crazy that you can sit in this heat and stare at someone else's house for such a long time. It's not normal. Maybe the scent has something to do with it. I must be sensing some sort of physical danger, and my body is responding to it through the sense of smell. I'm not into superstition, but there's no other way to explain it. Plus, you've committed a crime by trespassing. The thought of you continuing to hang around the house gives me the creeps. I get a headache just thinking about it. All of that must be connected to the smell. My head is starting to throb as we speak."

I was still looking at the ground.

"So what are you going to do about it?" the woman said after a pause, sounding exasperated.

I no longer knew what to think. Why was this woman asking me what I planned to do? I knew nothing of the scent she was talking about, nor was I interested in it. So what if there was a mysterious scent? What was surprising about not feeling well? Wasn't it simply that my house had not welcomed her? To state it more plainly, wasn't it a clear sign that she had no right to live in my house?

I raised my head and looked around the living room. Nothing had changed. It was as if time had stopped inside my house. Everything was as it had been, from the sofa to the cushions to the curtains to the light that stretched across the floor this time of day in the season.

Did I not just come down from the second floor? Had I not been sewing a moment ago in my atelier? Was this not my house? The inhabitants may have changed, but things remained the same. Now that I had returned, everything could go back to the way it used to be. Like the garden just a moment ago. The house felt alive once more—I felt alive. These past several months had all been a mistake . . . and just like waking from a bad dream, I could come back.

"What's over is over." The woman's voice interrupted my thoughts. "No matter how much you long for it, the house is no longer yours. It's all over. You need to move on."

"Move on?"

"That's right. I'm being greatly inconvenienced here. You're wasting my time as we speak. What you did was criminal. I could report you to the police, but I don't want to waste any more time."

I nodded in silence.

"You need to think about how you can refrain from coming here. Are you listening? You're hung up. You're still attached to the house psychologically."

"Yes . . ."

"That's right," the woman continued. "In TV shows or in novels, people like to burn and destroy things to get revenge—but you don't do that in real life. You've lost your house, and now it belongs to me. That's a fact. Period. If you killed me now, the house still wouldn't be yours. The only thing left to do, then, is for you to change. So the important question is, How can you make this change? How can you get over the attachment you have to the house?"

I nodded weakly at the woman's words.

"Listen, this is something you should be thinking about yourself. I just want to resolve this as quickly as possible. What does it take for you to move on? If this was a romantic affair, well . . . you could have closure by having sex or a huge blowout—something that aims for a final sense of unity before going separate ways. Once you've given it your all, you can move on, or so I hear. How about doing something like that?"

"Like what?" I asked. "Do what exactly?"

"That was just an analogy. I'm just thinking of ways for you to get over the whole thing. Let's see . . . what's your favorite thing about this house?"

"Everything," I answered. As I listened to the woman, my mind became foggy and my head was beginning to throb. What was she talking about? Although I felt my head tighten, the pain felt abstract and my body seemed to become more and more remote with every minute. I could no longer tell what was real and what was not.

"You can't say *everything*. Try to be more specific."

"The flower garden," I whispered after a while.

"The flower garden." The woman became thoughtful and fell silent. Then, she looked straight at me.

"The flower garden . . . That might work."

"Hmmm," I said vaguely.

"It could be a kind of therapy. More practical, even. Why don't you become the flower garden itself? Who knows if it will work, but then, one thing may lead to another . . . you might come out feeling better. It may be worth trying—becoming one with what's most important to you, something you normally can't attain unity with. Why don't we try it while the sun is out? Who knows, it may even be connected to that scent I've been talking about. Plus . . . this is the last time I'm offering you help. Next time, I'm handing you over to the police."

"But how?" I was puzzled.

"You become part of the flower garden," the woman snapped in a cold voice, "by burying yourself. Next to all of your precious flowers. To reach a catharsis, they say you either have to burn it or bury it. And we can't exactly burn you, can we? So instead, you can connect with what's most precious to you from a different perspective, a different approach. You might have an epiphany. Or, who knows, you might lose interest in the house altogether. It's worth trying in any case. I'm sure no other fifty-year-old housewife has done such a thing before."

With a chuckle, the woman glided across the living room and opened the sliding glass door to the garden. She turned around and motioned for me to follow. I walked toward her, dragging my feet, which were nearly asleep from standing for so long.

The woman stepped into the flower garden and put on the gardening shoes. She walked over to the shed where the gardening tools were kept, and brought over a large shovel and spade. I stared at the spade as she placed it in my hand. The memory of buying the tools came back to me. How I couldn't decide on the design of the handle. The first time I used them to dig up soil. How the ground was so tough because of all the roots. The sound of the soil being pierced through. Dirt crumbling. Digging up potatoes. Wait, wasn't I a child then? The gardening gloves. My husband. He was busy with work and rarely around, but sometimes I would turn and see him watching me with a pleased expression as I poked around in the ground. *The flowers are beautiful*, he would say. *Thanks to you, our garden is always in good shape.* Yes, that was here. The two of us. When I let my guard down, when I let my thoughts wander, all kinds of memories came flooding back. They enveloped me completely. Where were they taking me? The spade was rusty. They came rushing back. What did any of that have to do with the shovel and spade?

The woman stepped on the bed of thyme. Pointing to the ground with the shovel in her right hand, she drew an outline just above the ground. "Is this big enough? We can't dig too deep, so we'll have to bury you horizontally. A rectangular shape, like a coffin." I began digging into the bed of thyme as the woman directed. Because of the water I had just given it, the soil gave in to the spade easily and soon I could see the dark, moist part. In silence, I dug the edges of the rectangle, then began digging deeper. I dug and dug, in silence. The bed of thyme was shallow and came out without resistance, its white roots exposed and severed from the soil. All around me were piles of black soil mixed with green and white. After half an hour or so, there was a dark hole big enough for a person to lie in.

"Go ahead and lie down," the woman said.

I sat down on the dark, moist soil and stretched my legs, placing my arms to my side. I breathed in the gentle smell of the soil. *Stay still*, the woman said, *I'm going to bury you now*. It was that voice again. I felt a cool sensation on the back of my hands, my arms, my neck. The voice began to cover me with the soil mixed with thyme. At first it felt light, then I began to feel the weight on my chest and thighs. After a while, I felt a new sort of weight fall upon me with a thump. It seemed that she had added compost she found in the shed. The voice continued to cover me with soil as I lay in the middle of the garden.

The summer evening sky extended as far as my eyes could see. When I opened them wide, the sky became wider with them. The sky became so wide that, curious to see how far it would stretch, I opened my eyes as wide as I could, and opened my mouth along with them. The tinted cirrocumulus clouds appeared faint and ephemeral in the distance, and I could see a small airplane floating among the clouds. The voice continued to cover me with soil. My limbs became heavier and heavier as the hands pressed down the dirt meticulously. The seeds, the bulbs, the roots. I could see myself tending to the flowers wearing my gardening gloves. *May you bloom beautifully. May you take root.* Each time I dug the spade into the earth, fresh dirt would fall upon my body. *What have I done?* One scoop at a time, I became heavier and heavier. Then, I became lighter and lighter. My limbs were no longer free and I could hardly breathe, but somehow, somewhere, I could feel myself growing upward toward the sky. *What have I done?* The voice, now silent, covered me with dirt. I could hear it breathing. Whose voice was it? I couldn't see the face, but it seemed to be struggling. Whose voice was it? It covered me with dirt. I covered myself with dirt. Each time I breathed, each time the voice pressed down with its hands, I became heavier and heavier. One scoop at a time, I became lighter. Managing to shift my neck slightly to the side, I saw the leaves of petunia flowers. A water drop swayed and reflected the light. A newborn ladybug was about to spread its wings. I had a feeling that I had seen this moment long, long ago, but could no longer remember when. But I will tell him. When my husband comes home, I will tell him about the ladybug, about this tiny delicate creature ready to spread its wings and take off. Beyond the windows of my house, I hear the usual church bells ringing. I will leave my room, descend the stairs, and tell all kinds of stories. About these flowers that breathed gently, existing quietly in peace. About myself. About all that I can see from here. I will tell you everything.

Night Women

Edwidge Danticat

I cringe from the heat of the night on my face. I feel as bare as open flesh. Tonight I am much older than the twenty-five years that I have lived. The night is the time I dread most in my life. Yet, I must depend on it.

Shadows shrink and spread over the lace curtains as my son slips into bed. I watch as he stretches from a little boy into the broom-size of a man, his height mounting the innocent fabric that splits our one-room house into two spaces, two mats, two worlds.

For a brief second, I almost mistake him for the ghost of his father, an old lover who disappeared with the night's shadows a long time ago. My son's bed stays nestled against the corner, far from the peeking jalousies. I watch as he digs furrows in the pillow with his head. He shifts his small body carefully so as not the crease his Sunday clothes. He wraps my long blood-red scarf around his neck, the one I wear myself during the day to tempt my suitors. I let him have it at night, so that he always has something of mine when my face is out of sight.

I watch his shadow resting still on the curtain. My eyes are drawn to him, like the stars peeking through the small holes in the roof that none of my suitors will fix for me, because they like to watch a scrap of the sky while lying with their naked backs on my mat.

A firefly buzzes around the room, finding him and not me. Perhaps it is a mosquito that has learned the gift of lightning itself. He always slaps the mosquitoes dead on his face without even waking. In the morning, he will have tiny blood spots on his forehead, as though he had spent the whole night kissing a woman with wide-open flesh wounds on her face.

In his sleep he squirms and groans as though he's already discovered that there is pleasure in touching himself. We have never talked about love. What would he need to know? Love is one of those lessons that you grow to learn, the way one learns that one shoe is made to fit a certain foot, lest it cause discomfort.

There are two kinds of women: day women and night women. I am stuck between the day and night in a golden amber bronze. My eyes are the colour of dirt, almost copper if I am standing in the sun. I want to wear my matted tresses in braids as soon as I learn to do my whole head without numbing my arms.

Most nights I hear a slight whisper. My body freezes as I wonder how long it would take for him to cross the curtain and find me.

He says, "Mommy."

I say, "*Darling.*"

Somehow in the night, he always calls me in whispers. I hear the buzz of his transistor radio. It is shaped like a can of cola. One of my suitors gave it to him to plug into his ears so he can stay asleep while Mommy *works*.

There is a place in Ville Rose where ghost women ride the crests of waves while brushing the stars out of their hair. There they woo strollers and leave the stars on the path for them. There are nights that I believe that those ghost women are with me. As much as I know that there are women who sit up through the night and undo patches of cloth that they have spent the whole day weaving. These women, they destroy their toil so that they will always have more to do. And as long as there's work, they will not have to lie next to a man whose scent still lingers in another woman's bed.

The way my son reacts to my lips stroking his cheeks decides for me if he's asleep. He is like a butterfly fluttering on a rock that stands out naked in the middle of a stream. Sometimes I see in the folds of his eyes a longing for something that's bigger than myself. We are like faraway lovers, lying to one another, under different moons. When my smallest finger caresses the narrow cleft beneath his nose, sometimes his tongue slips out of his mouth and he licks my fingernail. He moans and turns away, perhaps thinking that this too is a part of the dream.

I whisper my mountain stories in his ear, stories of the ghost women and the stars in their hair. I tell him of the deadly snakes lying at one end of a rainbow and the hat full of gold lying at the other end. I tell him that if I cross a stream of glass-clear hibiscus, I can make myself a goddess. I blow on his long eyelashes to see if he's truly asleep. My fingers coil themselves into visions of birds on his nose. I want him to forget that we live in a place where nothing lasts.

I know that sometimes he wonders why I take such painstaking care. Why do I draw half-moons on my sweaty forehead and spread crimson powders on the rise of my cheeks. We put on his ruffled Sunday suit and I tell him that we are expecting a sweet angel and where angels tread the hosts must be as beautiful as floating hibiscus.

In his sleep, his fingers tug his shirt ruffles loose. He licks his lips from the last piece of sugar candy stolen from my purse.

No more, no more, or your teeth will turn black. I have forgotten to make him brush the mint leaves against his teeth. He does not know that one day a woman like his mother may judge him by the whiteness of his teeth.

It doesn't take long before he is snoring softly. I listen for the shy laughter of his most pleasant dreams. Dreams of angels skipping over his head and occasionally resting their pink heels on his nose.

I hear him humming a song. One of the madrigals they still teach children on very hot afternoons in public schools. *Konpè Jako, dormez vous?* Brother Jacques, are you asleep?

The hibiscus rustle in the night outside. I sing along to help him sink deeper into his sleep. I apply another layer of the Egyptian rouge to my cheeks. There are some sparkles in the powder, which make it easier for my visitor to find me in the dark.

Emmanuel will come tonight. He is a doctor who likes big buttocks on women, but my small ones will do. He comes on Tuesdays and Saturdays. He arrives bearing flowers as though he's come to court me. Tonight he brings bougainvillea. It is always a surprise.

"How is your wife?" I ask.

"Not as beautiful as you."

On Mondays and Thursdays, it is an accordion player named Alexandre. He likes to make the sound of the accordion with his mouth in my ear. The rest of the night, he spends with his breadfruit head rocking on my belly button.

Should my son wake up, I have prepared my fabrication. One day, he will grow too old to be told that a wandering man is a mirage and that naked flesh is a dream. I will tell him that his father has come, that an angel brought him back from Heaven for a while.

The stars slowly slip away from the hole in the roof as the doctor sinks deeper and deeper beneath my body. He throbs and pants. I cover his mouth to keep him from screaming. I see his wife's face in the beads of sweat marching down his chin. He leaves with his body soaking from the dew of our flesh. He calls me an avalanche, a waterfall, when he is satisfied.

After he leaves at dawn, I sit outside and smoke a dry tobacco leaf. I watch the piece-worker women march one another to the open market half a day's walk from where I live. I thank the stars that at least I have the days to myself.

When I walk back into the house, I hear the rise and fall of my son's breath. Quickly, I lean my face against his lips to feel the calming heat from his mouth.

"Mommy, have I missed the angels again?" he whispers softly while reaching for my neck.

I slip into the bed next to him and rock him back to sleep.

"Darling, the angels have themselves a lifetime to come to us."

The July War

Rabih Alameddine

In summer, our neighborhood quiets in phases. The quieting begins in May. Schools give their older kids, the seventeen- and eighteen-year-olds, a month off to prepare for the baccalaureate exams. Following a ritual as old as our parents, the students retreat to residences out of town, to peaceful chalets and cabins away from civilization for communal study and living. As noisily as migrating birds, they return for the state exams in June. Then school ends for the year; a couple of families travel abroad, a few more leave for the mountains. An outsider doesn't perceive the slow but sure change in the neighborhood's population until Beirut broils in August.

In early July, our neighbors across the landing, the Masris, left for the mountains. They wouldn't return from their summer home till late September with its cooling temperatures. That was the summer I was promoted to the apartment's caretaker, taking over from my brother. My father insisted that I look after the Masri home because he thought that at thirteen, I wasn't yet behaving as an adult should. I needed to become more responsible. I'd been receiving talking-tos, lectures with full arm waving and hand gestures, every day for a month.

In the mornings, in the bathroom, as my father in boxer shorts and T-shirt stood before the vanity mirror, words would bubble out of the snow-white shaving foam. "When I was your age, I didn't laze about all day doing nothing," he'd say. "Can't you find more mature friends? Do things that are more productive? You know, every action has a consequence, and the consequence of doing nothing is that you end up as nothing."

At lunch, in the dining room, as we sat around the oak table, "Sit up straight. Look at how Wajdi sits, like a man. Enough with this boyish slouching."

In the den, while watching television, he'd repeat the spiel, except after dinner he made it sound as if the thought had just occurred to him. "You should be thinking about what you want to do with your life," he'd say. His right arm, as was its wont every evening, held my mother in what I always considered a matrimonial embrace, and she regarded him with admiration, as though each word of his were a tumbling pearl. "It's never too early," he'd go on, his left hand wandering and questioning. "What do you like? Solving problems? You can become an engineer. Helping people? An attorney. You could raise your grades if you applied yourself. Consider your future."

I didn't mind taking care of our neighbors' apartment. My becoming-more-responsible chore for the summer involved little work: I had to open the windows once a week to air the place out and make sure that the two canaries were fed and their cage kept clean.

I SAT CROSS-LEGGED ON the leather couch in Dr. Masri's apartment, reading an ancient Harold Robbins novel where all the action happened in the Middle East—and I do mean action. In the best scene, Leila, who as a child refugee was traumatized by both Jews and Arabs, sucked a guy's sumptuous dick in delicious descriptive detail. Her PLO boyfriend had persuaded her to fellate a fine-looking Mossad agent to extract valuable information. That was the first time I came across the verb *fellate*. I'd read Jacqueline Susann and Jackie Collins, so I knew about oral sex in literature, but this book was different. These were Arabs giving blowjobs and saying things like *their mother's cunt*, which would have worked had it been written in Arabic but sounded utterly silly in English. Robbins was shooting for authenticity and ended up with anything but. Much fun.

I enjoyed reading a book from start to finish, unlike my brother, who read only the good parts. Wajdi would pick any book from Dr. Masri's library, new or classic, a Collins or a Robbins, and let it open to where the spine was most creased. His technique never failed to ferret out an act of coitus or fellatio, since it seemed that Dr. Masri concentrated on the same parts. My brother's interest in the books had waned the year before, when he turned seventeen and said he needed to concentrate on the real instead of the imaginary.

Dr. Masri's entire library was shelved in one piece of furniture in the salon, a breakfront that had been moved from the dining room; thick paperbacks had replaced china and silverware behind the glass, and every paperback contained at least one good sex scene. If, as my father advocated, being a responsible caretaker was the gateway to manhood, I was all for it—those paperbacks would be my Saint Peter.

I had reached the page where Leila gets recruited to be a terrorist when the doorbell rang. I tiptoed to the door, as quiet as a stalking Mossad, and didn't have to look through the peephole to know that it was Pipo, the bane of my existence. He had warned me to tell him as soon as the Masri family drove up to the mountains.

"If I don't hear from you as soon as they leave," he'd told me three days earlier, "I'm going to squeeze you with my hands like a little cockroach." It would have been funny, how he always used incorrect similes, if his threats hadn't usually been followed by unpredictable actions. I'd lied to the overweight monster and told him that Wajdi was the caretaker again this year—Pipo was afraid of Wajdi, who was the only boy in the neighborhood who was stronger and taller than the blob.

Pipo had this most annoying habit of talking to my face while lifting me by the collar of my shirt. That stopped when, during one lift, I told him I was wearing Wajdi's shirt—I lied then as well, of course, but it was looser than what I normally wore—and my brother would be terribly upset if the collar was crinkled.

"I know you're in there," Pipo said to the door. His tone was whispery and sinister; he couldn't yell because Wajdi or my father, ensconced in our apartment across the landing, would hear him. He rang the bell once more. "Open it."

I wasn't going to, for several reasons, one of which was ethical: I liked the Masris and wouldn't give Pipo the run of their home. I had no idea what his plans for the empty apartment were, but I could guarantee that they weren't savory. And I wasn't going to do what he wanted because I was going to get pummeled whether I opened the door or not. If a beating is inevitable, delay is always the better course of action.

"If you don't open the door," Pipo said, "I'll break Karl's legs."

"What?" squealed a damp voice. I held still, my back to the wall, resisting the urge to peek and confirm the presence of the traitor, my ex–best friend. "You can't break my legs. It's not fair."

"I will if he doesn't let me in."

"What if he's not there? He told me he has the key, but maybe he's reading in his room. You can't hurt me because the door isn't opening by itself."

I heard my father's voice. "What are you boys doing? The Masris aren't in." The sound of hurried footsteps—cowardly Karl rushed down the stairs. Pipo stuttered an incoherent reply. "I don't want to see you here, Philippe," my father said. "You're a man now. Start behaving like one."

THAT WAS KARL'S SECOND betrayal in less than a week. The previous Monday, we were sitting together on the wall across the street from our building, our feet dangling below us. He was a couple of months older than I, but two 501 inches wider. When cars sped by, he pointed and yelled out the make and year. His favorites, which you could tell by the inflection of his voice, were the new BMWs. He watched the cars. I watched him, his pimply face, as if seeing him for the first time. I thought he was so funny with his hair that hadn't seen a comb in days. "Buick, 1998," he announced. I smiled and rubbed my shoulder on his arm. He smelled of deodorant and armpit. "Peugeot, 2006, the latest model." I laughed and rubbed against his shoulder again. "Nissan, 2000." Laugh. Rub. Laugh. I stopped, though, because I felt my father staring at me from our balcony across the street. Like safari prey, I had developed, and nurtured, a sixth sense—an ability to feel his disapproval across large distances.

You always heard Pipo before you saw him. He rumbled toward us, his face aglow with sneer. His shirts were always white and blue, the colors of Lazio, his favorite soccer team, but since their sky blue was difficult to find in men's clothing, he made do with other shades.

"Are you two sucking each other's cocks?" he yelled.

Karl jumped off the wall, almost stumbled into a boxwood hedge. "It was him," he pleaded, flailing his finger in my general direction. "He did it."

Pipo whistled, not by puckering his lips but by folding his lower lip over his teeth in a manly way. He wiggled his black eyebrows, rubbed his hands like a sated housefly. "He sucked your cock, did he?"

I could feel my blood bubble. I slid off the wall, landing close to my tormentor. "Grow up, Pipo," I said. Karl gasped, but I soldiered on. "You think we're still in kindergarten?"

I turned and walked away. My father, still watching, probably had an unobstructed view of Pipo's fist landing on the back of my neck and my falling forward. The bitumen rushed to greet my face at a dizzying speed before my hands broke my fall.

My father yelled at Pipo to stop. I lifted myself off the ground, looking neither back at Pipo nor up at the balcony, and marched to our building, knowing that my father would be waiting with a lecture on how men stood up to bullies. I allowed my eyes to see only the large bougainvillea, which sprinkled discarded bracts and faded magenta flowers onto our balcony.

NOONISH, the sky was bone white and shadows were still shortening along the sand. The sea whispered, hissed, and lapped. I balanced on one foot, trying hard to look inconspicuous and not succeeding. I switched to the other, almost tipped over—my imitation of a crane with a middle-ear infection. I wasn't wearing my flip-flops and the sparkling sand burned my feet. In my hurry to spy on Wajdi and his new girlfriend, I'd forgotten how fiery the sand could get. I stood on my toes, hoping to see farther, but my brother was too distant. I hopped over to the shore.

The water temperature was perfect for swimming, but I wished it were a bit cooler so it could comfort my soles more quickly. It was a day to make angels smile and forgive. Indolent and somnolent, sunbathers basked all around. Everyone and their bottle of suntan oil was on the beach.

Wajdi and his new girl walked by me, close to each other but not holding hands like I'd expected. He was lean and muscled from years of swimming, his brown hair already sun-bleached on top. He ignored me, talked to the smiling girl. He shuffled his feet, looking both self-effacing and suave, as if he had spent the last hour soaking in a tubful of confidence. They parted and he swaggered in my direction, chest puffed out like an iguana's. I was still standing in the water. He stopped before his espadrilles got wet.

"She let me touch her," he declared.

I rushed over. "Touch her? Touch her where?"

"Only a baby would ask such a question." He turned and walked away. I ran after him, bobbing and bouncing. He looked so urbane. I admired his long fingers as he lit a cigarette. He walked straight, held his head up high. "She said she liked that I'm not wearing socks."

"What do you mean? I'm not wearing socks either."

"No, you baby. She likes that I'm not wearing socks with shoes. I'll never wear socks again. Never ever again."

THE FIRST REFUGEE WAS my sister, Nadia. After the Israelis bombed the airport, she and my one-year-old nephew, cheeks still swollen with sleep, arrived with three suitcases in tow. One contained her clothes and belongings, the second her son's clothes, and the third was bursting with disposable diapers. She lived only three buildings away, nowhere near the airport, but we knew it wouldn't take her long to come over. We didn't have to ask where her husband was.

"He can stay where he is," she huffed. "The Israelis have sophisticated weapons. I don't want to be there when one of their missiles finds him."

My sister had married a Shiite.

"You shouldn't be saying that," my father said. "Your husband is a good man, a wonderful man."

We all loved my brother-in-law, but Nadia found him annoying. She had been completely obsessed with him before the wedding, but not after. I found the situation, her constant irritation with her husband, somewhat confounding. He was decent, intelligent, and admirably gentle, not the most interesting man, one had to admit, but consistent, if anything. How a wedding could change her opinion so abruptly wasn't easy to explain. I assumed the intimacy and mundaneness of marriage had surprised her and she had yet to recover. It could have been worse, since he traveled quite a bit, being a commercial pilot. Still, she complained that he wasn't gone enough. My mother defended her by reminding everyone that she was a young bride and would grow up in time.

My sister rolled her suitcase into her old room, which she hadn't allowed anyone to claim when she moved out—understandably, since she still spent most of her days in our apartment. I followed her, carrying my nephew, and put him on his cot, under its ever-circling wooden airplanes. I moved my sister's old stuffed toys around to create space for him. The walls were baby pink, the color of her nail polish and lipstick—she avoided dark shades, claiming they emphasized the puffy aspects of her lips.

"Watch him," Nadia said. "I have to go hoarding."

"Your brother should go with you," my mother said. "He can carry. I'll stay here, but don't forget anything."

. . .

THE ENTIRE COUNTRY WAS on the road. It happened every time the Israelis bombed Beirut—never when they shelled the south, which they did on a more regular basis. Bombing the airport during high season, though, meant that every tourist was driving out of the city and out of the country.

My father raged against the traffic, and when we passed a gas station, he banged his head on the steering wheel. After dropping us at the supermarket, he'd have to wait in line for at least a couple of hours to fill up the tank. Wajdi, who had taken my mother's car, was probably stuck at a station already.

"I hate this," my father yelled.

"Are you sure we need to do this?" I asked.

"The Israelis won't stop. They never do. It's the right of the privileged. They're always the victims, which means they're going to rain the demons of hell upon us." He took deep breaths, trying to fill his lungs with calm. It rarely worked. "Bomb everything. Kill hundreds, thousands. Does anyone take any responsibility? Feel guilty? They blame everyone but themselves."

My father's heart found some relief in diatribes. He raged every time the Israelis attacked us, less at the actual casualties and damage than at their lack of concern. This time, my father was going to rage for quite a while.

MY SISTER AND I split up in the supermarket. I reveled in the excitement of upheaval, stacking my shopping cart with cases of drinking water, cartons of cigarettes for my father, sacks of flour, bulgur, and coffee. She would get everything else if we were lucky, since the market was emptying quickly. People had begun hoarding the evening before. The Lebanese had a lot of experience.

I was deciding how much rice to buy when I heard my sister shriek two aisles away. I rushed over, pushing my cart, finding her in the baby aisle. She held a package of Pampers as a tall, better-manicured woman in a tailored gray day dress tried to snatch it away. The woman blabbered and kept jerking her recently coiffed head at two packages of Huggies in my sister's cart, as if she had a neurotic twitch. My sister's fingers had punctured the plastic. Several strands of her hair had escaped their barrette. Customers whispered, not bothering to hide their sniggering. The woman's Filipina maid in a baby-blue uniform watched the melee with her hand over her mouth. The maid and her mistress must have shared a hairdresser, because they had the exact same coif, the latter in a much lighter tone, of course. They both had sweaters tied around their shoulders.

Nadia tugged and pulled and screeched. The woman finally released her grip. "You have three packages," she said, shocked at not getting what she wanted. "Give me one of them."

My sister snorted as she put the last package of Pampers in her cart. She turned her back and pushed the cart away. "Let's go," she said when she saw me.

The woman whispered to her maid, who nodded, then rushed my sister's cart, grabbed a diaper package, and disappeared down another aisle, the blue sweater floating on the air like a hero's cape. My sister screamed, tried to swing her cart around to follow the maid's cooling trail, but other customers got in the way. The woman laughed, beamed. I expected her to shout, "Who's the fairest of them all?"

A WEEK INTO THE BOMBING, my father's rage was spent. That evening he wore the black pants he'd had on the day before, the same starched white cotton shirt. His eyes were red from alcohol. Holding his glass with four fingers, he drank, kept it tilted for a while, quenching a thirst. The fingers were long, wrinkled, and swollen. His lips had shrunk and paled so that I couldn't trace them. He sat staring at the water-stained ceiling, lost in inebriated thought.

"Sometimes," he said quietly, "I feel so tired."

"I know."

He conversed with me by way of the ceiling, not lowering his head.

"Your mother keeps going to bed earlier and earlier."

He couldn't get to work, and when he was unable to work, he got bored, and when he was bored, he drank, and since he didn't drink often, he was a sad, boring drunk.

THERE WAS A LULL in the bombing. It was a Club Med–weather day and Wajdi wanted to go for a walk. He'd been cooped up too long. He left the apartment and I followed. We reached the corniche above our favorite beach, what used to be a long stretch of white sand. When the Israelis started bombing, one of the first things they hit was an oil depot at the port, and the resulting spill turned all our beaches black. We looked down on the goo, stared at the slick dark carcasses of fish. The sea that once sweetly whispered now grumbled and burped.

My brother descended to the beach to get a closer look. "Are you coming?"

I didn't reply. I didn't follow. I couldn't.

THE SECOND SET OF REFUGEES, the real ones, arrived two weeks after the bombing commenced. Dr. Masri asked that we open his apartment to two of his employees and their families, who had been left homeless by the ceaseless bombing of the southern suburbs. Our neighborhood had sustained damage but was now relatively safe. The bridge leading into the neighborhood had been blown up; the tall building two streets away, with a television antenna on its roof, had been leveled, but our area escaped the cluster bombs.

As the caretaker, I had to wait for the families. I'd expected children by the bushel, but there was only one, a taciturn boy of twelve. The two men worked in Dr. Masri's orchards in the south and had to return to the fields after they dropped off their wives.

"War or no war," the older man said, "we can't leave the blessings unattended."

Whereas a one-eyed man could tell that the men were brothers, their wives were a study in contrast. Both were harried and haggard, but the boy's mother looked as if she was ready to attend Friday prayers at the mosque, long skirt of brown and black, dusty beige shirt, and a dark blue chiffon scarf covering her hair. The younger, recently married, looked as if she was about to attend an afternoon disco party for the bad-taste crowd. Her slick skin was pale and white; her eyes, slightly slanted, were a light gray blue; and her wild blond hair was three shades to the left of peroxide, a spilled bottle. Black tights disappeared under a large white T-shirt with a rash of rhinestones.

As soon as I unlocked the door for them, the women toured the apartment, synchronizing their movements as if they had been refugee-ing together all their lives. I excused myself, but before I could close the door behind me, the older woman said, "Would you like to show Mohammad Ali around?"

He stood by his mother, staring at his shoes, looking smaller than his age. His chin almost disappeared into his concave chest, which made his head seem all hair—dirty and tangled hair, with strands reaching out like baby snakes. When he looked up briefly, he unnerved me. He had terrifying eyes, I thought—light, penetrating, like a wizard's.

"I can't," I replied. "Maybe later."

Against family advice, one morning my sister decided to go shopping up north, maybe as far as Tripoli, having exhausted the Beirut markets. The roads were damaged, but the Israelis hadn't attacked the north in almost ten days. Neither of our parents was willing to go with her. My brother refused as well, so she forced her husband to accompany her. "Make sure to leave your Shiite GPS locator in the apartment before you pick me up," she needled him. Usually my mother would have been needling her about her excessive cell phone usage, but the Israelis had destroyed all the landlines.

I'd spent the previous week telling my sister that she was nuts, AK-47 crazy, but she paid me no mind. My mother explained that every individual dealt with traumatic stress differently and one couldn't predict wartime behavior based on non-bombing personality. As the Israeli missiles hit, my father drank, my mother cooked, my brother brooded, and my sister shopped for diapers. During non-bombing she was probably as rational as any Lebanese, but with each missile she grew more and more erratic. Her pink room brimmed with disposable diapers, four distinct piles from floor to ceiling; one diaper bag at the top looked like it was suffocating because it couldn't fit between the ceiling and its brother below it. My sister had stuffed a dozen bags under the baby's cot and at least twice as many under her bed. She had enough diapers to ensure that her son would be wearing them until he was six years old, maybe seven. When I pointed that out to her, she shouted, "Well, I might get pregnant again. It happens."

But then this morning, we turned on the diesel generator to watch the television news and the announcer informed us that the Israelis had bombed the Johnson & Johnson warehouse the night before, incinerating everything in it.

"Why?" my mother asked the television.

My father looked at the bottle of scotch, but it was still early in the morning.

My brother sipped his coffee. "I'm sure terrorists were hiding between the shampoo and the Band-Aids. No more tears."

My sister beamed, seemed to have grown taller in her chair. "I told you we'll run out of diapers. Just you wait, they'll bomb the Procter & Gamble warehouse next." She was talking to us but looked as if she were addressing a large invisible audience. She pursed her lips and blew on newly painted fingernails.

I HAD TO SHOW Mohammad Ali around. My mother insisted that I spend time with the sullen boy. She thought he looked like a haunted creature, that he'd seen much more than a child should. "He must be lonely," she'd said. "His house has been destroyed. His family is all over the place. The least we can do is be kind and neighborly."

I didn't know what to show him. The Israelis were taking a break and we didn't have to stay indoors, but he didn't seem to care about seeing the neighborhood—his head rarely tilted anywhere but down. We sat silently on the wall facing our building. His legs were shorter than mine. He wouldn't look at me, instead leaned forward, his knuckles turning white where he held on to the wall. He was a nail biter. I glanced at my fingernails, then quickly looked away. My father had told me that men didn't worry about their fingernails.

The quiet bothered me. "You're an only son?" I asked.

"No." His strange vowels identified him as a southerner.

I waited, hoping he'd go on, but silence was his preferred companion. "Where are your siblings?"

"Not here."

I wanted to smack him. I could have been reading one of the doctor's books instead of spending time with him.

"Do you want me to leave you alone?" I asked, no longer trying to mask my irritation. "I could. It's no trouble. I'm just trying to be friendly."

He finally turned his head, his blue eyes measuring me. "Why do you want to be friends?" he asked.

"Because my mother said I had to."

A gold tooth shone way back in his mouth when he laughed.

"I have three brothers and two sisters," he said.

"That's more like it," I said.

"My eldest brother is in Nigeria, and so are my two sisters and their families. I have a brother who's a martyr. He would've been sixteen now, but he's dead."

I waited for a moment to see if he would go on. "That leaves one more," I said.

"He's fighting." He paused, sighed. "He's a man."

"Oh," I said. I leaned back and pretended nonchalance, as if it were every day that I talked about men fighting wars. "How old is he?"

"Fourteen."

"Hmm. Was your other brother a fighter, too?"

"I don't know."

"How could you not know?"

"No one knows who the fighters are until there's a war. I know that my brother is fighting now because he told me last week. He wanted me to protect my mother because he was going to kill the enemy."

"Oh," I said. "Fighting."

"You ask too many questions," he said.

"It's because you don't ask any."

"I'll ask," he said. "Why are you hiding from the fat boy?"

I didn't reply. I looked up at our balcony to see if anyone was up there.

"You shouldn't be afraid of him," he said.

LATER THAT DAY, I heard my father laughing like a crazy hyena on the balcony. He sipped a beer and leaned over the waist-level concrete wall that separated Dr. Masri's balcony from ours. The bougainvillea's flowers lay crumpled at his feet. On the other side, the newlywed listened to him tell the story of my meeting the American ambassador, an oft-repeated tale. My father waved me over to stand by him. He tousled my hair, held me close, and went on with the story.

I was in kindergarten, some years after the civil war ended, when the American ambassador came to visit our school with an entourage of reporters and sycophants. The ambassador engaged a number of kids in conversation. He surprised me at the bottom of the slide, asking me directly in English, "How much is two and two?" Without pausing I said, "Are you buying or selling?" There. I identified myself as one of the Lebanese, who would sell their souls for a good profit, descendants of the Phoenicians, who apparently had. I also identified myself as the son of my father, a moneychanger.

My father finished the story and burst into hyena laughter once more.

The laughter settled into comical hiccups. "You were such a funny boy," he said, caressing my cheek.

. . .

THE MORNING SUN FOUND Mohammad Ali and me sitting on the same wall as the day before, still not talking much. We were there for about twenty minutes before the bully showed up.

"Who's your friend?" Pipo yelled.

There was no escape. Mohammad Ali stared at his weathered shoes. My palms turned clammy.

"He's not my friend," I said. "His family moved next door because their house was bombed."

"So you found a younger boy to suck your cock?"

Something within that younger boy was unyoked. He lifted his head up and glared at Pipo.

"Don't look at me that way, you little—" Pipo's eyes looked unhinged suddenly as Mohammad Ali lunged with a Swiss Army blade and slashed his sleeve.

"If you talk to me again," Mohammad Ali said, "I'll kill you."

Pipo looked at the tear in his light blue shirt, put his finger right through it. There was no blood. "This is my favorite shirt," he said. "My mother bought it for me."

"If you talk to me again—"

This time it was Pipo who interrupted. For a fat boy, he was inordinately quick. He punched the younger boy in the face and sent him flying against the wall. That wasn't enough. Pipo jerked him to the ground, sat on him, and began an unforgiving assault. Blood erupted, bones broke. Pipo kept yelling, "You think you can scare me with a Swiss Army knife?"

I tried to stop Pipo, but he swung at me as soon as I got close to him. He was much too big. I screamed for help. I thought Mohammad Ali was already dead. I screamed so loud that practically everyone in the neighborhood showed up. Wajdi was the one who lifted Pipo off the unconscious boy.

Someone called for an ambulance. Someone else called his mother.

Pipo blabbered, "He stabbed me with a knife. He stabbed me. I'm going to tell my father."

. . .

EVEN THOUGH WE DIDN'T know his family well, my parents decided on the hospital visit as a show of support, and I was forced along. In the hospital bed, surrounded by machines and his watchful mother, he did not look like the boy of the day before. The contours of his face, its distinctive shadings, had been altered, as if I were looking at him in an aquarium. I couldn't bear to look directly at him. My father stared at Mohammad Ali lying in the coma and shook his head as if what was in front of him was inconceivable, as if his eyes were betraying him. He shook his head with his eyes closed, opened them, then repeated the process. I thought we should return home. He needed his drink.

My mother, on the other hand, wished to stay at the hospital because she felt sorry for Mohammad Ali's mother, being far from home without enough family around her.

I persuaded my father to take me home. As I followed him toward the car, the boy's aunt, the newlywed, ran after us, her body jiggling in a loud leotard, asking if she could get a ride.

Sitting in the front seat, Mohammad Ali's aunt chattered, couldn't remain quiet, giggled nervously, didn't seem worried about her nephew's condition. Every individual dealt with traumatic stress differently. You couldn't predict wartime behavior.

"JUST GO OVER THERE and fuck her," my father demanded with emphasis, but not in anger.

He and I were alone in the apartment. He wore his white sweat suit, which usually meant he was planning a brisk walk. The slicked-back hair, however, and the intensity in his eyes, made him look like an Eastern European, a Romanian or Bulgarian, about to go to a nightclub.

The Israelis were bombing the southern section of Beirut again—no one was going for a brisk walk.

I stood before my father, unable to move, even though I wanted desperately to retreat into a book. My tongue tasted chemicals. My father wanted me to walk across the hallway that separated our apartment from Dr. Masri's and fuck our neighbor, the boy's aunt. And he wanted me to do it right then.

"Get Wajdi to do it." My face flushed. How did one just walk over and have sex with a woman? What was the procedure? Was there a secret language between men and women that I was not privy to, an adult code of signs, of body hieroglyphs, announcing readiness to fuck? "Wajdi should go first."

"No, you. You're ready. Just go over there and fuck her." His eyes bored into me. Nothing else in his life mattered at that moment except this.

"I don't understand. How do I do it? How do you know she's ready to fuck? I don't know what to do." I whined like a baby, already defeated.

"She's ready and she wants it. There's no one else there and she's meowing like a cat in heat. Just go now."

"What about her husband?"

"She's not getting what she wants from her husband. He's a wimp. You can tell. Go over there and fuck her."

"Do I have to do it now? Why now? How do you know she's ready this minute?"

"Why not now? She's meowing. Go."

"I can't. I masturbated twice this morning."

Saved.

He raised his arms in exasperation and walked out. The sound of the closing door echoed in the apartment. I shut my eyes and concentrated on the afterimage. The white sweat suit turned black.

An hour later, he sat on the sagging armchair in the living room, a light sheen of sweat covering his face. He was wearing the same Adidas sweat suit but now unzipped. His undershirt showed, a few chest hairs forcing their way through the thin fabric. His potbelly looked more bloated than usual, as if he had swallowed a globe. His hair was plastered to his forehead.

"I don't usually do this." He spoke in a low voice.

"Do what?" I asked, not wanting to believe what I was seeing.

"I don't usually screw around when your mother and I are in the same town. I have too much respect for her. But I wanted to show you the girl was ready to get fucked. If only you'd listened to me." He regarded me with some compassion, but I was too stunned to utter anything. "She was meowing. I told you. All you had to do was go over there and you would've fucked her. She needed it. You could've had it. I didn't want to do it, but you forced me. I had to do it to show you."

The summer breeze slowly eddied the faded magenta flowers round and round the balcony like ghostly gowns waltzing at the ball. My father looked away from me, toward the window, toward the dance, toward Beirut, our city, falling apart.

Cattle Praise Song

Scholastique Mukasonga

Translated from French by Melanie Mauthner

I was seven years old and puffed up with pride; I was my father's little cattle herder. Every morning, when my father left the big hut, I woke with a start, reproaching myself bitterly for sleeping so soundly when I should have been up before him, like my older brothers, to tend to the cows in the kraal. I was convinced that my father never slept, that he was always on the alert. He would never let himself be caught out by cattle rustlers. Stealing cows was a serious sport in Rwanda. People feared these bandits and also admired them. They were very cunning. They had medicines that would put all the inhabitants of a kraal to sleep. The rustlers would make an opening in the fence, and the cows, under their spell, would follow them through it without a moo. The thieves left no trace: they were powerful sorcerers. They knew the secret paths that led through the swamps to Burundi, where they sold the stolen cows and bought new ones. In Rwanda, some herds grew bigger quickly, but you couldn't ask questions—it was too dangerous.

My father, though, knew how to counter the cattle rustlers' spells. He placed talismans in the acacia-thorn fence to protect the herd from attack. So what was I afraid of? My father always kept his staff and his spear within arm's reach near his bed. In those days, all the men carried a spear; they never went out without one. The Belgians hadn't outlawed them yet, as they did later on, to our great humiliation. My father's bow and arrows hung near the entrance of our hut. At my father's side—he armed with his spear and his bow, I with my small herder's staff—I was ready to defy all the thieves and their sorcery. But I was ashamed of the deep sleep I succumbed to every night instead of watching over the cows the way he did.

My father didn't need to count every cow in the large enclosure: he could tell at a glance if they were all there. They lay on the grass bedding that my mother and my sisters had prepared the day before, while the cows were in the pasture. My brothers were busy rousing them. A gentle tap of the stick was enough to prod the leader of the herd, and the rest then followed. My father made sure that, as they jostled, they didn't stab one another with their horns; he went from one to the next, his staff raised, protecting the gentle cows from those who were known to be skittish or feisty (we had carefully burned the tips of the horns of the most aggressive ones). As the master, he had nothing to fear, even from the most irascible cows. He worried about the cows who seemed to balk at standing up on all four legs. He spent a long time checking them, prodding, touching, and tapping them, inspecting their ears, eyes, and tongues. He examined their dung—its color, size, and consistency; he decided what medications to administer and indicated which cows he deemed too weak to go out and graze: they'd stay in the kraal to be fed hay and fresh-cut grass gathered as the herd returned.

"Karekezi," my father said, "look after Intamati."

I went to her immediately: she was one of those cows we call *isine*, with a shiny black hide. My father had likely assigned her to me because she was a heifer known for her strength, who might one day lead the herd. He was probably hoping that Intamati would augur well for me and bring me luck. I knew what to do. I stroked her neck and whispered, "Intamati, Intamati!" With a tuft of fresh, damp grass, I carefully wiped off the mud where cowpats had splashed her; I gently brushed her coat until it was silky and shining. She rewarded me with a generous spray of urine. That was what my father was waiting for. He always worried when a cow took too long to pee. He'd hold her tail high and boldly lean forward—never mind that if the cow finally decided to urinate she might shower him. Nobody dared to laugh. Anyway, isn't cow urine, *amaganga*, considered to be a potent remedy? That first warm morning urine is what we give to children whose swollen bellies indicate that they're harboring worms.

One of my brothers removed the barrier made of thick, cleverly intertwined branches that blocked the entrance to the big kraal, while the others, at my father's orders, corralled and channelled the impatient cattle. To reach the small kraal, they had to be herded between two bamboo poles that framed the entrance. I followed Intamati closely, since I was in charge of her, watching for any horn jabs she might give or receive, but, otherwise, she knew the way as well as I did. I admired her dancer's gait, her long, perfectly curved horns, her wide, dreamy eyes. She was my pride and joy, Intamati; she was my cow.

In the small kraal, a few feet from the cows, we lit a huge fire with wet grass; its thick smoke chased away the flies, which would otherwise have annoyed the cattle. This was the time to get rid of the ticks and the fleas around their ears and eyes, to lift their tails and hunt down all the parasites, to inspect their hooves and make sure that there were no stones or thorns embedded there. If my father spotted a wound, he rubbed it with some ointment made from the marrow of a banana-tree branch. Oh, how we enjoyed brushing their coats again and whispering proud and tender words.

Afterward, we led the cattle beyond the small kraal to a fallow field, where they could graze on the dew-drenched grass.

THEN CAME THE HOUR when the sun was climbing the sky but the freshness of dawn hadn't yet dissipated: *agasusuruko*, milking time.

By now, my mother and my sisters had joined us. They'd brought wooden milk pails, carved from flame trees, those beautiful trees with red flowers that shade the kraals. The youngest girls sat by the fire with their own pails, specially shaped to fit in their hands.

Milking could begin. This was a solemn moment for everyone, a formal ritual. It was a bit like going to Mass—which I do every morning now that I have no cows—with my father as the high priest, of course. He summoned the cows one by one, calling out their names: "Songa! Songa!" Songa slowly came toward him. He repeated her name, sweet-talked her, called her "my darling, my beloved." We brought her calf out of the stable and led it to the small kraal. Because we'd named him, too, at birth, we greeted him: "Rutamu! Rutamu!" He was hard to keep hold of, and as soon as he was released he ran under his mother and began to feed greedily. My father squatted beside the cow, observing the calf's muzzle. When the muzzle was blotted with creamy froth, we pulled him away from his mother's udder and placed a pail under her teat. It took all my older brother's strength to wrench the poor calf away from his feast. We'd console him with a handful of bulrushes and some bean stock, and, once the milking was over, he would return to his mother and glean whatever milk was left.

My father had hitched up his pagne in order to squeeze the wooden pail between his knees. He was a good milker. You can spot a good milker by his smooth, regular rhythm. You can hear a good milker in the *shyushyushyushyu* of the milk spurting from the udder in the milker's hands. How I wish I could hear that sound again here in Nyamata!

We always began the milking with the cow who had just calved, for she produced the most milk—honey-rich, creamy milk. This was the milk we saved for the youngest children. We quickly filled their pails and let them drink right away. But you couldn't receive such precious milk any old way. You had to be sitting—not squatting—with your legs straight in front of you and the rest of your body upright. It was my mother who gave her children this milk, murmuring, "*Akira amata! Nyakugira amata!* Here's your milk! May you always have milk!" The children held the milk pail in their small hands—you must always hold a milk pail with both hands, out of respect and reverence for the cow, so that she may live a long life. It was a bit like the priests with their chalices, but, for us, milk was what truly nourished us. The children drank it in one draught, without taking a breath. And their mothers felt reassured:

they had no reason to fear for their children's health. What joy it was to gaze at my mother as she gazed at her children's cheeks and noses splashed with creamy froth like the calf's. When their pails were empty, the little ones handed them to my mother, their eyes wide with pleasure.

My mother and my sisters would bow their heads respectfully as they carried the milk pails to the big hut. They set them in the place of honor on the *uruhimbi*, the dresser that wrapped around the curved wall of the house. A whole array of traps protected the milk from rats, for if a rat fell into a pail, the loss of the milk was less upsetting than the curse that would inevitably befall the family. The *uruhimbi* was like an altar to milk, and those big milk pails with pointy lids protected us, like statues of the saints in a church. What was there to fear? Milk, our life source, was abundant.

If man is the master of the cows, woman is the mistress of the milk. Until I was old enough to join my brothers in tending the herd, I followed my mother around in her daily chores, especially those to do with milk. The morning's fresh milk, what we hadn't drunk, she poured into a large, wide-rimmed pot. On the *uruhimbi*, in several identical vessels, milk had sat for several days. With a small wooden spoon, Maman skimmed the cream and slowly filled the *akabya*, a little black pot, with it. When there was enough cream, it was time to get out the milk churn: with as much caution as respect, my mother retrieved it from the net that was strung like a hammock over the *uruhimbi*. I saw the sun pass before me, the churn shining far more brightly than the monstrance that the priests carry on procession day. Well, not every gourd is destined to become a milk churn. Very few possess the requisite qualities: a young girl's hips, my mother said, and the neck of a crowned crane. Its curves must be as soft to the touch as a baby's dimpled thigh. Untarnished by water, it was wiped dry, like a cow, with a tuft of *ishinge*, the soft, fine grass that girls offered as a tribute to distinguished guests, and varnished with a layer of the butter that was mysteriously created inside it. My mother sat with her back against the partition that screened off my parents' big bed, her legs stretched out in front of her, her chest high, and the churn resting on her thighs, as she rocked it from side to side, like a baby. Fascinated, my little sisters and I would watch the swaying belly of the churn and wonder whether, as well as the anticipated butter, we would see emerge from it the poor orphan girl who, according to my mother's tales, had been locked up inside it by her evil stepmother.

AFTER MILKING, we led the cows to pasture. In those days, the land hadn't yet been overrun by huts and crop fields: there was still room for the cows to graze. Sometimes my father came with us, but most of the time he trusted my older brother to lead the herd. He had many other tasks to do. My father was a wise man. For the families from our hills and the surrounding areas, he was a kind of living memory. He knew who their ancestors were, their lineage and genealogy, the alliances and the rivalries. People came to him for advice. He could defuse a conflict with a well-chosen proverb. The men would gather in the shade of a tall ficus tree, on the meadow grass known as *agacaca*, and discuss the news from Nyanza and the royal palace, or the whites' latest tactic for adding to the misfortunes of Rwandans and their cattle. But, most important, they met to establish the borders of each man's grazing ground (this led to endless arguments, negotiations, and recriminations) and the order in which each herd would go to drink at the watering holes, to avoid any jostling or fighting among either the beasts or their herders.

It's not good for the head of a family to stay in his kraal with his wife. In any case, she wouldn't put up with it. In no time, her neighbors would be mocking her and whispering behind her back, "Her husband's like a dog, he's always hanging around at home, *sumugabo n'imbwa*." A man's role is to defend his family's interests outside the home, almost like a minister of foreign affairs. And a notable like my father had to put in an appearance with the chief, spend time with him, join his evening gatherings, and listen to what was being said over jugs of beer, and he had to offer cows and accept cows in exchange. But as soon as he could he returned to his herd.

The pastures stretched along the steep hillside, where it was hard to build a kraal. Grassy fields in the valley were rare, and reserved for the privileged few. During the rainy season—and you know how long the rains last in Rwanda—herders sought shelter under an *isinde*: this was a sort of individual shelter that you could carry with you, like a hood. It looked a bit like the sentry box for the soldier on guard at the Gako military camp. But this *isinde*, woven from dried banana-tree leaves, was much lighter: it was stored in a hole under a heavy rock. This was our hiding spot for staffs, bows and arrows, flutes. We also kept our day's meagre provisions there.

On the hill opposite us, above the swamp, there were other herds, other herders. It was the custom for the herdsmen to insult one another; I won't repeat what they said—it was always about your mother. . . . They also praised their cows, which were always one of a kind, and mocked their neighbors' cows. Some played the flute. They positioned themselves so that their insults, their boasts, and their melodies would echo and carry as far as possible. But they never took their eyes off their cattle. They made sure that the cows didn't wander too close to the steep slopes or graze on poisonous plants. Me, I always followed Intamati. My mother had given me a small pouch made from black-and-yellow banana leaves. I was meant to gather my cow's dung in it. My mother had noticed how beautifully bright green Intamati's cowpats were. "That's just what I need to coat the bottom of the big baskets with," she told me. "The ones I keep at the foot of the bed to store sorghum and goose-grass." I diligently filled my pouch and stored it in the shady hiding spot.

When the sun was burning hot, one of the herders took the calves back to the stable. The poor things hadn't been able to drink, because their mothers' teats were coated in white clay. This stretch, in the heat of the day, was when you had to be vigilant. Thirst could send the cows sliding down the hill to the swamp without waiting for the herders to take them to the watering holes.

For the families from our hills, it was out of the question to let our cows drink the muddy swamp water. We fetched fresh spring water in wooden buckets and poured it into the baked-clay water troughs, and then salted it with marsh-grass ashes.

This water was an object of envy. We had to keep a constant eye on the spring and the troughs. Luckily, the water supply was visible from most of the kraals on our hillside, and, as soon as any intruders came near it, we sounded the alarm. Herders would reach for their spears and staffs to chase away the invaders. This spring water was known for its miraculous properties. We were forbidden to boil it or use it for cooking. This water protected us from sickness and bad spells. I don't think the small bottle of water from Lourdes that the priests gave me is as effective.

After quenching their thirst, the cows rested and ruminated peacefully in a shady copse or on the slope, out of the sun. What happier moment is there for a herder than when, resting his staff on his neck and folding his right leg over his left thigh, he can relax and admire his herd?

At nightfall, the cows returned to the kraal, and every evening was a party. The herdsmen danced and improvised poems in the cows' honor, and the leader of the herd was celebrated. I selected the most tender tufts of grass for Intamati. Sometimes we assembled the cattle from all the kraals on the hill into a long procession; it was like a parade for the king. Children clapped as the cattle passed, and women cried out with joy. Then each herder reclaimed his cows. This could take a long time, but what a beautiful spectacle that forest of horns made! The men of our hill never tired of it.

The men were starving when they got back to the kraal, but the cows needed to be milked according to the same ritual as in the morning. Afterward, we'd enter the big kraal, which was smoky from the burning wet grass. The cows would lie down on their fresh bedding while we treated each one to a nice green tuft, as a final tribute. The herders stood at the threshold of the hut. I hoped that my mother would bring me my wooden plate with some *ibirunge*, beans soaked in rancid butter, one of my favorite dishes, but we didn't eat *ibirunge* every day. Still, for the herders, we always saved a pail of buttermilk, *ikivuguto*, which was a tonic for tiredness and replenished their energy. By this point, I was falling asleep. I lay on my mat in the entryway of our hut, beside the newborn calf, promising myself that the next morning I'd be the first one—before my brothers or my father—to tend to the cows.

On days when I didn't go to school, when Kalisa, my father, returned from Mass, which he attended every morning, he would say, "Karekezi, you're a man now. Come, it is high time for you to learn how to look after the cows." Of course, there were no cows in Nyamata—not among the Tutsi who had been resettled there, at least—but my father spent his days steering his ghost cows through meadows of memory and regret.

"Look," he'd say, as we passed the tall banana trees that Maman grew with such care in the back kraal, whose bananas were a real treat for us children. "Look, your poor mother tends those banana trees as if they were our calves. Oh, Lord! I've seen her watering them with bean stock, and look at this green grass that is rotting—she picks it as if she still had cows, but all she can do with it now is feed the banana trees!"

My father had rested his long herder's staff across his shoulders, and now he propped his hands on it. I could see his straight, skinny, calf-less legs below his immaculately white pagne. He exchanged the pagne for some old shorts and a tattered top only if he was doing heavy work, like clearing roots or planting a field. But when the agronomists came to inspect the plots of coffee trees we Tutsi were forced to cultivate he knotted his whitest pagne and leaned majestically on his staff. Scanning the horizon and smoking his pipe, he let the young technicians proffer their ceaseless directives, until he finally said, "So, you're not veterinarians, then?"

We'd take the track that ran through our village for the displaced. My father seemed to see nothing, neither the row of identical huts nor the coffee plots in front of each one. I could barely keep up with him. It was as if he'd been summoned for some urgent business and he didn't have a second to lose. If I bumped into a classmate, there was just enough time to greet him and toss a banana-leaf ball back and forth. "Come on, hurry up," my father would say quickly. "You'll have plenty of time to chat with Juvénal in the playground at school tomorrow. I want to show you something."

If we passed some young girls on their way back from fetching water from Lake Cyohoha, my father would thunder, "Look at what they've done to us! Did you see the calabashes those girls were carrying on their heads? At home in Rwanda, those calabashes were our milk churns. We would never have dared to fill them with water! Shame on us! Yes, I know what your mother gets up to, but it makes no difference—even the water from Ruganzu Ndori can't replace the milk from our cows."

Indeed, Maman gave us water from the Rwakibirizi spring, which, according to ancient myth, had gushed from the ground under King Ruganzu Ndori's spear. She hoped that this water from an ancestral source would have the same powers as milk. Thus, we had to follow the same ritual: sit straight, with our legs stretched out in front of us, and drink it in a single draught, without stopping to breathe. This, for my father, was a sacrilege. "It's as if the priests were to fill their chalices with beer," said my father, who had never drunk wine. Yet, powerless as he was, he let Maman perform this desecration. What milk could he find for us now, after all? He was grateful, though, for her respectful way of handling the churns. If a gourd had attained the plumpness that would have won it the quasi-sacred status of a milk churn in Rwanda, she did not allow it to be used to fetch water from Lake Cyohoha. Instead, she placed it on what, in this rectangular hut, was as close as we could get to our *uruhimbi* shelf, and only after innumerable recommendations did she entrust it to the person who was going to gather holy water at Rwakibirizi. Woe befall the water carrier who broke the gourd that had been anointed in this way: such clumsiness might set off the worst calamities. That bad luck had to be immediately exorcised. My mother would intone the appropriate incantations to drive out the evil spirits, and sprinkle our family, our home, and its surroundings with her lustral libations.

A single road ran through the village and past the row of huts, and that made it difficult to avoid the hut that belonged to Nicodème—Nicodème, the village pariah! My father conspicuously turned away so as not to risk seeing Nicodème degrading himself, as they said he did, morning and evening. Having mourned his cows, Nicodème now kept goats, which he had procured from the Bagesera people. Crafty Nicodème, in order to get the goats, had befriended a Mugesera man, a certain Sekaganda; he'd even managed to convince him that they were of the same lineage. So proud of this family tie was Sekaganda that he solemnly offered Nicodème his two most beautiful goats. Every morning and evening, Nicodème milked his two goats. Is there anything more shameful for a Tutsi than milking goats? Misfortune had led Nicodème to these dishonorable depths. From then on, we referred to him only, in low voices, as Sehene, Father Goat. And then there was the calabash that Nicodème used for his goats' milk: it became, for everyone, an object of loathing and disgust. We named the calabash Igikorwa, the Untouchable. We were sure that this cursed calabash would bring bad luck to all the cows—those we no longer had, as well as those we might one day own. Some of us thought about going over there one night to smash that sinister calabash. But no one could persuade himself to commit the crime. For the calabash could seek revenge and curse him. And who dared to touch Igikorwa, the Untouchable? Anyway, some women, including Maman, stood up for Nicodème. He had a child who was always ill: the boy was why Nicodème had gone to get goats from the Bagesera and why he didn't hesitate to milk them, despite the shame this brought him. At the Nyamata clinic, they said that goat's milk was good for children. This made the men anxious: were their wives also going to seek out goats if their children fell ill? They left Nicodème and his goats alone, but they let him know that on no account could his goats roam freely in the fields, and then no one spoke to him again.

On the way to Lake Cyohoha, at the edge of the village, the track ran past Rukorera's abandoned plot. There were no coffee shrubs by this ruin of a hut, but behind it a ramshackle fence of woven branches hid a large kraal. Rukorera! A Tutsi in exile who still kept cows! He who, for a time, had brought joie de vivre to our village! Of course, these cows didn't belong to us: they were Rukorera's cows, but, because we knew they were nearby, and the smell of them and even of their milk floated in the air, and their fresh dung was scattered around the track, it was as if a small piece of Rwanda had come to console us in our exile.

No one could forget the day that Rukorera arrived. The sun wasn't yet up. We were woken by a familiar noise that we hadn't heard for such a long time, but we hesitated before rushing out. Had an evil spirit imprisoned us in a dream we could not escape from? we wondered. Was it the ghosts of our cows, whom we'd left to be slaughtered, coming back to haunt us? Or was it soldiers coming to taunt us poor, cow-less Tutsi? "Don't go," my mother told Kalisa. "It's probably just buffalo or soldiers' boots."

At last we ventured outside, cautiously making our way beneath the coffee shrubs to the edge of the track. We were sure of it now: the sound was that of lowing cows, trampling hooves, and herders calling out names that are given only to cows. The cows had returned!

Men, soon followed by women and children, headed to where these wonderful sounds seemed to be coming from. A few unclaimed plots of land still skirted the village. All that remained of the sheet-metal roofs and wattle walls with which the displaced Tutsi had built their new homes was a few stakes. But that morning, in the golden dawn light, there were real cows grazing on the sparse grass, four youths were collecting dry wood, a man draped in a dusty pagne was leaning on his herder's staff, a woman was unrolling the grass mat in which she'd probably carried all her family's treasures, and next to her, on a bed of woven grass, slept a little girl.

The stunned villagers gathered along the track. The man who appeared to be the head of the family approached us: "I'm Rukorera. I come from Kibirizi, like you. We've travelled far. My cows are thirsty. Do you have water for them?"

Water for his cows! Of course we'd find water for his cows. Rukorera had won everyone's respect. Here was a true Tutsi: he thought of his cows first.

To welcome his cows as befitted the occasion and to provide them with an auspicious drink, all the children of the village, clutching every available container, were dispatched to Rwakibirizi, for there was no question of offering the cows the rainwater we kept in reserve.

So Rukorera decided to settle in our village with his cows. "After all, we understand one another here," Rukorera said. "We all love cows."

During the massacres, he explained to us—in 1962, that was—his kraal had been spared. No one knew why, but it was obviously an oversight that would soon be rectified. So Rukorera had thought it most prudent to disappear with his family and his cows before the killers came to finish off the job. He hid in the great swamps that stretch along the Burundi-Rwanda border. Rukorera and his family survived by hunting and by drinking their cows' milk. When the rains came, they fled the swamp. He'd heard that many Tutsi had been relocated to Nyamata, and he told himself that there, among them, he would find refuge for his family and his cows.

The entire village accepted Rukorera, and especially his cows, with enthusiasm. We helped him build a hut for his wife and young daughter, another for his four sons, and a stable for his calves. All the men wanted to help weave the fence. When we realized that he had no Christian name and that, therefore, he must not have been baptized, no one was offended, not even my pious father. On the contrary, we admired the heroic names that Rukorera had given to his big, strapping sons—the names of famous ancient warriors in epic poems: Impangazamurego, he who is armed with a powerful bow; Rugeramibungo, he who has perfect aim; Rutiru-kayimpunzi, he who never flees; and Rwasabahizi, conqueror of conquerors.

THE VILLAGERS FELT ALIVE again to the rhythm of the cows. In the morning, we'd rush to Rukorera's kraal to watch him rouse and milk them. Oh, the joy of breathing in the smoke from the fire that kept the flies away. The women would ask him for some precious warm urine, the deworming potion that was so hard to come by in Nyamata, which they'd immediately administer to their children. We'd follow the herd through the village and argue over who could gather the fresh cowpats. Children shoved and jostled one another so that they could at last touch the cows that their parents talked about all the time but they had never seen. Naturally, everyone went to Rukorera to barter for milk. And he was happy to trade milk for sweet potatoes, beans, or bananas. But his ten cows couldn't satisfy the needs of the whole village. We tried to regulate access to Rukorera's milk. The elders decided that pregnant women, small children, and old people would get priority. But, of course, we knew that, despite this strict rule, with a few jugs of beer we could secure extra milk. We also came up with a rota for the cows to graze our fallow fields—every man invited Rukorera to bring the cows to his patch, not just in order to fertilize the land and receive milk in return but because having cows again made us happy. We were sure that this would bring our families good fortune.

The evening milking drew the largest crowd, especially among the women and children. The young people longed to come close and touch the cows' teats, but, since they weren't invited, out of pride they kept their distance. Rukorera and his sons reserved the noble task of milking for themselves. And they were good milkers: you could tell from the smooth, regular *shyushyu* rhythm. Rukorera's wife handed them the milk pails—these were the treasures they'd rescued and carried in their grass mats—and once a milk pail was full she handed it to the women, who sat side by side, their backs straight and their legs stretched out in front of them, as custom dictated. Each woman in turn carefully passed the pail to her neighbor, while blessing this life source and wishing the family and the whole village health and prosperity. The last woman in the row handed the pail to Rukorera's little daughter, who carried it inside the hut. After that, it was hard to go home, where there was no sour-milk smell to greet us.

The mirage of Rwanda that Rukorera and his cows had conjured up among us during our exile was soon to evaporate. One morning, the small crowd that assembled to watch the milking found Rukorera's kraal deserted. He and his family and his cows had moved on, silently, during the night. A great sorrow descended upon us exiled Tutsi, but Rukorera's flight hardly surprised us. We knew that he felt threatened, that soldiers had vowed to come and slaughter his cattle. Later, we learned that he had crossed the border and found refuge with his herd in Burundi. He had always been a lucky man, Rukorera, and he managed to save his cows!

Once you passed Rukorera's plot, the path disappeared and you had to walk through prickly scrub. Kalisa would run his rosary beads through his fingers, muttering and repeating his Ave Marias, but his attention was elsewhere: with his staff, he pointed out the plants and herbs he wanted me to pick. He studied them at length, nodding as he chewed on a leaf or the end of a stalk: "You see, it's hard to find good plants for the cows here. It's not like at home in Rwanda. I will have to ask the Bagesera. This is their land, but, to a Tutsi, they really don't know how to take care of their cows."

My father was indignant at the way the Bagesera treated their cattle. "Poor cows," he'd lament. "They're just bags of bones that attract every kind of disease. That's the curse that hangs over this Bugesera region. Now I know why the king banished rebels and cowards here: all you can do in Bugesera is wither away, and that's what they probably hoped would happen to us. Those Bagesera have no respect for their cows: they lump them in with goats, they use their staffs to control them, and they can't even tell them apart. You have to call a cow by her name, flatter her, whisper in her ear, sing her praises. And when you take her to the chief, decorate her with a garland of flowers, a string of beads. But when they herd cattle, what a shameful sight to behold: they dress like the white man's boys, in short trousers and tattered tops, *isengeri*. They don't even know how to knot a herder's pagne. It's no wonder their cows give so little milk. And this saying is unknown to them: *Shaka inka aryama nkazo*—a good herder sleeps to the rhythm of his cattle."

Kalisa did acknowledge one good trait of the Bagesera: in this parched land, they knew how to build troughs. He had noted where the troughs were, and always arranged things so that we could make a stop at one of them. He'd dip his rosary beads into the cows' water and mumble a prayer in praise both of his cows and of the Virgin Mary.

By this point we would have almost reached our destination. We were heading for a marshy patch, pushing our way downhill through the thickets. The ground here was always wet, even at the height of the dry season. Leaning on his staff, Kalisa would survey the stagnant ponds for a long time. He was staring at what I was incapable of seeing. "This is a beautiful spot for cows," he said. "There's always plenty of thick green grass. And there's water—we can build drinking troughs. Don't tell anyone. Especially not your mother—she'd come here and plant beans and sweet potatoes. This spot is for our cattle. Karekezi, you are my son, this is a man's business, and this must be our secret. When the cows come back, this is where I will bring our herd. There is enough grass here, and they'll strengthen themselves for the return to Rwanda. Yes, it will be a long and difficult journey, but we'll get there, we Tutsi and our cows. I can see them all here, I know their names: Kirezi, Kagaju, Gatare, Mihigo, Rugina, Ndori, Rutamu. . . . When the cows come back, that will be the sign that it's time to head home to Rwanda."

My father would reluctantly pull himself away from this secret pasture where his ghost cows were already grazing. As we walked, he cut branches that would make good staffs. "You always need some spares," he advised me. "A staff can easily break." At home, he stripped the bark, smoothed the wood, and sharpened the tip. My mother would ceaselessly, mechanically weave *intumwa*, the lids for the churns. She chose banana leaves with the finest bronze and copper hues. The *intumwa* piled up, useless, in a basket on the *uruhimbi*. No one was allowed to touch them.

In the heat of the day, we'd return to the village—it was the hour when, in Rwanda, we would bring the calves in. "Go and fetch firewood," my mother said. "It will soon be time to cook the beans." And, while I gathered sticks in the bush, I'd repeat out loud the lessons I'd learned from the schoolmaster. Before long, my father would be off again; there was always something for him to attend to in Nyamata, at the mission, or at a neighbor's, he said, but I knew that often he was just wandering, guiding his missing cows with his staff.

When night fell, the men gathered in a circle under a tall ficus tree. They exchanged news, weighed up any imminent dangers the community might be facing, and sought ways to address them, but, when they had exhausted all these topics, they always came back to their cows. Every man had something to say about the cows he'd once owned and those he would perhaps, one day, own again. The men reminisced about the cow that had been offered as a gift by this or that chief, or even by the king himself, why not! They described her coat, her horns, her temperament, and the calves she'd birthed; they recited the poems they'd composed in her honor. And their glorious and familiar praise song for our beloved lost cows mingled with the French words the schoolmaster had given me to learn—a strange litany that I recited out loud.

Like so many other Rwandan Tutsi, I followed the path of exile. I extended my studies for as long as I could, because my stateless status, conferred by the travel documents the High Commission distributed to refugees, gave me little hope of finding work. Overqualified with useless degrees, I finally got a teaching job in the Republic of Djibouti, in a remote village surrounded by jagged black rocks, where they raised a few camels, and three stray cows grazed on cardboard. I cried at this desolate scene. I hadn't understood that the path of exile led to the gates of Hell. Through various convolutions, I managed to have my first paycheck sent to my father. When a letter from him finally reached me, he told me that—as I'd suspected he would—he had put most of the money toward the purchase of a cow.

My father, my mother, and the rest of my family were not spared by the genocide; nor were the other Nyamata Tutsi. I will never know what Kalisa named his only cow. I don't want to know whether she served as a feast for the killers.

I returned to Rwanda without a single cow. I hope that my father was not angered by this in the land of the dead. I live in Kigali, in the Nyamirambo neighborhood, and I teach at a private university. I married a widow, who lost her husband in the genocide. Our first son already has a sister and a brother—her two children who survived. I drink beer with my Hutu neighbor: he is my neighbor and that's all I want to know about him. I often dream about King Gihanga: according to legend, he was our first king, and he introduced cows to Rwanda. And in my dreams King Gihanga always asks the same question: "So it was you, the Tutsi, who chose to herd cows?" But I turn my head and pretend not to hear him.

Garments

Tahmima Anam

One day Mala lowers her mask and says to Jesmin, my boyfriend wants to marry you. Jesmin is six shirts behind so she doesn't look up. After the bell, Mala explains. For months now she's been telling the girls, ya, any day now me and Dulal are going to the Kazi. They don't believe her, they know her boyfriend works in an air-conditioned shop. No way he was going to marry a garments girl. Now she has a scheme and when Jesmin hears it, she thinks, it's not so bad.

Two days later Mala's sweating like it's July. He wants one more. Three wives. We have to find a girl. After the bell they look down the row of sewing machines and try to choose. Mala knows all the unmarried girls, which one needs a room, which one has hungry relatives, which one borrowed money against her wage and can't work enough overtime to pay it off. They squint down the line and consider Fatima, Keya, Komola, but for some reason or other they reject them all. There's a new girl at the end of the row but when Mala takes a break and limps over to the toilet she comes back and says the girl has a milky eye.

There's a new order for panties. Jesmin picks up the sample. She's never seen a panty like it before. It's thick, with double seams on the front, back, and around the buttocks. The leg is just cut off without a stitch. Mala, she says, what's this? Mala says, the foreign ladies use them to hold in their fat and they call them Thanks. Thanks? Yep. Because they look so good, in the mirror they say to the panties, Thanks. Jesmin and Mala pull down their masks and trade a laugh when the morning supervisor, Jamal, isn't looking.

Jesmin decides it won't be so bad to share a husband. She doesn't have dreams of a love marriage, and if they have to divide the sex that's fine with her, and if he wants something, like he wants his rice the way his mother makes it, maybe one of them will know how to do it. Walking home as she did every evening with all the other factory workers, a line two girls thick and a mile long, snaking out of Tongi and all the way to Uttara, she spots a new girl. Sometimes Jesmin looks in front and behind her at that line, all the ribbons flapping and the song of sandals on the pavement, and she feels a swell in her chest. She catches up to the girl. Her name's Ruby. She's dark, but pretty. Small white teeth and filmy eyes. She's new and eager to make friends. I need a room, she complains. My village is far. I know, Jesmin says. Finding a place to live is why I'm doing this.

The year Jesmin came to Dhaka she said to her father, ask Nasir chacha to give you his daughter's mobile contact. Nasir chacha's daughter Kulsum had a job in garments. Her father nodded, said, she will help you. Her mother, drying mustard in front of their hut, put her face in the crook of her arm. Go, go, she said. I don't want to see you again. Jesmin left without looking back, knowing that, once, her mother had another dream for her, that she would marry and be treated like a queen, that all the village would tell her what a good forehead she had. But that was before Amin, before the punishing hut.

Kulsum did help her. Put in a good word when she heard they were looking. She has a place, a room in Korail she shares with her kid and her in-laws. Her husband works in foreign so she lets Jesmin sleep on the floor. She takes half of Jesmin's pay every month. You're lucky, she tells her, I didn't ask for the money up front. But now her husband's coming back and Jesmin has to find somewhere else. She has another relative, a cousin's cousin, but he lives all the way out in Mogbajar and Jesmin doesn't like the way he looks at her. There's a shanty not far from the factory and she heard there were rooms going, but when she went to look, the landlord said, I can't have so many girls in my building. What building? Just a row of tin, paper between the walls, sharing an outside tap. But still he told her he wasn't sure, had to think about it. If you had a husband, he said, that would be a different story.

When Jesmin joined the line, she started as Mala's helper. She tied her knots and clipped the threads from her shirt buttons. The Rana strike was over and Mala's leg was broken and the bosses had their eye on her, always waiting to see if she'd make more trouble. Even now, Jamal gives her a look every time she walks by, waiting to see if she takes too long in the toilet. They would have got rid of her a long time ago if her hands weren't so good, always first in the line, seams straight as blades of grass, five, seven pieces ahead of everyone.

To make the Thanks you have to stretch the fabric tight against your left arm while running the stitch. Then you fold it, stretch again, run the stitch back up, till the whole thing is hard and tight. Jesmin trims the leg and takes a piece home. She pulls it up over her leg. Her thigh bulges in front and behind it. She doesn't understand. Maybe the legs of foreign ladies are different.

Jesmin and Mala know a foreign lady, Miss Bridgey. She came to the factory and asked them a few questions and wrote down what they said. How many minutes for lunch? Where is the toilet? If there's a fire, what will you do? In the morning before she came Jamal lined everyone up. There's an inspector coming, he said. You want to make a good impression. Jamal liked to ask a question and supply the answer. Are we proud of the factory? Yes we are! What do we think of Sunny Textiles? We love SunnyTex! That day they opened all the windows and did the fire drill ten times. Then Miss Bridgey showed up and Jesmin could see the laugh behind Jamal's face. He thought it would be a man in a suit, and there was this little yellow-haired girl. Nothing to worry. Aren't we lucky? Yes we are.

When Miss Bridgey comes back Jesmin is going to ask her about the Thanks. But right now they have to explain the whole thing to Ruby. Mala's doing all the talking. We marry him, and that way we can tell people we are married. We give him a place to stay, we give him food, we give him all the things a wife gives. If he wants sex we give him sex. When she mentions the sex Jesmin feels her legs filling up with water. Why don't we get our own husbands? Ruby asks. She's green, she doesn't know. Ruby looks like she's going to cry. Then she bites her full lip with a line of those perfect little teeth and she says, okay, I'll do it.

When Jesmin was born, her mother took a piece of coal and drew a big black mark behind her ear. Jesmin went to school and learned the letters and the sums before any of the other children. The teacher, Amin, always asked her to sing the national anthem on Victory Day and stand first in the parade. Amin said she should go to secondary. He said, meet me after school. He taught her sums and a, b, c. He put his hand over her hand on the chalk.

Miss Bridgey comes a few days later and she takes Jesmin aside. I'm worried about the factory, she says. Has it always been this bad? Jesmin looks around. She takes in the fans in the ceiling, bars on the windows, rows and rows of girls bent over their machines. It's the same, she says. Always like this. This place good. This place okay. We love SunnyTex! But why, she asks Miss Bridgey, do the ladies in your country wear this? She holds up the Thanks. Miss Bridgey takes it from her hand, turns it around, then she laughs and laughs. Jesmin, you know how expensive these are?

On the wedding day Dulal comes to the factory. He's wearing a red shirt under the gray sleeveless sweater they made last year when the SunnyTex bosses decided to expand into knitwear. Jesmin and Mala and Ruby stand in front of him, and he looks at them with his head tilted to the side. Take a look at my prince! Mala says. He's got a narrow face and small black eyes and hair that sticks to his forehead. Now it's time to get married so they set off on two rickshaws, him and Mala in the front, Jesmin and Ruby following behind. They are all wearing red saris like brides do, except nobody's family has showed up to feed them sweets or paint their feet.

Jesmin watches the back of Mala and Dulal. She knows that Mala's brother died in Rana. That Mala had held up his photo for seven weeks, hoping he would come out from under the cement. That she was at the strike, shouting her brother's name. That her mother kept writing from the village asking for money, so Mala had to turn around and go back to the line. Mala's face was cracked, like a broken eggshell, until she found Dulal. Now she comes to the factory, works like magic, tells her jokes, does her overtime as if it never happened, but Jesmin knows that once you die like that, on the street or in the factory, your life isn't your life anymore.

This morning Jesmin went to the shanty to talk to the landlord. I'm getting married. Can I stay? He looked at her with one side of his face. Married? Show me the groom. I'll bring him next week, she said. He took one more drag and threw his cigarette into the drain and Jesmin thought for sure he was going to say no, but then he turned to her and said, what, I don't get any sweets? Then he slapped her on the back, and she shrank, but it was a friendly slap, as if she was a man, or his daughter. Next she went to Kulsum. I found a husband. Good, she said, you're getting old. Now I don't have to worry about you.

Jesmin sees marriage as a remedy. If you are a girl you have many problems, but all of them can be fixed if you have a husband. In the factory, if Jamal puts you in ironing, which is the easiest job, or if he says, take a few extra minutes for lunch, you can finish after hours and get overtime, you can say, but my husband is waiting, and then you won't have to feel his breath like a spider on your shoulder later that night when the current goes out and you're still in the factory finishing up a sleeve. Everything is better if you're married. Jesmin is giving Ruby all this good advice as their rickshaw passes the Mohakhali flyover but the girl's eyes are somewhere else. Bet she had some other idea about her life. Jesmin puts her arm around Ruby's shoulder and notices she smells very nice, like the biscuit factory she passes on the way to SunnyTex.

Jesmin is the only one who can sign her name on the wedding register. The others dip their thumbs into ink and press them into the big book. The Kazi takes their money and gives them a piece of paper that has all their names on it. Jesmin reads it out loud to the others.

After, Dulal wants to stop at a chotpoti stall. Three men, friends of his, are waiting there. They look at the brides, up and down, and then they stick their elbows into Dulal's side and Dulal smiles like he's just opened a drawerful of cash. Who's first? they ask him. The old one, he replies, not bothering to whisper it. Then that one, he says, pointing to Jesmin. Next week Kulsum said she would let Jesmin string a blanket across and take half the bed. Her in-laws will be on the other half and she'll take the kid and sleep on the floor. Best for last, eh? his friend says. Dulal looks at Ruby like he's seeing her for the first time and he says, yeah, she's the cream.

The friends take off and then it's just the brides and groom. They sit on four stools along the pavement. Jesmin feels the winter air on her neck. Where's your village? Dulal asks, but before she can tell him, she hears Ruby's voice saying, Kurigram. Something in the sound of her voice makes Jesmin think maybe Ruby wants to be the favorite wife. She notices now that Ruby has tied a ribbon in her hair. They finish their plates and Mala holds hands with Dulal and they take off in the direction of her place. Jesmin and Ruby are taking the bus to Kulsum's. Ruby's giving Kulsum some of her pay so she can stay there too, just until they find her somewhere else.

Jesmin wants to say something to mark the fact that they are all married now. She can't think of anything so she asks Ruby if it gets cold in her village. Yes, she says, in winter sometimes people die. I'm from the south, Jesmin tells her, it's not so bad but still in winter, it bites. They hug their arms now as the sun sets. I wonder what they're doing, Ruby says. Do you think he's nice? He looks nice.

They're doing what people do, she tells Ruby, at night when no one is looking. They arrive at Kulsum's. She can share your blanket, Kulsum says, throwing a look at Ruby until Ruby takes the money out of her bag. They warm some leftover rice on the stove Kulsum shares with two other families at the back of the building. The gas is low and it takes half an hour to heat the rice, then they crush a few chilies into it. I have three younger sisters, Ruby says, even though Jesmin hasn't asked about her family. Where are they? Home and hungry, she says, and Jesmin gets a picture in her mind of three dark-skinned girls with perfect teeth, shivering together in the northern cold. What about you? Ruby asks. A snake took my brother, Jesmin says, remembering his face, gray and swollen, before they threw it in the ground. Hai Allah! Ruby rubs her hand up and down Jesmin's back. His forehead was unlucky, Jesmin says, pretending it wasn't so bad, like this wasn't the reason everything started to go sour, her parents with nothing to look forward to, just a daughter whose head was a curse and the hope that next year's rice would come up without a fight.

It's freezing on the floor. Jesmin is glad for Ruby's back spreading the warm into their blanket. You are kind, Ruby mumbles as she falls asleep, and Jesmin can see her breathing, her shoulders moving up and down. She lies awake for a long time imagining Mala with their husband. The watery feeling returns to her legs. Ruby shifts, moves closer, and her biscuit smell clouds up around them. Jesmin takes a strand of Ruby's hair and puts it into her mouth.

When she gets to SunnyTex the next morning Mala is already at her machine with her head down. Jesmin tries to catch her eye but she won't look up, and when they break for lunch she disappears and Jesmin doesn't see her until it's too late. Finally it's the end of the day and Mala is hurrying along in the going-home line. What d'you want? She squints as if she's looking from far away and when Jesmin asks her what the wedding night was like, she says, it wasn't so bad. That's all? You'll find out for yourself, don't let me go and spoil it, and then her face bends into a smile. She won't say anything else.

After their shift is over Jesmin tells Ruby, let's go to a shop. I don't have any money, Ruby says. Don't worry, we'll just look. They walk to the sandal shop at the end of the street. They stare at the wall of sandals. Ruby takes Jesmin's hand and squeezes her fingers. It's so nice she can almost feel the sandals on her feet.

The week is over and finally it's Jesmin's turn. She scrubs her face till Kulsum scolds her for taking too long at the tap. She wears a red shalwar kameez. Ruby wants to do her hair. She makes a braid that begins at the top of Jesmin's head and runs all the way down her back. Her fingers move quickly and Jesmin feels a shiver that starts at her neck and disappears into her kameez. Ruby reaches back and takes the clip out of her own hair and puts it into Jesmin's. She feels it tense her hair together.

All day while they're sewing buttons onto check shirts Jesmin can feel the clip pulling at her scalp. Mala, she says, I'm feeling scared. At first Mala looks like she's going to tell her something, but her eyes go back to her sewing machine and she says, all brides are scared. Don't worry, I tested him out for you. Equipment is working tip-top.

After work Dulal is standing outside the SunnyTex gate. He puts his finger under her chin and stares into her face like he's examining a leg of goat. His breathing is ragged and his cheeks are shining. She notices how dirty his shirt is under the sweater and she starts to wonder what sort of a man would want three wives all at once. She shakes her head to knock the thoughts out of it. She has a husband, that's what matters. The road unfolds in front of them as they walk home, his hand molded onto her waist.

Kulsum is wearing lipstick and she tells her kid, look, your khalu has come to visit, give him foot-salaam, and her kid kneels in front of Dulal and touches his sandal. In the kitchen they pass around the food. Jesmin puts rice on Dulal's plate, and the bigger piece of meat. Kulsum gets a piece too and the rest of them do with gravy. She's given him the mora from under the bed so he sits taller than everyone else. The gravy is watery but Jesmin watches Kulsum's kid run his tongue all across his plate. She thinks about Ruby. It's Thursday and she's gone home on the bus to spend the weekend with her sisters. Jesmin fingers the clip, still standing stiff on the side of her head.

Now it's time and they lie down together. The blanket is strung across but Jesmin can see the outline of Kulsum's mother-in-law, her elbow jutting into their side of the bed. Dulal turns his face to the wall and says, scratch my back. He squirms out of his shirt and she runs her fingers up and down his back and soon her nails are clogged with dirt. He takes her hand and pulls it over to the front of his body, and then he takes out his thing. His hand is over her hand, and she thinks of Amin and the chalk and the village, fog in the winter and the new season's molasses and everything smelling clean, the dung drying against the walls of her father's hut. Her arm is getting sore and Dulal's breath is slow and steady, his thing soft as a mouse. She thinks maybe he's fallen asleep but then he turns around and she feels the weight of him pressing down on her. He drags down her kameez and tries to push the mouse in. After a few minutes he gives up and turns back around. Scratch my back, he says, irritated, and finally he falls asleep with her hand trapped under his elbow.

The next day is Friday and Dulal says he's going to spend it with his sister, who lives in Uttara. Jesmin was hoping they could go to the market and look at the shops, but he leaves before she can ask. She takes the bus to Mohakhali. Mala's neighbor looks Jesmin up and down and says to her, so your friend is married now. Look at her, like a queen she is. Mala's wearing bright orange lipstick and acting like something good has happened to her. She's talking on her mobile and Jesmin waits for her to finish. Then she asks, is it supposed to be like that?

Mala looks up from the bed. You couldn't do it?

What, what was I supposed to do?

She grabs an arm. Did he put it in?

No.

She curses under her breath. But I told him you would be the one.

The one to what?

The one to cure his, you know, not being able to.

Jesmin struggles to understand. You told me his equipment was tip-top.

Mala shrinks from her. It occurs to Jesmin that she never asked the right question, the one that has been on everyone's mind. Why does a guy working in a shop, who doesn't get his hands dirty all day, want a garments girl, especially a broken one like Mala? Jesmin stares at her until Mala can't hold her eye anymore. Mala looks down at her hands. I paid him, she says.

You paid him?

Then he started asking for more, more money, and I didn't have it, so I told him you and Ruby would fix him. That's the only way he would stay.

She's got her head in her hands and she's crying. She rubs her broken leg, and Jesmin thinks of Rana, and Mala's brother, and her own brother, and she decides there's nothing to be done now but try and fix Dulal's problem, because now that they were married to him, his bad was their bad.

What next?

Try again, try everything. Mala hands her the tube of lipstick. Here, take this.

That night Jesmin asks Kulsum for a few sprays from the bottle of scent she keeps in a box under the bed and Kulsum takes it out reluctantly, eyeing her while she pats some of it onto her neck. Jesmin draws thick lines across her eyelids and smears the lipstick on hard. Dulal cleans his plate and goes outside to gargle into the drain. She stands with him at the edge of the drain and after he rinses and spits he looks up at the night. There's all kinds of noise coming from the compound, kids screaming, dogs, a radio, but up there it looks quiet. Maybe Dulal's looking for a bit of quiet, too. Fog's coming, she says. She asks about his sister. Alhamdulillah, he tells her, but doesn't say, I will take you to meet her. I hate winter, he says instead, makes my bones tired.

Winter makes her think of the sesame her mother had planted, years ago when she was a baby. The harvest was for selling, but after the first season the price at the market wasn't worth the water and the effort, so she gave it up. But still the branches came up, twisted and pointy every year, tearing the feet off anyone who dared walk across the field. Only Amin knew how to tread between the bushes, his feet unscarred, the soles of his feet always so soft. Jesmin ran them across her cheeks and it was like his palm was touching her, or the tip of his penis, rather than the underside of his big toe, that's how delicate his feet were. I'm only here to talk, he said, telling her the story of Laila and Majnu. From Amin she learned what it was to be swallowed by a man, like a snake swallowing a rat, whole and without effort. He pressed his feet against her face, showing her the difference between a schoolteacher and a farmer's daughter, and she licked the salt between his toes, and when she asked when they would get married, he laughed as if she had told him the funniest joke in the world. And then his wife went to the Salish, and the Salish decided she had tempted Amin, and they said, leave the village. But not before you are punished. And into the punishing hut she went, and when she came out, she looked exactly like she was meant to look, ugly and broken. Like a rat swallowed by a snake. Just like Mala looked after they told her the search was over and she would never see her brother again. Now Jesmin is wondering if something happened to Dulal that made him feel like the rest of them, like a small animal in a big, spiteful world.

Maybe that's why, she offers, speaking softly into the dark. He turns to her. What did you say?

Maybe that's why, you know, it's not—it's not your fault.

He comes close. His breath is eggy. That's when, out of nowhere, one side of her face explodes. When she opens her eyes she's on the ground and everyone is standing over her, Kulsum, her kid, her in-laws, and Dulal. The kid tugs at her kameez and she stands up, brushes herself off. No one says anything. Jesmin can taste lipstick and blood where she's bitten herself.

In the morning Jamal takes one look at her and runs her to the back of the line. You look like a bat, he says, you should've stayed home. What if that inspector comes nosing around? Her eye is swollen so she has to change the thread on the machine with her head tilted to one side. Ruby's back from her village and when she sees Jesmin she starts to cry. Don't worry, Jesmin says, it's nothing. She takes a toilet break, borrows a compact from Mala and looks at herself. One side of her face is swallowing the other. When she comes out Ruby's holding a chocbar. She presses it against Jesmin's cheek and they wait for it to melt, then they tear open a corner and take turns pouring the ice cream into their mouths.

They go home. Dulal isn't there. Now look what you did, Kulsum says. They wait until the mosquitoes come in and finally everyone eats.

When the kerosene lamp comes on and she's about to bed on the floor with Ruby, Dulal bursts in and demands food. She makes him a plate and watches him belch. The food's cold, he says. After, it's the same, lying there facing his back, holding his small, lifeless thing, except this time Ruby's on the floor next to Kulsum and her kid. Scratch my head, Dulal mutters. He falls asleep, and later, in the night, she hears him cry out, a sharp, bleating sound. She thinks she must have dreamt it because in the moonlight his face is as mean as ever.

On the day of Ruby's turn, she looks so small. When she's cut too much thread off her machine, Jamal scolds her and she spends the rest of the day with her head down. But after lunch she goes into the toilet and when she comes out she's got a new sari on and the ribbon is twisted into her hair like a thread of happy running all around the back of her head. Dulal comes to the gate and when he sees Ruby his face is as bright as money. Ruby says something to Dulal and he laughs. Jesmin watches them leave together, holding hands, her heart breaking against her ribs.

Jesmin covers her ears against the sound of laughter.

In the punishing hut, the Salish gathered. The oldest one said, take off your dress. When her clothes were on the ground he said, walk. They sat in a circle and threw words like rotten fruit. She's nothing but a piece of trash. Amin said: her pussy stinks like a dead eel. She is the child of pigs. She's a slut. She's the shit of pigs. Walk, walk. Move your hands. You want to cover it now? Where was your shame when you seduced a married man? Get out now. Get out and don't come back. Afterward, they laughed.

Jesmin covers her ears against the sound of laughter.

It's Friday. She packs her things and says goodbye to Kulsum. The kid wraps his legs around her waist and bites into her shoulder. She hands money to the landlord and he waves her to the room. There's a kerosene lamp in one corner, and a cot pushed up against another. Last year's calendar is tacked to the wall. The roof is leaking and there's a large puddle on the floor. She sees her face in the pool of water. She sees her eyes and the shape of her head and Ruby's clip in her hair. She opens her trunk and finds the pair of Thanks she stole from the factory. She holds it up. It makes the silhouette of a piece of woman. She pulls the door shut and the room darkens. She takes off her sandals, her shalwar. She lies on the floor, the damp and the dirt under her back, and drags the Thanks over her legs. When she stands up she straddles the pool of water and casts her eyes over her reflection. There is a body encased, legs and hips and buttocks. The body is hers but it is far away, unreachable. She looks at herself and hears the sound of laughter, but this time it is not the laughter of the Salish, but the laughter of the piece of herself that is closed. She knows now that Ruby will fix Dulal, that she will parade with him in the factory, spreading her small-toothed smile among the spools of thread that hang above their heads, and that Dulal will take Ruby to his air-conditioned shop, and her sisters will no longer be hungry, and Jesmin will be here, joined by the laughter of her own legs, no longer the girl of the punishing hut, but a garments girl with a room and a closed-up body that belongs only to herself.

The door opens. Jesmin turns to the smell of biscuits.

Rotten Stench

Eka Kurniawan

Translated from Indonesian by Annie Tucker

Bursting from the streets and the alleyways and the fields and the rice paddies and the garbage heaps, a rotten stench floated into kitchens and bedrooms where husbands and wives were making love and classrooms where children were studying and mosques and whorehouses; and from the gutters it flowed to the rivers and to the bay and then to the ocean and the entire city was suffused with that putrid odor, but the city folk weren't surprised at all because they had breathed in that horrible smell years ago, exactly eighteen years ago, when hundreds of people or more were found, already corpses, sprawled out in the streets and the alleyways and lying in the fields and the rice paddies and in the ditches and the rivers, completely decomposed and barely recognizable as human, because it wasn't just the maggots and flies that were crawling all over them but dogs were fighting over their flesh too, and vultures, scorpions, crocodiles, and even chickens were pecking at those poor corpses' genitals and if you have forgotten, that happened after half of the communists in Halimunda were killed, some were shot in their houses while they were taking a shit or lathering their privates up with soap and others' necks were slashed while they were sleepwalking or sitting in a barber's chair and maybe one of them was stabbed with a bayonet while he was teaching his daughter how to ride her bike and most of the communists who died were just doing silly things like that because if they hadn't been, then surely they would have escaped into the jungle or even fled to a foreign country in a small boat while praying that a hurricane didn't come to destroy them, but in fact it is better to die at sea than die in some absurd fashion at the hands of your cowardly fellow men who only have the courage to live alongside dead communists, not living ones—so they killed them and left their corpses to rot with a foul stink that spread and wouldn't go away for the next five years, sticking to the leaves and the walls of houses and the clothes that they were wearing, a stink from the corpses left lying there just like that as if to let everyone know, both locals and visitors alike, that this is the fate you will meet if you are a communist who doesn't believe in God, because people who profess to believe in God will finish you off just that viciously, horrifically, totally and mercilessly, and leave your corpse lying there just like all those corpses were left, without even one person attempting to bury them because to touch them would be unclean, more unclean than touching a pig or a dog, so they were just left lying there in every corner of the city for months, and even after the dogs and the vultures were full of enough meat for seven generations the corpses still weren't gone, but the city folk truly couldn't have cared less about that rotten stench and that sordid sight, what's more they threw cheerful garden parties and ate grilled goat, with a headless corpse lying there all torn apart right beside the dining table while their children used its head as their soccer ball, as the people of Halimunda who had survived the years of slaughter looked at the corpses that were more disgusting than demons in hell as if they were looking at piles of trash on the side of the road and they never gave them a second thought because they were the corpses of communists, and they still didn't care even though the smell was so pungent that all visitors found it difficult to breathe when they first arrived in the city and the next day they would put on a mask and black sunglasses so that they didn't have to confront such a horrifying sight, and when they asked the people passing by how it could be that they weren't bothered by that revolting stink coming from those corpses, the people of Halimunda would just smile as if dead communists were completely commonplace and the visitors would just shake their heads, unable to hide their disbelief, and wonder what kind of wax the people of the city had used to plug their nostrils so that they didn't smell that most foul rotten stench, but the city folk never answered, and in fact they began to forget that there had ever been a massacre in their city, and they lived in a contented peace, not caring that the rice they ate every day now also stank because of it, and that mass amnesia took an even firmer hold once those corpses were finally gone, not because they were buried or thrown away or cremated, but because they were finally eaten up by the worms and decomposed by the maggots and after five years the rotten stench had disappeared, swept away by the ocean breeze . . . even though sometimes that same ocean breeze occasionally carried the smell back to the city too, but then the city folk would only sniff it with a sense of nostalgia for the past, which of course was the time when those corpses were still strewn about, maybe still warm with blood that was still red even though their stomachs had already been ripped open by dogs' teeth and their hearts had already been pecked at by ducks and their eyes and ears had already been made into key chains that the witch-doctors sold as talismans and charms and things like that, and perhaps there were a few corpses that were buried properly and given gravestones, but they had to be buried in private backyards or under a cluster of bamboo since the public cemetery would certainly refuse them because the virtuous ghosts that guarded the graveyard would never be willing to share a home with the souls of such infidel scum and the people who buried them were usually their devoted children or their wives who truly loved them or their friends who, although they had taken a different path in life, were still loyal to them, but whoever buried these corpses ended up meeting a fate that was more tragic than the dead because then the other city folk wouldn't associate with them, the women were forbidden to go to the market and the children were forbidden to attend school because they were considered even more unclean and more rotten than the corpses of their fathers or their husbands or their friends, so that ultimately most of the corpses were not taken care of, they just slowly decayed in the grass or were crushed by car wheels in the street, but then even though their surviving family members hadn't buried them—yes, even those who hadn't claimed or buried their loved ones, were still seen as the scourge of the city—they were forbidden to enter the city hall, forbidden to become city employees, denied care at the city hospital, and if you were a communist who survived and didn't become a corpse, you would suffer more than those who had died because you would be treated more or less like a living corpse and even if dogs attacked you the police and the neighbors would not come to your aid and more than that the city government would actually order a sign stuck on you, maybe on your neck or your forehead or on your identity card, indicating that you were one of those accursed atheists, as if inviting the dogs to bark at you and attack you, a sign that good people should stay at least fifteen meters away from the tips of your outstretched fingers, even though sometimes there were ignorant folks, most likely from the new generations who thought of those events as being in the past or who hadn't even experienced them at all because they were newcomers, and one day they would suddenly be startled by the foul odor carried ashore by the ocean breeze and they would ask other people in the city where it came from, and these idiots would be considered lucky if they were then quickly captured by three or four soldiers and thrown into a holding cell behind the military headquarters, the place where more executions were held than in any other place, usually on merciless charges of sedition because if they weren't, then the city folk would think of these ignorants as crazy people and their lives would ultimately end in shackles, eating in chains and shitting on themselves and the children would throw rotten eggs at them, until eighteen years after the massacre of hundreds of communists in that city, the rotten stench came again, not the same old rotten stench that was usually carried in by the occasional ocean breeze, but a rotten stench that came from corpses that were sprawled in the streets just like before, and just as might be suspected, the people of Halimunda were not at all surprised by that rotten smell, even the newborn babies were not surprised because they had inherited an immunity to it from their parents, who had grown accustomed to the rotten stench that had come eighteen years ago and was sometimes blown in by the ocean breeze, and now they were smelling that smell again as if in a quiet nostalgia for the past, and the people still woke up in the morning as usual and when they went out onto their verandas to read the national newspaper or the local one that was published in the provincial capital, they of course would read about the rotten smell coming from the corpses that were strewn about in every corner of their city, but they would read about it as if it was news from a distant place, or a fiction that hadn't actually happened, or worse than that they would only think of it as a small tragedy on par with the local soccer club's defeat in the independence day tournament, and they would quickly set that newspaper down onto the table before drinking their coffee made with water that came from a well that was contaminated by those melting corpses, by their flesh and blood that had liquefied into porridge, but they didn't care and said how delicious the coffee was that morning, just as they didn't care that the only thing that differentiated the current rotten stench from the one eighteen years ago was the fact that the current rotten stench wasn't coming from the bodies of wretched communists, but from criminals, rapists, thieves, racketeers, pickpockets, pirates, and all kinds of bad guys that you can find described in the holy books and so the virtuous city folk didn't care about them, as if saying that it was right for them to die, just like it had been right for those accursed communists to die eighteen years ago, so they left them there untouched because they too were more unclean than dogs and pigs and more misguided than even the demons in hell, so nobody buried them either, they just noted the fact that most of them had died riddled with bullet holes or with rusty bullets lodged inside their flesh and not one of them died from being stabbed or hung, and even though there was no formal report as to who had finished off that human trash the city folk could guess that the soldiers at the military headquarters were probably behind all this even though not even one soldier had ever discussed it, because the fact was that they were the only ones who had firearms and ammunition and the people of Halimunda, who were quick to speculate different scenarios about it all, were caught in a labyrinth of hearsay when someone said that the soldiers were angry because the criminals had cheated at the gambling table—

both the soldiers and the criminals placed bets on cockfights, pig fights and dice—and someone else said that the murders started with a scuffle over some prostitute at the whorehouse, but whatever was the story behind those corpses and that rotten stench that was once again engulfing the city, soon the people of Halimunda weren't really that interested in knowing any more about it, and preferred to carry on with their lives just like always without caring that huge green flies were now buzzing over their heads and occasionally dropping down to land on their lunch rice, because the men were truly happy that those cursed people were finally dead and now there was no one left to bother their women if they came out of the movie theater and their skirts were accidentally lifted for a moment by the wind, there was no one who would demand their money every time they took the train or rode the bus, and there was no one to confiscate their cigarettes at knifepoint on Saturday nights when they were getting romantic with their girlfriends on the beach, and the good and proper housewives were relieved because there was no longer anybody stealing the chickens out of their coops or swiping clothes off the laundry line or pots out of their kitchens, and the whole time the newspaper kept calling the killers "mysterious shooters," who must have hidden in the dark and crawled through the brush, attacking in an ambush and when one morning those corpses were filling the city again, overrun with flies and worms and dogs and crocodiles who were now gorging themselves in a merry orgy just like their ancestors had eighteen years ago, even though it could be appreciated that this time at least the assassins were a little more civilized about the whole thing because even though they didn't bury the corpses and they were happened upon by vegetable sellers heading to market early in the morning, and newspaper boys and the people coming home from the mosque, at least they were wrapped in old gunny sacks used for rice at harvest time and there they were temporarily safe until the dogs that roamed everywhere throughout the city began to sniff the sacks and rip them open and the smell began to spill out from inside, spreading throughout the air and the water and the sunlight until the entire city had a rotten stench, making the visitors once again put on their masks and some of them vomited and then suffered attacks of diarrhea and fever because of the food and water that was contaminated by human remains, but the city folk didn't seem to suffer at all because they just kept eating and drinking and they weren't bothered in the slightest by that pungent foul stink, as if they wanted to tell the whole world: we the people of Halimunda don't care how many you kill or how horrible they smell, because history has taught us to endure all kinds of horror and evil and we are used to forgetting it all just as quickly as we forget every act of piety, because everyone ultimately dies in the end and all corpses ultimately give off a rotten stench, and we will still read our newspapers and drink our coffee and play soccer and make babies, in other words we will continue to enjoy our lives in the middle of this rotten stench, if you really think that the way this air smells can in fact be described as a rotten stench.

Amira Who Knows

Rawaa Sonbol

Translated from Arabic by Katharine Halls

Amira knows that something different is going to happen today. She's known since she woke up, perhaps because she had a dream that her mind won't let her fully remember—she believes bad dreams need to be forgotten so that they don't come true—or perhaps it's because the first thing she saw in the garden that morning was a dove's nest blown to the ground by the night wind, her heart thumping when she saw the cracked egg and heard the mother's agonized cooing.

Amira, in her seventies now, knows many things, not because she's had any education—she can barely read, just a few words—and not because she has talkative neighbors who visit or children and grandchildren who are always around—she's been alone for years—and not because she has a TV to keep her abreast of entertainment and news—she just has a small transistor radio, which she inherited from her husband twenty years ago, and sometimes she manages to pick up one of the stations that broadcast pop music and horoscopes as well as the hourly local news roundup, which tirelessly assures listeners that all is well.

Amira, with her big bulky body, knows many things, even though she rarely leaves her spot against the filthy wall at the edge of the public garden. She sits permanently on a large, tattered sofa beneath the words PUBLIC TOILET, which are scrawled in large letters, and two wonky arrows pointing toward the metal door, which remains ajar all day but which, at night, Amira locks behind her on her way to the narrow rusted frame that is her bed, inside the damp toilet block, where she hunts down a few hours of rest if she's lucky, because sleep takes flight at night, only to settle comfortably on her head during the day, weighing down her eyelids and sapping the energy from her body, so that she dozes off on the spot, though nobody glancing at her from a distance would guess she was sleeping, because her pose is so dignified: shoulders straight, back resting on the back of the sofa that's held her body these past two years; before that, she used to spend her days sitting on a plastic garden chair, but one morning she found the sofa abandoned among the aged trees that surround the toilet block, and a single glance told her the whole story: somebody had pulled the sofa from the rubble after a battle on the outskirts of the capital, and then, having failed to sell it in the Thieves' Market, had dumped it here in the garden, where Amira beat the dust from the upholstery, wiped it down with soapy water so its gold blooms gleamed against the blue background, carefully sewed up the tear in the back, glued the carved wooden ornament back in place, and finally threw away the plastic chair; the sofa became her friend.

Amira, with the long faded black robe that's belted below the waist, knows some things that might not interest anybody: she knows without moving from her seat, for instance, which bathroom stall is going to be used, by listening to the footfalls and the squeak of the door, and she knows that the men who visit her toilets are few and far between, because men have the luxury of relieving themselves in other locations, as the weary stones of the ancient city walls next to the garden can attest. She also knows that in the early mornings, nobody comes to the public toilets except similar-looking young women with tired faces and smudged eyeliner, and near-threadbare skintight clothes, the high heels of their decrepit shoes wobbling so wildly it looks like they're planning to detach themselves and scuttle away; she knows that it's hunger that drives them out of their homes, that the night draws them in and lures them down dark, narrow alleys, that the morning disavows them, that the city sticks its fingers down its throat and meanly vomits them up before the office workers and schoolchildren appear; yet Amira greets them with a kind, commiserating smile, and although they spend an age in the bathroom, Amira doesn't mind: after five years of this she knows that it's not just about a full bladder or heaving bowels or a pad that needs changing, because one of those girls, with the help of nothing more than lipstick, cheap eyeliner, and a cracked mirror on a grimy wall, can come out of an ugly place like this looking lovelier, and another can have a long intimate phone call that makes her body hot despite the unpleasant cold seeping from the walls; Amira also knows that a cramped bathroom stall is as good a place as any for a woman to set free the pain in her chest, no matter how huge. Amira loves these women—especially the young ones, who aren't even twenty yet—who deposit their secrets with her, who come to her when they're pregnant, for home remedies that will make them miscarry: Amira is generous with her knowledge, and because ginger and cinnamon sticks are expensive, she makes do with onion skins, which she boils for them herself.

Amira, with her wide, gappy smile, knows how to listen properly; she takes an interest in the stories of passersby who use her toilets, pulling at the coarse hairs on her chin while she listens, and is never stingy with the tea she prepares over a small stove at her feet, or indeed with sympathy or advice, but she does, however, know not to get too attached to anyone, because people come and go, and others come in their place—beggars and garbage men, bus drivers, office workers and street traders, night girls, soldiers, schoolchildren—while she alone remains, guarding the filthy toilets like the old trees guard the river Barada, which cleaves through the garden here. Amira wishes that somebody would stay with her, which happened on occasion in years past, when war rained down from the city's skies, and Amira knew that a strange deserted place like her public toilet could feel safe and familiar; Amira would be as happy as those toilet-block refugees were afraid, and when the stink brought looks of disgust to their faces, Amira would smile sadly, because she knew that that stink was the smell of the city, the whole city, and she knew it would make no difference as she hurried to shut the three toilet stalls, because as she always says, with the wisdom age brings: *You can keep things behind closed doors, but they'll find their way out in the end.* Amira knows that all sorts of things can wriggle out, like the thin line of blood that trickled out one time under the door of the third stall, where a rose of a woman in her twenties had slashed her wrists—she died and found peace, but Amira was summoned for lengthy interrogations, and spent the night at the local precinct—or like the shriek of alarm that came from the second stall, that time when a trail of something clear and viscous slid across the dirty tiles, and Amira opened the door to find a terrified face, round belly, and crossed legs, and realized the woman was about to give birth; some kind souls called the Red Crescent, but the baby was in a hurry, and it was Amira whose arms welcomed it joyfully to the world, Amira who cradled it tenderly to her breast and whispered the words of the azan in its ear, Amira whose clothes were stained with blood and goo and whose heart nearly burst with happiness, because she hadn't known until that moment whether she would ever hold a grandchild to her bosom, because Muhammad was long gone—Muhammad her one and only, Muhammad her heart's joy and anguish.

Amira knows her work inside out: she unlocks the metal door early in the morning and wedges it open with a rock; she takes one hundred lira from each visitor in exchange for a smile and a gesture indicating they can go on in; she isn't too profligate with her toilets' share of the cleaning products the municipality hands out every few months, only cleaning when the filth becomes unbearable, but every night before going to sleep she makes a circuit of the toilets with a bleach-soaked cloth and checks each stall in turn, carefully examining the walls and the inside of the doors, because she knows that people leave things behind, they draw hearts and lips and signatures, they write crude phrases and cell phone numbers with names—Amira takes care never to erase the numbers, because one day she'll buy a cell phone, and then she'll call these numbers, one each day, and though she doesn't know what she'll say, she's certain she'll find plenty to talk about with people who must be as lonely as she is—but anyhow the names and numbers really aren't a problem, the real problem is those phrases she comes across from time to time: she laboriously unpicks the words, and when she's understood what they say she can't stop her hands from trembling as she scrubs them away in fright, for Amira knows that just one of these sentences is enough to guarantee her a place in a dark underground room. She finds other phrases too, and she usually ignores their vulgarity, because she believes that God doesn't have dark underground rooms and is too great to be perturbed by some blasphemy scribbled on a toilet wall in a moment of despair; and because she believes, too, that He is by nature merciful, she doesn't bother scrubbing them off until Ramadan approaches.

Amira knows many things, including some she wishes she didn't know; like everyone here she'd heard a lot about the dark underground rooms, but five years ago she memorized them, visited them all while looking for Muhammad before finding out he'd been swallowed up by the one with the worst reputation of all, and today, just before nine in the evening, a skinny pale young man shows up carrying a bag of bananas and another of apples, says hello, goes awkwardly into the toilet, then comes out a few minutes later looking like someone relieved of a heavy burden and gives her everything all at once: plastic bags, a few laconic words, and a small key. *Say God is one, Auntie*, he says in a trembling voice, his eyes filling with tears as he rubs her on the shoulder, and that's enough for Amira to know.

Amira knows many things, but she ignores them sometimes, tricks herself; she knows that the war crushed her home, leaving a heap of rubble in its place, a few months after Muhammad disappeared, and that these toilets are her home now, but still she's glad to have the key to the house, and hides it between her large, sagging breasts; she knows equally that Muhammad died two years ago, because that's what she was told by the skinny young man who was in there with him, and who spent three months looking for her once he got out, and yet she beams when she sees Muhammad as the dawn azan sounds, and when he holds out a hand, she takes it and gets up, and now Amira knows that although her body is there on the bed, she has Muhammad's arm through hers, and she's going with him, and she doesn't need to worry.

Petite Mort

Zanta Nkumane

When your father dies on a Friday night, you are choking on a stranger's dick in the backseat of a car, on a dark road just off 7th in Melville. New feelings dance on your skin, and you want to name them so when they return you can greet them properly, but his moans remind your mouth it can only do one thing at a time. As he thrusts in the back of your throat, the choking emboldens you. If death tastes like black smoke and defecation, then living tastes musty and hard, you decide. You hold onto this life with your tongue, pulsing and phallic, as if you can hear death knocking on the overcast window. When his breathing becomes frantic, you intensify your efforts. Tremors careen through his body and you pull your face away to watch him trickle milky treacle over your hands. You want to lick it, to taste briny life on your tongue, but you don't want to be too much, too soon. 'Too Much' was your father's other name for you. He collapses against the seat, his body quietening from the stupor. An orgasm is called a small death precisely because you briefly stop existing. He reaches for wet wipes in his cubby, takes your hands and quietly wipes himself off them. His kindness makes the need for more of his solidness insistent, so at least you can wake up next to something breathing.

'What's your name, by the way?' you ask as the car pulls out of the parking. When he responds you cough and pretend he didn't just say your father's name back to you.

The next morning, dread blisters in the air and you inhale its ominous stench as you roll out of bed. Your bedroom feels small and fills your lungs with cloying humidity. You open the windows. Chirpy avian melodies seep through the gaping glass, as does a surge of new air that makes the curtains unfurl. You settle on the edge of the bed and clink the sleep out of your body while your hangover booms against your head. Today is a different day. Your father is dead and a man with his name sleeps in your bed. You haven't told him he shares your father's name, not wanting to scare him off. You look outside at the summer sun, searing colour into the day's morning cells. Your father always said boys must spend their days outside, getting dirty, being inside was a girl's business. But you loved being inside, watching your three older sisters cook meals, listening to their stories of being heartbroken by men and triumphing over those men by getting under new men. You sometimes spend winter weekends following the sun's heat around your apartment, but it's not the same as being under its direct gaze, rolling in heaps of grass or climbing to the top of your neighbour's guava tree to catch its twilight farewell. That's why you can tell the time by looking up to the sky. Right now, the sun's rays ricochet across the room and everything sparkles, even you, even the sleeping man. Touching something to transfer their heat gives sun rays their meaning. Until that moment of contact, they're just accidental scraps of light falling from the sky. They only become tangible in the moment of touch. Like love. Like death only becomes real when it touches your life.

The cold floors are a welcome coolness under your feet as you walk to the kitchen. Sometimes, when it gets too hot and sweat slicks on your skin, you lie on the floor to let the slabs caress your cheek. You pry the fridge door open for some orange juice. You grab the concoction of pills you usually use to quell your hangovers after a night out or after a long call at the hospital. The pills glint in your hand like new coins. One is green, like photosynthesis. The second one a soft pink, like marshmallows. The third, an earnest purple like the jacaranda flower. The rest colourless, like teardrops. This is how life starts today, five little tumours and a sleeping stranger who has your father's name.

He appears from the bedroom, finds you on the floor, your body rolled into itself like a fist. You watch newborns roll their tiny bodies like this during your paediatrics rotations, so you assume it helps adults too. You feel him take steps towards you, but you can't bear to sit up, you don't care if this man you met last night sees you on the floor. He settles next to you and begins to tenderly rub your back. 'Thula, thula, ncesi,' he chants, like a soft mantra beckoning comfort back into your body, like you are a baby he gathers from the floor after a thudding fall. You remember telling him your father had died but there were no tears then. You repeated the words of the text message from your sister before you passed out next to him after a few sloppy rounds of sex. His back rub makes you want him inside you again. Maybe the heat of his hardness can incinerate the grief in your gut. Under the sheets of your tears, your mouth reaches for his, when you find it he lets you have his tongue because he knows you need it. Because he wants to be of use. He lets you use him to substitute the grief with pleasure, even if it's momentary. It's funny how an unrepentant desire in the midst of loss makes being alive so urgent. You pull his briefs down as he tears at yours, your mouths woven together. You are still open from last night. A stream of spit falls onto his hand and he wraps his dick with that wetness. He instructs you to sit on it and you do as he says. He stretches his legs out under you, while you straddle him like he is freedom. He starts swirling in you and your moans bang against your teeth. He grinds at you with too much carefulness, your father is dead, you want to feel pain. You unwrap your legs from behind his back, grind them on either side of his thighs. You instruct him: more, more. He obliges and has at you, like he owes you this act of erotic sympathy, like he is recompensing for some past transgression and each thrust is his redemption. You clench your hands against the fridge at his back, its contents shaking like your own. *Up, down, thrust, moan. Up, down, thrust, ah yes.* Your orgasm starts to build from your chest, somewhere next to the engorged loss. It bulges, filling your throat, filling the bottom of you. 'Don't stop.' This thrills him, your seemingly immense threshold for pain. His body smashes harder against yours. If death tastes like black smoke and defecation, then living tastes musty and hard. He grabs your mouth to hush your screams as you briefly pass away, tears still leaking from your eyes. On the kitchen floor, you both die small deaths while your father is dead for real.

'Please come with me to my father's funeral next week,' you ask in the sweaty, breathy afterglow.

'I've never been to a funeral as a first date. That strangely sounds intimate. I hope you know that I am a gentleman—I don't fuck on the first date.'

'But you fuck on the first night? Classy.'

All your three older sisters have boy's names. Your father wanted a son so desperately he named you three times before you arrived. His stubbornness has three names and perseveres whenever they are spoken. Your oldest sister, Menzi, is the one who instructs, like God, but unlike God she doesn't need worship to feel good about herself. You are not that close, but she is the one who messaged you about your father's death, because it was her duty. Like a firstborn son without the privileges. Sabelo is the one who sacrifices; she always does more than she should, like Jesus, but unlike Jesus she wants to know why she has to do it. You enjoy her spirit of fun, she slipped you your first drink at sixteen during her lobola ceremony, and how you passed out on the veranda, where your father found you, after one bottle of Smirnoff Storm, remains her favourite story to tell. But you really don't know her beyond memories of parties, dancing or sending you money during varsity. Mqondisi is the one who is silent, quiet to the point of not being there, but weighty in her presence, like the Holy Spirit, but unlike the Holy Spirit she is more tangible of heart. She is the one you are close to, your father said it was the smaller age difference, but you know it is because she treats you as an equal and not a baby brother. When she calls you the morning after your father's death, you remember why she is your favourite. *I know you're not okay. What do you need from me?* Her own grief clanging over the phone. She always knows how to be granular and doesn't care about the fluff of things or the obvious. *I'm fine. I'm with someone*, you say, like someone means a magic that will conjure your father back, back to his unwanted trinity of daughters. Yet he loved them as if he had wanted them, even if their names bore his true desires. If Menzi needed school shoes, your father would buy Sabelo and Mqondisi something new too, be it underwear or a T-shirt, no one ever felt unconsidered. When Sabelo told the family that her husband had lost their house because of his gambling habit, your father sat in their matrimonial bedroom, Sabelo curled on his shoulder, while Menzi and Mqondisi packed up her life. (She went back two months later, much to everyone's disapproval, even yours.) Even in their difference, your sisters move with the emotional synchronicity of one, like a coven of witches, because your father carved each of them into his likeness.

But, you, the wanted one. The one he waited for. The one he named three times before you came. There was something about you that refused to swing with his stride, how your form didn't chip under his chisel. When you refused to attend the university he had attended, as did your sisters, you unleash a flood of unkindness he flings back to you.

'Why is everything work with you?' he yells. On the television, a football match between a yellow team and one in black is on. The derby.

'I feel like I won't be happy there,' you explain, hoping it is enough.

'It's always feelings with you! Last week you didn't feel like going to church, another time you didn't feel well enough for rugby practice, now this. When do you ever feel willing to work with me? You are just like your mother. Your sisters never gave me this kind of nonsense and there were three of them!' His yellow team misses a shot and he grimaces. He still doesn't look at you.

'I'm normal. I am sorry you couldn't choose a better son, but I am all the son you will get right now. It's your sad spirit that can't handle me, no wonder mom left us.'

'She should have taken you with her then because you're too much for me. I'm also the only parent you'll get right now—you're going, that's final. As if it's not enough I have to see her face every time I look at you!'

It's been four days since your father died, two days before his funeral. You have masturbated five times today and your dick throbs from overuse. You shower after each time and hope the water will take the shame with it down the drain. By midday, you have smoked a whole pack of Marlboro Gold and you have just opened a second box, your lungs heave from misuse. You have somehow only listened to Peter Tosh all day. Your father had an ear for him, Marley and Lucky Dube, there was a rebelliousness he related to. You wonder if your father ever smoked weed, and try to imagine him high, but no image materialises. You never knew him well enough. When a virus infiltrates a host cell, the host cell is unaware of the virus' impending duplicity. The process whereby substances are brought into a cell is called endocytosis. That's how your grief feels, like an infection your body can't fight off. Today it feels like madness. Everyone has a madness about them, we all abandon a bit of our sanity when we reckon with how much pain it requires to stay alive. You miss your father's madness today because it made you, but you know it is tucked somewhere in the cupboard or under the mirror or behind your eyes. You know this is true because you laugh alone and talk to the ants scuttling along your windowsill. You ash them with your cigarette when they don't respond, their insect forms sizzling under your insanity.

The funeral is in two days, it's been four nights since your father died. You are waiting to go home till the last minute, much to Menzi's annoyance. *You better be here to help dig your father's grave, you're his only son!* she instructs over the phone one night, after sharing the funeral duties in the family WhatsApp group. Out of your three sisters, she is most like your father. Even her voice jumps from her throat with the same force like his used to—and she hasn't looked at you in years either. As the only son, you are expected to be seen, to perform certain things, like announcing your father's arrival to the ancestors in the family kraal, and your name has to hang at the bottom of the funeral announcement in the newspaper. *Announcement by his son Sifiso Fakudze on behalf of the Fakudze family*, it reads. Menzi feels she has earned these things. But culture was not on her side.

That evening finds him holding your hand as you walk back to your apartment after dinner, a plastic bag carving into your other hand, bottles of wine clanking inside. You move at the pace of lovers in a park, savouring the breeze. He insists on taking the long way home, he says it's good to get out from under the rafters of your grief-bent house, but all you can think of is him folding you to the command of his hardness again. For someone as sad as he seems to be, he is fascinatingly buoyant. Some would call him unhappy but that is a misnomer. Unhappy suggests the knowledge or the experience of happiness. There is no trace of it in him. Sad people like to be of use, as you know. That's why you became a doctor. Saving lives channels your sadness into something important, morphs it into healing—even if that healing is not your own. He is a man of minimal words, he somehow articulates himself fully using the smallest amount of them. An economical speaker. You enjoy that about him most because it reminds you of Mqondisi. When you tell him this, he says he enjoys your unnecessary thoughts and the words that flow out of you like a burst water pipe.

'Fuck off.' Your voice warps with misplaced defensiveness. 'You don't know me like that. All my thoughts are necessary, and my words.'

'See how tender the most vulgar of words sound when you say them? You like to pretend you are tough. Who taught you that shame?' he responds.

'My father,' you say.

Plot 140. Mangwaneni Cemetery. That's your father's final address. The cemetery is just outside of Mbabane, on a hill overlooking the city, near a power station. The graves swoop in and out of view as if they are riding a wave. Some hang dangerously on the edge of the hill, holding on for dear life. Some have tombstones and others are heaps of rocks. It feels colder up here. You are not sure if it's because of the height or the congregation of icy bodies underneath the ground. The vegetation is oddly lush. You are with the other men in your family, but you are standing watching them carve the soil into your father's final bed because there aren't enough tools to dig. You are here because Menzi instructed you to go straight to the cemetery, before you even walk into the house or greet anyone. You are also here because it's outside, and digging graves is *what men do*, you imagine your father saying. Your companion watches from the car, you found it too bizarre to ask him to join you. His support is yet to fray. It is strange to bring someone you barely know to your father's funeral, but funerals are strange themselves. They are a celebration of life that can't be too celebratory, a farewell with no return, and one of the only places crying is the expected, most appropriate reaction. Your cousins and uncles trample on the neighbouring graves like it's a construction site. One of your cousins even keeps his beer on the tombstone behind him, a catacomb coaster. You start apologising profusely to the earth under your breath every time you see someone stomp on a grave with no regard. It strikes you how casual they are, how normal it all seems. When someone dies in the hospital, after you call the time of death, you have a moment of silence. Most times you have to rush off to attend something else, and it becomes just a murmur. But it is a moment nonetheless.

'yeMsa wami,' your uncle calls, from the bottom of the unfinished grave, a milk stout bottle dangling from his hand. 'Sondzela la.' You walk carefully between two graves towards him. 'I'm happy to see you, it's been years since you were home. Akulungi Ntolo, you are ours too. Home is home, there is nothing you can do to change that,' he says. The use of your clan name is purposeful, a reinforcement that you are theirs, they live alongside you in your surname.

You nod. It's not necessarily in agreement. You want him to feel he isn't alone in the conversation. He is your father's younger brother and the last of his generation now, the heaviness of that responsibility is palpable in him like the red in his eyes and the sudden creases on his face. He steals a glance at your car then looks at you, his eyebrows raised.

'He is just a friend, please do not make it more awkward than it already is, Babe Lomncane.'

'A friend who keeps guard like that? In my time, I only gave the gift of such inconvenience to girls I *really* loved.'

You sneak into the house because you want to show him your bedroom. You also want to shield yourselves from further questions—especially about his name. Your bedroom remains untouched, except for the walls. When you lived in it, you remember choosing the colour because you liked the idea of waking up to a burning sky. After you left for university, your father painted them beige. Your small desk is still in the corner, empty of the books that used to congest it. You are both sitting on the double bed, taking in the room like you have never been there before.

'This is where the "self-magic" used to happen,' you tease.

'Who did you fantasise about then?' he asks.

'Many, many boys. But there was this boy in my class, Phila. He wore these thick glasses, always sat in the front, but he was big and tall, and teachers moved him to the back, near my friends and me. He sat alone during lunch and it never looked awkward, you know? I found that so attractive. One day he sat next to me during prep and our legs kept brushing against each other. Everything tingled and I was embarrassingly hard. At some point, I put my hand in his shorts and he didn't move it—he was also hard.'

'Did anything else ever happen between you two?'

'No, just that day, then he avoided me until we left school. Anyways, after that, every time I wanked I would imagine Phila and his warm dick and how much I wanted him on top of me right here.' You tap the bed.

'Like this?' he presses you down onto the bed and his whole weight is suddenly surrounding you. You kiss him and scramble to unbutton his shirt. He shakes his head and says, 'There's no time for that.'

He unbuckles your pants and flips you over, your body malleable. He kisses the back of your neck and pulls your pants down to expose half your buttocks. His own buckle clinks and you spread your legs for his entry. Your pants constrain the radius of your spread, which only heightens the delight. Without warning he is inside you and a loud gasp escapes you and meets his now familiar grunt above you. His thrusts are fast and frustrated. His arm wraps under your neck, choking you, exerting his power, to bring you close to death and draw you back with desire. His arm flexes tighter against your throat and the pressure on your breathing scares and excites you at the same time. If death tastes like black smoke and defecation, then living tastes musty and hard, you decide. He curves his torso over and to the right of you, so that his face is near your face. You taste chardonnay, soil and sweat on his breath. His eyes glare a whole universe at you while he plunges a bit of that universe inside you. You have never had sex in your room before and something about that makes this moment daring, even though now there isn't a father to catch you. The noise of funeral preparations below suddenly rises, you can hear clanking pots, boiling rice and your family's heartbeat. You know your father would find this infinitely disrespectful and that arouses you more. Doing something forbidden always feels like you are finally doing what you *actually* want. He interlocks his hands with yours. His grunts begin to soar faster and you close your eyes to feel it all. You think about your mother, who left because her husband forgot to love her until she gave him a son but by then it was too late.

'When were you going to tell me your father and I have the same name?' He chucks the question at you as buckles and pants are shifting back into place.

'I don't know. All I know is it felt deeply uncomfortable to say, "Hey Lwandle, you know my dead father? His name was also Lwandle" after sucking your dick.'

'At least it would have prepared me for the awkward stares everyone gives me when I introduce myself.'

'I'm sorry. If you knew, would you have still come?'

'Maybe. But would you go somewhere where your name makes everyone want to cry?'

The funeral service of Lwandle Fakudze begins at 4 a.m., after a night vigil. By tradition, he has to be buried before the sun comes up to have a full day of light to travel the final stretch home. Multitudes of people fill the cemetery. Your father's popularity is unexpected but you understand that a person can be a different experience for everyone.

Your sisters sit in order of birth in the small tent. You are standing with the men around the coffin. This is the last time you will be this close to your father. The coffin is covered with a thick blanket, to keep him warm. You are not sure when mourning starts and when it ends. As they lower his casket into the ground, you wonder if the parts a person contributes to you die with them too. Maybe that's why it feels like a part of you disappears. The procession to sprinkle a handful of earth on the coffin begins with your family. Sabelo and Mqondisi hold Menzi up, her body flickering away. They lean over the grave like they will all jump in. You've heard this happens at many funerals. But they don't. You search for the alive Lwandle, you see his shiny head move in and out of sight as he helps collect the funeral programmes that go into the grave before they cover it. Your father was an ocean when he was alive, exactly like his name. He drowned and cleansed. Now that ocean rests beneath you while another ocean will sleep next to you tonight.

You look up at the sky, it's 5:15 a.m.

Girl

Jamaica Kincaid

Wash the white clothes on Monday and put them on the stone heap; wash the color clothes on Tuesday and put them on the clothesline to dry; don't walk barehead in the hot sun; cook pumpkin fritters in very hot sweet oil; soak your little cloths right after you take them off; when buying cotton to make yourself a nice blouse, be sure that it doesn't have gum on it, because that way it won't hold up well after a wash; soak salt fish overnight before you cook it; is it true that you sing benna in Sunday school?; always eat your food in such a way that it won't turn someone else's stomach; on Sundays try to walk like a lady and not like the slut you are so bent on becoming; don't sing benna in Sunday school; you mustn't speak to wharf-rat boys, not even to give directions; don't eat fruits on the street—flies will follow you; *but I don't sing benna on Sundays at all and never in Sunday school*; this is how to sew on a button; this is how to make a buttonhole for the button you have just sewed on; this is how to hem a dress when you see the hem coming down and so to prevent yourself from looking like the slut I know you are so bent on becoming; this is how you iron your father's khaki shirt so that it doesn't have a crease; this is how you iron your father's khaki pants so that they don't have a crease; this is how you grow okra—far from the house, because okra tree harbors red ants; when you are growing dasheen, make sure it gets plenty of water or else it makes your throat itch when you are eating it; this is how you sweep a corner; this is how you sweep a whole house; this is how you sweep a yard; this is how you smile to someone you don't like too much; this is how you smile to someone you don't like at all; this is how you smile to someone you like completely; this is how you set a table for tea; this is how you set a table for dinner; this is how you set a table for dinner with an important guest; this is how you set a table for lunch; this is how you set a table for breakfast; this is how to behave in the presence of men who don't know you very well, and this way they won't recognize immediately the slut I have warned you against becoming; be sure to wash every day, even if it is with your own spit; don't squat down to play marbles—you are not a boy, you know; don't pick people's flowers—you might catch something; don't throw stones at blackbirds, because it might not be a blackbird at all; this is how to make a bread pudding; this is how to make doukona; this is how to make pepper pot; this is how to make a good medicine for a cold; this is how to make a good medicine to throw away a child before it even becomes a child; this is how to catch a fish; this is how to throw back a fish you don't like, and that way something bad won't fall on you; this is how to bully a man; this is how a man bullies you; this is how to love a man, and if this doesn't work there are other ways, and if they don't work don't feel too bad about giving up; this is how to spit up in the air if you feel like it, and this is how to move quick so that it doesn't fall on you; this is how to make ends meet; always squeeze bread to make sure it's fresh; *but what if the baker won't let me feel the bread?*; you mean to say that after all you are really going to be the kind of woman who the baker won't let near the bread?

The Fruit of My Woman

Han Kang

Translated from Korean by Deborah Smith

1

It was late May when I first saw the bruises on my wife's body. A day when the lilacs in the flower bed by the janitor's office sprayed out petals like severed tongues, and the paving slabs at the entrance to the senior citizen's centre were clotted with rotting white blooms, trampled beneath the shoes of passers-by.

The sun was almost at its zenith.

Sunlight, soft as the flesh of a ripe peach, was spilling languidly across the living room floor, allowing countless grains of sand, dust and pollen to cling to its body as it oozed in. That sickly sweet, lukewarm sunshine streamed onto the back of my white vest as my wife and I flicked through the Sunday morning paper.

The week just gone had been marked by the same exhaustion I'd been feeling for months now. On weekends I allowed myself a lie-in, and I had woken up only a few minutes ago. Lying on my side, I inched my languid limbs into a more comfortable position, scanning the newspaper as slowly as possible.

'Would you take a look at this? I don't know why these bruises haven't faded.'

I registered my wife's words as a mere disturbance in the fabric of silence rather than processing their meaning. I glanced up at her absent-mindedly.

I sat bolt upright. Marking what I'd been reading in the paper with a finger, I scrubbed my eyes with the palm of my hand. My wife had lifted her vest up to her bra; deep bruises mottled her back and stomach.

'How did you get those?'

She twisted her torso and drew the back zipper of her pleated skirt down to her tailbone. Pale blue bruises the size of a newborn's palm, as distinct as though they'd been printed in ink.

'Well? How did you get them?' My sharp, insistent tone ruptured the still space enclosed in our eighteen-p'yong flat.

'I don't know . . . I just assumed I must have knocked into something without realising, and the bruises would go away . . . but they're actually getting bigger.'

My wife avoided my gaze like a child caught doing something wrong. Slightly regretting having seemed to scold her, I made an effort to soften my tone.

'Doesn't it hurt?'

'No, not at all. There's actually no sensation at all in the bruised parts. But, you know, that's even more worrying.'

The guilty expression I'd noticed a few moments ago had vanished without a trace, replaced by a gentle, incongruous smile. That smile played around my wife's lips as she asked if she ought to go to the hospital.

Feeling oddly withdrawn from the whole situation, I examined my wife's face with a cool, dispassionate gaze. The face I was confronted with felt unfamiliar, almost unreal; nothing like what one would expect given that we were in our fourth year of cohabitation.

My wife was three years younger than me, she had turned twenty-nine this year. Her face used to make her look embarrassingly young when we went out together, before we were married—she was frequently mistaken for a schoolgirl. It now bore clear signs of fatigue, which jarred with her look of wide-eyed innocence. It seemed unlikely that anyone would mistake her for a schoolgirl anymore, or even a university student.

If anything, she actually looked older than her age. Her cheeks, the colour of unripe apples into which the red has just begun to rise, were sunken, like knocked-in clay. The waist that had been as soft and pliant as a sweet potato seedling, the stomach that once had such an appealing set of curves, were now pitifully lean.

I struggled to recall the last occasion that I'd seen my wife naked, and it had been bright enough to see her properly. Not this year, for sure; I wasn't even certain that it had happened the year before.

How could I have failed to notice such deep bruises on the body of the only person I lived with? I tried to count the fine wrinkles radiating out from the corners of my wife's eyes. Then I told her to take off all her clothes. A red flush appeared along the line of her cheekbones, which her weight loss had left indecently sharp. She tried to remonstrate with me.

'What if someone sees?'

Unlike most flats, which are laid out facing a garden or car park, our balcony looked out onto the main eastern road. Since we were three streets away from the nearest apartment block, separated from it by both the main road and Chungnang stream, it would be impossible for anyone to pry without a high-powered telescope. There was certainly no danger of anyone catching a glimpse of our living room from inside one of the cars speeding along the road. So I simply took my wife's protest as a sign of her embarrassment on my account. On weekends as newlyweds, in this selfsame living room, with both the glass door leading onto the veranda and the window on its far side flung wide open in an attempt to mitigate the sweltering August heat, we used to make love several times in the middle of the day, clumsily exploring this thing that was so new to us until we eventually succumbed to the weight of exhaustion.

After a year or so had passed we were no longer so unaccustomed to our love, and the fervour of those early days gradually dissipated. My wife went to bed quite early, and she was an unusually deep sleeper. If I returned home late, I could take it as a given that she would already have fallen asleep. When I turned my key in the front door's lock and stepped into the flat, alone and with no one to greet me, washed myself and entered the darkened bedroom, the even cadences of her breathing struck me as inexplicably desolate. If I made love to her, hoping to ease this loneliness, her half-open, sleep-clouded eyes gave me no clue as to whether she was rejecting my embrace or passionately returning it. She only swept her silent fingers through my hair until the movements of my body stopped.

'Everything? You want me to take everything off?'

Her crumpling face struggling to suppress an outburst of laughter, my wife rolled the underwear she'd just removed into a ball, and covered her pubic area.

And there was her naked body, fully exposed in the spring sunshine. It really had been a long time.

And yet I was unable to feel even the faintest stirrings of desire. Seeing the yellowish-green bruises not only on her buttocks but also on her ribs and shins, marring even the white flesh on the insides of her thighs, anger seized me, then just as suddenly relinquished its grip, leaving in its wake an unwarranted melancholy. For this woman, whose mind so easily wandered, had sleep dissolved even the memory of walking along the street early one evening—senses already dulled by sleep's descending curtain—blundering into a slow-moving car, or perhaps of losing her step and tumbling down the unlit emergency stairs in our building?

The figure of my wife, standing there shielding her pubic area as the late spring sunshine streamed onto her back, absent-mindedly asking whether she ought to go to the hospital, was just too wretched, pitiful, sorrowful for words, so that I was touched with a sadness I hadn't felt in a long time. I could only hold her skinny body against me.

2

I assumed everything would be fine. And that was why I'd taken my wife's bony frame in my arms that spring day and said, 'If they're not hurting then no doubt the bruises will fade soon enough. It's hardly the first time you've ended up with a few here and there from clumsiness.' I softened the reproach with a loud laugh.

One night in early summer the heat-saturated wind rubbed its sticky cheeks against the leaves of tall sycamores and the bloodshot eyes of the streetlamps blinking among them. My wife, who sat across from me at the table as we shared a late dinner, laid her spoon down with a clatter. I'd completely forgotten about her bruises.

'Well, it's strange . . . have another look.'

Having examined the two gaunt arms protruding from her short sleeves, my wife briskly stripped off her T-shirt and bra. A brief moan escaped me before I could swallow it back.

The bruises that had been the size of a newborn's palm the previous spring were now more like large taro leaves. On top of that, they'd darkened. They were a dull green, like the color that pale blue-green willow branches of spring deepened into with the onset of summer.

I stretched out a trembling hand and stroked my wife's bruised shoulder, feeling as though it were a stranger's body I was touching. How painful must it have been, for bruises like these?

Now I come to think of it, I noticed that my wife's face, too, was burnished with blue that day, as though suffused with lead water. Her formerly glossy hair was as brittle as dried radish leaves. The whites of her eyes were so pale they carried a faint indigo hue, making her pupils gleam even darker in their sheen of moisture.

'Why is this happening to me? I keep wanting to go outside, and as soon as I do . . . as soon as I see the sunlight, in fact, I get the urge to take my clothes off. It's as though my body wants them off.' My wife stood up, giving me the plainest view I'd had all year of her withered, naked frame. 'The day before yesterday, I went out onto the balcony with nothing on and stood next to the drying rack. Not knowing if anyone could see me . . . and not even trying to hide myself . . . I mean, like I was some crazy woman!' I did nothing but sit and stare at my wife's scrawny upper half as it approached me, nervously running my fingers along the edges of the chopsticks I was holding. 'I've lost my appetite, too. I'm drinking more water than I used to, though . . . I can't even manage half a bowl of rice in a whole day. And because I'm not eating, I guess my stomach acid isn't being secreted properly or something. Even if I force myself to eat, it doesn't get digested properly and I just keep throwing it back up again.' She crumpled to her knees like a puppet whose strings had been cut and buried her face in my thigh. Surely she wasn't crying? A warm, damp patch formed on my tracksuit bottoms.

'Do you know what it feels like to be throwing up several times a day? It's like having motion sickness even though you're standing on solid ground; you have to walk hunched over, it's impossible to straighten up. Your head hurts like . . . like your right eye is boring into it. Your shoulders are stiff as a board, you salivate, yellow stomach acid on the paving slab, on the roots of the roadside trees . . ."

The fluorescent lamp, its filament worn thin, gave off a buzz like an insect's cry. Under its murky glow, my wife, a blood-dark bruise marking her back, managed to kill the whimpering sound trickling out of her.

'Go to the hospital,' I told her, looking her in the face. 'Tomorrow, go straight to the internal medicine department.'

Her wet, blotchy face was unsightly. As my splayed fingers ran through my wife's brittle hair, I gave her a toothy smile. 'And do be careful how you go. You don't want to be hurting yourself again. It's not as though you're a child, to be falling over and bumping into things.'

My wife's wet face trembled into a smile, and a single tear that clung to her lips elongated and detached itself.

3

Had my wife always had such a propensity for tears? No, she hadn't. The first time I saw her cry, she was twenty-six.

As a young girl she'd been more easily moved to laughter, her voice always shot through with that bright undertone, laughter as a wash of colour. I heard that voice, its calm maturity usually at odds with her youthful looks, quaver for the first time when she told me, 'I hate living in the Sanggye-dong high-rises.'

'Seven hundred thousand people all crammed together, I feel like I'm going to wither and die. I hate these hundreds and thousands of identical buildings, identical kitchens, identical ceilings, identical toilets, bathtubs, balconies and lifts, and I hate the parks, the rest areas, the shops, the pedestrian crossings. I hate them all.'

'What's brought this on, hmm?' I spoke as if soothing a fractious child, having paid more attention to the softness of my wife's voice than to what she was actually saying. 'What's there to dislike about a lot of people living near each other?'

I adopted a somewhat stern expression as I looked into my wife's eyes. Her guileless, gentle eyes.

'I would always make sure the rooms I rented stood near the entertainment district. I'd only move to places that were swarming with people, where thumping music spilled out into the streets and the cars clogged the roads and blared their horns. I couldn't have coped otherwise. I couldn't have coped with being alone.' From those gentle eyes rolled a tear that felt almost like a lie. Even as my wife dashed the tears from her cheeks with the back of her hand, they were replaced in continuous flow. 'And now, it's like I'm going to fall into some lingering illness and die. Like I won't be able to get down from this thirteenth floor, like I won't be able to get outside.'

'Why are you making such a song and dance about it? Seriously, it's a bit much.'

In our first year here in these high-rise flats, my wife was quite often ill. She'd been used to the natural environment of a rented room in one of Seoul's hillier districts, and her body seemed unable to adjust to a central-heated, tightly sealed flat. Her body, hardened by the daily climb up and down steep hills to her underpaid publishing job, soon lost its vigour.

But it wasn't because of our marriage that she quit her job. It was only after she quit, not long after, in fact, that I'd talked of marriage concretely. She'd taken out all the money she had—whatever she'd put aside from her monthly salary and pension allowance, plus any extra from part-time work at weekends—and was planning on leaving the country.

'I want to go and get some new blood in my veins,' she said. This was the evening of the day when she'd finally given her letter of resignation to her immediate superior. She told me she wanted to transfuse the bad blood that was clotting up her veins like cysts and flush out her tired old lungs with fresh air. Living and dying freely had been her dream ever since she was a child, she said; she'd been putting it off because the time wasn't right, but now she felt that she'd saved up enough to make her dream a reality. She planned to pick a country, stay there for six months or so, then move on somewhere else, and so on. 'I want to do it before I die, you know,' she said, and gave a low chuckle. 'I want to see the very edge of the world. To get as far away as possible, bit by bit.'

But in the end, instead of setting out for the world's edge, my wife poured all her meagre funds into the deposit for this flat and our wedding costs. She'd explained this all to me in a single short sentence, saying she'd done it 'because it's not like I can part from you'. How real had been this dream of hers, this dream of freedom? Considering that she'd been able to relinquish it so easily, I assumed not very. The plans she'd made toward that dream would have been childlike. An unrealistic, romantic delusion. In the end, she must have realised all this by herself, and I felt vaguely moved and proud to think that I must have been the one who'd prompted this belated realisation.

It was probably all down to her frequent aches and pains, but when I saw my wife standing with her cheek pressed against the glass door to the balcony, her narrow shoulders drooping like wilted cabbage leaves as she stared down at the speeding cars, my heart sank. She was so still, only the incredibly faint sound of her breathing confirmed she was still alive; as though a pair of invisible arms pinioned her shoulders, as though a massive iron ball attached to an invisible chain prevented her from so much as flexing a single muscle.

In the depths of night and the small hours of the morning, my wife would awake with a start, disturbed by the occasional taxi or motorbike as it roared down the otherwise deserted street. 'It's like the road's speeding rather than the cars, like this flat is being swept away with the road,' she said. Even after the noise of the engines had receded into the distance and sleep had reclaimed her, my wife's lovely face was deathly pale.

On one such night, my wife mumbled as though in a dream, her hoarse voice only barely audible: 'All that stuff, where did it come from . . . where is it all running off to?'

4

The next evening, when I opened the front door and stepped inside the flat, I saw that my wife had come to the door to greet me, presumably having heard my footsteps in the corridor. She was barefoot and the curve of her toenails, which she hadn't been trimming as often as she should have, gleamed white.

'What did they say at the hospital?'

No answer. Having studied me in silence as I removed my shoes, my wife turned away, tucking behind her ear a lock of dull hair which had been resting on her cheek.

That profile, I thought to myself. I remembered how, when we were first introduced, a smooth silence elapsed after my senior at work—he played the role of the intermediary—got up and left us alone, and how disconcerted I'd been by the secretive expression on my future wife's face. It made her look as though she was wandering somewhere far away, in some undisclosed location. In that face, which at first glance had seemed merely bright and lovely, I was able to read an unlooked-for loneliness, seemingly that of an entirely different person, and it was this that gave me the momentary conviction that she understood me. Then, too, when this conviction and the alcohol I'd drank led me to blurt out a confession, that I'd been lonely my whole life, the twenty-six-year-old woman who was to become my wife turned away to face some distant horizon, leaving me confronting the same cold, desolate profile I was faced with now.

'You did go to the hospital, right?' My wife inclined her head in the barest hint of a nod. Had she turned away in order to conceal her unhealthy complexion, or was there something I'd done? 'Come on, please, talk to me. What did the doctor say?'

'That it's fine,' she said, more like an exhalation than a statement. Her voice was frighteningly flat.

At that initial meeting, it had been her voice that most attracted me to her. It was a senseless comparison, but her voice put me in mind of an elaborately glazed and lacquered tea table; one of those elegant pieces of furniture which you begrudge getting out for any but the most important guests, and on which it only seems right to serve the very best tea, in the very best cups. That night, apparently not the least ruffled by the confession I'd let slip, my wife's response had been perfectly matter-of-fact, and delivered in her usual composed tone of voice. And I, she'd said, I want to live my whole life without settling in a single place.

After that, I'd talked about plants. I told her I'd had a dream where the balcony was crowded with large flowerpots, each of them filled with green lettuces and perilla. In summer, tiny flowers would unfurl on the perilla plants like drops of snow. And there would be bean sprouts growing in the kitchen, I added. That finally wrung a faint laugh from my wife, who'd been fixing me with a sceptical stare as if all this talk of plants was very much at odds with her idea of me. Trying to cling on to the trailing end of that innocent, fragile laugh, I said the words again: 'I've been lonely my whole life.'

After we were married, I put flowerpots out on the balcony as discussed, but neither of us proved to be particularly green-fingered. For whatever reason, even hardy greenstuffs, which I presumed would need nothing more than regular watering, withered and died without providing us with a single crop.

One person said that our upper-floor flat was too far removed from the ground's energy; another told us our plants were all dying because the air and water were bad. We were even told that we lacked the good faith necessary to tend living things, but that simply wasn't true. The wholehearted manner in which my wife devoted herself to caring for those plants exceeded all expectations. If a lettuce or perilla plant withered, this would be enough to plunge her into depression for half a day, while if one seemed to be still clinging tenaciously to life she would wander around humming a bright tune.

For whatever reason, nothing now remained on the balcony other than rectangular flowerpots filled with dry soil. Where had they all gone, I wondered, all those dead plants? And what about those rainy days when I'd set the flowerpots up on the windowsill, dipping my hands in the cold streaks of rain, where had all those young days gone?

My wife had turned to me and said, 'Let's go somewhere far away, the two of us.' Unlike the plants, which revived at least a little as their leaves took in that invigorating rain, my wife looked to be withering into an ever deeper state of depression. 'It's impossible to live in this stifling place. Even the mucus from my nose and throat is black,' she said, stretching her haggard hand out over the lettuce leaves to intercept the falling rain, which she then shook onto the balcony. 'This rain is filthy,' she said. Her eyes sought my agreement. 'This isn't living,' she spat out, 'it only looks like it.' Her voice was edged with hostility, like a drunk's slurring declamation, *This country's rotten through!* 'There's no way anything could grow here, don't you see? Not trapped here in this . . . in this stifling, deafening, *place*!'

I couldn't stand it any longer.

'What's stifling?' I couldn't stand her sharp little jabs, blindly shattering my precarious newfound happiness, nor the sight of her gaunt frame, coursing with the blood she claimed was of a worn, melancholic strain. 'Tell me.' I splashed the rainwater I'd collected in my cupped hands over my wife's shoulders. 'What's stifling? What's deafening?'

A low moan escaped from my wife, her startled hands flailing at her face. Cold rainwater splashed onto the balcony windowpane, onto my face. The flowerpot on the windowsill struck my wife's foot before crashing to the balcony floor. Rough potsherds and clumps of soil clung to my wife's clothes, her bare feet. She bent over, gripped the injured foot in both hands and bit her lower lip.

Biting her lip was a long-standing habit of hers; even back before we were married, she would do it whenever I got angry or raised my voice. Worrying at her lip seemed to help her set her thoughts in order, and after a while she would begin to reply to whatever it was I'd said or done, listing her points calmly and logically. But after that incident on the balcony, her bitten lip became the only response I could draw from her. We stopped arguing after that day.

'The doctor said there's nothing wrong?' I felt an intense wave of fatigue and loneliness. When I shrugged off my suit jacket, my wife didn't take it from me.

'He said he couldn't find anything wrong,' she confirmed, her face still turned away.

5

My wife gradually lost what little speech she'd retained. She didn't speak unless she was spoken to, and even then her only reply was a nod or shake of the head. If I raised my voice, demanding that she answer me, she would just stare off into the distance, an equivocatory look in her eyes. Her steadily worsening complexion was now clearly perceptible even under the dim light of the fluorescent lamp.

Given that the doctor had said he couldn't find anything wrong, perhaps, rather than there being some physical problem with my wife's stomach or intestines, it was a simple case of being troubled. But what on earth could she be troubled about?

The past three years had been the warmest and most peaceful of my life. My work was not too taxing, I was lucky enough to have a landlord who didn't try and hike up the deposit for the flat, I'd almost paid off the mortgage for the new flat and I had a wife who, though she had little in the way of playful charm, was devoted to me; my contentment was like warm water lapping gently at the inner sides of a deeply filled bathtub, caressing my exhausted body.

So what was my wife's problem? I couldn't figure out what distress could be so severe as to bring about a psychogenic illness. Every time I questioned whether this woman really had the right to make me so lonely, or by what right she did so, all I felt was a desolate abhorrence, accumulating like layers of old dust.

The following Sunday morning, the day before I was due to take a weeklong business trip abroad, I watched my wife shaking the laundry out on the balcony. The bruises now covered so much of her arms that the white parts of skin seemed like bruises in reverse, small white blotches among all that blue. I caught my breath. As she carried the empty laundry basket back into the living room, I blocked her way and demanded she take off her clothes. She resisted, but I got her T-shirt off, revealing a shoulder dyed a dark, dull blue.

I staggered back and stared at her body. More than half of her once-thick armpit hair had fallen out, and the colour had leached from her brown nipples, formerly soft and tender.

'Things can't go on like this. I'm going to phone your mother.'

'No, don't, I'll do it,' my wife shouted hastily, her pronunciation garbled as though she were chewing on her tongue.

'Go to the hospital, understand? Go to a dermatologist. No, go to a general hospital.' She nodded, mute. 'You know I don't have time to go with you. You know your own body, so you have to keep it in order, no?' She nodded again. 'Listen to me. Call your mother.' My wife carried on nodding, her lips pressed together. Did the nodding mean she was listening? Most likely, my words had gone in one ear and out the other; I could hear them falling to the living room floor, crumbling like cheap biscuits.

6

The doors of the lift rattled open. I walked down the darkened corridor carrying my cumbersome suitcase, and rang the bell. No response.

I pressed my ear against the door's gelid steel. I kept on pressing the bell, two times, three times, four times, checking that it was still working; it was, I could hear it ringing inside the flat, though the muffling effect of the door made it sound as though it was coming from somewhere much further away. I propped the suitcase against the door and looked at my watch. Eight in the evening. Granted, my wife was a heavy sleeper, but this was surely a bit much.

I was worn out. I hadn't eaten, either. Just this one time, I didn't want the hassle of having to fish out my key.

Perhaps my wife had called her mother and gone to the hospital as I'd told her to, or gone to stay with her relatives in the countryside. But no—as soon as I stepped through the door, I took in the familiar jumble of her slippers, trainers and smart shoes.

I eased my feet out of my own shoes and into my slippers, unconsciously registering the flat's usual chill. Before I'd taken a few steps, though, I became aware of a disgusting smell. Opening the fridge, I saw courgettes, cucumbers, and other side-dish ingredients, withered and rotting from the middle of their backs outward.

Around half a bowl of rice had been left in the rice cooker; clearly it had been there for some time, as it had dried and stuck to the inner pan. When I opened the lid, the distinct smell of days-old rice flooded my nostrils along with the still-warm steam. There was a pile of dirty dishes in the sink and the sweet smell of rot was coming from the plastic washbowl on top of the washing machine, where the laundry sat puddled in grey soapy water.

My wife wasn't in the bedroom, the bathroom, or the spare room which we used for various things. I called out her name; no answer. In the living room there was only the morning newspaper, spread out as I'd left it the week before; an empty 500ml milk carton; a glass cup flecked with droplets of congealed milk; one of my wife's white socks, inside-out; and a red faux-leather purse; all scattered here and there.

The roar of car engines as they sped down the main road cut a sharp incision into the solid mass of the flat's contained emptiness.

Because I was tired and hungry, because the crockery was all rusting in the sink's dishpan, without a single clean spoon for me to scoop up some rice, I felt lonely. Because I'd come back to an empty house after travelling such a great distance, because I wanted to talk about all those trivial things that happen on long distance flights, about the landscapes that had scudded past the window on foreign trains, because there was no one to ask 'Are you tired?', robbing me of the opportunity to demonstrate my endurance with a stoic 'I'm okay,' I was lonely. And because of this loneliness, I got angry. Because of the feeling that, owing to my body's insignificance, I was fundamentally unable to enmesh myself within the fabric of this world, because of the chill that was leaching through my suddenly flimsy clothes, and because of the thought that all I had managed in my life so far was to successfully kid myself that I was appreciated, I felt angry. Alone, and with no one to love me, my existence might as well have already been snuffed out.

Just at that moment, I heard a feeble voice.

I turned in the direction of the sound. It was my wife's voice. A faint murmuring carried in from the balcony, impossible to decipher.

Instantly, that intense loneliness morphed into a feeling of relief, and as I stomped over to the balcony I felt a burst of irritation come spiralling off the tip of my tongue. 'Why didn't you answer me if you've been there all this time?' I flung the veranda door open. 'Is this any way to run a household? What on earth have you been living on?'

Then I saw my wife's naked body, and stopped.

My wife was kneeling down, facing the grille that stretched across the balcony window, her two arms raised as though she was cheering. Her entire body was dark green. Her formerly shadowed face now gleamed like a glossy evergreen leaf. Her dried radish-leaf hair was as lustrous as the stems of wild herbs.

Her two eyes glittered pale in her green face. Turning to face me as I shrank back, she shifted as though to get up. But instead, spasms flinched uselessly up and down her legs. She seemed unable either to stand or walk.

Her pliant waist torqued painfully. Her atrophied tongue swayed like a water plant between her deep blue lips. Already, there was no sign of her teeth.

A single cry, little more than a moan, escaped from between those puckering pale-flecked lips.

'. . . water.'

I ran to the sink, turned the tap on all the way and filled the plastic washbowl until it overflowed. The water slapped at the sides with each of my hasty footsteps, sloshing onto the living room floor as I hurried back to the balcony. As soon as I splashed it onto my wife's chest, her entire body underwent a quivering revival, like the leaf of a huge plant. I went back and refilled the washbowl, returning to pour it over my wife's head. Her hair sprang up, as though some invisible weight had been compressing it. I watched her glittering green body bloom afresh with my baptism. I felt dizzy.

My wife had never been so beautiful.

7

Mother.

I'm not able to write you letters anymore. Or to wear the sweater you left here. That orange woollen sweater, the one you accidentally left behind when you came up to visit last winter.

I wore it the day after he went on his business trip. You know how I feel the cold.

It hadn't been washed, so it still had that smell of stale side dishes mixed in with the scent of your skin. On a different day I probably would have washed it, but it was too cold, and besides, I wanted to keep breathing in that scent, so I kept it on, and even fell asleep wearing it. The next morning, the frost still hadn't relaxed its grip, and perhaps it was because I was so cold and thirsty that, when the morning sunlight eventually shone through the bedroom window, that stifled cry broke out from me: *mother.* Wanting to be enfolded in that warm light, I went out onto the balcony and took off my clothes. The sun's rays penetrating my bared flesh were so much like your scent, I knelt there and called out *mother, mother.* No other words.

I wonder how much time passed. Days, weeks, months? Having noticed that the air didn't seem particularly warm, all I registered after that was a slight rise in temperature, followed by a comparable dip.

Any moment now, the windows of the distant flats over the Chungnang stream will blaze with an orange light.

Can the people who live there see me? What about the cars that race along the main road, light streaming from their headlights? What do I look like now?

He's been extremely kind. He bought a huge flowerpot and planted me in it. On Sundays, he spends all morning sitting on the balcony threshold catching aphids.

He, who used to be so exhausted all the time, climbs the mountain behind our block every morning, returning with a pail of mineral water to water my legs (he's remembered that I don't like tap water). A while ago, he emptied my flowerpot and replaced my soil with an armful of rich new loam. When the previous night's rain has scrubbed some of the dirt from the city air, he throws the front door and windows wide open to let the fresh air circulate.

It's strange, mother. Even without seeing, listening, smelling and tasting, everything feels fresher, more alive. I sense the rough friction of the car tyres as they skim over the tarmac, the minute reverberations of his footsteps as he opens the front door and walks over to me, the rain-saturated air swelling with fertile dreams, the grey half-light of dawn.

I feel buds sprouting and petals unfurling in places both near and distant, larvae emerging from chrysalises, dogs and cats giving birth to their young, the trembling stop-start of the pulse of the old man in the next building, the spinach parboiling in a pan in the kitchen above, a bunch of snapped-off chrysanthemums being put in a vase beside the gramophone in the flat below. Day or night, the stars describe a calm parabola, and every time the sun rises the bodies of the sycamores at the side of the highway incline their craving bodies eastwards. My own body responds in a similar way.

Can you understand? Soon, I know, even thought will be lost to me, but I'm alright. I've dreamed of this, of being able to live on nothing but wind, sunlight and water, for a long time now.

Thoughts of when I was young: when I ran into the kitchen and buried my face in your skirt, that delicious smell; the smell of sesame oil, of stir-fried sesame seeds. I always had my hands in the earth, you know. My soil-smeared hand dirtying the hem of your skirt.

How old would I have been? That spring day hazed with drizzle, father lifting me up onto the power tiller and driving us down to the shore. The unconcerned laughter of adults in rainwear, children with wet hair plastered to their foreheads, skipping around and waving, their faces whirling, blurring.

That poor village by the sea was your whole world. You were born there and grew up there. You gave birth there, worked there, grew old there.

At some point, you will be laid there at the foot of our family burial ground, side by side with father.

It was fear of ending up like you, mother, that made me put such a distance between myself and my home. Leaving home at seventeen, the urban districts of Busan, Daegu, Gangneung, where I wandered aimlessly for over a month, have remained in my memory. Lying about my age to work as a server at a Japanese restaurant, evenings dozing fitfully in a cubicle at an all-night study hall—yet I liked being there. The dazzling lights of the urban districts, the glittering glamour of their inhabitants.

I don't know when I first became aware that I would end up old and ruined, roaming these stranger-thronged streets. I was unhappy at home and equally unhappy elsewhere, so tell me, where should I have gone?

I've never been happy. Is there some tortured soul forever at my back, clutching at my throat, my limbs? I've only ever wanted to run away, an extremely basic impulse, the pain that provokes a cry, the pinch that produces a scream. Hunched at the back of the bus, looking as though I wouldn't hurt a fly, and all that time longing to shatter the window with my fist. Greedy for the blood that would stream down my palm, I would have lapped it up as a cat does milk. What was it that I was trying to run away from, what was it that tormented me so much I longed to flee to the other side of the world? And what held me back, hobbling me, crippling me? What were the fetters that weighed me down, preventing the leap that would transfuse this sickening blood?

The elderly doctor repeatedly rapped the stethoscope with his finger, muttering that my insides were as silent as the grave. That the only sounds were the echoing gusts of a distant wind. He put the stethoscope down on the table and shifted the ultrasound monitor. I lay still as he smeared a clammy gel onto my stomach then rubbed a cold stick-shaped tool over my flesh, methodically travelling down from my solar plexus to my lower stomach. Through that tool, it seemed, an image of my insides was transmitted to the monitor, in black and white.

'It's normal,' he muttered, clicking his tongue. 'What we're looking at now is your intestines . . . there's nothing wrong with anything there.'

Everything was declared 'normal'.

'Stomach, liver, uterus, kidneys, they're all fine.'

Why couldn't he see that these organs were slowly atrophying, soon to disappear? He wiped most of the gel off with a handful of tissues, but when I tried to get up he told me to lie back down again. He pressed down on my stomach in a few different places; it wasn't particularly painful. I glared at his bespectacled face as he flung out a casual 'Does it hurt?', and kept shaking my head.

'Is it okay here?'

'It doesn't hurt here?'

'It doesn't hurt.'

I got an injection, and on the way home I vomited again. I crouched down in the subway station, back braced against the tiled wall. I counted as I waited for the pain to subside. The doctor had told me to relax, you see, to think cozy, calming thoughts. Everything is down to the mind, he'd said, intoning it like some Buddhist master. Calming thoughts, comfortable thoughts, one, two, three, four, endless peace, counting while trying not to throw up . . . the pain brought tears to my eyes, convulsions gripping me as I retched up stomach acid, again, again, until finally there was nothing left and I could let myself sink to the floor. I waited for the shaking ground to stop, damn it, just to stop.

How long ago was that?

Mother, I keep having the same dream. I dream that I'm growing tall as a poplar. I pierce through the roof of the balcony and through that of the floor above, the fifteenth floor, the sixteenth floor, shooting up through concrete and reinforcing rods until I break through the roof at the very top. Flowers like white larvae wriggle into blossom at my tallest extremities. My trachea sucks up clear water, so taut it seems it will burst, my chest thrusts up to the sky and I strain to stretch out each branching limb. This is how I escape from this flat. Every night, mother, every night the same dream.

The days are growing colder. Today, too, this world will have seen many leaves fall to the ground, many snakes shed their skins, many insects shed their tiny lives, and many frogs begin their winter hibernation, a little ahead of time.

I keep thinking of your sweater. The memory of your scent is no longer so clear. I want to ask him to drape it over me, but speech is lost to me now. What can I do? He cries to see me wasting away, and he gets angry, too. As you know, I was all the family he had. I can detect his warm tears mingling in the mineral water he pours on me. I can sense the air molecules being disarranged, his clenched fist flailing without a target.

I'm scared, Mother. My limbs have to fall out. This flowerpot is too cramped, its walls too hard. Shooting pains at the tips of my roots. Mother, I will die before winter comes.

And I doubt that I will bloom again in this world.

8

Later that night when I'd arrived back from my business trip, after dousing my wife with three washbowls full of water, she vomited a slew of yellow stomach acid. I watched her lips pucker and quickly knit themselves back together, flesh into flesh, before my very eyes. My trembling fingers fumbling at those pale-flecked lips, I at last heard a feeble voice, so faint I couldn't make out what it might be saying. That was the last time I heard my wife's voice. After that, there wasn't so much as a moan.

A thick white spray of roots sprouted out of her inner thighs. Dark red flowers blossomed from her chest. Twin stamens, white at the ends, yellowish and thick at the roots, pierced out through her nipples. When her raised hands were still able to exert a tiny amount of pressure, my wife wanted to clasp my neck. Looking into those eyes, in which a faint light still remained, I bent forwards into the embrace of those camellia-petal hands. 'Are you okay?' I asked. Her eyes, a pair of well-ripened grapes; glimmering on their lacquered surfaces, the ghost of a smile.

As autumn deepened, I witnessed a clear orange light gradually imbue my wife's body. When I opened the window, her upstretched arms would sway ever so slightly, moving with the wind currents.

As autumn drew to a close, her leaves began to fall in twos and threes. Her body slowly changed from its former orange to an opaque brown.

I thought about the last time I'd slept with my wife.

Instead of the sour tang of bodily fluids, an unfamiliar, faintly sweet scent had been coming from my wife's lower half. At the time, I just assumed she must have changed to a different brand of soap, or else that she'd had a bit of time on her hands and chose to spend it in sprinkling some drops of perfume down there. How long ago was all that?

Now, her form retains barely a trace of the biped she once was. Her pupils, which seemed to have metamorphosed into shining round grapes, are gradually being buried in brown stems. My wife cannot see anymore. She can't even flex the ends of the stems. But when I go out onto the balcony I feel a hazy sensation that defeats all language, like a minute electric current pulsing out from her body and into mine. When the leaves which were once my wife's hands and hair all fell out, and the place where her lips had meshed together split open, releasing a handful of fruit, that sensation ended like a thin thread snapping.

The tiny fruits had burst out en masse like pomegranates; I gathered them in my hands and sat down across the threshold that connects the balcony to the living room. These fruits, which I was seeing for the first time, were a yellowish green. And they were hard, like the sunflower seeds they serve alongside popcorn as an accompaniment to beer.

I picked out one and popped it into my mouth. The smooth rind was entirely devoid of taste or smell. I crunched down on it. Fruit of the only woman I'd ever had on this earth. The first thing my palate picked up was an acidic, almost burning flavour, and the juice that clung to the root of my tongue had a solely bitter aftertaste.

The next day I bought a dozen small, round flowerpots, and after filling them with fertile soil, planted the fruits in them. I lined the small flowerpots up next to that of my withered wife, and opened the window. I leant out over the railing and smoked a cigarette, savouring the smell of fresh grass that had suddenly bloomed from my wife's lower parts. The chill wind of late autumn ruffled my cigarette smoke, my long hair.

When spring came, would my wife sprout again? Would her flowers bloom red? I just didn't know.

Vertical Motion

Can Xue

Translated from Chinese by Karen Gernant and Chen Zeping

We are little critters who live in the black earth beneath the desert. The people on Mother Earth can't imagine such a large expanse of fertile humus lying dozens of metres beneath the boundless desert. Our race has lived here for generations. We have neither eyes nor any olfactory sense. In this large nursery, such apparatus is useless. Our lives are simple, for we merely use our long beaks to dig the earth, eat the nutritious soil, and then excrete it. We live in happiness and harmony because we have abundant resources in our hometown. Thus, we can all eat our fill without a dispute arising. At any rate, I've never heard of one.

In our spare time, we congregate to recall anecdotes of our forebears. We begin by remembering the oldest of our ancestors and then run through the others. The remembrances are pleasurable, filled with outlandish salty and sweet flavours, as well as some crispy amber—the immemorial turpentine. In our recollections, there is a blank passage that is difficult to describe. Broadly speaking, as one of our elders (the one with the longest beak) was digging the earth, he suddenly crossed the dividing line and vanished in the desert above. He never returned to us. Whenever we remembered this, we fell silent. I sensed that everyone was afraid.

Even though people never descended to our underground, we actually gained all kinds of information about the mortals above us. I don't know what sort of channel this information came from. It is said that it was very mysterious, and that it had something to do with our builds. I'm an average-sized, ordinary individual of my genus. Like everyone else, I dig the earth every day and excrete. Recalling our ancestors is the greatest pleasure in my life. But when I sleep, I have some odd dreams. I dream of seeing people; I dream of seeing the sky above. Human beings are good at movement. They feel bumpy to the touch. I'm extremely jealous of their well-developed limbs, because our limbs have atrophied underground. We all move about by wiggling and twisting our bodies. Our skin has become too smooth, easily injured.

We make these kinds of remarks about humankind:

'If you approach the border of the yellow sand, you can hear camel bells ringing: this is what our grandfather told me. But I don't want to go to such a place.'

'Human beings reproduced too quickly: it is said that their numbers are immense. They've consumed all of earth's food, and now they're eating yellow sand. It's dreadful.'

'If we don't think about the sky and the people on earth, doesn't that ultimately mean that those things don't exist? We have enough memories and knowledge of this kind of thing. It's pointless to go on exploring.'

'The yellow sand above us is more than ten metres deep. It's just like the end of the world to those of us who live in the warm, moist, deep soil. I've been to the boundary and have felt the desire to thrust upward. Here and now, I'd like to recall that time.'

'Our kingdom of the black earth didn't always exist. It came into being only later. Our oldest ancestors didn't always exist, either. They, too, came into being only later. And so here we are. Sometimes I think that maybe one of us should take a risk. Since we came from nowhere, taking risks is part of our obligation.'

'I want to take a risk, too. I've begun fasting recently. I hate my sweaty, damp, and slippery body. I want a change. Whenever I think of yellow sand dozens of metres deep, I'm terrified. But the more terrified I am, the more I want to go to that place. There, I would certainly lose all sense of direction. Probably my only sense of direction would come from gravity. But would gravity change in such a place? I'm very worried.'

'We remember all of the history and all of the anecdotes. Why have we forgotten only our long-beaked grandpa? I always feel that he's still alive, but I can recall nothing about him. Recollections concerning each of us are preserved only in our hometown. Once one leaves here, one is thoroughly invalidated by history.'

'When I grow quiet, whimsical ideas come into my mind. I would like our collective to ease me into oblivion. Yet, I know this can't be done here. Here, my every word and action will be preserved in everyone's memories, and will be passed on from generation to generation.'

'I think I can grow bumpy skin; I just have to make a point of exercising every day. Recently, I've been rubbing and scraping against the rigid clods in the earth. After my skin bleeds, scabs form. It seems this is working.'

It's worth pointing out that we critters don't congregate in a certain space for our meetings (as the human beings above us do), for our kingdom of the black earth has no spaces. Everything is packed together. When we do assemble for recreation or discussion, the earth still blocks us off from each other. The black earth is a very good medium for transmitting sound. Everyone can hear every single one of our utterances, even if it's in the feeblest voice. Sometimes while we're digging, we accidentally run into another body. At such times, both sides may feel really disgusted. Ah, we really don't care to have any bodily contact with our own race! It's said that the people above us had to have sexual intercourse in order to propagate: this is much different from our asexual reproduction. Indeed, what does sexual intercourse look like? We don't yet have any detailed information about this. Sometimes when I think of being entangled with my own kind, I start squealing from nausea.

When we stop digging, we don't move. We're like pupae as we dream in the black earth. We know that our dreams are similar, but our dreams have never been strung together. Each of us has his or her own dreams. During those long dreams, I can bore deep into the earth and then fuse into a single body with the earth. In the end, my dreams are about only the earth. Long dreams are great, for they are sheer relaxation. But if this goes on for a long time, I feel vaguely discontented, because a dream of earth can never give me the joy that I most want to experience.

Once, we gathered together and talked of our dreams. After I related one of mine, I began crying in despair. What kind of dream was it? It was blacker and blacker until finally it became the black earth. In my dream, I wanted to make a sound, but my mouth had vanished. One after another they consoled me, referring to our ancestors to prove nothing was wrong with our lives. I stopped crying, but something ice-cold settled into my body. I thought it would be difficult to hang onto my previous optimistic attitude toward life. Subsequently, even during working hours, I could feel the heavy black earth pushing down on my heart. Even my rigid beak was weakening, and it itched now and then. I wanted the relaxation that comes from dreaming, but I didn't want the fatigue that comes after waking from a dream. I didn't want to lose interest in life. I must have been possessed. Was I going to disappear in the boundless yellow sand just as our missing ancestor had?

I had recently lost weight, and I was sweating a lot—more than usual. Perhaps because of my mood, I was about to fall ill. When I dug the earth, I heard my companions encouraging me, but for some reason this didn't cheer me up. Instead, I felt sorry for myself and was sloppily sentimental. At break time, an elder talked to me of my late father. He had a lovely buzzing voice, much like the sound sometimes made by the black earth. I called that sound a lullaby. The elder said my father had had a last wish, but he'd been unable to express it. Those beside him didn't probe, either, and thus his last wish hadn't been preserved in our memories. Near death, my father made an odd sound. This old man had been nearest to him, so he heard the sound the most distinctly. He understood immediately that my father wanted to fly like a bird in the sky.

'So did he want to become a bird?' I asked.

'I don't think so. He had a higher purpose.'

I talked with the elder for a long time about what my father's last wish might have been. We spoke of sandstorms, of giant lizards, of a certain oasis that had existed, and also of certain minor disturbances involving our ancestors in remote antiquity—because a qualitative change in the earth brought about a scarcity of food. Each time we broached a new topic, we felt we had almost reached my father's last wish. But as we continued talking, it eluded us even more. It really made us uneasy.

Thanks to the elder's information, I gradually calmed down. After all, there *was* a last wish! This made me feel less nihilistic.

'M! Are you digging?'

'Ah, I am!'

'That's good. We've all been worried about you.'

These dear friends, associates, kin, and confidants! If I didn't belong to them, who would I belong to? The hometown was so serene, the soil so soft and delicious! I felt that I became a better self. Although my chest still ached dully, the disease had left me. This didn't mean, however, that I was unchanged. I *had* changed. Hidden in me now was an obscure plan that even I couldn't explain.

I was still like everyone else—working, resting, working, resting . . . I heard subtle transformations taking place in our hometown. For example, the tribes decreased in number; the desire to procreate declined; unreasonable complaints spread among us; and so on. Recently, we had begun to amuse ourselves by measuring the lengths of our beaks with the width of our atrophied fingers. 'Ha, ha! Mine is three fingers long!' 'Mine is four!' 'Mine is even longer—four and a half!' Even though our fingers weren't the same width, this activity was still fun for everyone. I discovered that my beak was longer than those of all of my brethren. Was it possible that the elder who had disappeared was my great-grandfather?! Because of my discovery, I broke out in a cold sweat and kept this secret to myself.

'M, how many fingers is your beak?'

'Three and a half!'

I kept my body vertical and continued rushing upward. Everyone soon discovered this change in my motion. I felt the fear all around me.

I heard them say: 'Him!' 'Scary, scary!' 'I feel the land wobbling. Will there be an accident?' 'M, you need to get hold of yourself.' 'It isn't in our nature to move straight up!'

I heard all of this. I was engaged in a dangerous activity and couldn't stop this impulse. I ascended, ascended—until, worn out from this work, I slept a dreamless sleep. It was a sound sleep—like death. It was free of confusion and anguish. And I couldn't estimate how long I had slept. After I awakened, my body once more rushed up. This had become a conditioned reflex.

Before long, I noticed a deathly silence all around me; they were probably deliberately staying away from me. Because I was far from the border, others must have been here, too. For the first time in my life, I was alone in an absolutely quiet place. Two large things—black, certainly blacker than the earth—settled over my head all the time. I thought those two things must be heavy and impenetrable. The bizarre thing was that as I kept digging upward, they kept backing off. I couldn't touch them. If I touched them with my beak, would we be together for all eternity? Sometimes, they fused into one huge thing and sometimes they separated again. When they were fused together, they made a *gege* grinding sound; when they were separated, they moaned unhappily. I couldn't think about so many things: I just continued darting ahead as though they weren't there. I thought, *I wasn't supposed to die so soon.* Was I perhaps implementing my father's last wish?

More time passed, and I was working in the deathly quiet and sleeping soundly in the deathly quiet. Scrupulously controlling my feelings so as not to think too much, I knew I was approaching the boundary. Ah, I nearly forgot those two black things! Did I take them to be myself? It was obvious that one could become accustomed to anything. To be sure, I was also sometimes weak, and at such times, I would utter a heartfelt lament: 'Father, ah, Father, your last wish is such a terrifying black hole!' This lament gave rise to a misconception: the layers of black earth were twisting me, as if they would twist off my body. I also felt that my ancestors' corpses were hidden in the earth's folds. The corpses emitted spots of phosphorescence. I never hallucinated for very long: I didn't like sentimentality. Most of the time, I ascended step by step. Ascended!

Since beginning vertical motion, I felt that my life was more disciplined—work, sleep, work, sleep . . . Because of this regularisation, my mind was also transformed. In the past, I loved to have rambling daydreams—about the layers of black earth, about the ancestors, about Father, about the world above, and so forth. Daydreaming was a way to relax, a kind of entertainment, a kind of tasty turpentine. Now everything had changed. My daydreams were no longer rambling; now they had an objective. As soon as I began resting, those two black things above me started suggesting a direction, and they towed my thoughts in that direction. What was above? Simply those two things. As I was musing, I heard them make the bizarre sound of a watchman's wooden clapper: it was as if someone were striking clappers on an ancient mountain on the ground above and the sound actually reached us underground. Listening attentively, I was thinking of the huge black things. While I was enthralled in this, the sound of the clapper would suddenly stop and become the sound of us insects—many, many insects—boring into the ground. Sometimes I also heard the obscure sound of insects talking—a sound that I seemed to have heard before. Ah, that sound! Wasn't it the very sound that I had heard not long after I split away from my father's body? It appeared that Father was still among us. He brought me a sense of stability, confidence, and a kind of special excitement. A new realm of imagination lay in this. I realised that I liked my present life. When you were about to achieve your objectives, when you incessantly extended your beak toward the things that interested you so much: Didn't you feel happy? To be sure, I didn't think of this too much: I merely felt satisfied with my new circumstances.

I realised tardily that the two black things above were not just totally black, but they contained infinite hues that were in constant flux. The closer I came to the boundary, the weaker and flimsier the core parts seemed to be, as if they would pass through light. Believe me, my body was close to sensing light, which was pink and a little hot. Once, when I overexerted myself, I felt I had torn one of the cores. I even heard a breaking sound—*cha*. I was both excited and afraid. But after a while, I realised that nothing had happened: they were still above me. All was well. I was being silly: How could there be light underground? Now these two things were so exquisite, so seductive. Wasn't Father's obscure voice echoing once again?

Before long, something happened: while I was digging upward, there was a sudden landslide. It was only afterwards that I concluded it was a landslide. At the time, I realised only that I was falling and I didn't know where I had fallen. I remember that at first I'd been excited and had faintly heard the noise that was told of in our ancient legends: the sound of people above congregating for singing and dancing. At the time, I thought, *How can there be a congregation in the desert?* Or perhaps it wasn't a desert over us, after all? Now, the two black things above me really did let light through. I am speaking merely of my conclusion, because I wasn't aware of it. This light wasn't pink, nor was it yellow or orange. It was a thing that you couldn't sense, wedged between the two black things. The sound of the musical accompaniment became increasingly intense, and I grew increasingly excited. I exerted all of my strength to thrust upward . . . and then there was the landslide.

I was despondent, for I thought I had certainly fallen to the place where I was before I started my vertical motion. But a long time passed, and silence still lay all around me. Did another kingdom lie beneath the desert, a dead kingdom? It was very dry here, and the earth was not the black earth of before. All of a sudden, it came to me: this wasn't earth, it was sand! Right. This was shapeless sand! I had clearly fallen down, so how had I ended up in this kind of place? Could gravity have changed direction? I didn't want to think about this too much. I had to start my work as soon as possible, for it was only work that could put me in a good mood with a steady self-confidence.

I began digging—still in the upward, vertical motion. Motion in the desert was quite different from motion in the earth. In the earth, you could sense the track—and the sculpture—your motion left behind. But this heartless sand submerged everything. You couldn't leave anything behind, and so you couldn't judge the direction of your motion. Of course, with my present lifestyle, vertical motion was just fine, because my inner body was attuned to gravity. As this went on, I felt that this work was harder and tenser than before. And what I ate was sand: flavour was out of the question. I ate it just to fill my stomach. I was tense because I was afraid of losing my direction by mistake. I had to keep paying attention to my sense of gravity: it was the only way to maintain the vertical route. This sand would seemingly choke all of my senses. I had no way to know if I was even in motion. And so my feelings shrank inward. There was no longer a track, not to mention the sculpture, but only some blurred throbbing innards, along with flashes of faint light in my brain.

And so, was I squirming in the same spot or was I moving up? Or sinking down? Was I capable of determining this? Of course not. Every so often I made expanding and contracting motions, which I thought meant I was moving up. Of course the sand's resistance was not nearly as great as the earth's, but this slighter resistance left me uneasy. If you have nowhere to stand, then you have no way, either, to confirm the results of your exertions, and there's likely to be no result. After tiring from my activity, I ate some sand and then fell into a death-like sleep. After my skin cracked, it healed again, and after healing it cracked again. Little by little, it was thickening. The humankind above me wears thick skin. Had they all gone through what I was experiencing? Ah, this quiet, this desolation! One can probably endure it for a short time, but if it persists, isn't it the same as being dead? Uneasiness germinated tardily in my mind. I reflected on the one who had disappeared: Perhaps he was still alive? One possibility was that he and I were both living and that we would never actually die. Buried by this boundless yellow sand, each of us leapt on his own, and we would never be able to see each other. When I considered this possibility, I began twitching all over. This occurred a number of times.

The last time it happened, it was really dreadful. I thought I would die. I became aware of the mountain, which was the two black things that had formerly been above me. After disappearing for a time, they had returned. They pressed down toward me, but didn't press me to death. They were just suspended above. At this time, I stopped having spasms at once. As this eased, at first my consciousness functioned rapidly, and then it was entirely lost. I leapt up with all my strength! At once, the mountain weakened so much that it was like two leaves—leaves of the phoenix tree above ground. Indeed, I sensed that they were drifting. As I saw it, a miracle was taking place. In my excitement, I leapt again, and now there were four phoenix leaves! There were actually four. I heard the sound of each one. It was the metallic sound mentioned in legends. I knew I hadn't lost my way: I was on the correct path! Soon, the metallic leaves would split and I would see light! Although I had no eyes, this wouldn't preclude my 'seeing.' I—an insect underground—would see light! Ha ha! Not so fast. How would I do this? With my scarred, haggard, restless body? Or was it just my mirage? Who could guarantee that the instant I emerged from the earth wouldn't be the moment of my death? No, I didn't want to get to the bottom of this question. It would be fine if I could just keep sensing the phoenix leaves above me. Ah, those eternal metallic leaves: the cool breeze on Mother Earth shuttled among the leaves . . .

I fainted. When I came to, I heard sand buzzing all around me, and in this sound an old, low voice spoke:

'M, is your beak still growing?'

Who was it? Was it he? Who else could it be? So much time had passed. This desert, this desert . . . How could things be like this?

'Yes, my beak, my beak! Please tell me: Where am I?'

'You're on the uppermost crust of the earth. This is your new home.'

'Can't I bore my way out of it? Are you saying that from now on I can only wander around in this sand? But I'm accustomed to vertical motion.'

'You can only engage in vertical motion here. Don't worry, there's more sand on top of this sand.'

'Are you saying I cannot break out completely? Oh, I see. You've tried it. How long have you lived in this region? It must be a very long time. We can't measure the time, but we know we lost you long ago. Dear ancestor, I never imagined, never imagined that in this—how to say it?—that in this extremity, I would come across you. If my father . . . ah, I can't mention him. If I do, I'll faint again.'

He didn't say any more. I heard his far-off voice: *cha, cha, cha* . . . as he dug the sand with his long, senile beak. My bodily fluids were boiling. It was bizarre: I'd stayed in such an arid place for so long and yet I still had fluids in my body. Judging by the sound I heard, this ancestor had fluids in his body, too. This was really miraculous! Somewhere above me, he walked away. He must have seen the phoenix leaves, too.

Ah, he returned! How wonderful—now I had a companion! I had someone to communicate with. The boundless yellow sand was no longer so frightening! Who . . . who was he?

'Grandpa, are you the one who disappeared?'

'I am a wandering spirit.'

This was great: I spoke, and someone answered me. How long had I been without this? Someone of the same species would engage in the same activity and live with me in this desert . . . Father's last wish was for me to find him: I realised this!

I was a little critter submerged in the desert. This was the outcome I had pursued. In this mid-region, I was envisioning the phoenix leaves on Mother Earth. Yet, I didn't forget my kindred in the dark.

You Can't Get Lost in Cape Town

Zoë Wicomb

In my right hand, resting on the base of my handbag, I clutch a brown leather purse. My knuckles ride to and fro, rubbing against the lining . . . surely cardboard . . . and I am surprised that the material has not revealed itself to me before. I have worn this bag for months. I would have said with a dismissive wave of the hand, 'Felt, that is what the base of this bag is lined with.'

Then Michael had said, 'It looks cheap, unsightly,' and lowering his voice to my look of surprise, 'Can't you tell?' But he was speaking of the exterior, the way it looks.

The purse fits neatly into the palm of my hand. A man's purse. The handbag gapes. With my elbow I press it against my hip, but that will not avert suspicion. The bus is moving fast, too fast, surely exceeding the speed limit, so that I bob on my seat and my grip on the purse tightens as the springs suck at my womb, slurping it down through the plush of the red upholstery. I press my buttocks into the seat to ease the discomfort.

I should count out the fare for the conductor. Perhaps not; he is still at the front of the bus. We are now travelling through Rondebosch, so that he will be fully occupied with white passengers at the front. Women with blue-rinsed heads tilted will go on telling their stories while fishing leisurely for their coins and just lengthen a vowel to tide over the moment of paying their fares.

'Don't be so anxious,' Michael said. 'It will be all right.' I withdrew the hand he tried to pat.

I have always been anxious and things are not all right; things may never be all right again. I must not cry. My eyes travel to and fro along the grooves of the floor. I do not look at the faces that surround me, but I believe that they are lifted speculatively at me. Is someone constructing a history for this hand resting foolishly in a gaping handbag? Do these faces expect me to whip out an amputated stump dripping with blood? Do they wince at the thought of a hand, cold and waxen, left on the pavement where it was severed? I draw my hand out of the bag and shake my fingers ostentatiously. No point in inviting conjecture, in attracting attention. The bus brakes loudly to conceal the sound of breath drawn in sharply at the exhibited hand.

Two women pant like dogs as they swing themselves onto the bus. The conductor has already pressed the bell and they propel their bodies expertly along the swaying aisle. They fall into seats opposite me—one fat, the other thin—and simultaneously pull off the starched servants' caps, which they scrunch into their laps. They light cigarettes and I bite my lip. Would I have to vomit into this bag with its cardboard lining? I wish I had brought a plastic bag; this bag is empty save for the purse. I breathe deeply to stem the nausea that rises to meet the curling bands of smoke and fix on the bulging bags they grip between their feet. They make no attempt to get their fares ready; they surely misjudge the intentions of the conductor. He knows that they will get off at Mowbray to catch the Golden Arrow buses to the townships. He will not allow them to avoid paying, not he who presses the button with such promptness.

I watch him at the front of the bus. His right thumb strums an impatient jingle on the silver levers; the leather bag is cradled in the hand into which the coins tumble. He chants a barely audible accompaniment to the clatter of coins, a recitation of the newly decimalized currency—like times tables at school, and I see the fingers grow soft, bending boyish as they strum an ink-stained abacus; the boy learning to count, leaning earnestly with propped elbows over a desk. And I find the image unaccountably sad and tears are about to well up when I hear an impatient empty clatter of thumb-play on the coin dispenser as he demands, 'All fares, please,' from a sleepy white youth. My hand flies into my handbag once again and I take out the purse. A man's leather purse.

Michael too is boyish. His hair falls in a straight blond fringe into his eyes. When he considers a reply, he wipes it away impatiently, as if the hair impedes thought. I cannot imagine this purse ever having belonged to him. It is small, U-shaped and devoid of ornament, therefore a man's purse. It has an extending tongue that could be tucked into the mouth or be threaded through the narrow band across the base of the U. I take out the smallest note stuffed into this plump purse, a five-rand note. Why had I not thought about the bus fare? The conductor will be angry if my note should exhaust his supply of coins, although the leather bag would have a concealed pouch for notes. But this thought does not comfort me. I feel angry with Michael. He has probably never travelled by bus. How would he know of the fear of missing the unfamiliar stop, the fear of keeping an impatient conductor waiting, the fear of saying fluently, 'Seventeen cents, please,' when you are not sure of the fare and produce a five-rand note? But this is my journey and I must not expect Michael to take responsibility for everything. Or rather, I cannot expect Michael to take responsibility for more than half the things. Michael is scrupulous about this division; I am not always sure of how to arrive at half. I was never good at arithmetic, especially this instant mental arithmetic that is sprung on me.

How foolish I must look sitting here clutching my five-rand note. I slip it back into the purse and turn to the solidity of the smoking women. They have still made no attempt to find their fares. The bus is going fast and I am surprised that we have not yet reached Mowbray. Perhaps I am mistaken; perhaps we have already passed Mowbray and the women are going to Sea Point to serve a nightshift at the Pavilion.

Marge, Aunt Trudie's eldest daughter, works as a waitress at the Pavilion, but she is rarely mentioned in our family. 'A disgrace,' they say. 'She should know better than to go with white men.'

'Poor whites,' Aunt Trudie hisses. 'She can't even find a nice rich man to go steady with. Such a pretty girl too. I won't have her back in this house. There's no place in this house for a girl who's been used by white trash.'

Her eyes flash as she spits out a cherished vision of a blond young man sitting on her new vinyl sofa to whom she serves ginger beer and koeksisters, because it is not against the law to have a respectable drink in a coloured home. 'Mrs Holman,' he would say, 'Mrs Holman, this is the best ginger beer I've had for years.'

The family do not know of Michael, even though he is a steady young man who would sit out such a Sunday afternoon with infinite grace. I wince at the thought of Father creaking in a suit and the unconcealed pleasure in Michael's successful academic career.

Perhaps this is Mowbray after all. The building that zooms past on the right seems familiar. I ought to know it, but I am lost, hopelessly lost, and as my mind gropes for recognition, I feel a feathery flutter in my womb, so slight I cannot be sure, and again, so soft, the brush of a butterfly, and under cover of my handbag I spread my left hand to hold my belly. The shaft of light falling across my shoulder, travelling this route with me, is the eye of God. God will never forgive me.

I must anchor my mind to the words of the women on the long seat opposite me, but they fall silent as if to protect their secrets from me. One of them bends down heavily, holding on to the jaws of her shopping bag as if to relieve pressure on her spine, and I submit to the ache of my own by swaying gently while I protect my belly with both hands. But having eyed the contents of her full bag carefully, her hand becomes the beak of a bird dipping purposefully into the left-hand corner and rises triumphantly with a brown paper bag on which grease has oozed light-sucking patterns. She opens the bag and her friend looks on in silence. Three chunks of cooked chicken lie on a piece of greaseproof paper. She deftly halves a piece and passes it to her thin friend. The women munch in silence, their mouths glossy with pleasure.

'These are for the children,' she says, her mouth still full as she wraps the rest up and places them carelessly at the top of the bag.

'It's the spiced chicken recipe you told me about.' She nudges her friend. 'Lekker, hey!'

The friend frowns and says, 'I like to taste a bit more cardamom. It's nice to find a whole cardamom in the food and crush it between your teeth. A cardamom seed will never give up all its flavour to the pot. You'll still find it there in the chewing.'

I note the gaps in her teeth and fear for the slipping through of cardamom seeds. The girls at school who had their two top incisors extracted in a fashion that raged through Cape Town said that it was better for kissing. Then I, fat and innocent, nodded. How would I have known the demands of kissing?

The large woman refuses to be thwarted by criticism of her cooking. The chicken stimulates a story so that she twitches with an irrepressible desire to tell.

'To think,' she finally bursts out, 'that I cook them this nice surprise and say what you like, spiced chicken can make any mouth water. Just think, it was yesterday when I say to that one as she stands with her hands on her hips against the stove saying, "I don't know what to give them today. I've just got too much organizing to do to bother with food." And I say, feeling sorry for her, I say, "Don't you worry about a thing, Marram. Just leave it all in cook's hands"—wouldn't it be nice to work for really grand people where you cook and do nothing else? No bladdy scrubbing and shopping and all that—". . . in cook's hands," I said,' and she crows merrily before reciting, 'And I'll dish up a surprise / For Master Georgie's blue eyes.

'That's Miss Lucy's young man. He was coming last night. Engaged, you know. Well, there I was on my feet all day starching linen, making roeties and spiced lentils and sweet potato and all the lekker things you must mos' have with cardamom chicken. And what do you think she says?'

She pauses and lifts her face as if expecting a reply, but the other stares grimly ahead. Undefeated, she continues, 'She says to me, "Tiena," because she can't keep out of my pots, you know, always opening my lids and sniffing like a brakhond, she says, "Tiena," and waits for me to say,

"Yes, Marram," so I know she has a wicked plan up her sleeve and I look her straight in the eye. She smile that one, always smile to put me off the track, and she say, looking into the fridge, "You can have this nice bean soup for your dinner so I can have the remains of the chicken tomorrow when you're off." So I say to her, "That's what I had for lunch today," and she say to me, "Yes, I know, but me and Miss Lucy will be on our own for dinner tomorrow," and she pull a face. "Ugh, how I hate reheated food." Then she draws up her shoulders as if to say, *That's that.*

'Cheek, hey! And it was a great big fowl.' She nudges her friend. 'You know for yourself how much better food tastes the next day, when the spices are drawn right into the meat, and anyway, you just switch on the electric and there's no chopping and crying over onions; you just wait for the pot to dance on the stove. Of course, she wouldn't know about that. Anyway, a cheek, that's what I call it, so before I even dished up the chicken for the table, I took this'—and she points triumphantly to her bag—'and to hell with them.'

The thin one opens her mouth, once, twice, winding herself up to speak.

'They never notice anyway. There's so much food in their pantries, in the fridge and on the tables; they don't know what's there and what isn't.' The other looks pityingly at her.

'Don't you believe that. My marram was as cross as a bear by the time I brought in the pudding, a very nice apricot ice it was, but she didn't even look at it. She know it was a healthy grown fowl and she count one leg, and she know what's going on. She know right away. Didn't even say, "Thank you, Tiena." She won't speak to me for days, but what can she do?' Her voice softens into genuine sympathy for her madam's dilemma.

'She'll just have to speak to me.' And she mimics, putting on a stern horse face. '"We'll want dinner by seven tonight," then, "Tiena, the curtains need washing," then, "Please, Tiena, will you fix this zip for me. I've got absolutely nothing else to wear today." And so on the third day she'll smile and think she's smiling forgiveness at me.'

She straightens her face. 'No,' she sighs, 'the more you have, the more you have to keep your head and count and check up because you know you won't notice or remember. No, if you got a lot, you must keep snaps in your mind of the insides of all the cupboards. And every day, click, click, new snaps of the larder. That's why that one is so tired, always thinking, always reciting to herself the lists of what's in the cupboards. I never know what's in my cupboard at home, but I know my Sammie's a thieving bastard—can't keep his hands in his pockets.'

The thin woman stares out of the window as if she has heard it all before. She has finished her chicken, while the other, with all the talking, still holds a half-eaten drumstick daintily in her right hand. Her eyes rove over the shopping bag and she licks her fingers abstractedly as she stares out of the window.

'Lekker, hey!' the large one repeats. 'The children will have such a party.'

'Did Master George enjoy it?' the other asks.

'Oh, he's a gentleman all right. Shouted after me, "Well done, Tiena. When we're married, we'll have to steal you from Madam." Dressed to kill he was, such a smart young man, you know. Mind you, so's Miss Lucy. Not a prettier girl in our avenue and the best dressed too. But then she has mos' to be smart to keep her man. Been on the pill for nearly a year now; I shouldn't wonder if he don't feel funny about the white wedding. Ooh, you must see her blush over the pictures of the wedding gowns, so pure and innocent she think I can't read the packet. "Get me my headache pills out of that drawer, Tiena," she say sometimes when I take her cup of cocoa at night. But she play her cards right with Master George; she have to 'cause who'd have what another man has pushed to the side of his plate. A bay leaf and a bone!' Moved by the alliteration, the image materializes in her hand. 'Like this bone,' and she waves it under the nose of the other, who starts. I wonder whether with guilt, fear or a debilitating desire for more chicken.

'This bone,' she repeats grimly, 'picked bare and only wanted by a dog.'

Her friend recovers and deliberately misunderstands, 'Or like yesterday's bean soup, but we women mos' know that food put aside and left to stand till tomorrow always has a better flavour. Men don't know that, hey. They should get down to some cooking and find out a thing or two.'

But the other is not deterred. 'A bone,' she insists, waving her visual aid, 'a bone.'

It is true that her bone is a matt grey that betrays no trace of the meat or fat that only a minute ago adhered to it. Master George's bone would certainly look nothing like that when he pushes it aside. With his fork he would coax off the fibres ready to fall from the bone. Then he would turn over the whole, deftly, using a knife, and frown at the sinewy meat clinging to the joint before pushing it aside towards the discarded bits of skin.

This bone, it is true, will not tempt anyone. A dog might want to bury it only for a silly game of hide-and-seek.

The large woman waves the bone as if it would burst into prophecy. My eyes follow the movement until the bone blurs and emerges as the Cross where the head of Jesus lolls sadly, his lovely feet anointed by sad hands, folded together under the driven nail. Look, Mamma says, look at those eyes molten with love and pain, the body curved with suffering for our sins, and together we weep for the beauty and sadness of Jesus in his white loincloth. The Roman soldiers stand grimly erect in their tunics, their spears gleam in the light, their dark beards are clipped, and their lips curl. At midday Judas turns his face to the fading sun and bays, howls like a dog for its return as the darkness grows around him and swallows him whole with the money still jingling in the folds of his saffron robes. In a concealed leather purse, a pouch devoid of ornament.

The buildings on this side of the road grow taller, but oh, I do not know where I am and I think of asking the woman, the thin one, but when I look up, the stern one's eyes already rest on me while the bone in her hand points idly at the advertisement just above my head. My hands, still cradling my belly, slide guiltily down my thighs and fall on my knees. But the foetus betrays me with another flutter, a sigh. I have heard of books flying off the laps of gentle mothers-to-be as their foetuses lash out. I will not be bullied. I jump up and press the bell.

There are voices behind me. The large woman's 'Oi, I say' thunders over the conductor's cross 'Tickets, please.' I will not speak to anyone. Shall I throw myself on the grooved floor of this bus and, with knees drawn up, hands over my head, wait for my demise? I do not in any case expect to be alive tomorrow. But I must resist; I must harden my heart against the sad, complaining eyes of Jesus.

'I say, miss,' she shouts, and her tone sounds familiar. Her voice compels like the insistence of Father's guttural commands. But the conductor's hand falls on my shoulder, the barrel of his ticket dispenser digs into my ribs, the buttons of his uniform gleam as I dip into my bag for my purse. Then the large woman spills out of her seat as she leans forward. Her friend, reconciled, holds the bar of an arm across her as she leans forward shouting, 'Here, I say, your purse.' I try to look grateful. Her eyes blaze with scorn as she proclaims to the bus, 'Stupid, these young people. Dressed to kill maybe, but still so stupid.'

She is right. Not about my clothes, of course, and I check to see what I am wearing. I have not been alerted to my own stupidity before. No doubt I will sail through my final examinations at the end of this year and still not know how I dared to pluck a fluttering foetus out of my womb. That is if I survive tonight.

I sit on the steps of this large building and squint up at the marble facade. My elbows rest on my knees flung comfortably apart. I ought to know where I am; it is clearly a public building of some importance. For the first time I long for the veld of my childhood. There the red sand rolls for miles, and if you stand on the koppie behind the house, the landmarks blaze their permanence: the river points downward, runs its dry course from north to south; the geelbos crowds its banks in near-straight lines. On either side of the path winding westward plump little buttocks of cacti squat as if lifting the skirts to pee, and the swollen fingers of vygies burst in clusters out of the stone, pointing the way. In the veld you can always find your way home.

I am anxious about meeting Michael. We have planned this so carefully for the rush hour, when people storming home crossly will not notice us together in the crush.

'It's simple,' Michael said. 'The bus carries along the main roads through the suburbs to the City, and as you reach the post office, you get off and I'll be there to meet you. At five.'

A look at my anxious face compelled him to say, 'You can't get lost in Cape Town. There'—and he pointed over his shoulder—'is Table Mountain, and there is Devil's Peak, and there Lion's Head, so how in heaven's name could you get lost?' The words shot out unexpectedly, like the fine arc of brown spittle from between the teeth of an old man who no longer savours the tobacco he has been chewing all day. There are, I suppose, things that even a loved one cannot overlook.

Am I a loved one?

I ought to rise from these steps and walk towards the City. Fortunately I always take the precaution of setting out early, so that I should still be in time to meet Michael, who will drive me along de Waal Drive into the slopes of Table Mountain, where Mrs Coetzee waits with her tongs.

Am I a loved one? No. I am dull, ugly and bad-tempered. My hair has grown greasy, I am forgetful, and I have no sense of direction. Michael, he has long since stopped loving me. He watched me hugging the lavatory bowl, retching, and recoiled at my first display of bad temper. There is a faraway look in his eyes as he plans his retreat. But he is well brought up, honourable. When the first doubts gripped the corners of his mouth, he grinned madly and said, 'We must marry,' showing a row of perfect teeth.

'There are laws against that,' I said unnecessarily.

But gripped by the idyll of an English landscape of painted greens, he saw my head once more held high, my lettuce-luscious skirts crisp on a camomile lawn and the willow drooping over the red mouth of a suckling infant.

'Come on,' he urged. 'Don't do it. We'll get to England and marry. It will work out all right,' and betraying the source of his vision, 'and we'll be happy for ever, thousands of miles from all this mess.'

I would have explained if I could, but I could not account for this vision: the slow shower of ashes over yards of diaphanous tulle, the moth wings tucked back with delight as their tongues whisked the froth of white lace. For two years I have loved Michael, have wanted to marry him. Duped by a dream, I merely shook my head.

'But you love babies, you want babies sometime or other, so why not accept God's holy plan? Anyway, you're a Christian and you believe it's a sin, don't you?'

God is not a good listener. Like Father, He expects obedience and withdraws peevishly if His demands are not met. Explanations of my point of view infuriate Him so that He quivers with silent rage. For once I do not plead and capitulate; I find it quite easy to ignore these men.

'You're not even listening,' Michael accused. 'I don't know how you can do it.' There is revulsion in his voice.

For two short years I have adored Michael.

Once, perched perilously on the rocks, we laughed fondly at the thought of a child. At Cape Point where the oceans meet and part. The Indian and the Atlantic, fighting for their separate identities, roared and thrashed fiercely so that we huddled together, his hand on my belly. It is said that if you shut one eye and focus the other carefully, the line separating the two oceans may rear drunkenly but remains ever clear and hair-fine. But I did not look. In the mischievous wind I struggled with the flapping ends of a scarf I tried to wrap round my hair. Later that day on the silver sands of a deserted beach he wrote solemnly, *Will you marry me?* and my trembling fingers traced a huge heart around the words. Ahead the sun danced on the waves, flecking them with gold.

I wrote a poem about that day and showed Michael. 'Surely that was not what Logiesbaai was about,' he frowned, and read aloud the lines about warriors charging out of the sea, assegais gleaming in the sun, the beat of tom-toms riding the waters, the throb in the carious cavities of rocks.

'It's good,' he said, nodding thoughtfully. 'I like the title, "Love at Logiesbaai (Whites Only)," though I expect much of the subtlety escapes me. Sounds good,' he encouraged. 'You should write more often.'

I flushed. I wrote poems all the time. And he was wrong; it was not a good poem. It was puzzling, and I wondered why I had shown him this poem that did not even make sense to me. I tore it into little bits.

Love, love, love, I sigh as I shake each ankle in turn and examine the swelling.

Michael's hair falls boyishly over his eyes. His eyes narrow merrily when he smiles and the left corner of his mouth shoots up so that the row of teeth forms a queer diagonal line above his chin. He flicks his head so that the fringe of hair lifts from his eyes for a second, then falls, so fast, like the tongue of a lizard retracted at the very moment of exposure.

'We'll find somewhere,' he would say, 'a place where we'd be quite alone.' This country is vast and he has an instinctive sense of direction. He discovers the armpits of valleys that invite us into their shadows. Dangerous climbs led by the roar of the sea take us to blue bays into which we drop from impossible cliffs. The sun lowers herself on to us. We do not fear the police with their torches. They come only by night in search of offenders. We have the immunity of love. They cannot find us because they do not know we exist. One day they will find out about lovers who steal whole days, round as globes.

There has always been a terrible thrill in that thought.

I ease my feet back into my shoes and the tears splash on to my dress with such wanton abandon that I cannot believe they are mine. From the punctured globes of stolen days these fragments sag and squint. I hold, hold these pictures I have summoned. I will not recognize them for much longer.

With tilted head I watch the shoes and sawn-off legs ascend and descend the marble steps, altering course to avoid me. Perhaps someone will ask the police to remove me.

Love, love, love, I sigh. Another flutter in my womb. I think of moth wings struggling against a windowpane and I rise.

The smell of sea unfurls towards me as I approach Adderley Street. There is no wind, but the brine hangs in an atomized mist, silver over a thwarted sun. In answer to my hunger, Wellingtons looms on my left, the dried-fruit palace that I cannot resist. The artificial light dries my tears, makes me blink, and the trays of fruit, of Cape sunlight twice trapped, shimmer and threaten to burst out of their forms. Rows of pineapple are the infinite divisions of the sun, the cores lost in the amber discs of mebos arranged in arcs. Prunes are the wrinkled backs of aged goggas beside the bloodshot eyes of cherries. Dark green figs sit pertly on their bottoms peeping over trays. And I too am not myself, hoping for refuge in a metaphor that will contain it all. I buy the figs and mebos. Desire is a Tsafendas tapeworm in my belly that cannot be satisfied, and as I pop the first fig into my mouth, I feel the danger fountain with the jets of saliva. Will I stop at one death?

I have walked too far along this road and must turn back to the post office. I break into a trot as I see Michael in the distance, drumming with his nails on the side of the car. His sunburnt elbow juts out of the window. He taps with anxiety or impatience and I grow cold with fear as I jump into the passenger seat and say merrily, 'Let's go,' as if we are setting off for a picnic.

Michael will wait in the car on the next street. She had said that it would take only ten minutes. He takes my hand and so prevents me from getting out. Perhaps he thinks that I will bolt, run off into the mountain, revert to savagery. His hand is heavy on my forearm, and his eyes are those of a wounded dog, pale with pain.

'It will be all right.' I try to comfort and wonder whether he hears his own voice in mine. My voice is thin, a tinsel thread that springs out of my mouth and flutters straight out of the window.

'I must go.' I lift the heavy hand off my forearm and it falls inertly across the gearstick.

The room is dark. The curtains are drawn and a lace-shaded electric light casts shadows in the corners of the rectangle. The doorway in which I stand divides the room into sleeping and eating quarters. On the left there is a table against which a servant girl leans, her eyes fixed on the blank wall ahead. On the right a middle-aged white woman rises with a hostess smile from a divan that serves as sofa, and pats the single pink-flowered cushion to assert homeliness. There is a narrow dark wardrobe in the corner.

I say haltingly, 'You are expecting me. I spoke to you on the telephone yesterday. Sally Smit.' I can see no telephone in the room. She frowns.

'You're not coloured, are you?' It is an absurd question. I look at my brown arms, which I have kept folded across my chest, and watch the gooseflesh sprout. Her eyes are fixed on me. Is she blind? How will she perform the operation with such defective sight? Then I realize: the educated voice, the accent has blinded her. I have drunk deeply of Michael, swallowed his voice as I drank from his tongue. Has he swallowed mine? I do not think so.

I say, 'No,' and wait for all the cockerels in Cape Town to crow simultaneously. Instead the servant starts from her trance and stares at me with undisguised admiration.

'Good.' The woman smiles, showing yellow teeth. 'One must check nowadays. These coloured girls, you know, are very forward, terrible types. What do they think of me, as if I would do every Tom, Dick and Harry. Not me, you know; this is a respectable concern and I try to help decent women, educated, you know. No, you can trust me. No coloured girl's ever been on this sofa.'

The girl coughs, winks at me and turns to stir a pot simmering on a Primus stove on the table. The smell of offal escapes from the pot and nausea rises in my throat, feeding the fear. I would like to run, but my feet are lashed with fear to the linoleum. Only my eyes move, across the room, where she pulls a newspaper from a wad wedged between the wall and the wardrobe. She spreads the paper on the divan and smooths with her hand while the girl shuts the door and turns the key. A cat crawls lazily from under the table and stares at me until the green jewels of its eyes shrink to crystal points.

She points me to the sofa. From behind the wardrobe she pulls her instrument and holds it against the baby-pink crimplene of her skirt.

'Down, shut your eyes now,' she says as I raise my head to look. Their movements are carefully orchestrated, the manoeuvres practised. Their eyes signal and they move. The girl stations herself by my head, and her mistress moves to my feet. She pushes my knees apart and whips out her instrument from a pocket. A piece of plastic tubing dangles for a second. My knees jerk and my mouth opens wide, but they are in control. A brown hand falls on my mouth and smothers the cry; the white hands wrench the knees apart and she hisses, 'Don't you dare. Do you want the bladdy police here? I'll kill you if you scream.'

The brown hand over my mouth relaxes. She looks into my face and says, 'She won't.' I am a child who needs reassurance. I am surprised by the softness of her voice. The brown hand moves along the side of my face and pushes back my hair. I long to hold the other hand; I do not care what happens below. A black line of terror separates it from my torso. Blood spurts from between my legs and for a second the two halves of my body make contact through the pain.

So it is done. Deflowered by yellow hands wielding a catheter. Fear and hypocrisy, mine, my deserts spread in a dark stain on the newspaper.

'OK,' she says, 'get yourself decent.' I dress and wait for her to explain. 'You go home now and wait for the birth. Do you have a pad?' I shake my head uncomprehendingly. Her face tightens for a moment, but then she smiles and pulls a sanitary towel out of the wardrobe.

'Won't cost you anything, lovey.' She does not try to conceal the glow of her generosity. She holds out her hand and I place the purse in her palm. She counts, satisfied, but I wave away the purse, which she reluctantly puts on the table.

'You're a good girl,' she says, and puts both hands on my shoulders. I hold my breath; I will not inhale the foetid air from the mouth of this my grotesque bridegroom with yellow teeth. She plants the kiss of complicity on my cheek and I turn to go, repelled by her touch. But have I the right to be fastidious? I cannot deny feeling grateful, so that I turn back to claim the purse after all. The girl winks at me. The purse fits snugly in my hand; there would be no point in giving it back to Michael.

Michael's face is drawn with fear. He is as ignorant of the process as I am. I am brisk, efficient and rattle off the plan. 'It'll happen tonight, so I'll go home and wait and call you in the morning. By then it will be all over.' He looks relieved.

He drives me right to the door and my landlady waves merrily from the stoep, where she sits with her embroidery among the potted ferns. 'Don't look,' she says anxiously. 'It's a present for you, for your trousseau,' and smiling slyly, 'I can tell when a couple just can't wait any longer. There's no catching me out, you know.'

Tonight in her room next to mine she will turn in her chaste bed, tracing the tendrils from pink and orange flowers, searching for the needle lost in endless folds of white linen.

SEMI-DETACHED HOUSES WITH red-polished stoeps line the west side of Trevelyan Road. On the east is the Cape Flats line, where electric trains rattle reliably according to timetable. Trevelyan Road runs into the elbow of a severely curved Main Road, which nevertheless has all the amenities one would expect: butcher, baker, hairdresser, chemist, library, off-licence. There is a fish-and-chip shop on that corner, on the funny bone of that elbow, and by the side, strictly speaking in Trevelyan Road, a dustbin leans against the trunk of a young palm tree. A newspaper parcel dropped into this dustbin would absorb the vinegary smell of discarded fish-and-chip wrappings in no time.

The wrapped parcel settles in the bin. I do not know what has happened to God. He is fastidious. He fled at the moment that I smoothed the wet black hair before wrapping it up. I do not think he will come back. It is 6 a.m. Light pricks at the shroud of Table Mountain. The streets are deserted and, relieved, I remember that the next train will pass at precisely six twenty-two.

Squatting

Diao Dou

Translated from Chinese by Brendan O'Kane

Summer is high season for criminal offences, particularly at night. I'm not just referring to crimes of a sexual nature.

THAT SEXUAL ASSAULT IS more prevalent during the summer months, and especially on summer nights, is a fact in need of little explanation. Indeed, summer nights facilitate many other forms of crime, as may also go without saying.

Brawling, for example. On summer nights, when the heat lifts a little and a light breeze blows, when outdoor barbecue stands line both sides of the street and fill the air with the aroma of roasting meat, even people who have already eaten dinner will take the chance to slip away from their stifling homes and sit out on the benches by the barbecue stands, drinking beer and husking boiled peanuts or brined flatbeans, nibbling at skewers of roast chicken or slices of kidney or grilled fish, gossiping with friends, playing drinking games, growing louder and rowdier as the night wears on. The combination of strangers in close quarters, alcohol fanning the flames, and a conversational milieu consisting largely of idle chatter, boasts, and swagger is ripe for disagreements, for conflict, for violence, for incidents leading to injury or even grievous bodily harm.

Or robbery. It is considerably harder to rob someone's person in the winter, when layers of heavy clothing pile up so thickly that no sooner has one shoved the victim into a narrow alleyway or a grove of trees or a tight corner, than one has to rifle through a dozen pockets in different layers of clothes—tissues in this pocket, handkerchief in that one, nothing at all in that one over there—and there's no guarantee one will even find the money before a patrolman comes running. Much more straightforward in the summer, when people only have a couple of places to store things on their person and the pickings are easier by far.

Breaking and entering likewise. Doors and windows are shut tight in the wintertime but left quite agape in the summer. Many individuals who might be merely satisfying their own vulgar curiosity by peeking through other people's windows will find, after discovering the ease of egress and the convenient placement of mobile phones on tables and wallets in handbags, that one thing simply leads to another, a problem of morality becoming a problem for the courts.

Or homicide. Chinese people don't possess guns, or at any rate don't generally have access to them, so most murder weapons are improvised—clubs, hammers, axes, screwdrivers and whatnot. The padded jackets and insulated hats of winter wrap their wearers so thickly that an attacker using insufficient or improperly applied force will find that even with a perfectly timed attack, these improvised weapons will let them down almost every time. They may manage to tear a hole in the victim's cotton-stuffed vest or down jacket, or to knock the victim's cotton or leather or woollen cap out of shape, but the victim will remain physically unharmed, possibly reeling for an instant before understanding the situation. Whereupon most people will bolt like startled rabbits. But from time to time a victim made of tougher stuff will respond by rearing up like a horse and pouncing like a tiger, and then there's no telling who will end up killing whom. Summer homicides are a different matter altogether, and a malefactor of sufficient strength and accuracy will be able to effect the expiration of their victim with nothing more than a single well-placed blow.

Summer is beautiful, and summer nights more beautiful still, but in our city it was a deadly beauty.

THE ABOVE SHOULDN'T BE TAKEN to reflect the primary characteristics of summer nights in our city—merely a single aspect, incidental, a footnote to a greater whole. In principle, I believe, the overall mainstream big picture situation of our city at the macro level is hardly different from Paris or Warsaw, Pyongyang or London, Tokyo or Beijing, Baghdad or Port-au-Prince, Canberra or Kabul, Sarajevo or Caracas, Addis Ababa or Buenos Aires. Not that I've been to any of these cities—but insofar as issues of public security are concerned I am confident, going by common sense, deductive reasoning, and what I've seen in books and television, that the problem of increased crime during summer months is by no means limited to the city in which I live. That it is a general phenomenon by whose very commonness we may see that conflicts will arise anywhere people are gathered, and that promoting public morality and social progress is not as simple a matter as, say, acquiring a new production line for the manufacture of televisions or refrigerators or washing machines. Far from it. The road to a better world, as the poet said, is a long and winding one. My colleagues and I therefore composed a delicately couched, politely worded, mildly phrased letter along these lines to the highest-ranking municipal administrator—not to criticise or assign blame or complain or bellyache or grumble; merely an earnest, sincere, humble, written reminder that summer was nearly upon us and, with it, peak season for crimes, and that we hoped the highest-ranking municipal administrator and the relevant departments would find the time to note the passing of the seasons and make such preparations as might be needful.

We sent the letter in the middle of April, when the air was cool and crisp.

. . .

Every year summer comes to our city a few days earlier than the year before, owing supposedly to the greenhouse effect. Meteorological authorities had already said it would be another veritable scorcher: even our far-northern city would be running into temperatures of 25 degrees Celsius or higher by the start of May, and authorities couldn't—or wouldn't, or at least couldn't honestly—say how hot it would be come July and August. Indeed, by the beginning of the May Day holiday week anyone setting foot outside was instantly inspired to change into shorts and undershirts; meanwhile air conditioners, fans, window-screens, and cool bamboo sleeping mats sold out overnight. During those first few days of the May Day holiday, all of our city's media outlets—the 'three mouthpieces' of newspapers, radio, and television—began replacing front page and prime time coverage of tourism revenues with reports on a new regulation from the municipal Counter-Criminal Crackdown Command Office, stipulating that starting after the May Day holiday week, all public buses, motorcycles, bicycles, and other human-powered vehicles would be barred from city streets between the hours of 8pm and 5am.

There was a public outcry, in response to which 'CrackCom' issued a full explanation of the new regulation.

The explanation was faithfully transmitted by all news outlets. Through a barrage of interviews, special features, opinion pieces, letters from the editor, recorded lectures, public service announcements, televised exposés, and topical artistic performances, newspapers and radio and television stations informed the masses that while the new regulation would, most certainly, result in minor public inconvenience, any honest comparison against the major public inconvenience of rampant nocturnal criminality would conclude that the restrictions on the 'three categories of vehicles' were merely a small inconvenience. The brilliance of the new regulation, in other words, lay in using a minor inconvenience to the public to utterly eliminate the major inconvenience of criminal activity; in employing a minor curtailing of the public's ability to do its business in order to allow the authorities to discharge their duty of wiping out criminal elements; in engineering a beneficial trade-off between inconvenience and convenience.

The logic behind the regulation was straightforward. Having buses, motorcycles, and bicycles on the roads at night contributed to crime: some vehicles, such as buses, were sites of criminal activity; some, such as motorcycles and bicycles, were implements of crime; some, such again as motorcycles and bicycles, were targets of crime. There were pickpockets and hooligans on buses by day, but at night they ran rampant; likewise, there were daytime thefts of motorcycles and bicycles, and thieves who snatched at people's wallets, necklaces, and mobile phones from moving bicycles and motorcycles during the daytime, but under cover of night the snatching and thievery became downright brazen. If, during the dark hours from 8pm to 5am, these three categories of vehicle were barred from city streets, then the problems might be resolved, and the ability of criminal elements to commit crimes effectively restricted. Gesturing with his hands as he addressed the television cameras, a CrackCom spokesman said: 'Ladies and gentlemen, citizens of our fair city, we have every reason to expect a sharp drop in crime rates this summer.'

The residents of our city are understanding, law-abiding sorts—except for the criminals—and after an initial period of stunned silence the public came to appreciate the municipal government's concern, and took to the media to express its full support for CrackCom's new regulation. Public support or no, however, the new regulation undeniably gave rise to more than a few new problems—most obvious of which, and anticipated by CrackCom, was the massive inconvenience caused to the work and everyday life of people throughout the city.

The inconvenience to people who began or ended their work shifts at night may be imagined. Even for those who didn't, the inconvenience will be readily apparent. People couldn't just barricade themselves indoors talking or making love or watching TV or playing mahjong as soon as the sky began to darken. Many enjoyed taking evening strolls in the city's parks or commercial districts—but how, once outside, were these ordinary citizens to get there without buses or motorcycles or bicycles or other everyday means of transport? More troublesome still: if, at 8pm, a bus or a motorcycle or a bicycle or a cargo tricycle was out on the roads, it would be compelled to stop where it was by the sight of a police car zooming by on its rounds, or by the deafening blast of sirens that signalled the beginning of the curfew. This was no problem for people who were within sight of their homes—they could simply get off and walk, or gun the throttle a couple of times and slip in under the wire—but what about those left stranded between work and home? Unable to afford taxi fare, bus passengers would have to disembark and contemplate the long road ahead of them; riders of bicycles, motorcycles, and tricycles faced the additional question of what to do with their vehicles. The regulation banned even pushing a bicycle between the hours of 8pm and 5am, since any moving motorcycles, bicycles, or even tricycles would place patrolling officers in a position of having to ascertain whether the people pushing the vehicles were thieves or the vehicles' rightful owners.

And then there were secondary issues not to be overlooked. In one instance, the sudden blast of the curfew alert startled an old lady so severely as to affect her heart. Some drivers, lacking proper respect for CrackCom's new regulation, would gleefully follow the curfew alert by leaning on their horns, resulting in a blast of urban noise pollution in excess of the regulated three minutes. A young boy on a bicycle forgot what the 8pm alert was for and kept pedalling through the streets while other cyclists throughout the city stopped in their tracks—presenting a problem for the patrolling officer who caught him, since detention or fines would be inappropriate given the boy's status as a minor. An old scrap collector pedalling back to the little shack he rented was so startled by the alert that he overturned his cargo tricycle, scattering rubbish all over the roadway and bringing the remaining legitimate traffic to a halt for 15 minutes, infuriating the motorists on the scene. One woman chained her scooter to a sapling by the side of the street; upon returning to retrieve it in a car two hours later, she and her husband found that the scooter and the newly planted tree it had been chained to were both gone, leaving only a shallow pit.

Though by no means common, such problems could only lead to greater problems in the future if they continued to go unaddressed. After spending nights compiling a list of such cases, my colleagues and I wrote an urgent letter to the highest-ranking municipal administrator, which we passed to one of his secretaries through the secretary's wife in order to ensure prompt delivery. It was our hope that the highest-ranking municipal administrator would receive our report on recent conditions from his secretary the following morning.

(It should be noted that one of our number had attended university with the wife of one of the highest-ranking municipal administrator's secretaries, and had for some years been romantically involved with her.)

My colleagues and I weren't People's Congress delegates or People's Political Consultative Committee members, nor indeed were we employees of any governmental authority. We were writers of reportage, teachers of history, players of oboes, designers of computer software, extractors of teeth, translators of foreign languages, creators of advertisements, students of calculus, researchers of pharmaceutical compounds. We'd all gone to university and taken at least undergraduate degrees, and if forced to give an account of ourselves we would shyly admit to being intellectuals. Engaged in different lines of work, living in different neighbourhoods, of different ages and genders, we shared nonetheless a common concern for the development and growth of our city, and wrote regular letters to a succession of highest-ranking municipal administrators addressing the strengths and shortcomings of our city and the strengths and shortcomings of municipal policy in the hopes that our suggestions would aid them in the performance of their duties. Our efforts were motivated not by a desire for official recognition or pecuniary reward, but by a sense of righteousness and justice, of responsibility, of social morality, and of love for our fellow man.

Our little group had its roots in a happy coincidence some years before.

While other parts of our city had prospered, the west side was at the time still a desolate swathe of brick shacks, linked together by a few secondary roads, that stared out uncomfortably at the rest of the city. Any attempt to change the fortunes of the west-side slums was bound to be an uphill battle—but, we felt, a battle well worth fighting! Leaving aside more complex issues like housing and employment for the time being, we felt that the simpler issue of transportation could be readily addressed through public transit links between the west side and the rest of the city, and that the remaining problems might not seem so insoluble once this had been accomplished. In virtually every other part of the city, even the unimportant roads were immaculately paved, bordered by gleaming sidewalks lined with emerald trees stretching as far as the eye could see, punctuated at intervals by red and green lights merrily a-twinkle. But on the west side of the city, even arterial roads like Huashan Road or Qishan Road or Buyunshan Road were little better than the dirt roads of the wild Northwest: on clear days, they were covered in thick clouds of dust; on rainy days, water pooled waist-deep; and they were so pitted and rutted, rain or shine, that even any senior cadres driving over them would find their sedans being tossed to and fro like boats on a choppy sea. Not that senior cadres took these roads—their residences and offices weren't in the area. Even when municipal inspection teams visited our city from the Central Committee, and foreign guests and overseas compatriots came, saying that they wanted to see every nook and cranny of the city, nobody ever visited that part of town. But we felt that a lack of visits from officials and foreign friends shouldn't mean that the west side never got to see brighter days. A city is a single organism. Allowing one part of an organism to wither away while the rest of the organism develops might seem to have no effect in the short term—other than a possible saving in development expenditures—but if matters continued as they had been, the imbalance could potentially cause incalculable damage to the appearance, structure, and overall progress of the whole. Consider a family in which the majority of members never touch tobacco or strong drink, but one member becomes addicted to drugs. The addict's cash-flow and health problems may not initially affect the other members of the family, but as his money runs low and his health begins to fail, he becomes progressively likelier to drag all the others down with him. Seeing the condition of the west side of our city and its key roads in much the same light, we wrote down our observations in letters which we sent to the official then serving as the highest-ranking municipal administrator, humbly requesting that he consider the west side of town and its pitiful roads.

None of us had ever met any of the others at the time, I hasten to add. Each of us was perfectly unaware of the others' existence. We were making our proposals as individuals, and so naturally our letters went out separately.

The letters' common addressee was nonplussed, as you may imagine, to receive so many letters containing roughly the same content at more or less the same time. His bemusement gave way to nervousness and suspicion, and he turned the letters over to the Public Security Bureau. Someone who was with him at the time told us later that he had suspected us of being American spies or Russian special agents before deciding that we were working with a political rival, or were at the very least plants hired to stir up the waters and force him to resign. After analysing the letters, the Public Security Bureau agreed that the evidence suggested a conspiracy. The cover story—that a group of people from disparate backgrounds had written letters for purposes other than pleading their own cases, complaining about their own mistreatment, or making personal demands—was transparently flimsy, and yet the PSB had no idea what to make of letters from authors scattered all around the city—except for the west side, where none of them lived—on the subject of roads on the west side of the city that had nothing to do with them. The more the PSB analysed the letters, the more serious the situation grew: they raised the municipal security alert level and deployed officers on the west side of town, particularly around Huashan, Qishan, and Buyunshan Roads, while also employing every available method of detection to investigate the senders of the letters and conduct round-the-clock surveillance and tracking operations. Fortunately none of us had sent our letters anonymously, and fortunately we were all cleaner than a fresh sheet of paper and purer than water. The PSB realised soon enough that it had blown matters out of proportion, and reported to the highest-ranking municipal administrator that we posed no threat whatsoever. In its report, the PSB attributed the coincidence of our letters to the fact that we were a bunch of intellectuals who minded other people's business for fun instead of playing mahjong or going out with friends or getting massages or singing karaoke. Embarrassed at his own over-reaction, and perhaps eager to create an impression of being open to good advice, the highest-ranking municipal administrator actually did take our suggestions to heart. In addition to repairing Huashan, Qishan, and Buyunshan Roads, he drafted an urban rejuvenation plan for the west side of the city with the stirring slogan of 'One Small Step in One Year, One Medium Step in Two Years, and One Big Step in Three Years.'

His successors must have heard the story, because subsequent letters were not forwarded to the PSB, and the urban rejuvenation plan ultimately did make the transition from paper to reality. Like anywhere else in this changing city of ours, the west side today is full of bright lights and all the trappings of healthy prosperity, of families living together in peace and loving kindness in the high-rises that dot the area, and citizens co-existing in amicable fraternity on the streets outside. The public order and strong governance our city enjoys today is due in no small measure to the way the west side was reunited with the rest of the city. Despite improvements, crime rates are admittedly still higher than average—especially during summer, and most especially on summer nights—but this is merely a small bump in the road, the brief darkness before the dawn. I will extend the analogy I laid out earlier: the addict's family has successfully prevailed upon him to change his ways, and he finally understands the importance of just saying 'no'—but he can hardly be expected to quit cold turkey.

But of this, no more. I still have to say how my colleagues and I found one another.

During the PSB's distressing investigation of us, we'd had to submit evidence proving ignorance of one another, lack of organisational structure, freedom from external control, and absence of malicious intent. But there was an unexpected benefit—namely, discovering that there were others out there who shared our goals and our sensibilities. The woman who did computers and the man who did ads were the first to meet each other after the investigation wrapped up, and they promptly fell in love. Using the list of names the PSB had compiled, they contacted us one by one and brought the whole group together. From then on, acting as a loose collective of friends sharing a mutual concern for the public welfare, we resumed offering advice to the highest-ranking municipal administrators with renewed vigour and enthusiasm. We never received any response from the relevant departments, other than the investigation; nor did we come in for any praise or criticism. But we believed that many of our suggestions had been taken seriously by a succession of highest-ranking municipal administrators and the relevant departments, meaning that at least a tiny smidgen of the credit for the continued prosperity, rejuvenation, modernisation, and growing cultural sophistication of our city belonged to us—or rather, to our letters.

We wrote letters beyond counting in the years that followed, and countless numbers of people joined or left our loose collective as their interests changed or their passions shifted. Throughout all of this, whether our ranks were swollen or depleted, we continued not to form a civilian organisation or even to admit that we were an organisation of any description. We had no name, no program, no charter, no stated goal. Every letter we sent to the highest-ranking municipal administrators of our city was a personal letter: if it was written by one person, then one person would sign; if by three people, then three people would sign; if by seven, then seven would sign. If there were disagreements on an issue, but people felt that the issue needed to be aired, then we would each write our own letters, or one faction would write a letter expressing its views and another group would write its own letter. Our members exercised the strictest self-discipline: never once did anybody attempt to seek personal gain by means of their 'public service letters.'

NEVER BEFORE HAD WE SEEN such a rapid response!

Three days after we sent off our letter, CrackCom published a set of supplementary recommendations that rendered the new regulation instantly more humane. Firstly: the sudden three-minute siren at 8pm was to be replaced with three snippets of classical music, each one minute long, starting at 7:50pm. Specifically: at 7:50pm, there would be a minute of the Czerny études; at 7:54pm, a minute of the allegro from Chopin's 'Les Sylphides'; at 7:59pm another minute, this time of the famous Fate-knocking-at-the-door motif from Beethoven's Fifth. In this way citizens would be reminded and given advance warning before the curfew, and instead of harsh sirens, the alerts would promote high art in a clear case of killing two birds with one stone. Secondly: the city had recruited 10,000 migrant workers on short notice, and set them working around the clock to put up simple shelters anywhere around the city there was sufficient empty space. These were to be used by cyclists as 8pm drew near for the free storage of their motorcycles, bicycles, and cargo tricycles, to which end CrackCom and the Urban Law Enforcement Bureau had also hired, at no small expense, a crop of strapping young unemployed men—priority given to those with martial arts training—to act as night-watchmen for the bicycles. Finally: people who were caught on buses at 8:00, or who locked their motorcycles or bikes in a shed far from home or work, would be eligible for partial reimbursement of taxi fare. Anyone who could present a taxi receipt time-stamped after 8pm, marked with the starting point, destination, and circumstances of the cab ride, and stamped with the official seal of their work unit or the residential committee where they lived, would be eligible for reimbursement of two-thirds of the fare by CrackCom. At the discretion of representatives of the person's work unit or residential committee, two-thirds of the remaining one-third of the fare could also be reimbursed, with a full report of expenses incurred in the reimbursement thereof to be presented to CrackCom by the applicable work unit or residential committee at the end of the month.

Once the new recommendations were announced, what little public resentment there had been simply evaporated, and people went happily back to their everyday work and life routines with relatively minor changes. No less happily, my colleagues and I discussed writing a letter of thanks in the form of a poem expressing our gratitude at having city fathers and mothers who cared for us more deeply than our own parents had. The person drafting the letter likened the city leaders to 'father and mother' and 'dad and mum,' and cast us and our fellow citizens as 'children' and 'sons and daughters,' a rhetorical flourish that set our little group of thin-skinned intellectuals squabbling. The war of words ended with a decision to leave the phrasing in, even though it did betray a rather serf-like mentality, if only because the government leaders' solicitous concern for their citizens really did reflect nothing so much as parental love.

We mailed our encomium with a long sigh of contentment in the knowledge that at long last, our city's public security problems had been solved, and promptly split into separate groups to apply our minds—there were nine of us at this point—to other pressing issues that required our attention. Two of us conducted an investigation; three of us engaged in research; the other four sank into wild cogitation. But just as our three groups began drafting letters based on the fruits of our investigations, research, and cogitation, and as our three groups began to draft our three letters of advice, we found that the state of law enforcement in the city remained grim.

We knew, of course, that the size and scope of the problems facing municipal law enforcement meant that they might never be completely resolved. Naive—not to say childlike—we may have been, but we still lived in the same society as everybody else, and we knew enough to be sceptical of utopias and panaceas. Still, the negligible effect of the new CrackCom order on night-time crime rates came as a shock to us. Statistics showed a nearly vertical drop-off in crimes related to the 'three vehicles'—buses, motorbikes, and bicycles—but a nearly vertical increase in unrelated crimes, as if the miscreants who'd been committing vehicle-related crimes had suddenly all decided to move into new lines of criminality.

First among these was an upswing in brawls: at roadside kebab stands, in street-side parks, at night market stalls, outside the entrances of internet cafes—anywhere crowds of people gathered for fun, shoving would turn to arguments, would turn to shouting, would turn to cursing, would turn to bloodshed. Second was an increase in rape. Not all the women on the streets after 8pm were able to take cabs, or might not find it so easy to get that second two-thirds reimbursed, and a lack of transportation meant more women spending more time in dangerous areas, which meant more targets for sex offenders. Breaking and entering was up: without transportation, many people didn't get home from work until late in the evening, providing a window of opportunity for criminal elements to climb onto balconies, squeeze through windows, pry doors off the hinges, drill locks, and strip homes bare—in some cases arranging for moving trucks to haul away their takings. Following the promulgation of the CrackCom order, overall crime was down from the previous summer by one-fifth but brawls, rapes, and robberies had increased by one-fifth, three-fifths of a fifth, and five-tenths of a fifth, respectively.

THE NINE OF US RECONVENED: what to do? Social order was the most pressing issue of the day, and we devoted all of our free time to thought on this new front. This resulted in a new letter, and upon learning that our city's highest-ranking municipal administrator would attend a ribbon-cutting ceremony for a new bathhouse, we took collective, concealed, coordinated action. One of us darted forward, lightning-fast, delivering the letter directly and vanishing back into the crowd before the highest-ranking municipal administrator's three bodyguards and three secretaries could stop him. In addition to our usual report on on-the-ground conditions, this letter put forth several suggestions, including cancelling restrictions on the 'three vehicles,' removing the current ineffectual head of CrackCom and appointing a new CrackCom leader who might be more effective, and expanding the police force to guarantee no fewer than three patrolmen per square kilometre. We had twelve suggestions in all, several of them eminently practicable.

Not all of these were the product of unanimous agreement. The nine of us had originally planned to write separate letters, as usual, with different groups signing their names to letters representing their own viewpoints. The circumstances of this letter, however, seemed clearly to require an exception. Even if we got past the secretaries and bodyguards, we could hardly expect the highest-ranking municipal administrator to stand there next to the young female compère, holding his oversized pair of golden scissors, celebratory firecrackers going off on all sides, while we each submitted our own letter—and presenting a united front with a joint letter might underscore the importance of the letter and convince the highest-ranking municipal administrator to take it more seriously. And so, in an unprecedented turn of events, we composed a joint letter without unanimous agreement on its content. Our disagreements were on points of principle, naturally, rather than on fundamental issues. Democratically minded intellectuals that we were, we took pains to indicate at the end of the letter which signatories agreed with which suggestions.

THIS TIME WE SAW no immediate effect. Days passed, and CrackCom continued to implement the original regulation. The office's revised recommendations made the regulation more palatable to the general public, but did nothing to address the newly created problems of social order. Brawling, rape, and robbery continued to fill the nights with terror and besmirch the civility and social harmony of our city.

Our minds raced. We had never worried too much about the letters that we'd sent out before, since any misgivings we might have could be explained by the possibility that the highest-ranking municipal administrator had never received the letter. After all, he worked night and day with the pressures of a thousand weighty matters bearing down upon him; where would he find the time to read a letter from a group of nobodies? This time we knew to a moral certainty that he had received the letter himself—so why, when he had always responded to us through real-world policy changes in the past, was there now only silence? Some among us suggested that we write another letter, something more strongly worded than the last, but most of us were against this—indeed, one of us suggested worriedly that we not get ideas above our stations. After careful reflection, we decided unanimously that the highest-ranking municipal administrator had read our letter and chosen not to take any of our suggestions—possibly out of annoyance at us, and quite possibly out of annoyance at the way we had delivered the letter. We guessed, also, that the CrackCom director we had judged ineffectual might keep his position and could retaliate against us at any time—his background was something of an open secret, and his backers outranked those of the highest-ranking municipal administrator. And after all, we weren't as young as we had been. Our passions had cooled, our impulsiveness given way to rationality. Memories of our time as the focus of the municipal PSB's attentions elicited a twinge or two of retrospective terror. In the end, the people who had advocated writing another letter abandoned the idea owing to a lack of support and a shortage of new suggestions.

At the same time, of course, we reproached ourselves for our timidity and selfish hesitation. As patriotic intellectuals concerned for our country and our fellow citizens, we felt, we lacked the craft and courage of our literati forebears, who staked their lives on their words. For a while, our loosely knit collective threatened to fall apart in a storm of recriminations. Our manners may have been the only thing that kept us together—all of us were too embarrassed to make the first move to disband the group, secretly hoping it would happen through a gradual distancing and cooling, a shifting of the subject, a slow disassociation.

It was just at this time that CrackCom issued a new regulation, which the three mouthpieces of state media promptly broadcast at full volume, and at once we were back to our old selves again, like balloons re-inflating. Regardless of the content of the regulation, our letter had produced at least one visible effect: the new CrackCom regulation bore a new signature. We couldn't help but blame ourselves once again, this time for our lack of faith. As for the original director of CrackCom, there was a sense of concern that we might have ended his career with our focus on his shortcomings. Not until we heard that he had taken up a new position—a minor promotion, albeit to a post without many of the perks of his former job—did our sense of guilt lessen slightly. We debated whether or not to write another letter to the highest-ranking municipal administrator expressing our thanks in the form of a poem, but our new found caution convinced us not to write.

The new regulation was: in addition to strict enforcement of the previous regulation, all individuals engaged in outdoor activity between the hours of 8pm and 5am would be required to do so while squatting.

. . . To do so while squatting? How were people supposed to do everything squatting? *Why* were people supposed to do everything squatting? Wasn't the ability to rise from a squat to a stand the very trait that separated men from apes? The broad masses of the public didn't understand or accept the new regulation, and expressed their discontent through murmurs and grumbles and other means of silent protest. Being more incisive thinkers, however—I'm sorry, but we really are just a bit smarter than most—the nine of us instantly understood the reasoning behind the new requirement, which was precisely the same as that offered by the mass media.

First, the drawbacks. There are two major drawbacks to doing things while squatting: how much slower it renders all movement, and the numb legs and aching joints that result from protracted squatting. The negative aspects of squatting are familiar to everyone and will require no further description—unlike the positives, which merit further enumeration. The positive aspects of squatting are complementary to the negative aspects: slow movement, numb legs, and sore joints are objectively positive factors in preventing criminal elements from committing crimes. A group of drunks looking for a fight, for instance, will shortly ascertain that a persistent squatting position renders one unable to move with any physical strength. Even if armed with knives, they will find that the sudden motion of attacking meets with painful protest from their numbed, cramping legs, causing them to drop their knife hands reflexively to maintain balance, and nipping neatly in the bud what might have otherwise been a bloody incident. Imagine a rapist squat-rushing at a woman in short, mincing steps, backing her into a corner, and then—but how would sexual relations occur between two squatting people? Of course, the rapist could throw the woman to the ground and throw himself on top of her, but even ignoring the effects of protracted squatting on the human sex drive and sexual performance, how intimidating could a lowlife be, so close to the ground? Especially when the woman could resist by simply standing up—an option open to her, but not him, under the same legal principle permitting violence in the cause of legitimate self-defence? Even if he dared stand up, patrolmen would descend upon him for violating the regulation before circulation ever returned to his legs, and our would-be rapist would end up worse off than when he had started. Imagine a group of thieves planning to rob the empty home of a wealthy man. They have done reconnaissance, planned their escape route, prepared a car to transport their takings and a full set of pliers, screwdrivers, crowbars, scissors, and other implements of crime; they have waited for just the right moment, and now—but how are they to get up onto the balcony? How will they squeeze through the window? Their sole option will be to enter the building and attempt to pry the iron anti-theft door off its frame, a time-consuming and difficult proposition. Any ideas of climbing onto a balcony or squeezing through the window are doomed to failure: either of these would require them to stand up straight while outdoors, a move that would instantly mark them as thieves to any law-abiding citizen or police officer within the vicinity. Clearly, evil-doers of all varieties would find their ambitions thwarted, were squatting to be generally enforced.

It took only a week for the results of the new regulation to become clear in the form of a pronounced improvement in the state of public security in our city. Criminals of all kinds had simply scattered in all directions and vanished without a trace, like cockroaches after the light comes on. It appeared that squatting was a true panacea for crime. Some of the more arrogant criminals, lacking a full appreciation for the seriousness of squatting, continued in their wanton behaviour, but no sooner had they made their move—which is to say, before they had left the scene of the crime and in some cases before the crime had even been committed—than they were caught red-handed by patrolmen. Some would even manage to flee the scene, but the act of standing, even under cover of darkness, caused them to be noticed and promptly reported by law-abiding members of the public, and in the end all were caught up in the sweeping nets of justice. As you can imagine, all eyes will instantly lock onto a man who stands while everyone else is squatting, and he will be left with nowhere to hide.

But after our initial excitement had abated and we had reflected upon our individual experiences, we came to feel that there was a major flaw in the new squatting regulation. For the majority of the public that had no criminal designs, the matter of numb legs and sore joints was a minor one, and easily addressed with a bit of rest, a slap or two with the hands, some rubbing and stretching—but the slowness the squatting caused was an intolerable inconvenience. An example. When a girlfriend came to visit me at my home one night, the security guard at the gate of my residential compound refused to allow her cab to enter the development. Her only option was to disembark and enter the gate at the northwest corner of the compound, squat down, and proceed towards Building 23, where I lived. Building 23 was in the southeast corner of the compound. She had walked there from the northwest corner of the compound before. While large, the compound could be traversed in three to five minutes. But this time, she had to do it in a squat, simultaneously contending with high heels, a long dress, long hair that kept spilling down over her face, and a handbag that kept slipping off her shoulder no matter how she carried it, all of which contributed to her bursting into tears halfway across the compound. It was a full 20 minutes before she arrived inside the gateway of my building and was able to stand up straight again. I asked her why she hadn't called for me to go down and get her, and she replied, still sobbing: 'Wha-what g-good would th-that do when you d-don't have a c-car? You'd j-just be keeping me c-company . . .'

She referred to squat-walking as 'crawling.' She crawled over to my bed and started crying her heart out, and wouldn't let me wipe her tears away. We only got to spend the night together once every couple of weeks, and all she did that night was cry.

After compiling together many such reports, we wrote another letter to the highest-ranking municipal administrator to express our firm opposition to the squatting regulation. In heated tones, we said that preventing crime by forcing citizens to squat-walk was a modern variation on the fable of the man who swore off food for fear of choking, or of the policy that would kill 3,000 innocent men to prevent a single guilty man from escaping, and that continuing to enforce the regulation would hold back the development of our society and inhibit the growth of our city.

But when I say 'we' here, I am being imprecise: it still refers to our group of nine, but although we were by and large of the same mind, there was such disagreement over how to express our sentiments that only one or two of us were willing to co-sign letters. The majority of us opted to write our own letters, and three of us decided that although they supported our views, they would not write any more letters—that is, that they would leave our loose collective.

We knew they must have heard the news—all of us had, though we didn't say anything about it. A few days earlier, the highest-ranking municipal administrator had invited a famous singer to a banquet in our city. She complimented him on the progress our city had made, and joked that the sight of all the people squat-walking under the starry, moonlit night sky made her feel as if she were watching a colossal work of performance art. She called our highest-ranking municipal administrator one of the great postmodern artists of our time. Recognising a kindred spirit, the highest-ranking municipal administrator replied unhappily that he had worn himself out in the cause of promoting good and repressing evil, of protecting the land and securing the common people. But still there were people who, being given an inch and taking a mile, being given a bit of face and taking a whole nose, being insufferably given to picking nits and finding fault wherever they could, were in the habit of constantly writing negative letters. 'I envy you your stalkers,' the highest-ranking municipal administrator sighed to his guest. At least they understood love and loyalty. If only the people of his city could be more like them.

The news filled us with a sense of foreboding, but still—times were changing and society was progressing, and if the involvement of the PSB years before hadn't made us fall apart, then we could hardly allow a bit of back-alley gossip to scare us into silence now. On the other hand, since there was strength in numbers and we didn't want to be accused of attempting to sow discontent by sending separate letters, we stuffed the four letters that the remaining six of us had written into a single large envelope and sent them out as one communiqué. As we mailed the letters off, another two members of our group told us this would be their last letter to the highest-ranking municipal administrator.

Our sense of foreboding was basically correct. As I said, we are more incisive thinkers than most. Two weeks went by without any sign that the highest-ranking municipal administrator had considered our views—but on the other hand we didn't see any signs of a new investigation into us, either. There were only four of us left, and two were married to each other. Many evenings we gathered together in a high building that overlooked the streets, and gazed out to see, under the shimmering lights, parallel to the streams of vehicles, on the streets that stretched out as far as the eyes could see, the ever more familiar sight of crowds of men and women, young and old, shifting their weight from side to side and rocking backward and forward as they squat-walked to and fro. It was a funny sight, but we weren't laughing. We knew that if we needed to go out to work or visit friends or family, and we couldn't catch a ride with a friend or put together money for a cab, then we would join the freaks squat-walking outside. Even as we stood inside, looking out from the air-conditioned comfort of the apartment, we might already be among them. It was a chilling, gloomy realisation.

We wrote another letter, a joint missive signed by the four of us. We expressed our firm moral convictions by means of heated, even confrontational language—phrases like 'human dignity,' 'the difference between man and beast,' 'no different from mindless tortoises,' 'slowness equals death,' and 'adapting to numbness is a sign of a tacit acceptance of atrophy and regression.' We even wrote that 'an even surer way to protect the streets might be to keep the entire populace as house pets, or to declare martial law outright.' But after finishing, we looked at each other and decided we didn't have the courage to mail off anything so fiery. After a long silence, the wife in the husband and wife couple—our group's only female member, the bright young computing prodigy who had joined us all those years before—burst into tears.

'Why don't we just play mahjong?' she said. 'We've got the right number of people.'

AND SO WE BEGAN to enliven our otherwise dull night lives with our new found hobby of mahjong—no wonder so many people found it addictive. Hunting under the sofa for a dropped tile one evening, we found the letter that we had written but never sent out. After re-reading it, we all agreed that despite a certain elegance and moral force, it was undeniably a work of juvenilia—trite, ill-considered, focusing on details at the expense of the big picture.

As we played round after happy round of mahjong one evening, two of our old comrades—the two who had sent out the last letter with us—called to say they'd heard we were all together, and to ask if they could drop by. We'd missed them since their departure, we said, but it was already 10pm, and to get to where we were gathered there was a stretch of road that cabs were barred from, meaning they'd have to cover the distance in a squat. Our mahjong club usually got together before 8pm so that we could avoid squat-walking. Never mind that, they said. Just wait for us.

We assumed they wouldn't arrive before 11, but at 10:17 there they were—driving, each in his own car! They grinned wildly as they parked their cars beside our building so that they only had to squat-walk for ten or twenty metres before stepping inside and stretching their limbs to stand back up in front of us. They had become members of the driving classes, and night-time excursions no longer presented any inconvenience to them.

We were by no means poor, intellectuals that we were, but neither were we politicians or big shots. Though tempted to join the growing number of private car owners, we had decided to wait and learn to drive first, and to date this was as far as any of us had allowed ourselves to go. Partly this was out of a desire to wait until prices fell; partly it was because new expenses kept cropping up—new houses to replace old work-unit housing, private school tuition for children, savings to help parents enjoy a comfortable retirement—and none of us felt particularly wealthy. So how had these two become big spenders?

They sat down across from us and explained how they had come to buy the cars. Big spending didn't enter into it, they said: their new luxury cars had been practically free, thanks to special vouchers they'd been given by the director of CrackCom. This flummoxed us—what did cars have to do with CrackCom, and why would they have vouchers from CrackCom anyway?

They squirmed a little at the question.

'Maybe the letter?' one of them said.

The last letter we wrote to the highest-ranking municipal administrator? we said. But we wrote to him too, we said. How come we didn't get anything?

Their new car-owning self-assurance returned, and they began to look amused.

'You want to join the driving classes too, is that it?'

But before we could accuse them of having forgotten who their friends were, they leaned forward earnestly.

'After all the years we've known each other, after all we've done together,' said the one who was the lover of the highest-ranking municipal administrator's secretary's wife, 'what's ours is yours. We were just worried that you were going to say we'd sold out, or that we'd just driven over here to lord it over you. You know the saying about the bravest person in human history being the first man to eat a crab? That's us—we tried the bourgeois crab first so you wouldn't have to.'

As he spoke, he pulled out four vouchers authorising low-cost car purchases and slapped them down on the mahjong table, where we could see the red seal of CrackCom and the signature of the CrackCom director on each.

The secretary's wife's lover explained that a few days earlier he had received a call from the secretary asking him to come in for a chat. Naturally he found this unsettling, but the secretary's wife assured him that he had nothing to worry about—her husband knew they were old classmates, but had no clue that they were sleeping together. So he went and sat down with the husband of his lover, the secretary of the highest-ranking municipal administrator, in an office just across from the administrator's own. After a prodigious amount of small talk and conversation filler, the secretary finally brought up the topic of the squatting regulation.

'I understand that you intellectuals may have a hard time getting used to the regulation,' he said. 'The leaders don't have to squat, because they have cars; the big shots don't have to squat, because they have cars; the labouring classes mostly don't mind squatting because they've got strong knees and waists, but you intellectuals . . . CrackCom has made an internal decision to periodically offer batches of high-quality cars to select intellectuals at borderline suicidal discounts—so what do you say? If you're interested, I'll get the director of CrackCom to write you out a voucher right now.'

'Not interested,' our comrade nobly replied without giving the offer even a moment's thought. 'There are plenty of intellectuals out there like me, and if they have to squat, then I'll squat along with them.'

'You're a stand-up guy,' the secretary/husband laughed. 'No wonder my wife is always saying good things about you. How about this: there are five cars in the first batch. I'll get CrackCom to give them all to you, and if five's not enough then you can have the second and third batches too. How about that? Any problems with that arrangement?'

Our comrade immediately called the other comrade who had left our group with him, and they went to CrackCom to get their vouchers. Instead of startling us with the sudden news, the two decided that they would each take a car home first. After 8pm they took their new cars out for a long spin around the city. Then they called us.

The four of us rushed forward to shake their hands. Tears filled our eyes as emotion overwhelmed us.

Our sole female member broke the silence some moments later, her eyes sparkling as she stroked one of the vouchers with a fingertip.

'Even if he'—she meant the secretary/husband—'didn't mention the letter, it's obviously what all this is about. But'—she laid a hand gently on her husband's chest—'how on Earth could he have known that two of the six authors were married to each other? And that no matter how cheap the cars were, the married couple would only be able to afford one?'

She spoke seriously, but we all laughed, including her husband. Sometimes being a little naive, a little silly, a little dumb, just makes women more lovable. Even if they're former computer geniuses.

IN NO TIME AT ALL, we became members of the car-owning classes. The five of us would go out for drives together, enjoying our new status. When we got together in the evenings, we could drive wherever and whenever we wanted, without having to concern ourselves with being unable to take a cab down this street, or having to squat-walk down that street. So far as squat-walking was concerned, I had it better than the others: there were times when they couldn't avoid squat-walking—like when the two of us who had first received cars had come to visit: they'd still had to hunker down and squat-walk the ten or twenty metres from their cars to the doorway. It was a short distance, and it was inside the residential compound, but not squatting was still against the rules. I, on the other hand, had simply hired a chauffeur, since I'd never learned to drive. When I came or went, the chauffeur would drive to the front of my building. The burden of squat-walking to and from the parked car was his, and I never had to squat down again—one long stride would be sufficient to carry me from my building into the car, or from the car back into the building.

My comrades joked that I was acting like a leader or a big shot. They were right—leaders and big shots had chauffeurs and people to do the squatting for them, too.

'Never mind leaders and big shots,' our sole female member said. 'Why not just say he's acting like me?'

We laughed, after a moment of surprised silence. That was our former computer genius—an analytical thinker. She was right, I was like her. Her husband was her chauffeur, and any place or any time she didn't feel like it, she didn't have to squat down either.

Sparks

Carol Bensimon

Translated from Portuguese by Beth Fowler

All we did was take the BR-116, passing beneath bridges that showed slogans of cities we hadn't the slightest intention of visiting, or which told of Christ's return or counted down to the end of the world. We left behind the suburban streets whose beginnings are marked by the highway and which then disappear in an industrial estate or among the abandoned shacks along a stream where stray dogs crawl and rarely bark, and we carried on, on until the straight road turned a corner. I was driving. Julia had her feet on the dashboard. I could only look at her occasionally. When she didn't know the words to the song, she hummed instead. 'You've changed your hair,' I said, glancing at her fringe. Julia replied: 'About two years ago, Cora.' We laughed as we climbed into the hills. That was the start of our journey.

My car had been out of action for some time, under a silver waterproof cover, like a big secret you just can't hide or a child trying to disappear by putting her hands over her eyes, surrounded by junk in the garage at my mother's house. Initially, my mother was desperate to resolve the situation. It's a bad business leaving a car off the road for so long, she would say, although she understood very little about business and even less about getting rid of things. She lived in a house that already seemed too big when there were still three of us. When you opened certain wardrobes in that house, you could see the entire evolution of ladieswear from the mid-sixties onwards. Lovely jackets, pretty dresses that didn't fit my mother any more. I was direct about the car. I said: 'Maybe I'll come back.' I could sense her breath crossing the ocean and almost capsizing before returning to dry land. Perhaps it was a mistake to offer hope to a single mother, given that I wasn't even considering the possibility of moving home at that point. We never spoke about the car again.

Three years later, I was back and found the garage fuller than ever, so much so that I could barely see the terracotta floor tiles for the bags full of papers, the boxes of all sizes. There were balls of dust, an electric heater, a small bicycle, a minibar missing a leg. I got the impression I could have written WASH ME in the air with my index finger. I pushed open the wooden concertina doors and let in the light. I stood looking at the street for a while. It was no longer the same street, I mean, it was the same street, but in place of the houses belonging to my childhood friends—where were they now?—an apartment block had been built. It scared me to think that one person's aesthetic preferences could be summed up in that white, seventeen-floor mastodon, which stuck out on the block like a naked woman in an order of nuns, or a nun at the First Brazilian Meeting of Polyamorists.

Apart from that, there were other subtle changes to that section of the street. They did not date from the last three years, however, the three years I had spent away from Porto Alegre and that house, during which time I had rarely imagined my return and the exhausting list of comparisons that would almost certainly stem from it. For some reason, what I was trying to do was rebuild the street of my adolescence and my difficulty in achieving that made me think about those little books you get in Rome where, by superimposing two images, you can see something that was once grandiose where now there are only remains of columns, marble blocks or a sizeable area of grass.

Then I went back into the garage. I pulled the waterproof cover off the car. It was very clean. A strange, metallic blue body in the midst of all that dusty chaos. The battery, though, or whatever it was, had gone to pot.

Even though the car was unfit to drive right then, I adjusted the back of the seat and stayed sitting there. I very nearly put my hands on the wheel. But cars weren't my obsession. You ask me what model just went past and I'll never be able to say. It was their mobility that appealed to me, mobility as an end. And I was thinking how obscure that is when you are first presented with a car, how, at eighteen, with your driving licence in a flawless plastic sheath and that ridiculous photo with the haircut you'll regret later, all you want to do is cruise along open roads at dawn without ever getting anywhere. Or rather, your anywhere is an album to be heard in full, your anywhere is a river you watch as you smoke, with as many friends as you can fit in the back seat. The curious thing is that keeping these habits beyond their expiry date makes them seem, in the eyes of others, to be nothing more than a sign of eccentricity in someone who never knew how to grow up.

My mother entered the garage as I was reminiscing. In the rearview mirror, I saw her running her fingers over the dust-covered boxes, head bowed, giving the impression that she was reading what might be written there, as if until that moment she had ignored their contents or didn't even know why they were piled up in her garage. I got out of the car and waited for her to approach. She gave me one of her out-of-context smiles. 'Won't it start?' It was quite common for bad news to come out of my mother's mouth accompanied by a smile. Not out of spite, quite the opposite; there was some notion of compensation in it.

'I think it would have been a miracle if it had,' I said.

We agreed that it probably wasn't anything serious, nothing a mechanic couldn't sort with the turn of a spanner. We stayed standing there. I looked around me. Funny I couldn't remember that tiny bicycle. No one other than me had been a child in this house.

'Is Julia going with you?'

'Mmhm.'

'I thought you'd fallen out.'

It was a bicycle with stabilizers and there was a bell attached to the handlebar.

'I thought you weren't speaking any more. You had a fight once, didn't you?'

'Yes. But it's fine now.'

I asked what was in all those boxes. My mother raised her eyebrows and looked down. They were papers she had collected from the office. She opened a box, as if she needed to illustrate what she was saying. I saw part of a beige folder labelled INVOICES 2002. The box was probably full of them, right to the bottom. Only the years changed.

'Do you miss the office?'

She thought about it.

'I miss having an obligation to leave the house.'

I RANG JULIA FOUR DAYS later from a petrol station. The sky was blue, it was Saturday, the clouds glided until they scattered into pieces. I asked her to wait for me in front of the hotel. The attendant soon finished filling my tank and I left.

All great ideas seem like bad ones at some point.

Julia was staying in one of those little hotels in the centre. Not the kind that has decayed to the point of being considered elegant, but something a bit more functional, near the bus station, frequented by executives in suits that are too broad for their shoulders. There were half a dozen of those right at the entrance, laughing loudly as they milled about the red carpet, rather worn in the middle but new-looking at the edges. A cluster of fake palm trees, too, whose plastic leaves looked more rigid than Tupperware, gave a tropical welcome to those arriving by car at the main door. Julia was waiting for me next to one of the palms. She was wearing a denim jacket buttoned up to the neck and burgundy skinny jeans. She had radically changed her hair; it fell to her shoulders in a slight wave and a substantial fringe hung over her forehead, almost covering her eyebrows. Never in a million years would you guess that this girl had grown up in the depths of Rio Grande do Sul.

Julia was biting her cuticles. That hadn't changed. When she saw me, the tip of her finger was released from between her teeth, she nodded, grabbed her bag by the handle and walked towards me. I got out of the car. She was from Soledade, Capital of Precious Stones—all cities in the interior feel the need to proclaim themselves capital of something and naturally the reason for their singularity is a compulsory source of pride for their residents. So there was no one in Soledade who didn't see in an amethyst coaster or a rose-quartz obelisk the most beautiful, sensitive art.

I received a lengthy embrace and a 'Paris was good to you', a subject I thought best to hold at bay with a stock smile. A few metres away, a man wearing the baggy gaucho trousers known as *bombachas* was watching us with a certain sad interest.

For a few moments, I imagined what it would have been like if she had been there too, in the small apartment on the Rue du Faubourg du Temple, from which you heard a babble of Chinese voices going on about what may well have been their regular business, but which assumed a tense quality due to the fact that I couldn't make out any variety in their intonation. Julia would certainly have liked the grand boulevards, the gilt detailing on the facade of the opera house and a pastry in six perfect, shiny layers sitting in the window of a patisserie just as much as she would a metro station in urgent need of renovation or an argumentative beggar raising his finger to an old lady. She was an adaptable girl, who took the best from whatever she was presented with. Put her in any city in the world and, within three months, she'll be calling it home.

We carried Julia's bag to the back of the car and positioned it in the boot, at which point there was time to exchange a few banal questions and answers about how our lives were going. Paris is lovely, Montreal is freezing, the course is great. Then we got into the car. The previous day, I had bought a road map of Rio Grande do Sul. I hadn't taken a GPS with me because receiving any kind of instruction would go against the idea of the trip. I wanted a map on which we could circle the names of towns with a red pen, a map that starts tearing at the folds on long journeys. Julia looked at it with a faint smile and shut the door.

'Where are we off to first?'

I replied that we were going to Antônio Prado, up in the hills. Julia began to unfold the map.

'But you've never been there, right?'

'Neither of us has been there.'

My attempt to say something of consequence ended with the click of my seat belt, which only made it sound more ridiculous. To prevent any echo, I added, almost without breathing: 'And your parents?'

She laughed.

'Oh, they're quite furious. Hurt, actually.' Julia looked at the map, like someone flicking uninterestedly through a magazine in a white waiting room. 'But I don't care about that as much as I used to, you know? They went to live by the beach.'

'I know.'

'It's nice there, but there's nothing to—'

We were interrupted by three successive knocks on my window. I looked round and recognized the guy in *bombachas*. He was the only person left after all the initial hubbub, other than two employees in kepis, the kind chauffeurs wear, but which definitely seemed to suggest something else, perhaps two boys dressed up for a carnival dance at the Friends of Tramandaí Society. I lowered the window.

'Those boots you're wearing are for men,' he said, pointing into the car, his finger withdrawing and returning twice. From his expression, my boots seemed to have ruined his day.

Slightly shocked, I looked at my feet to check what I was actually wearing, and saw it was my Doc Martens, for which I had paid a small fortune in one of the brand's shops in Paris. Those boots were iconic in almost all counterculture movements, but it was too much to expect that such a symbolic connotation would penetrate the weary carcass of someone who, at best, had seen boots like this protecting the feet of the military police as they shot rubber bullets into the tents of the Landless Workers' Movement. That's the problem with fashion: you depend on others. If they don't get the message, all your efforts go down the drain.

I let out a short, resigned laugh.

'I hardly think you're a fashion expert.'

So I was sitting there confronting his prematurely wrinkled face, when I felt Julia place a hand on my leg and heard her say quietly that we should get out of there. A few minutes later we were leaving the city on the BR-116, a noisy grey line following the train tracks, cutting the suburbs down the middle, which, like any exit route from any big Brazilian city, makes apparent the country's determination to emulate the United States, although what becomes even more apparent is the failure of that mission.

I was still in shock over the incident with the man in *bombachas*, even though I had the strongest convictions about fashion and style, about gender and the rulebook of life. But reading *The Second Sex* or whatever doesn't make you immune to idiotic opinions. To be honest, the thing I found most discomfiting was not knowing exactly what Julia thought about it all. It's true that she had unleashed her anger once we moved off in the car ('I can't believe he knocked on the window just to give his opinion on your boots!'). It's true that she had made it clear I shouldn't pay any attention to the words of a stranger ('What an accent he had, my God!') and, on top of that, she thought very differently ('I love your boots'). But that effusiveness ended up producing the opposite effect: it increased my distrust.

Meanwhile, outside, the buildings by the edge of the road seemed as though they were being consumed by soot, broken down by a kind of urban erosion, in which two seconds were equivalent to hundreds of years. Some of them held advertising boards showing amateur models in rather grotesque positions, desperately striving to look attractive. If someone appears at one of those windows, I thought, I won't be able to help feeling a twinge of commiseration.

'You'll never guess what was going on in that hotel,' said Julia, and I was prepared to continue with the subject, whatever it was, until we recovered our Reserves of Intimacy, frozen some years earlier. 'No idea.'

'A meeting of chinchilla breeders.'

She started laughing like one of those people who chuckle alone as they walk, and you're never quite sure whether it's because they have earphones in (what could they be listening to that's so funny?).

'They were negotiating pelts with a *Serbian*. Actually, it was two Serbians, father and son. And the teenager was the expert.' Julia picked up my iPod. 'How do you plug this in?'

'With that cord there,' I pointed. 'But carry on, please.'

'It only gets better.'

'I can imagine.'

The un-nuanced joy of an indie band dribbled through the speakers like a viscous liquid. I thought: glad we kept the good tunes for when we're leaving the city limits. Then she continued her story about the chinchillas, which was particularly long and juicy. She had followed almost the entire transaction from a distance, leaning against the entrance to the convention room as the breeders took turns in front of the Serbians. They were carrying suitcases, which they opened on a large table, and they were overflowing with pelts, kind of like chinchillas in plan, chinchillas in 2D, get it? said Julia, to which I replied, yes, unfortunately I could picture it. 'So the boy picked up the pelts one by one and smacked them. Sometimes he blew. I think that was how he worked out whether it was a good or a bad pelt. Then each one was given a label with a value. They were separated into piles. So many dollars for this pile, so many dollars for the other, and in the midst of it all there was a red-haired interpreter, trying to make them understood, but occasionally someone would get carried away and bang on the table, and she seemed completely lost.'

I HAD BEEN UP into the hills many times, when I was a child and my parents still had a bit of energy. In those days, money came in without them having to make much of an effort and turned into articulated Ninja Turtle figures and five-star hotels. I never asked for a sibling. My father was an ENT doctor, an *otorrinolaringologista*, twenty-two letters long, five fewer than *inconstitucionalissimamente*, although he insisted his profession was the longest word in the Portuguese language.

'Cora, listen. *Inconstitucionalissimamente* is an adverb.'

'So?'

'So, it's not even in the dictionary.'

'But it exists.'

'It exists, yes, but it's a word whose only use is to be long, understand?'

I really liked having that conversation over and over again.

It was funny the way that my father's professional success gave me the false impression that otorhinolaryngology was booming during that period of my childhood, like pet shops and private security firms today. Not that the whole city was suffering from tonsillitis, sinusitis and tumours of the ear canal, but everyone who woke up one day coughing or half deaf seemed to have my father's number on their fridge door. Because of this, whenever someone mentions the difficult days of frozen savings, the dollar through the roof, all I can think about is how we had it easy in my house at the start of the nineties. This contributed to a curious feeling that I always lived my life upside down; the decline of the majority was my most prosperous period and, when things started to improve around me, I was already in free fall.

When I say the three of us went to the hills frequently, I'm of course talking about the resorts of Canela and Gramado. Few families attempt anything more than that. On those trips, my father was the guy who drove with his arm hanging outside the car, and my mother was the woman who thought that that posture wasn't correct or safe. My father was the guy who saw a stall and wanted to drink sugar cane juice and eat cake, and my mother was the woman who reminded him that my aunt and uncle were expecting us for lunch.

Julia and I stopped to eat at a place by the roadside. It was begging to be visited, a pastiche of German architecture, the front of which was overcrowded with flowerpots and garden gnomes and rugs made of squares of hide. We got out of the car and inhaled the fresh mountain air, as if we had spent the last six months in an airless cave. Two signposts fixed in the gravel ('Give us a try!') left no doubt that they also served lunch and snacks as well as offering cheese, salami, honey, phone cards and batteries to take away. I took a few steps forward and looked at the valley below us, speckled with wooden houses. Chimneys were smoking, dogs were barking, children were running around, a girl whose outstretched arms, open palms and short steps gave the impression that she was wearing a blindfold. Julia came up to me, dragging her feet over the gravel.

'Perhaps we should look for something outside the town. When we get to Antônio Prado,' I said.

'Like cabins?'

I nodded.

'I second that.'

Between the ages of eighteen and twenty-one, I think we must have planned the famous Unplanned Journey a hundred times. And when something like that is repeated so often, with minimal variations, it's natural that everything compacts into a single powerful memory, the setting for which is determined at random—it only needs to have happened once in the place in question—while its dramatic charge comes from the sum of all the nights that eventually led us to the idea of the journey, plus the number of years separating us from those nights. In my case, the memory is this: Julia and me lying on the rug in her spartan room on the third floor of the exclusive Maria Imaculada all-girls residence, where she lived the whole time she was at university. We're looking at the ceiling. To my left, there's a record player that Julia's family was thinking of throwing away, and the vinyl that's spinning once belonged to her brother and brought great delight to the small parties where her parents served Coca-Cola and a boy who was more devious than the rest adulterated his friends' plastic cups with palm cachaça. *Houses of the Holy*, Led Zeppelin's 1973 album, lived in between Pink Floyd and Metallica in a typical teenager's bedroom in Soledade, often smelling of the sweat of forgotten football shirts under the furniture. But then Julia's brother supposedly stopped listening to music after he got married.

The day we listened to *Houses of the Holy* lying on the floor, we got carried away again over the Unplanned Journey. There was an infinite number of uninteresting cities to be discovered, and that album seemed like fuel for our plans for freedom. But yet again, we didn't leave the room, we didn't run downstairs, we didn't reach the car before the spark went out. To tell the truth, we stayed staring at the ceiling, even though the volume and tone of our voices betrayed a good deal of excitement.

It was as if you'd spent months thinking about whether to dye your hair blue, and suddenly you realize that all that time spent deliberating, analysing, imagining, has ended up completely satisfying your desire to rebel. And so the trip was left for another time, a safe distance away from disappointment, after all, having blue hair was perhaps not such a great way to break from the status quo and uninteresting places were perhaps just uninteresting places, nothing more. I breathed deeply. It was mountain air, and we were there, five or six years late, but there, finally. We had survived a fight that was still hanging over us, Paris, Montreal, the madness of our families. That journey was another irresistible failure.

Exhalation

Ted Chiang

It has long been said that air (which others call argon) is the source of life. This is not in fact the case, and I engrave these words to describe how I came to understand the true source of life and, as a corollary, the means by which life will one day end.

For most of history, the proposition that we drew life from air was so obvious that there was no need to assert it. Every day we consume two lungs heavy with air; every day we remove the empty ones from our chest and replace them with full ones. If a person is careless and lets his air level run too low, he feels the heaviness of his limbs and the growing need for replenishment. It is exceedingly rare that a person is unable to get at least one replacement lung before his installed pair runs empty; on those unfortunate occasions where this has happened—when a person is trapped and unable to move, with no one nearby to assist him—he dies within seconds of his air running out.

But in the normal course of life, our need for air is far from our thoughts, and indeed many would say that satisfying that need is the least important part of going to the filling stations. For the filling stations are the primary venue for social conversation, the places from which we draw emotional sustenance as well as physical. We all keep spare sets of full lungs in our homes, but when one is alone, the act of opening one's chest and replacing one's lungs can seem little better than a chore. In the company of others, however, it becomes a communal activity, a shared pleasure.

If one is exceedingly busy, or feeling unsociable, one might simply pick up a pair of full lungs, install them, and leave one's emptied lungs on the other side of the room. If one has a few minutes to spare, it's simple courtesy to connect the empty lungs to an air dispenser and refill them for the next person. But by far the most common practice is to linger and enjoy the company of others, to discuss the news of the day with friends or acquaintances and, in passing, offer newly filled lungs to one's interlocutor. While this perhaps does not constitute air sharing in the strictest sense, there is camaraderie derived from the awareness that all our air comes from the same source, for the dispensers are but the exposed terminals of pipes extending from the reservoir of air deep underground, the great lung of the world, the source of all our nourishment.

Many lungs are returned to the same filling station the next day, but just as many circulate to other stations when people visit neighboring districts; the lungs are all identical in appearance, smooth cylinders of aluminum, so one cannot tell whether a given lung has always stayed close to home or whether it has traveled long distances. And just as lungs are passed between persons and districts, so are news and gossip. In this way one can receive news from remote districts, even those at the very edge of the world, without needing to leave home, although I myself enjoy traveling. I have journeyed all the way to the edge of the world, and seen the solid chromium wall that extends from the ground up into the infinite sky.

It was at one of the filling stations that I first heard the rumors that prompted my investigation and led to my eventual enlightenment. It began innocently enough, with a remark from our district's public crier. At noon of the first day of every year, it is traditional for the crier to recite a passage of verse, an ode composed long ago for this annual celebration, which takes exactly one hour to deliver. The crier mentioned that on his most recent performance, the turret clock struck the hour before he had finished, something that had never happened before.

Another person remarked that this was a coincidence, because he had just returned from a nearby district where the public crier had complained of the same incongruity.

No one gave the matter much thought beyond the simple acknowledgement that seemed warranted. It was only some days later, when there arrived word of a similar deviation between the crier and the clock of a third district, that the suggestion was made that these discrepancies might be evidence of a defect in the mechanism common to all the turret clocks, albeit a curious one to cause the clocks to run faster rather than slower. Horologists investigated the turret clocks in question, but on inspection they could discern no imperfection. In fact, when compared against the timepieces normally employed for such calibration purposes, the turret clocks were all found to have resumed keeping perfect time.

I myself found the question somewhat intriguing, but I was too focused on my own studies to devote much thought to other matters. I was and am a student of anatomy, and to provide context for my subsequent actions, I now offer a brief account of my relationship with the field.

Death is uncommon, fortunately, because we are durable and fatal mishaps are rare, but it makes difficult the study of anatomy, especially since many of the accidents serious enough to cause death leave the deceased's remains too damaged for study. If lungs are ruptured when full, the explosive force can tear a body asunder, ripping the titanium as easily as if it were tin. In the past, anatomists focused their attention on the limbs, which were the most likely to survive intact. During the very first anatomy lecture I attended a century ago, the lecturer showed us a severed arm, the casing removed to reveal the dense column of rods and pistons within. I can vividly recall the way, after he had connected its arterial hoses to a wall-mounted lung he kept in the laboratory, he was able to manipulate the actuating rods that protruded from the arm's ragged base, and in response the hand would open and close fitfully.

In the intervening years, our field has advanced to the point where anatomists are able to repair damaged limbs and, on occasion, attach a severed limb. At the same time we have become capable of studying the physiology of the living; I have given a version of that first lecture I saw, during which I opened the casing of my own arm and directed my students' attention to the rods that contracted and extended when I wiggled my fingers.

Despite these advances, the field of anatomy still had a great unsolved mystery at its core: the question of memory. While we knew a little about the structure of the brain, its physiology is notoriously hard to study because of the brain's extreme delicacy. It is typically the case in fatal accidents that, when the skull is breached, the brain erupts in a cloud of gold, leaving little besides shredded filament and leaf from which nothing useful could be discerned. For decades the prevailing theory of memory was that all of a person's experiences were engraved on sheets of gold foil; it was these sheets, torn apart by the force of the blast, that was the source of the tiny flakes found after accidents. Anatomists would collect the bits of gold leaf—so thin that light passes greenly through them—and spend years trying to reconstruct the original sheets, with the hope of eventually deciphering the symbols in which the deceased's recent experiences were inscribed.

I did not subscribe to this theory, known as the inscription hypothesis, for the simple reason that if all our experiences are in fact recorded, why is it that our memories are incomplete? Advocates of the inscription hypothesis offered an explanation for forgetfulness—suggesting that over time the foil sheets become misaligned from the stylus which reads the memories, until the oldest sheets shift out of contact with it altogether—but I never found it convincing. The appeal of the theory was easy for me to appreciate, though; I too had devoted many an hour to examining flakes of gold through a microscope, and can imagine how gratifying it would be to turn the fine adjustment knob and see legible symbols come into focus.

More than that, how wonderful would it be to decipher the very oldest of a deceased person's memories, ones that he himself had forgotten? None of us can remember much more than a hundred years in the past, and written records—accounts that we ourselves inscribed but have scant memory of doing so—extend only a few hundred years before that. How many years did we live before the beginning of written history? Where did we come from? It is the promise of finding the answers within our own brains that makes the inscription hypothesis so seductive.

I was a proponent of the competing school of thought, which held that our memories were stored in some medium in which the process of erasure was no more difficult than recording: perhaps in the rotation of gears, or the positions of a series of switches. This theory implied that everything we had forgotten was indeed lost, and our brains contained no histories older than those found in our libraries. One advantage of this theory was that it better explained why, when lungs are installed in those who have died from lack of air, the revived have no memories and are all but mindless: somehow the shock of death had reset all the gears or switches. The inscriptionists claimed the shock had merely misaligned the foil sheets, but no one was willing to kill a living person, even an imbecile, in order to resolve the debate. I had envisioned an experiment which might allow me to determine the truth conclusively, but it was a risky one, and deserved careful consideration before it was undertaken. I remained undecided for the longest time, until I heard more news about the clock anomaly.

Word arrived from a more distant district that its public crier had likewise observed the turret clock striking the hour before he had finished his new year's recital. What made this notable was that his district's clock employed a different mechanism, one in which the hours were marked by the flow of mercury into a bowl. Here the discrepancy could not be explained by a common mechanical fault. Most people suspected fraud, a practical joke perpetrated by mischief makers. I had a different suspicion, a darker one that I dared not voice, but it decided my course of action; I would proceed with my experiment.

The first tool I constructed was the simplest: in my laboratory I fixed four prisms on mounting brackets and carefully aligned them so that their apexes formed the corners of a rectangle. When arranged thus, a beam of light directed at one of the lower prisms was reflected up, then backward, then down, and then forward again in a quadrilateral loop. Accordingly, when I sat with my eyes at the level of the first prism, I obtained a clear view of the back of my own head. This solipsistic periscope formed the basis of all that was to come.

A similarly rectangular arrangement of actuating rods allowed a displacement of action to accompany the displacement of vision afforded by the prisms. The bank of actuating rods was much larger than the periscope, but still relatively straightforward in design; by contrast, what was attached to the end of these respective mechanisms was far more intricate. To the periscope I added a binocular microscope mounted on an armature capable of swiveling side to side or up and down. To the actuating rods I added an array of precision manipulators, although that description hardly does justice to those pinnacles of the mechanician's art. Combining the ingenuity of anatomists and the inspiration provided by the bodily structures they studied, the manipulators enabled their operator to accomplish any task he might normally perform with his own hands, but on a much smaller scale.

Assembling all of this equipment took months, but I could not afford to be anything less than meticulous. Once the preparations were complete, I was able to place each of my hands on a nest of knobs and levers and control a pair of manipulators situated behind my head, and use the periscope to see what they worked on. I would then be able to dissect my own brain.

The very idea must sound like pure madness, I know, and had I told any of my colleagues, they would surely have tried to stop me. But I could not ask anyone else to risk themselves for the sake of anatomical inquiry, and because I wished to conduct the dissection myself, I would not be satisfied by merely being the passive subject of such an operation. Auto-dissection was the only option.

I brought in a dozen full lungs and connected them with a manifold. I mounted this assembly beneath the worktable that I would sit at, and positioned a dispenser to connect directly to the bronchial inlets within my chest. This would supply me with six days' worth of air. To provide for the possibility that I might not have completed my experiment within that period, I had scheduled a visit from a colleague at the end of that time. My presumption, however, was that the only way I would not have finished the operation in that period would be if I had caused my own death.

I began by removing the deeply curved plate that formed the back and top of my head; then the two, more shallowly curved plates that formed the sides. Only my faceplate remained, but it was locked into a restraining bracket, and I could not see its inner surface from the vantage point of my periscope; what I saw exposed was my own brain. It consisted of a dozen or more subassemblies, whose exteriors were covered by intricately molded shells; by positioning the periscope near the fissures that separated them, I gained a tantalizing glimpse at the fabulous mechanisms within their interiors. Even with what little I could see, I could tell it was the most beautifully complex engine I had ever beheld, so far beyond any device man had constructed that it was incontrovertibly of divine origin. The sight was both exhilarating and dizzying, and I savored it on a strictly aesthetic basis for several minutes before proceeding with my explorations.

It was generally hypothesized that the brain was divided into an engine located in the center of the head which performed the actual cognition, surrounded by an array of components in which memories were stored. What I observed was consistent with this theory, since the peripheral subassemblies seemed to resemble one another, while the subassembly in the center appeared to be different, more heterogenous and with more moving parts. However the components were packed too closely for me to see much of their operation; if I intended to learn anything more, I would require a more intimate vantage point.

Each subassembly had a local reservoir of air, fed by a hose extending from the regulator at the base of my brain. I focused my periscope on the rearmost subassembly and, using the remote manipulators, I quickly disconnected the outlet hose and installed a longer one in its place. I had practiced this maneuver countless times so that I could perform it in a matter of moments; even so, I was not certain I could complete the connection before the subassembly had depleted its local reservoir. Only after I was satisfied that the component's operation had not been interrupted did I continue; I rearranged the longer hose to gain a better view of what lay in the fissure behind it: other hoses that connected it to its neighboring components. Using the most slender pair of manipulators to reach into the narrow crevice, I replaced the hoses one by one with longer substitutes. Eventually, I had worked my way around the entire subassembly and replaced every connection it had to the rest of my brain. I was now able to unmount this subassembly from the frame that supported it, and pull the entire section outside of what was once the back of my head.

I knew it was possible I had impaired my capacity to think and was unable to recognize it, but performing some basic arithmetic tests suggested that I was uninjured. With one subassembly hanging from a scaffold above, I now had a better view of the cognition engine at the center of my brain, but there was not enough room to bring the microscope attachment itself in for a close inspection. In order for me to really examine the workings of my brain, I would have to displace at least half a dozen subassemblies.

Laboriously, painstakingly, I repeated the procedure of substituting hoses for other subassemblies, repositioning another one farther back, two more higher up, and two others out to the sides, suspending all six from the scaffold above my head. When I was done, my brain looked like an explosion frozen an infinitesimal fraction of a second after the detonation, and again I felt dizzy when I thought about it. But at last the cognition engine itself was exposed, supported on a pillar of hoses and actuating rods leading down into my torso. I now also had room to rotate my microscope around a full three hundred and sixty degrees, and pass my gaze across the inner faces of the subassemblies I had moved. What I saw was a microcosm of auric machinery, a landscape of tiny spinning rotors and miniature reciprocating cylinders.

As I contemplated this vista, I wondered, where was my body? The conduits which displaced my vision and action around the room were in principle no different from those which connected my original eyes and hands to my brain. For the duration of this experiment, were these manipulators not essentially my hands? Were the magnifying lenses at the end of my periscope not essentially my eyes? I was an everted person, with my tiny, fragmented body situated at the center of my own distended brain. It was in this unlikely configuration that I began to explore myself.

I turned my microscope to one of the memory subassemblies, and began examining its design. I had no expectation that I would be able to decipher my memories, only that I might divine the means by which they were recorded. As I had predicted, there were no reams of foil pages visible, but to my surprise neither did I see banks of gearwheels or switches. Instead, the subassembly seemed to consist almost entirely of a bank of air tubules. Through the interstices between the tubules I was able to glimpse ripples passing through the bank's interior.

With careful inspection and increasing magnification, I discerned that the tubules ramified into tiny air capillaries, which were interwoven with a dense latticework of wires on which gold leaves were hinged. Under the influence of air escaping from the capillaries, the leaves were held in a variety of positions. These were not switches in the conventional sense, for they did not retain their position without a current of air to support them, but I hypothesized that these were the switches I had sought, the medium in which my memories were recorded. The ripples I saw must have been acts of recall, as an arrangement of leaves was read and sent back to the cognition engine.

Armed with this new understanding, I then turned my microscope to the cognition engine. Here too I observed a latticework of wires, but they did not bear leaves suspended in position; instead the leaves flipped back and forth almost too rapidly to see. Indeed, almost the entire engine appeared to be in motion, consisting more of lattice than of air capillaries, and I wondered how air could reach all the gold leaves in a coherent manner. For many hours I scrutinized the leaves, until I realized that they themselves were playing the role of capillaries; the leaves formed temporary conduits and valves that existed just long enough to redirect air at other leaves in turn, and then disappeared as a result. This was an engine undergoing continuous transformation, indeed modifying itself as part of its operation. The lattice was not so much a machine as it was a page on which the machine was written, and on which the machine itself ceaselessly wrote.

My consciousness could be said to be encoded in the position of these tiny leaves, but it would be more accurate to say that it was encoded in the ever-shifting pattern of air driving these leaves. Watching the oscillations of these flakes of gold, I saw that air does not, as we had always assumed, simply provide power to the engine that realizes our thoughts. Air is in fact the very medium of our thoughts. All that we are is a pattern of air flow. My memories were inscribed, not as grooves on foil or even the position of switches, but as persistent currents of argon.

In the moments after I grasped the nature of this lattice mechanism, a cascade of insights penetrated my consciousness in rapid succession. The first and most trivial was understanding why gold, the most malleable and ductile of metals, was the only material out of which our brains could be made. Only the thinnest of foil leaves could move rapidly enough for such a mechanism, and only the most delicate of filaments could act as hinges for them. By comparison, the copper burr raised by my stylus as I engrave these words and brushed from the sheet when I finish each page is as coarse and heavy as scrap. This truly was a medium where erasing and recording could be performed rapidly, far more so than any arrangement of switches or gears.

What next became clear was why installing full lungs into a person who has died from lack of air does not bring him back to life. These leaves within the lattice remain balanced between continuous cushions of air. This arrangement lets them flit back and forth swiftly, but it also means that if the flow of air ever ceases, everything is lost; the leaves all collapse into identical pendent states, erasing the patterns and the consciousness they represent. Restoring the air supply cannot recreate what has evanesced. This was the price of speed; a more stable medium for storing patterns would mean that our consciousnesses would operate far more slowly.

It was then that I perceived the solution to the clock anomaly. I saw that the speed of these leaves' movements depended on their being supported by air; with sufficient air flow, the leaves could move nearly frictionlessly. If they were moving more slowly, it was because they were being subjected to more friction, which could occur only if the cushions of air that supported them were thinner, and the air flowing through the lattice was moving with less force.

It is not that the turret clocks are running faster. What is happening is that our brains are running slower. The turret clocks are driven by pendulums, whose tempo never varies, or by the flow of mercury through a pipe, which does not change. But our brains rely on the passage of air, and when that air flows more slowly, our thoughts slow down, making the clocks seem to us to run faster.

I had feared that our brains might be growing slower, and it was this prospect that had spurred me to pursue my auto-dissection. But I had assumed that our cognition engines—while powered by air—were ultimately mechanical in nature, and some aspect of the mechanism was gradually becoming deformed through fatigue, and thus responsible for the slowing. That would have been dire, but there was at least the hope that we might be able to repair the mechanism, and restore our brains to their original speed of operation.

But if our thoughts were purely patterns of air rather than the movement of toothed gears, the problem was much more serious, for what could cause the air flowing through every person's brain to move less rapidly? It could not be a decrease in the pressure from our filling stations' dispensers; the air pressure in our lungs is so high that it must be stepped down by a series of regulators before reaching our brains. The diminution in force, I saw, must arise from the opposite direction: the pressure of our surrounding atmosphere was increasing.

How could this be? As soon as the question formed, the only possible answer became apparent: our sky must not be infinite in height. Somewhere above the limits of our vision, the chromium walls surrounding our world must curve inward to form a dome; our universe is a sealed chamber rather than an open well. And air is gradually accumulating within that chamber, until it equals the pressure in the reservoir below.

This is why, at the beginning of this engraving, I said that air is not the source of life. Air can neither be created nor destroyed; the total amount of air in the universe remains constant, and if air were all that we needed to live, we would never die. But in truth the source of life is *a difference in air pressure*, the flow of air from spaces where it is thick to those where it is thin. The activity of our brains, the motion of our bodies, the action of every machine we have ever built is driven by the movement of air, the force exerted as differing pressures seek to balance each other out. When the pressure everywhere in the universe is the same, all air will be motionless, and useless; one day we will be surrounded by motionless air and unable to derive any benefit from it.

We are not really consuming air at all. The amount of air that I draw from each day's new pair of lungs is exactly as much as seeps out through the joints of my limbs and the seams of my casing, exactly as much as I am adding to the atmosphere around me; all I am doing is converting air at high pressure to air at low. With every movement of my body, I contribute to the equalization of pressure in our universe. With every thought that I have, I hasten the arrival of that fatal equilibrium.

Had I come to this realization under any other circumstance, I would have leapt up from my chair and ran into the streets, but in my current situation—body locked in a restraining bracket, brain suspended across my laboratory—doing so was impossible. I could see the leaves of my brain flitting faster from the tumult of my thoughts, which in turn increased my agitation at being so restrained and immobile. Panic at that moment might have led to my death, a nightmarish paroxysm of simultaneously being trapped and spiraling out of control, struggling against my restraints until my air ran out. It was by chance as much as by intention that my hands adjusted the controls to avert my periscopic gaze from the latticework, so all I could see was the plain surface of my worktable. Thus freed from having to see and magnify my own apprehensions, I was able to calm down. When I had regained sufficient composure, I began the lengthy process of reassembling myself. Eventually I restored my brain to its original compact configuration, reattached the plates of my head, and released myself from the restraining bracket.

At first the other anatomists did not believe me when I told them what I had discovered, but in the months that followed my initial auto-dissection, more and more of them became convinced. More examinations of people's brains were performed, more measurements of atmospheric pressure were taken, and the results were all found to confirm my claims. The background air pressure of our universe was indeed increasing, and slowing our thoughts as a result.

There was widespread panic in the days after the truth first became widely known, as people contemplated for the first time the idea that death was inevitable. Many called for the strict curtailment of activities in order to minimize the thickening of our atmosphere; accusations of wasted air escalated into furious brawls and, in some districts, deaths. It was the shame of having caused these deaths, together with the reminder that it would be many centuries yet before our atmosphere's pressure became equal to that of the reservoir underground, that caused the panic to subside. We are not sure precisely how many centuries it will take; additional measurements and calculations are being performed and debated. In the meantime, there is much discussion over how we should spend the time that remains to us.

One sect has dedicated itself to the goal of reversing the equalization of pressure, and found many adherents. The mechanicians among them constructed an engine that takes air from our atmosphere and forces it into a smaller volume, a process they called "compression." Their engine restores air to the pressure it originally had in the reservoir, and these Reversalists excitedly announced that it would form the basis of a new kind of filling station, one that would—with each lung it refilled—revitalize not only individuals but the universe itself. Alas, closer examination of the engine revealed its fatal flaw. The engine itself is powered by air from the reservoir, and for every lungful of air that it produces, the engine consumes not just a lungful, but slightly more. It does not reverse the process of equalization, but like everything else in the world, exacerbates it.

Although some of their adherents left in disillusionment after this setback, the Reversalists as a group were undeterred, and began drawing up alternate designs in which the compressor was powered instead by the uncoiling of springs or the descent of weights. These mechanisms fared no better. Every spring that is wound tight represents air released by the person who did the winding; every weight that rests higher than ground level represents air released by the person who did the lifting. There is no source of power in the universe that does not ultimately derive from a difference in air pressure, and there can be no engine whose operation will not, on balance, reduce that difference.

The Reversalists continue their labors, confident that they will one day construct an engine that generates more compression than it uses, a perpetual power source that will restore to the universe its lost vigor. I do not share their optimism; I believe that the process of equalization is inexorable. Eventually, all the air in our universe will be evenly distributed, no denser or more rarefied in one spot than in any other, unable to drive a piston, turn a rotor, or flip a leaf of gold foil. It will be the end of pressure, the end of motive power, the end of thought. The universe will have reached perfect equilibrium.

Some find irony in the fact that a study of our brains revealed to us not the secrets of the past, but what ultimately awaits us in the future. However, I maintain that we have indeed learned something important about the past. The universe began as an enormous breath being held. Who knows why, but whatever the reason, I am glad that it did, because I owe my existence to that fact. All my desires and ruminations are no more and no less than eddy currents generated by the gradual exhalation of our universe. And until this great exhalation is finished, my thoughts live on.

So that our thoughts may continue as long as possible, anatomists and mechanicians are designing replacements for our cerebral regulators, capable of gradually increasing the air pressure within our brains and keeping it just higher than the surrounding atmospheric pressure. Once these are installed, our thoughts will continue at roughly the same speed even as the air thickens around us. But this does not mean that life will continue unchanged. Eventually the pressure differential will fall to such a level that our limbs will weaken and our movements will grow sluggish. We may then try to slow our thoughts so that our physical torpor is less conspicuous to us, but that will also cause external processes to appear to accelerate. The ticking of clocks will rise to a chatter as their pendulums wave frantically; falling objects will slam to the ground as if propelled by springs; undulations will race down cables like the crack of a whip.

At some point our limbs will cease moving altogether. I cannot be certain of the precise sequence of events near the end, but I imagine a scenario in which our thoughts will continue to operate, so that we remain conscious but frozen, immobile as statues. Perhaps we'll be able to speak for a while longer, because our voice boxes operate on a smaller pressure differential than our limbs, but without the ability to visit a filling station, every utterance will reduce the amount of air left for thought, and bring us closer to the moment that our thoughts cease altogether. Will it be preferable to remain mute to prolong our ability to think, or to talk until the very end? I don't know.

Perhaps a few of us, in the days before we cease moving, will be able to connect our cerebral regulators directly to the dispensers in the filling stations, in effect replacing our lungs with the mighty lung of the world. If so, those few will be able to remain conscious right up to the final moments before all pressure is equalized. The last bit of air pressure left in our universe will be expended driving a person's conscious thought.

And then, our universe will be in a state of absolute equilibrium. All life and thought will cease, and with them, time itself.

But I maintain a slender hope.

Even though our universe is enclosed, perhaps it is not the only air chamber in the infinite expanse of solid chromium. I speculate that there could be another pocket of air elsewhere, another universe besides our own that is even larger in volume. It is possible that this hypothetical universe has the same or higher air pressure as ours, but suppose that it had a much lower air pressure than ours, perhaps even a true vacuum?

The chromium that separates us from this supposed universe is too thick and too hard for us to drill through, so there is no way we could reach it ourselves, no way to bleed off the excess atmosphere from our universe and regain motive power that way. But I fantasize that this neighboring universe has its own inhabitants, ones with capabilities beyond our own. What if they were able to create a conduit between the two universes, and install valves to release air from ours? They might use our universe as a reservoir, running dispensers with which they could fill their own lungs, and use our air as a way to drive their own civilization.

It cheers me to imagine that the air that once powered me could power others, to believe that the breath that enables me to engrave these words could one day flow through someone else's body. I do not delude myself into thinking that this would be a way for me to live again, because I am not that air, I am the pattern that it assumed, temporarily. The pattern that is me, the patterns that are the entire world in which I live, would be gone.

But I have an even fainter hope: that those inhabitants not only use our universe as a reservoir, but that once they have emptied it of its air, they might one day be able to open a passage and actually enter our universe as explorers. They might wander our streets, see our frozen bodies, look through our possessions, and wonder about the lives we led.

Which is why I have written this account. You, I hope, are one of those explorers. You, I hope, found these sheets of copper and deciphered the words engraved on their surfaces. And whether or not your brain is impelled by the air that once impelled mine, through the act of reading my words, the patterns that form your thoughts become an imitation of the patterns that once formed mine. And in that way I live again, through you.

Your fellow explorers will have found and read the other books that we left behind, and through the collaborative action of your imaginations, my entire civilization lives again. As you walk through our silent districts, imagine them as they were; with the turret clocks striking the hours, the filling stations crowded with gossiping neighbors, criers reciting verse in the public squares and anatomists giving lectures in the classrooms. Visualize all of these the next time you look at the frozen world around you, and it will become, in your minds, animated and vital again.

I wish you well, explorer, but I wonder: does the same fate that befell me await you? I can only imagine that it must, that the tendency toward equilibrium is not a trait peculiar to our universe but inherent in all universes. Perhaps that is just a limitation of my thinking, and your people have discovered a source of pressure that is truly eternal. But my speculations are fanciful enough already. I will assume that one day your thoughts too will cease, although I cannot fathom how far in the future that might be. Your lives will end just as ours did, just as everyone's must. No matter how long it takes, eventually equilibrium will be reached.

I hope you are not saddened by that awareness. I hope that your expedition was more than a search for other universes to use as reservoirs. I hope that you were motivated by a desire for knowledge, a yearning to see what can arise from a universe's exhalation. Because even if a universe's lifespan is calculable, the variety of life that is generated within it is not. The buildings we have erected, the art and music and verse we have composed, the very lives we've led: none of them could have been predicted, because none of them were inevitable. Our universe might have slid into equilibrium emitting nothing more than a quiet hiss. The fact that it spawned such plenitude is a miracle, one that is matched only by your universe giving rise to you.

Though I am long dead as you read this, explorer, I offer to you a valediction. Contemplate the marvel that is existence, and rejoice that you are able to do so. I feel I have the right to tell you this because, as I am inscribing these words, I am doing the same.

The Ugliest Woman in the World

Olga Tokarczuk

Translated from Polish by Antonia Lloyd-Jones

He married the ugliest woman in the world. As a known circus impresario, he made a special trip to Vienna to see her. It wasn't a premeditated act at all—it never occurred to him beforehand that he might make her his wife. But once he had seen her, once he had weathered the first shock of astonishment, he couldn't tear his eyes away from her. She had a large head covered in growths and lumps. Her small, ever running eyes were set close under her low, furrowed brow. From a distance they looked like narrow chinks. Her nose looked as if it were broken in many places, and its tip was a livid blue, covered in sparse bristles. Her mouth was huge and swollen, always hanging open, always wet, with some sharply pointed teeth inside it. To cap it all, as if that were not enough, her face sprouted long, straggling, silken hairs.

The first time he saw her she had emerged from behind the cardboard scenery of a traveling circus to show herself to the audience. A cry of surprise and disgust went rolling over the heads of the crowd and fell at her feet. She may have been smiling, but it looked like a woeful grimace. She stood very still, conscious of the fact that dozens of eyes were staring at her, avidly drinking in every detail, in order to describe that face to their friends and neighbors later on, or to their own children, to be able to summon it up again, as they compared it with their own faces in the mirror—and then breathe a sigh of relief. She stood patiently, perhaps with a sense of superiority, as she gazed over their heads towards the roofs of the houses beyond.

After a lengthy silence, swollen with astonishment, someone finally shouted: "Tell us about yourself!"

She peered into the crowd, to the spot where the voice had come from. She was searching for the person who had said it, but just then a stout lady compère ran out from behind the cardboard wings and answered for the Ugliest Woman in the World: "She doesn't talk."

"Then you tell us her story," the voice repeated its request, so the compère cleared her throat and started speaking.

AFTERWARDS, as he drank a cup of tea with her by the little tin stove that heated the inside of the circus caravan, he found her to be not at all stupid. Of course she could speak, and with perfect sense too. The whole time he observed her closely, wrestling with his own fascination with this freak of nature. She could see right through him.

"You thought my speech would be just as bizarre and repulsive as my face, didn't you?" she said.

He didn't answer.

She drank her tea in the Russian manner, pouring it from a samovar into small cups with no handles, and nibbled at a sugar lump between each sip.

He quite soon noticed that she spoke many languages, but apparently none of them well. Now and then she shifted from one language into another. It was no cause for surprise—since early childhood she had grown up in the circus, in an international troupe full of grotesques of every possible shade of skin, never in the same place twice.

"I know what you're thinking," she said again, looking at him with those puffy little animal eyes. After a short silence she added: "Anyone who hasn't got a mother has no mother tongue either. I use many languages, but none of them is my own."

He didn't dare reply. Suddenly she had begun to get on his nerves, though he wasn't sure why. She was making witty remarks, she was coherent and specific—not what he'd been expecting.

So he bid her farewell, and to his astonishment she gave him her hand with a very feminine gesture. The gesture of a lady, and a perfectly pretty hand it was, too. He bowed down towards it, but didn't even touch it with his lips.

As he lay on his back in the hotel bed he was still thinking about her. He stared ahead into the damp, stuffy hotel darkness, the sort of deep void that gave fire to his imagination. He lay there wondering what it must be like to be her, what it felt like from inside, how the world might look through eyes like a pig's eyes, what it must be like to breathe in air through such a misshapen nose—would it be aware of the same smells? And what would it be like to touch yourself every day while washing, or scratching, while doing all the usual little things?

Never once did he feel sorry for her. If he had sympathized with her, he never would have thought of making her his wife.

Some people used to tell this story afterwards as the tale of an unhappy love affair, saying that his heart gazed into hers and that he fell in love with the sweet-natured angel inside her, in spite of her repulsive face. Nothing of the kind—that first night after meeting her he simply imagined what it would be like to make love to such a creature, to kiss her and undress her.

He hovered around the circus for the next few weeks. He would leave, and come back again. He gained the trust of the manager, and negotiated a contract for them in Brno, where he went with them and where the circus people regarded him as one of their own. They let him sell the tickets, then later he took over from the fat lady compère—and it has to be said he did it well, warming up the audience before the shoddily painted curtain was raised.

"Close your eyes," he cried. "Especially the women and children, because the ugliness of this creature is hard for sensitive eyes to bear. No one who has seen this freak of nature is ever able to fall asleep in peace again, but keeps waking up with a shock. Some people have even lost their faith in the Creator . . ."

At this point he hung his head, and the sentence seemed to be incomplete, though in fact it wasn't—he didn't know what else to say. He reckoned the very word "Creator" put everything in its proper light. But what he actually thought was that the Creator, in whom some people were supposed to lose their faith, had singled him out by bestowing this opportunity on him. The Ugliest Woman in the World. Some fools fought duels and killed each other over the most beautiful women. Some idiots gave away their entire property at the whim of a woman. But he was the exact opposite—the Ugliest Woman sought his affection like a sad, domesticated animal. She was different from all other women, and she even provided a money-earning opportunity into the bargain. If he made her his wife he'd be distinguished, he'd be special. He'd have something other people didn't have.

He started buying her flowers, not special bouquets, but just cheap little bunches wrapped in foil with a flimsy tissue paper bow, or he'd give her a cotton neckerchief, a glossy ribbon or a small box of pralines. Then he'd watch, hypnotized, as she tied the ribbon round her forehead, and instead of being an adornment, the colorful bow would look shocking. And he'd watch as she crushed the chocolates with her oversized, bulging tongue, causing brown saliva to form between her wide-spaced teeth and dribble down her bristle-coated chin.

He liked to look at her when she didn't know he was watching. He'd disappear in the morning and hide behind the tent or the caravan, he'd go off merely in order to lurk nearby and watch her for hours on end, even through the cracks in the wooden fence. She used to sunbathe, and while she did she'd spend ages very slowly combing her straggly hair, as if in trance, plaiting it into skinny braids and immediately undoing it again. Or else she would knit, the needles glittering in the sunlight as they stabbed at the noisy air of the circus. Or in a loose shirt, with her arms bare, she would launder her clothes in a washtub. The skin on her arms and upper chest was covered in pale fur and looked pretty. Soft, like an animal's.

He needed this spying, because day by day his disgust was lessening, melting in the sun, disappearing from sight like a puddle on a torrid afternoon. Gradually his eyes were growing used to the painful asymmetry, the broken proportions, the shortcomings and the excesses. Sometimes he thought she looked ordinary.

Whenever he began to feel uneasy, he told them all he was going away on important business, that he had a meeting with so and so—here he'd mention a stranger, or by contrast, a well-known name—that he was doing deals and holding talks. He'd polish his boots, launder his best shirt and set off on his way. He never went far. He'd stop in the nearest town, steal someone's wallet and drink. But even then he was never free of her, because he'd start talking about her, as if he couldn't do without her, even during these escapades.

And the strange thing was, she had become his most valuable possession. He could even pay for wine with her ugliness—more than that, by describing her face he could mesmerize beautiful young women, who told him to go on talking about her even later on, when they were lying beneath him naked.

When he got back he would always have a new story about her ugliness ready, mindful of the fact that no thing fully exists until it has its own special story. At first he told her to learn them by heart, but he soon realized that the Ugliest Woman wasn't good at telling stories; she spoke monotonously and burst into tears at the end, so he started telling them for her. He'd stand to one side, point his hand towards her and recite: "The mother of the unfortunate creature whom you see before you, whose appearance is so hard for your innocent eyes to bear, lived in a village on the edge of the Black Forest. And there one summer's day, as she was picking berries in the woods, she was hunted down by a savage wild boar who attacked her in a frenzy of mad, bestial lust and possessed her."

At this point he invariably heard muffled, horror-stricken cries, and some of the women, wanting to leave already, would start tugging at their reluctant husbands' sleeves.

He had several other versions too.

"This woman comes from a place that is severely tried by God. She is the descendant of some evil, heartless people who showed no mercy to a sickly pauper, for which Our Lord punished their entire village with this terrible hereditary ugliness."

Or: "This is the fate that befalls the children of women of loose morals. Here you see the harvest of syphilis, a terrible illness that punishes impurity into the fifth generation."

He never felt guilty. Any version could have been true.

"I don't know who my parents were," the Ugliest Woman told him. "I've always been like this. I was found at the circus as a baby. No one can remember what happened."

WHEN THEIR FIRST SEASON together was at an end and the circus was traveling in an idle curve back to Vienna for its annual hibernation, he proposed to her. She blushed to the roots and trembled. Then she quietly said "all right", and gently rested her head on his arm. He could smell her fragrance—it was soft and soapy. He endured this moment, then drew back and excitedly began to tell her his plans for their life together, listing all the places they would visit. As he paced about the room she kept her eyes fixed on him, but was sad and silent. Right at the end she took him by the hand and said she'd like the exact opposite—for them to settle somewhere in the sticks, and never have to go anywhere or see anyone. And that she would cook, they'd have children and a garden.

"You'd never be able to cope with it," he retorted indignantly. "You grew up in the circus. You want, you need to be looked at. You'd die without people's eyes on you."

She didn't answer.

. . .

THEY WERE MARRIED AT CHRISTMAS, in a tiny little church. The priest who conducted the ceremony almost fainted, and his voice was trembling. The guests were people from the circus, because he told her he didn't have any family and was just as alone in the world as she was.

When they were all swaying in their seats, when all the bottles were empty and it was time to go to bed (even she was tipsily tugging at his sleeve), he held them all back and sent for more wine. He couldn't get drunk, though he tried. Something inside him remained at the ready, tensed like a string. He couldn't even relax his shoulders or cross his legs, but sat bolt upright, his cheeks flushed and his eyes glittering.

"Let's go now, my love," she whispered in his ear.

But he seemed to cling to the edge of the table, as if pinned to it by invisible tacks. So the more attentive guests might have thought he was afraid of being close to her naked, afraid of the obligatory post-nuptial intimacy. Was that in fact the case?

"Touch my face," she asked him in the darkness, but he didn't do it. He raised himself above her on his hands so that all he could see was the outline of her silhouette, a little lighter than the obscurity of the room, a faint patch with no distinct edges. Then he closed his eyes—she couldn't see that—and possessed her, like any other woman, as usual, without a single thought.

THEY BEGAN THE NEXT season on their own. He had some photographs of her taken and distributed them worldwide. The answers came by telegraph. They had numerous appearances and traveled first class. She always wore a hat with a heavy, gray veil, from behind which she saw Rome, Venice, and the Champs Elysées. He bought her several dresses, and laced up her corset himself, so as they walked about the crowded streets of the cities of Europe they looked like a proper human couple. But even then, in the best times they ever had, he still had to escape. That's the type he was, the eternal runaway. A sort of panic would suddenly rise in him, an unbearable case of the jitters, then he'd start sweating and choking, so he'd take a wad of banknotes, grab his hat and run down the stairs, unerringly finding his way to the drinking dives near the port. Here he'd at once relax, his face would go flabby, his hair would get ruffled and the bald patch hidden under his slicked-down strands would insolently emerge in public. Joyfully and innocently he would sit and drink, letting himself ramble on, then be slapped on the wrists by a persistent prostitute.

THE FIRST TIME the Ugliest Woman reproached him, he punched her in the stomach, because even this way he was afraid to touch her face.

He no longer told stories about syphilis or the boar in the woods. He had received a letter from a professor of medicine in Vienna, and nowadays he presented his wife in scientific terms.

"Ladies and gentlemen, here we have a freak of nature, a mutant, an error of evolution, the real missing link. Specimens of this kind are very rare. The probability is as small as the likelihood of a meteor hitting this spot right now. So here you have the opportunity of viewing a living mutation."

Of course they used to go and see the professor at the university. There they posed for some photographs together, she sitting and he standing behind her, with his hand on her shoulder.

Once, while she was being measured, the professor had a word with him.

"I wonder if this mutation is hereditary?" he said. "Have you not thought about a child? Have you tried? Does your wife . . . er . . . ? Do you in fact . . . er . . ."

Not long after, as if unconnected with this discreet exchange with the professor, she told him she was pregnant. From then on he was split in two. He wanted her to have a child just like herself—then they'd have even more contacts, even more invitations. If the need arose he'd be guaranteed a long living, even if something happened to her. Perhaps he'd become famous? But then at once he'd have the panic-stricken thought that the child would be a monster, and that he'd really prefer to rip it from her belly, to protect it from her poisonous, defect-infested blood. And he had dreams that he was that son in her belly, imprisoned there, doomed to her dismal mercy, and that by confining him in there she was gradually changing his face. Or else he'd dream he was the wild boar in the forest, violating an innocent girl. He'd wake up in a sweat and pray for her to miscarry.

HER BELLY GAVE THE AUDIENCE courage, and made it easier for them to forgive her monstrous ugliness. They started asking her questions, which she would shyly answer in a quiet, unconvincing way. Their closer acquaintances began to make bets on what sort of child she'd have and of what gender. She took it all as meekly as a lamb.

In the evenings she sewed baby clothes.

"You know," she would say, stopping still for a moment, and fixing her eyes on a single faraway spot, "people are so fragile, so alone. I feel sorry for them as they sit there in front of me, staring at my face. It's as if they themselves are empty, as if they have to take a good look at something, fill themselves up with something. Sometimes I think they envy me. At least I'm something. But they're so lacking in anything exceptional, so lacking in special attributes."

As she said it he winced.

She gave birth in the night, without any fuss, quietly, like an animal. The midwife only came to cut the umbilical cord. He gave her a wad of notes to make sure she didn't spread any stories too early. His heart thumping, he lit all the lamps at once, to be able to give it a close inspection. The child was horrible, even worse than the mother. He had to close his eyes because his stomach was rising to his throat. Only much later did he satisfy himself that the newborn child was a girl, as she said it was.

So here's what happened: he went into the dark city, it was Vienna, or maybe Berlin. Light, wet snow was falling. His shoes trailed pitifully over the cobblestones. He was split inside again—he felt happy, but at the same time desperate.

He drank and remained sober. He daydreamed and felt afraid. When he came back several days later, he had ideas for the itinerary and promotion all ready. He wrote to the professor, and arranged for a photographer to call, who with shaking hands and flash after flash of magnesium recorded the monstrous ugliness of both creatures.

As soon as winter ends, as soon as the forsythia blooms, as soon as the cobbles of the great cities are dry, he thought. Petersburg, Bucharest, Prague, Warsaw, further and further, all the way to New York and Buenos Aires . . . As soon as the sky stretched tight above the earth like an enormous azure sail, the whole world would be bewitched by the ugliness of his wife and daughter, and would fall before them on its knees.

At more or less this point he kissed her on the face for the first time ever. Not on the lips, no, no, but on the brow. She looked at him with a brightened, different gaze, almost human. That was when the question arose in his head that he could never ask her. "Who are you? Who are you? Who are you?", he kept repeating to himself, failing even to notice when he started mentally putting it to others, even himself in the mirror while shaving. It was just as if he had discovered a secret—that everyone is in disguise, that human faces are just masks, as if the whole of life were one big Venetian ball. Sometimes he drunkenly fantasized—because he never allowed himself this sort of nonsense when sober—that he was removing the masks, and with a gentle crackle of glued-on paper they were revealing—what? He didn't know. It began to bother him so much that he couldn't bear to be at home with her and the child. He was afraid that one day he'd give in to a bizarre temptation and start trying to scratch the ugliness off her face. His fingers would rummage in her hair, seeking out the hidden edges, the straps and the strips of glue. So he'd slip out for a drink and then think up the next itinerary, design the posters and draft the telegrams.

But in early spring came the terrible epidemic of Spanish flu, and mother and child fell ill. They lay beside each other in a fever, breathing heavily. From time to time out of some panic-stricken instinct she would cuddle the child to her, trying to feed it in her delirium, not understanding that it had no strength left to suck and was dying. And when it finally died, he gently took it and laid it on the edge of the bed, then lit a cigar.

That night the Ugliest Woman briefly regained consciousness, but only to start sobbing and whining in desperation. It was more than he could bear—it was the voice of the night, the sound of darkness, straight from the black abyss. He blocked his ears, until finally he grabbed his hat and ran from the house, but he didn't go far. He walked up and down beneath the windows of his own apartment until morning, and in this way he helped her to die too. It happened quicker than he could have expected.

He shut himself in their bedroom and gazed at both bodies; suddenly they seemed heavy, troublesome and oddly material somehow. He was surprised how much the mattress appeared to be sagging. He had no idea what to do now, so he told no one but the professor; drinking straight from the bottle, he sat and watched as the twilight gradually effaced the contours of both the motionless shapes on the bed.

"Save them," he pleaded incoherently once the professor was there, performing a post mortem.

"Have you gone mad? They're no longer alive," he snapped.

Afterwards the professor handed him a piece of paper and he signed it with his right hand, while taking the money with his left.

But that same day before vanishing into the port, he helped the professor to convey the bodies by droshky to the university clinic, where soon after they were secretly stuffed.

For a long time, almost twenty years, they stood in the chilly basement of the building, until better times came and they went to join the main collection, including Jewish and Slavonic skulls, two-headed babies and conjoined twins of every possible race and color. They can still be seen today in the storerooms of the Pathologisches Museum—a glass-eyed mother and daughter, frozen still in a perfectly dignified pose, like the unsuccessful start of a brand-new species.

The Good Denis

Marie NDiaye

Translated from French by Jordan Stump

When—after I'd long hesitated, lost my nerve, thought better of it—I finally gathered the strength to ask my decreasingly lucid mother if she remembered a certain scene that still brought an ache to my grownup heart, she gave me a mystified, offended stare, a stare of virtuous indignation, and then, collecting herself, answered gently, as you might answer a very old person who, you realize, didn't mean to say such a ridiculous thing, that what I was talking about not only hadn't happened but could not, in any case, possibly have happened.

My father, of whose face and voice I had no memory, who was preserved in my childhood recollections only as a tall form, enormous, eminent, and dark, could not have walked out of our apartment in 1969, could not, closing the door behind him, have left the weeping woman I could only vaguely picture but whose sobs, whose despair, in the tiny entryway of that modest apartment, had always had for me the sting of a genuine memory. My father could not have abandoned her, my mother claimed, since in the first month of that year she herself had gone to live with another man, a certain Denis, who with the deepest goodness had also taken in the very young child that I then was.

It was she, my unsteady-minded mother asserted, who had left my father, not the other way around.

And how, she murmured in a voice now disappointed, now accusing, depending on whether the morning had found her weak and drained or full of vigor, how was it that I had not the slightest memory of that exceptionally kind and decent Denis?

Denis, a custodian at the Malakoff primary school where my mother had spent a few months substituting for the fourth-grade teacher, had immediately agreed—since he'd fallen in love with my mother, had even fallen under her spell, she would say with a sort of pained modesty, and apparently had no children—to learn to love and care for me as if I were his own daughter.

Those words would often return to my confused mother's tongue: Denis had treated me "like his own daughter." How, she asked, could I have forgotten a man like that while imagining I remembered some pathetic scene of her keening and hiccupping before a door that my father had closed behind him? No such scene could ever have happened, she assured me, because my father had disappeared from our lives as soon as he'd realized that she wouldn't be leaving Denis, that admirable man whom, to her deep disappointment, I couldn't recall even though he'd loved me far more than my father ever did.

For example, Denis, unlike my father, talked to me. Yes, my mother said, he looked you straight in the eye and talked to you, even though you were only one or two years old and few fathers did such things in those days. Your biological father never spoke to you, said my mother, whose memories were perhaps corrupted by senility, and he never put his face near yours to tell you things or just give you one of those tender little smiles which even the most indifferent parents lavish on their young ones.

Only from a distance, my mother said, did he gaze on the sweet, lovable little girl you were, and it seemed, she went on despite my mumbled attempts to interrupt her, that there was something about you that repelled him. Yes, my doddering old mother added pensively, there was something about you, beautiful though you were, that inexplicably disgusted him. Did that aversion spring from something of himself that he saw in you or something of me or, my uncertain, unsound mother said, did he see in you some element of the wider world which displeased or eluded him? He didn't like the wind, or cold shadows, or ice under the thin soles of his shoes. Any fondness for twilight made him cackle with horror, with scorn.

As best I could, I spoke up in my own defense.

I had to intercede on behalf of the baby I'd been, whose flaws were still insidiously being held against me.

I could not, I assured my musing mother, have been so unsavory a child that my father, in his wholesomeness, should feel obliged to keep his distance from me. At the dawn of my life, I could not, I insisted tremulously, have been visibly dangerous, strange, depraved.

I don't know, I don't know, she would sigh, and then add, moved, that Denis had chosen not to see those putative failings in me. He had accepted me, she said, as I was.

But who was I that anyone should have to deign to accept me, and that raising me for two short years should seem the work of a saint?

Oh, you were nice, you were very pretty, my mother said hesitantly, as if to reassure me, as if she didn't entirely believe what she was claiming. No, you weren't unpleasant, far from it.

A long time (decades!) had gone by before I'd dared to have these brief talks with my mother, and certainly nothing had prepared me, when I finally ventured to bring up my father's leaving, for the eruption into our shared history of Denis Rouxel, since that was his name.

And now my surprise, perplexity, and vague rancor could no longer be expressed—as they used to be, for other reasons, when I was younger—in the form of caustic retorts, whining reproaches, or long, sonorous sighs.

I had to make do with a stunned little laugh.

I looked away from my mother's vacant face and turned toward the window, but there I found her reflection, since darkness had fallen—she was scowling, thinking I couldn't see her, perhaps in sorrow.

Or was this her way of getting back at me?

For having moved her, with her consent, to be sure, and at the cost of much complicated paperwork, into this first-class rest home?

There were very old trees on the grounds, and benches designed by artists of some renown.

Two or three times already I'd lunched with my mother in the dining room, where we were served quail with grapes, strawberry cake, and very fresh goat cheese, all on elegant dishware.

My mother, with her failing mind and her wobbly legs, had pronounced herself satisfied with this haven, though in a voice so stiff and stolid that I could only conclude, as she wanted me to, that no such thing was true, that she hated the place and had resigned herself to it only out of politeness and respect for my efforts.

Some of her clothes disappeared from the dresser.

"All the nicest things," she told me with a shrug. "My sky-blue cardigan with the mother-of-pearl buttons, my lace-cuffed blouse, my silk nightgown."

"I'll tell the floor monitor," I said, unable to conceal my rage.

In the long, silent hallway, I came across a resident who gave me a cheery hello.

She was wearing my mother's cardigan, despite her own girth and height—the little mother-of-pearl buttons weren't done up and the sleeves came just halfway down her forearms.

Then I passed by a room with an open door and, reflexively glancing inside, glimpsed a very old woman sitting on her bed, wearing a cream-colored silk nightgown with long balloon sleeves which I immediately recognized, since it had been a present from me, as my mother's.

I turned back.

I lied to my mother, told her I couldn't find the floor monitor.

She said it didn't matter, I could forget the whole thing, it didn't trouble her in the least.

She still had more nice clothes than she'd ever get a chance to wear in this place of death.

"Are you sure," I asked meekly, pretending to see no disturbing implications in her use of the word "death," "are you sure you couldn't have given those clothes to your neighbors?"

"Why would I do that?" my mother exclaimed.

She laughed, indulgently, thinking me very silly.

"I have no friends in this squalid place. There's no one I spend time with. I don't know anyone's name," she added, sourly pleased.

I refused to back down, suggesting that she might have given away clothes that she herself admitted she didn't need.

"Maybe you don't remember," I said, looking away from her face toward the face in the dark window, which was again horribly deformed, upper lip pulled back over diseased teeth, eyes cynically narrowed, as if, while pretending to listen, my mother were mocking me, closing her ears to arguments she'd already foreseen, weaving the threads of her future—secret, hateful, and meticulously planned.

She coolly replied that she remembered everything.

She hadn't taken those three outfits out of the dresser since she'd arrived at this facility, and she hadn't for a moment thought of giving anything to her "prison mates," whom she wanted nothing whatever to do with.

Because the few friends she'd had in the course of her life, nearly all dead now, had been chosen on the basis of subtle, exacting affinities. Out of self-respect, she would not even contemplate the possibility of allowing a friendship to develop in this lugubrious place.

Better to know no one than to resign herself, thanks to an excess of solitude, to fraternizing with "not very interesting" people.

You're wrong, you're wrong, I shouted at her silently, as I always had. Any perfectly ordinary person is more "interesting" than you think you are, in your tedious, predictable vanity, you who, on the pretext of not wanting to encourage other people's supposedly improper curiosity about you, never tell a single story from your drearily respectable life.

Then I saw that her face, whose vicious reflection I was still staring at in the window, had turned peaceful.

I whirled around, full of hope.

I saw my mother's face smooth and pink, almost satiny with good will.

She calmly explained that she herself lacked the generosity of, for example, since we'd been talking about him, the good Denis.

I whispered, "Denis Rouxel?"

"If you like," she said impatiently. "I'm talking about just Denis. He gave away what few clothes he had. He didn't like owning things, you see. If he were in my place, yes, he would have handed out the cardigan and the blouse and the nightgown. But I'm not good like Denis, and I would never have done such a thing. Why should I? I'm not him."

When, later, I told my husband the things my mother had said that had so shaken me—first, that it was she who'd broken up with my father, rather than the other way around, and then that the good Denis had been the loving, vigilant guardian of my first two or three years—he stepped away from the picture window in our living room, making an effort that I could see, and that touched me, to suspend his numb, torpid contemplation of our neglected gray yard and the cornfields beyond and the mauve hills in the distance.

I took his hand, put it to my cheek.

It pulsed against my skin like a startled heart.

Short of any more meaningful pleasure, I found myself not unhappy that I could share with my husband something that was troubling me and, by rousing his concern for me, extract him from his gloom, if only briefly.

For twenty-five years, he'd run an antique shop on the ground floor of our house, in a small city in the Gers which I've since left.

Austere, sombre, moral, and ardently pure, the shop sold only representations of the Virgin Mary—painted, marble, plaster, wood, or glass—even some that were blasphemous or clumsily obscene, which offended certain people.

My husband had no fondness for smut, for assaults on the sacred. He often railed against indecency and, particularly, the obsession with provocation that he saw in some of the profane, heavy-handed works he offered for sale.

But the profound integrity and even, perhaps, the maniacal rectitude that fuelled his pleasure in selling useless old things had always forbidden him from excluding works that repulsed him, with the result that his shopwindow sometimes displayed a Virgin masturbating under her plaster dress, on the ground that his aversion to such an image not only shouldn't prevent him from showing it but made showing it a sort of duty: were he to follow only his own deeply wholesome tastes, he would categorically ban that outrageous object from his shop, even though it lay squarely within the domain of his mania (Maria!), and so he felt obliged to exhibit it, lest people think he chose his merchandise according to a conventional morality, private and uninteresting, rather than his rigor as a specialist.

That was how my husband was, conscientious to the point, sometimes, of exaltation, of blindness, such was the man who, that evening, would pretend to set aside his melancholy and tell me what he knew of the good Denis.

First, he let me take his hand, let me hold it delicately between my own hands like a precious little organ.

It had been months since we'd touched in any way.

He was bankrupt.

His shop had not survived the lockdowns, and beneath our feet stood a stock of Virgins that he struggled to sell on the Internet and lacked the energy even to dust. To be honest, we both felt a strange terror at the thought of approaching them, now that the shop was likely closed forever, as if they might suddenly awaken and call us to account, their dull-blue, animated eyes looking into ours, perhaps murmuring, Why do we fascinate you so?

"I know about this good Denis," he said. "I never met him, no, of course."

He smiled at me, as he hadn't done, I thought, for a very long time.

"Your mother told me about him a few years back, when we had that little party at our house, you remember?"

"Yes," I answered immediately. "The third of June, 2017."

"She'd had a few that evening," my husband said, still smiling, not at me but at the memory, which I immediately thought impossible, of seeing my mother drunk.

"She never drinks," I said quietly.

"I'm more than happy to believe that," he said, slightly amused, "but I'm telling you she was smashed that evening, and maybe, oh, yes, it might be, I hadn't thought of that, maybe because she wanted to hide from you and your certainty that she never drinks she sought shelter or maybe, yes, cover at the far end of the yard, you know, where we dump the grass clippings, and I happened to stroll over that way, and there she was, very friendly, hammered but lighthearted and funny, all alone at the far end of the yard, with her very full glass, and, I must say, we chatted more freely than we ever had before."

"She was drinking iced tea," I said, deeply disoriented but knowing that with those naïve words I could amuse my husband after months of despondency.

"Then her tea was heavily spiked with vodka or gin," he merrily shot back.

Some long minutes went by in silence.

"So," I said, surprised that I had to get him started again, "what about the good Denis?"

"Oh, yes."

My husband stepped away from me and back toward the window, staring out with his bewildered, mournful gaze.

"That evening your mother told me, yes, that she'd taken up with a certain Denis when you were a baby. As I said, she was very drunk, so I was only half listening, and I don't recall the details, but, as I remember them, her words made it clear that Denis's goodness, since that vague quality seemed to define him completely, could never have been expressed by some triviality like donating clothes in a retirement home. It seems your mother left Denis because she didn't think she could live up to the moral heights that life with that man—not that he ever said a word about it, not that he ever asked anything of her, not that he even realized it, perhaps—evidently entailed."

"Meaning? She didn't give you any examples?"

"Examples?"

From his muted, weary voice, I sensed that the subject had lost its hold on him, that he had even, possibly, in his discreet way, stopped listening to me, that he'd forgotten I was there, very present, beside him.

"Yes," I said, "some concrete manifestation of his goodness. What form did it take in their day-to-day life? Maman had nothing specific to tell you?"

"Oh, no, no, nothing specific. I don't know if she could have."

"Why?" My tone was suddenly more tense than I would have liked. "Because she was drunk?"

I saw him making another earnest, laudable effort to remember what exactly we were talking about, to summon what little energy he had in him to consider my question and answer it as honestly as he could.

"No, everything she said of him was astute and judicious. Being drunk made her clear-eyed, cruel, vaguely tormented but ironic about it. I don't believe there were any examples. This Denis was apparently an ordinary man, perhaps, I believe, even shy, retiring, his goodness was like . . . a scent."

"A scent?"

"That emanated from him, though he was the only one who couldn't sense it. Evidently, to anyone who noticed it, that essence felt like an obligation they didn't always have the courage for, or the strength, or who knows, who knows. . . ."

My husband let his voice fade away, making a bit of a show of it, no doubt overplaying it a little, in order to tell me, Summoning up for you these memories of little consequence has exhausted me—now leave me in peace with my gloom.

But in our thirty-five years together hadn't I done far more than that for him? Many times, for his benefit, I'd recalled pieces of my life that weren't pleasant, and so often I'd supported him, encouraged him, consoled him, caressed him.

Why didn't he want to help me understand the nature of Denis Rouxel's goodness, what I'd got from it, and from him, and if I owed that man anything, if I had some obligation to seek him out because he'd looked after me, or if, on the contrary, I had to banish any thought of finding him because he was responsible, despite or because of his goodness, for my most grievous flaws, my most hidden failings, most hidden but most condemned in the courtroom of my conscience?

The idea of a consoling kiss didn't even enter my husband's mind. He went back to his grim, silent contemplation of the violet hills in the distance, his hunched, emaciated back suddenly, subtly straightening to throw off any attempt to make him tell me more.

But he, at least, had had a reasonable conversation with my mother, something now forbidden to me, or almost, and the fact that, according to my husband, she had been drunk that night in the garden in no way implied she wasn't a more reliable source—surely more precise and sincere—than the suspicious, crafty old lady I had to deal with now.

I thought that she was making up secrets to keep me from guessing the real secrets, the ones she'd defiantly sealed away in her now savage, proud, and primitive heart.

I suspected that she didn't remember those deep, true secrets.

She remembered that she had secrets but not what they were, and she didn't care.

Secrets have to be hidden—this much she knew, like a disoriented high priestess, mechanically performing the rituals of her cult.

Which was why, when I went back to see her in her "funereal home" (as she liked to call the facility), I not only brought along a bottle of champagne and two crystal flutes but popped the cork nonchalantly, without a glance at my mother, as if all this were an everyday routine between the two of us.

She looked on coldly as I held out her glass.

She simply sat there, shaking her head.

"I never drink, my poor girl, have you forgotten that? Do you know anything about me?"

She let out a sardonic little laugh even as, I could see, her gaze grew troubled.

She looked toward the dark window for help, tried to twist her lips into an intimidating rictus.

So she knew I could see her! She was manipulating her reflection to deceive me!

That's all over, Maman, that's all over now! I cried mutely.

And then, It's no good trying to scare me!

I set on her nightstand the champagne flute she'd declined.

I calmly filled my glass, drank it down in one go, and concluded with an expansive "Mmm" of delectation.

Turning back toward me, she fixed me with a defiant, reproachful stare while her right hand stealthily moved toward her left and clasped it to stop it from trembling.

"Maman," I said offhandedly, pouring myself another glass, "tell me about Denis Rouxel."

"The good Denis?"

She gave me a sarcastic smile, but her eyes seemed as unquiet as her hands.

It occurred to me then that she might have refused the champagne not because she didn't want it or because she had so long pretended she didn't drink but because her fingers could no longer hold a delicate glass without the risk of dropping it or spilling its contents.

Chiding myself for not having thought of this earlier, I went into the bathroom for her tooth glass, a solid plastic goblet. I half filled it with champagne.

"Here, Maman," I said plainly.

And I feigned a perfectly neutral expression, forcing myself not to look at her so that she wouldn't have to put on an act.

She took the glass in both hands and raised it to her lips.

Before her first sip, she whispered, in a voice I thought mischievous, "Cheers, my girl!"

Then: "You don't need to get me drunk to make me talk about the good Denis, you know. I'll listen to all your questions, but, my poor girl, I won't have many answers."

"But," I said, with a touch of impatience, "you lived with him for a while, and I was there. You must have some memories of the three of us together."

"Well, really . . ."

To my great joy, she kept her grip on the glass and drank it down.

And I hurried to pour her a bit more, so she wouldn't have to ask.

No sign, now, of her turning toward the dark transforming window!

No aspiration to some metamorphosis that would erect a wall of terror between her and me!

Only the formal, superior, ingratiating welcome she reserved for my curiosity: "What would you like me to tell you, my girl?"

"Well, for one thing, why do you call him the good Denis?"

She gave a little laugh, coquettish or cunning or maybe sweet—I wasn't sure of anything.

"Because to me he was the incarnation of the purest goodness."

"Maman, those are just words. What, in your everyday life, made you think that man exceptionally good? How did he treat you, treat us?"

She reached toward me with both thin, ropy, trembling arms, summoning, I thought, what was left of their strength to help the two hands holding the glass.

"This champagne of yours isn't bad."

Had she ever held out loving, consoling arms to embrace me?

She must have, even if I had no memory of it.

I poured her another glass.

A faint pinkness rose to her cheeks, not as if she'd been rouged but as if the young, still vital woman inside her, encased in a sheath of decrepitude, had, thanks to the champagne, found a crack through which to appear.

"Well," she began.

She closed her eyes, slowly drank down her glass.

I took it from her so she wouldn't have to go through the effort of setting it down.

She was smiling, distant, gracious.

She bent toward me, murmured, "Denis, you see, was a liberal."

"Is that all?" I gasped.

"Oh!"

Suddenly her lips were quivering in shock.

She waved her hands in front of her face, now drained of its color, and whispered, dismayed, "Isn't that enough?"

Tears came to my eyes, tears less of sadness than of cruel disappointment.

"Maman," I pleaded, abandoning all dignity, "tell me something! Just one single scene, I don't know, one single moment with Denis!"

"A moment?"

She sat down on the bed.

Her bony knees seemed about to poke through the fabric of her skirt—and those thighs, skeletal. . . . My mother had never been very solid, as they say, but I couldn't help noticing that since moving to this beautiful retirement home she'd become drastically thinner.

"Do you like the food here, Maman? Is everything good?"

"I don't know. I don't care about that."

Irritated, she raised her index finger beside her temple to indicate that my bland questions were disturbing her ruminations.

Her gaze was cool and stern. To my relief, she seemed to be not looking at me but watching for her memories to appear on my bare, blank, indeterminate face, a screen onto which her mind, commanded to remember, would project the images I was waiting or hoping for.

"Well, speaking of food," she began, now wearing a forthright, pure, amused smile that was, I sensed, addressed not to me but to the visions taking shape on my face, "Denis is a fine chef. He won't let me do the cooking. I don't have his talent, it's very true. He whips up wonderful dishes for my little girl. 'Only the best foods can go into that little body,' he sweetly repeats. Oh, yes, what a cook is my good Denis!"

She closed her eyes and opened them again, coming back to me and to the new expression on her face, a look of quiet terror at the thought of what I might be expecting from her. Now she was afraid of disappointing me!

Wouldn't I have preferred to see the reflection of her cruel gaze in the dark window?

Wouldn't I have preferred to see her savage, unjust, unfeeling, and unhinged?

Wouldn't that be preferable to this pleading look, even if, for the moment, all she wanted was to satisfy my wish, my need to learn more about myself than I could remember?

"Thank you, Maman. Tell me, do you have any idea where Denis lives now?"

My voice was gentle, beguiling, so low that she didn't understand.

Simpering, she pretended to have heard.

"Yes, yes, Denis is still alive, I'm sure of it. You see, my girl"—she gave a little laugh—"the good Denises of this world always outlive the others, and that's only right! Your father wasn't good. He died. And what will that mean for me?"

Two days later, my husband tried, unsuccessfully, to be dead.

He was trying not to die, I'm quite sure—that's too hard—but to go directly from living to dead, from one moment to the next.

He wasn't young anymore, but he wasn't yet old.

So, for my mother, he was neither a good man nor a bad man but simply a nobody.

"He jumped out the window, you say? My girl, I know your house, and I know he had no chance of killing himself that way. The worm! What a sorry excuse for a man, never did well at anything!"

"Maman, I don't want you talking about my husband that way! I love him, I love him so! I have no choice but to love him, to love him so!"

"Then, my girl, ask this one little thing of him: that he not fail at dying the way he's failed at everything else."

"Maman, this attitude of yours is quite simply fascist. A successful death, a glorious suicide . . ."

"Yes, yes. . . . 'Fascist' is just the word you're using right now. It doesn't in any way alter the truth of what I'm telling you about your husband, about that particular man who happens to be your husband.

As you see, unlike you, I'm not generalizing. I'm telling you about that man whom I knew well, my son-in-law, whom I never thought much of. I never understood how you could feel such a fanatical love for him, when, unlike Denis, there was nothing special about him, apart from a few ridiculous manias, like his passion for the Virgin Mary or his much vaunted knowledge of wines and varietals or whatever they're called, which made me sick with boredom when, too often, too pleased with himself, he lectured me about it, though he had to have noticed my disgusted indifference to the whole subject. Whereas the good Denis never talked to anyone, not even a child, not even a dog, unless he was sure that what he was saying had some chance of interesting them. The good Denis would never have failed at his own suicide. But, of course, the good Denis would never have wanted to die."

"What connection are you making, Maman, between Denis's goodness and his taste for life?"

"But, my girl, it's obvious. How could you of all people not understand? You're sometimes cowardly, you lack backbone. You're not good like Denis—you're just weak and ordinary and tormented because you think too much of yourself, your little anxieties take you over, you torture yourself and coddle yourself. You'll never be a good person. Unfortunately, I was like you! The good Denis would never have forced anyone to find his dead body, to deal with his 'suicide,' would never have left others wondering whether they could have prevented that fatal act. But your failure of a husband! What a joke!"

I spent the next few weeks trying to add to what little I knew of Denis by means of a careful, unhurried, groping search through the infinite space of the Web.

My husband, whose attempt had fortunately left him physically unscathed, now needed treatment and a stay in the country, for the good of us all, for our peace of mind. How I wished never to have to think of his well-being again!

How I wished never to have to think about anything that concerned him, be it his love for me, which I felt responsible for and duty bound to maintain, for his good and his peace of mind, or be it his future, which I secretly, scandalously hoped he might envisage without me in it, without my playing even a minor role in it.

How I wished he would forget me!

Yes, how I wished his various hurts and his irrefutable age might make him miraculously forget I existed!

Maybe not that I *had* existed, since I liked to think that our many happy years together had given my otherwise colorless life (my face, my figure, my profession: all insipid) a density, a significance, a singularity that I could attribute only to my particular capacity for affection.

My husband had a similar capacity, and so, although we were, alas, childless, we had always been quiet champions of long-term love.

I hoped now that he would preserve a memory of me that might soothe his bitter heart, and that once in a while, from around the corner of a hospital hallway, or through the window of his room, or when he reached for the remote on his bedcovers, there would come a fleeting assurance that the two of us had been stout-hearted and valiant in our journey through married life.

But I also wished, fiercely, that he would believe I was dead, for my peace of mind.

Oh, not that I wanted him to suffer, no!

Only that he might hear in his disturbed mind a blithe, carefree voice, an obliging whisper informing him that I was no longer a woman on this earth but a soul in the cosmos, for his peace of mind and my own.

P.F.H.! P.F.H.! Pray for her!

And then, miraculously, I made the acquaintance of Régine.

"How did you find me?"

"By chance and persistence, which is to say that the tenacity I devoted not to finding you, exactly, since I had no idea you existed, but to following the trail of the good Denis led me to you, by accident, by fortune."

"Yes, Denis. Why do you call him the good Denis?"

"That's how people speak of him to me. Is it not true?"

"Oh, it is, it is. Oh, yes, yes. The too good Denis, if you see what I mean, the excessively good Denis, perhaps, but, yes, he was good, I suppose."

"You're not sure?"

"Oh, I am, I am. His goodness was like a thunderbolt, you see. No, I'm wrong, his goodness was like the slow fire that descends from the heavens and settles over your soul and convinces you, numbs you, makes you feel you're nothing much but gives you hope that with meditation, integrity, and honor you may eventually become blessed yourself. You see, Denis, without knowing it or wanting it, was truly a saint. Like any saint, I suppose, he could be fearsome and terrifying in his greatness, that greatness of which he was unaware. Implacably rigorous in pursuing a goodness he clearly didn't register. That's where you come in."

"Me? But, you understand, I don't know him."

"You did, though, even if you were too young to remember. And what matters in all this is that he knew you well, he raised you, he cared for you like his own daughter, and he loved you the same way, happily, passionately. It was because of you that he refused to have a child with me, out of a monstrously virtuous fidelity to his memory of that tiny girl, you. 'I can't let another child into my memory,' he would tell me. 'I can't think of creating any competition between my memory of Mimi and the memory I might have of another little girl.' And I answered, 'But what makes you think you'd lose our child, too?' And he said, 'It happens. I owe it to Mimi to forever think of her as the only child I ever loved.'"

"But I'm not dead!"

"He lost you—it's the same thing. As I understand it, your mother took you away one day, left him just like that, and of course you went with her. Denis's glorious simplicity shielded him from hard feelings, and even from pointless anguish, from vainly protracted grief. He endured his lot with a smile. And, at the same time, he resolved to remain forever the father of only one child, you. Oh, not, as you must already understand, to spare himself other sorrows. He never gave that a thought. He had no fear of sorrow, and he didn't wallow in it. It's just that the inexorable, unyielding nature of his marvellous humanity had led him to decide that because he'd loved you desperately, and because you'd been taken away from him without your wanting it at all, he owed it to you never to attach himself to any other child, ever."

"That's ridiculous! It's absurd!"

"I don't know. That was Denis. That was why I left him. I went on to have the children I wanted, of course, with other men. But I miss the child Denis and I would have had, so I can't help resenting you a little. Forgive me, it's not your fault."

The strange damage that goodness can do!

When I asked Régine how she felt about my wish to meet in person, she seemed surprised and shocked, as if I were proposing something utterly immoral.

"What reason would I have for meeting you? The adult that you are has no place in my life, you don't interest me. And also I want to forget the good Denis—I've been working on that all this time. Meet you? Who do you think you are? How indecent! You do not interest me, Madame. To me, Madame, you are only the faded reflection of a child who caused my unhappiness. I couldn't hate the little girl Denis so loved that he couldn't imagine giving the smallest share of his unlimited tenderness to any other, even his own—I couldn't hate her, because you can't hate a child. But the woman you've become I can only resent, however unfair that may be."

Although it was hard, I decided not to ask for Régine's forgiveness.

I asked only if she knew where the good Denis lived.

"I do not, and I have no wish to. I'm not good. I haven't entirely freed myself from anger and acrimony, brooding and pointless self-pity. I'm quite sure that Denis, in his radiant, indifferent goodness, never broods. Happy are the blessed! Does he remember me? Or has he, for my own good, erased me from his memory? If you meet him, tell him about me, I'm begging you, mention Régine. . . ."

I wasn't good, either.

If ever I did have the chance to meet Denis, I would certainly not speak the name of this Régine, who had, there's no other word for it, cursed me.

I wasn't good, either.

I tried not to be proud of that.

I would have been ashamed of my pride, but still proud.

Some of my dreams left me, in the morning, clammy with unease and a strange sort of timidity toward myself—yes, the self I now barely recognized and didn't know quite how to address in my thoughts.

Because, in those intense, pleasant dreams, I was, alas, copulating with the good Denis.

It would have been more than enough to make me uncomfortable if those dreams showed me *making love* with the good Denis—but there were only absurd, impossible couplings, in which one sole thing was manifestly obvious, which was that Denis was pushing his strange genitals into mine, and I was delighted, alas.

Long, cold, haunted years went by. I visited my mother as often as my husband, in their miseries.

"The good Denis, the good Denis," my mother said again and again, "does he remember me sometimes?"

"My Virgins, all my Virgins, so patiently assembled, and I've abandoned them! My Marys, forgive me!" my husband intoned in a murmur that never failed to lull me to sleep, though he was entirely unaware, I was convinced, that he was doing so.

A start, the shadow of a fear, an irrational mistrust wrenched me awake.

And, from the armchair covered in gray vinyl—identical to the one I sat in while pretending to have stopped listening to my mother, hoping she might reveal secrets that were real and not imagined—from the hard armchair that had become mine in my husband's room, I saw myself tugging at my own hair, jerking my face back and forth, forcing myself to see with eyes no longer veiled by easy sympathy: my husband had become a mysteriously disturbing man.

And in those days, in my misery, I thought I saw the good Denis everywhere.

And although, every morning, I tried to forget how I'd appropriated him in my dreams, how my sick dreams had pawed and besmirched his impeccably respectable body, the day found ways of reminding me how much he should, if he knew, fear my fantasies.

Because I thought I saw the good Denis everywhere.

"Does he remember me?" my mother kept asking.

"Just let this good Denis show up now!" I sometimes answered.

I looked for him in the inexhaustible expanses of the Web.

I thought I found him in the person of a certain Flora, a beautician in Saint-Jean-Pied-de-Port.

Because why, I said to myself, should the good Denis not be incarnated in bodies other than the one my mother had known? Why should he not manifest himself in a variety of forms, perhaps ambiguous, perhaps straightforward and clear, as that lady from the Pyrénées-Atlantiques seemed to be, her personality in every way one with the good Denis's?

Did he know, wherever he was, that I was on a quest to find him?

Was he entertaining himself by testing my imagination?

I had so little, so little, alas.

But enough to convince myself that Flora—whose Facebook account I'd come across, either accidentally or because it was the will of a fate governed by Denis—that Flora was one of the forms the good Denis had taken to reveal himself to my consciousness.

Unlike Régine, the good Flora had no objection to meeting.

But then—nothing, alas.

It wasn't him, couldn't be him—I could see that straightaway.

It was only Flora, absolutely, utterly, and unquestionably, in her own thoughtful, decent, humble goodness, a Flora who could not compare with what I expected from the good Denis.

After that, I met Régis, Sylviane, Maria, Alain.

The good Denis was not in them, no matter how hard I tried to draw him out.

He wasn't there. He wasn't anywhere.

"Big news, darling," my mother then told me. "Denis is coming to visit me. He'll be here Friday, in my room."

"No, Maman, that's not possible. You must be confused. I don't know who's coming to see you, but it can't be Denis."

My whole body was trembling, not because I saw in my mother's claim evidence of cognitive decline but because I was afraid that she was telling the truth.

She shrugged her slender shoulders, smiling, impassive, understanding me but not pitying me—with the serene, almost indifferent hardness that now marked her dealings with me, as if, resigned to finding me foolish, pointlessly complicated, she had, without vain regret, abandoned all hope of seeing me change.

On the day she'd named, which I wished I could put off forever, I found myself at her side, perched on the gray armchair as she sat on her bed, shrunken but valiant, bold, unafraid.

"I don't know, my girl," she said quietly, "if the good Denis will leave me in peace or torment me, but whatever his choice it will be the right one."

Then my racing heart, understanding before my mind, which was automatically formulating a sarcastic or perhaps infuriated answer, my enlightened, aware heart, prudent and sensible, began to pound so hard that I jumped up and ran from the room.

In the hallway, I met all the women wearing my mother's clothes, the cardigan, the nightgown, the lace-sleeved blouse—no, not all the women, maybe two? I don't know anymore.

I went home, making plans to flee.

Where could I go that the good Denis would never find me? Frantic, I called my mother, even as I suspected she might be more on Denis's side than on mine and would betray me without meaning to, without even knowing it.

I called her all the same, thinking that she was the only one who could give me, innocently, without thinking she was rescuing me or even wanting to rescue me, the best advice on how to escape the good Denis's embrace.

"Maman, don't give Denis my address."

"It's no use, my girl. Apparently, he has a date with you."

"Is he there in your room?"

"Yes, of course, he always did come on time." (She thought she'd lowered her voice, but she was whispering loudly, like a little girl who thinks she need only put on a costume in order not to be recognized or blindfold herself to keep from being seen.) "He said he'd come and join you in the place you decided on together."

"I never decided on anything with him, ever, not even in my thoughts!" I cried.

"I don't know, my girl, what am I supposed to say?" my mother whispered with what sounded like a last sigh, and then, to wrap things up, again called me "darling," which had always vaguely implied that she'd had enough of my questions. Because she never called me "darling" as much as when she wanted to be rid of me, rid of the sight of a woman she vaguely remembered she was supposed to love but in whose face or expression or anything else she found nothing to justify that love or even to suggest that the woman was particularly likable.

"The good Denis has a date with you, darling, wherever you are. He actually just told me that. And now, darling, let me talk to him, let me, darling, enjoy my reunion with the good Denis, please, darling."

And so, knowing there was no way my mother could flee, locked in the home I'd put her in, I gave up on warning her about the good Denis's intentions. In truth, I accepted the painful thought that not only had my mother resigned herself to her deadly fate but her weary heart, her bored old heart, had eagerly welcomed it.

As for me, oh, no, I wasn't ready yet. The sense that a great injustice was being plotted against me so outraged me that I imagined bursting into my mother's room, furious and triumphant, stronger than the good Denis, and spitting at him, "You won't get me! Impostor! My death will not wear your face!"

I imagined barricading myself in my house, turning a deaf ear to all coaxing entreaties, to all voices, unctuous or urgent, and, especially, to those that eloquently evoked a long-ago bond. But then, collecting my thoughts, I realized that the good Denis, if he was someone I should now fear, would know just how to convince me to open my door to him, and that my lost, desperate, submissive mind could never win a fight against his subtle brain, would never even dream of trying.

I went to visit my husband in the home, where they were doing their best to make him understand that he had no reason to want to die before his time.

I found him glum, plaintive, sometimes strangely boastful.

He confessed that he was happy to be alive, in spite of everything.

All the same, he said, he was proud that he'd wanted to die, and he seemed determined to make something heroic of that intention, as if, having had to choose between the mindless reflex to stay alive and the noble aspiration to kill himself, he'd settled for the former only to make things easier for us—for me and the rest of the world.

I sat down in the gray armchair while he lay stiffly on his bed of lamentations, not ailing in any way, held down by nothing.

Oh, my husband!

I loved him so when we were young.

Now he was nothing like the man I knew then—his very eyes, once brown, seemed bereft of color, always full of fierce tears that never flowed.

"Denis will be coming here," I said to him. "You know, the good Denis?"

And I savagely, furiously hoped that when Denis entered he would take my husband in his grim embrace, forget about me, not even see me.

Wasn't that only right?

Because I myself, ardently, wanted to live.

Frogs

Mo Yan

Translated from Chinese by Howard Goldblatt

I have to admit that, though I did not make it public, I was personally opposed to my Aunty's marriage plans. My father, my brothers and their wives shared my feelings. It simply wasn't a good match in our view. Ever since we were small we'd looked forward to seeing Aunty find a husband. Her relationship with Wang Xiaoti had brought immense glory to the family, only to end ingloriously. Yang Lin was next, and while not nearly the ideal match that Wang would have provided, he was, after all, an official, which made him a passable candidate for marriage. Hell, she could have married Qin He, who was obsessed with her, and be better off than with Hao Dashou . . . we were by then assuming she'd wind up an old maid, and had made appropriate plans. We'd even discussed who would be her caregiver when she reached old age. But then, with no prior indication, she'd married Hao Dashou. Little Lion and I were living in Beijing then, and when we heard the news, we could hardly believe our ears. Once the preposterous reality set in, we were overcome by sadness.

Years later, Aunty starred in a TV program titled 'Moon Child,' which was supposed to be about the sculptor Hao Dashou, though the camera was always on her, talking and gesturing as she welcomed journalists into Hao's yard and gave them a guided tour of his workshop and the storeroom where he kept all his clay figurines, while he sat quietly at his workbench, eyes glazed over and a blank look on his face, like a dreamy old horse. Did all master artists turn into dreamy old horses once they became famous? I wondered. The name Hao Dashou resounded in my ears, though I'd only met him a few times. After seeing him late on the night my nephew Xianquan hosted a dinner to celebrate his acceptance as a pilot, years passed before I saw him again, and this time it was on TV. His hair and beard had turned white, but his complexion was ruddy as ever; composed and serene, he was a nearly transcendent figure. It was during that program that we learned why Aunty had married Hao Dashou.

Aunty lit a cigarette, took a deep drag, and began to speak, sadness creeping into her voice. 'Marriages,' she said, 'are made in Heaven. By this, I'm not promoting the cause of idealism for you youngsters, for there was a time when I was an ardent materialist, but where marriage is concerned, you must trust in fate. Just ask him,' she said, pointing to Hao Dashou. 'Do you think he ever dreamed of one day getting me as his wife?'

'In 1997, when I was sixty,' she said, 'my superiors told me to retire, whether I wanted to or not. I was already five years past the retirement age, and nothing I said would have made any difference. You know the hospital director, that ungrateful bastard Huang Jun, the son of Huang Pi from Hexi Village. Just who do you think dragged that little shit—they called him Melon Huang—out of his mother's belly? Well, he spent a couple of days in a medical school, and when he came out, almost as stupid as the day he went in, he couldn't find a vein with a syringe, couldn't locate a heart with a stethoscope, and had never heard the terms "inch, bar, and cubit" when checking a patient's pulse. So who better to appoint as hospital director! He was admitted into the school thanks to my personal recommendation to Director Shen of the Bureau of Health. Only to be ignored by him when he was the man in charge. The wretched creature has limited talents: playing the host, giving gifts, kissing ass and seducing women.'

. . .

At this point, Aunty thumped her breast and stomped her foot. 'What a fool I was,' she said angrily, 'letting the wolf in my door. I made it easy for him to have his way with all the girls in the hospital. Wang Xiaomei, a seventeen-year-old girl from Wang Village, had nice, thick braids, a pretty oval face, and skin like ivory. Her lashes danced like butterfly wings, her eyes could talk, and anyone who saw her would believe that if film director Zhang Yimou discovered her, she'd be a hotter commodity than Gong Li or Zhang Ziyi ever were. Sadly, Melon Huang, the sex fiend, discovered her first. He rushed off to Wang Village, where, with a glib tongue that could bring back the dead, he talked Xiaomei's parents into sending her to his hospital to learn from me how to treat women's problems. He said she'd be my student, but she never spent a single day with me. Instead, the lecher kept her to himself, his daily companion and nightly lover. If that weren't bad enough, he even took her during the daytime; people had seen them. Then once he'd had enough fun with her, he was off to the county seat, where he hosted banquets for high officials with public funds, in hopes of being transferred to the big city. Maybe you haven't seen what he looks like: a long, donkey face with dark lips, bloody gums, and toxic breath. Even with a face like that, he figured he had a chance of becoming assistant director at the Bureau of Health! Each time he dragged Wang Xiaomei along to drink and eat and entertain the officials, probably even offering her up as a gift for their pleasure. Evil! That's what he was, pure evil!'

'One day the little wretch called me to his office. Other women who worked in the hospital were afraid to be in his office. But not me. I kept a little dagger handy, and wouldn't have hesitated to use it on the bastard. Well, he poured tea, smiled, and laid it on thick. "What did you want to see me about, Director Huang? Let's get to the point." "Heh-heh." He grinned. "Great Aunt"—damned if he didn't call me "Great Aunt"—"you delivered me the day I was born, and you've watched me grow into adulthood. Why, I could be your own son. Heh-heh" . . . "I don't deserve such an honour," I said. "You're the Director of a big hospital, while I'm just an ordinary woman's doctor. If you were my son I'd die from the honour. So, please, tell me what you have in mind." More heh-heh-heh, before he got around to revealing the shameless reason he'd summoned me. "I've made the mistake all leading cadres make sooner or later—through my own carelessness Wang Xiaomei got pregnant." "Congratulations!" I said. "Now that Xiaomei is carrying your dragon seed, the hospital is guaranteed leadership continuity." "Don't mock me, Great Aunt, I've been so upset the past few days I can't eat or sleep." Can you believe the bastard actually said he had trouble eating and sleeping? "She's demanding that I divorce my wife, and if I won't she's threatened to report me to the County Discipline Commission." "Really?" I said. "I thought having 'second wives' was popular among you officials these days. Buy a villa, install her in it, and you've got it made." "I asked you not to make fun of me, Great Aunt," he said. "I couldn't go public with a 'second' or a 'third' wife, even if I had the money to buy a villa." "Then go ahead and get a divorce," I said. He pulled that donkey face longer than ever and said, "Great Aunt, you know full well that my father-in-law and those pig-butcher brothers-in-law of mine are violent thugs. My life wouldn't be worth a thing if they found out about this." "But you're the Director, an official!" "All right, that's enough, Great Aunt. In your old eyes the director of a hospital in a piddling, out-of-the-way town is about as important as a loud fart, so instead of mocking me, why don't you help me come up with something!" "What in the world could I come up with?" "Wang Xiaomei admires you," he said. "She's told me that many, many times. You're the only person she'll listen to." "What do you want me to do?" "Talk her into having an abortion." "Melon Huang," I complained through clenched teeth, "I will never again soil my hands with that atrocious act! Over the course of my life I've already been responsible for more than two thousand aborted births, and I'll never do it again. Just wait her out until you're a father. Xiaomei is such a pretty girl, she's bound to present you with a lovely boy or girl, and that should make you happy. You go tell her that when the time comes, I'll be there to deliver the child."'

'With that, I turned on my heel and walked out of the office pleased with myself. But that feeling lasted only till I was back in my own office and had drunk a glass of water. My mood turned dark. No one as bad as Melon Huang deserved to have an heir, and what a shame that Wang Xiaomei was carrying his child. I'd learned enough delivering all those children to know that a person's core—good or bad—is determined more by nature than nurture. You can criticize hereditary laws all you want, but this is knowledge based on experience. You could place a son of that evil Melon Huang in a Buddhist temple, and he'd grow up to be a lascivious monk. No matter how sorry I felt for Wang Xiaomei or how unwilling I was to put ideas in her head, I simply couldn't let that fiend find an easy way out of his predicament. If the world had another lascivious monk, so be it.'

'But Xiaomei herself came to me, wrapped her arms around my legs, and dirtied my trousers with her tears and snivel. "Aunty," she sobbed, "dear Aunty, he tricked me, he lied to me. I wouldn't marry that bastard if he sent an eight-man sedan chair for me. Help me do it, Aunty, I don't want that evil seed in me."'

'So that's how it was.' Aunty lit another cigarette and puffed away savagely, until I couldn't see her face for all the smoke. 'I helped rid her of the fetus. Once a rose about to bloom, Wang Xiaomei was now a ruined, fallen woman.' Aunty reached up and dried her tears. 'I vowed to never do that procedure again, I couldn't take it any longer, not for anyone, not even if the woman was carrying the offspring of a chimpanzee. I wouldn't do it. The slurping sound as it was sucked into the vacuum bottle was like a monstrous hand squeezing my heart, harder and harder, until I broke out in a cold sweat and began to see stars. The moment I finished I crumpled to the floor.'

'You're right, I do digress when I'm talking—I'm old. After all that chatter, I still haven't told you why I married Hao Dashou. Well, I announced my retirement on the fifteenth day of the seventh lunar month, but that bastard Melon Huang wanted to keep me around and urged me to formally retire but remain on the payroll at eight hundred yuan a month. I spat in his face. "I've slaved away enough for you, you bastard. You have me to thank for eight out of every ten yuan this hospital has earned all these years. When women and girls come to the hospital from all around, it's me they've come to see. If money was what I was after, I could have made at least a thousand a day on my own. Do you really think you can buy my labour for eight hundred a month, Melon Huang? A migrant worker is worth more than that. I've slaved away half my life, and now it's time for me to rest, to go back home to Northeast Gaomi Township." He was upset with me and has spent much of the past two years trying to make me suffer. Me, suffer? I'm a woman who's seen it all. As a little girl I wasn't scared of the Jap devils, so what made him think I was scared of a little bastard like him now that I was in my seventies? Right, right, back to what I was saying.'

'If you want to know why I married Hao Dashou, I have to start with the frogs. Some old friends got together for dinner on the night I announced my retirement, and I wound up drunk—I hadn't drunk much, less than a bowlful, but it was cheap liquor. Xie Xiaoque, the son of the restaurant owner, Xie Baizhua, one of those sweet-potato kids of the '63 famine, took out a bottle of ultra-strong Wuliangye—to honour me, he said—but it was counterfeit, and my head was reeling. Everyone at the table was wobbly, barely able to stand, and Xie Xiaoque himself foamed at the mouth till his eyes rolled up into his head.'

Aunty said she staggered out of the restaurant, headed to the hospital dormitory, but wound up in a marshy area on a narrow, winding path bordered on both sides by head-high reeds. Moonlight reflected on the water around her shimmered like glass. The croaks of toads and frogs sounded first on one side and then on the other, back and forth, like an antiphonal chorus. Then the croaks came at her from all sides at the same time, waves and waves of them merging to fill the sky. Suddenly, there was total silence, broken only by the chirping of insects. Aunty said that in all her years as a medical provider, traveling up and down remote paths late at night, she'd never once felt afraid. But that night she was terror-stricken. The croaking of frogs is often described in terms of drumbeats. But that night it sounded to her like human cries, almost as if thousands of newborn infants were crying. That had always been one of her favorite sounds, she said. For an obstetrician, no sound in the world approaches the soul-stirring music of a newborn baby's cries. The liquor she'd drunk that night, she said, left her body as cold sweat. 'Don't assume I was drunk and hallucinating, because as soon as the liquor oozed out through my pores, leaving me with a slight headache, my mind was clear.' As she walked down the muddy path, all she wanted was to escape that croaking. But how? No matter how hard she tried to get away, the chilling *croak—croak—croak*—sounds of aggrieved crying ensnared her from all sides. She tried to run, but couldn't; the gummy surface of the path stuck to the soles of her shoes, and it was a chore even to lift up a foot, snapping the silvery threads that held her shoes to the surface of the path. But as soon as she stepped down, more threads were formed. So she took off her shoes to walk in her bare feet, but that actually increased the grip of the mud. Aunty said she got down on her hands and knees, like an enormous frog, and began to crawl. Now the mud stuck to her knees and calves and hands, but she didn't care, she just kept crawling. It was at that moment, she said, when an incalculable number of frogs hopped out of the dense curtain of reeds and from lily pads that shimmered in the moonlight. Some were jade green, others were golden yellow; some were as big as an electric iron, others as small as dates. The eyes of some were like nuggets of gold, those of others, red beans. They came upon her like ocean waves, enshrouding her with their angry croaks, and it felt as if all those mouths were pecking at her skin, that they had grown nails to scrape her skin. When they hopped onto her back, her neck, and her head, their weight sent her sprawling onto the muddy path. Her greatest fear, she said, came not from the constant pecking and scratching, but from the disgusting, unbearable sensation of their cold, slimy skin brushing against hers. 'They covered me with urine, or maybe it was semen.' She said she was suddenly reminded of a legend her grandmother had told her about a seducing frog: a maiden cooling herself on a riverbank one night fell asleep and dreamed of a liaison with a young man dressed in green. When she awoke she was pregnant and eventually gave birth to a nest of frogs. Given an explosion of energy by that terrifying image, she jumped to her feet and shed the frogs on her body like mud clods. But not all—some clung to her clothes and to her hair; two even hung by their mouths from the lobes of her ears, a pair of horrific earrings. As she took off running, she sensed that somehow the mud was losing its sucking power, and as she ran she shook her body and tore at her clothes and skin with both hands. She shrieked each time she caught one of the frogs, which she flung away. The two attached to her ears like suckling infants took some of the skin with them when she pulled them off.

Aunty screamed and she ran, but she couldn't break free of the reptilian horde. And when she turned to look, the sight nearly drove the soul out of her body. Thousands, tens of thousands of frogs had formed a mighty army behind her, croaking, hopping, colliding, crowding together, like a murky torrent rushing madly toward her. As she ran, roadside frogs hopped into the path forming barriers to block her progress, while others leaped out of the reedy curtain in individual assaults. She told us that the loose-fitting black silk dress she was wearing that night was being shredded by the assault. Attacking frogs swallowed the strips of silk, and were thrown into a frenzy of cheek scraping before they rolled on the ground and exposed their white undersides.

She ran all the way to a riverbank, where she spotted a little stone bridge washed by silvery moonlight. By then hardly anything remained of her dress, and when she reached the bridge, stark naked, she ran into Hao Dashou.

Thoughts of modesty did not enter her mind at that moment, nor was she aware that she had been stripped naked. She spotted a man in a palm-bark rain cape and a bamboo coned hat sitting in the middle of the bridge kneading something in his hands. 'I later learned that he was kneading a lump of clay. A moon child can only be made from clay bathed in moonlight. I didn't know who he was, but I didn't care. Whoever he was, he was bound to be my salvation.' She rushed into the man's arms and crawled under his rain cape, and when her breasts came into contact with the warmth of his chest, in contrast to the damp, foul-smelling chill of the frogs on her back, she cried out, 'Help, Big Brother, save me!' She promptly passed out.

Aunty's extended narration called up images of frog hordes in our minds and sent chills up and down our spines. The camera cut to Hao Dashou, who still sat there like a statue; the next scenes were close-ups of clay figures and of the little stone bridge, before returning to Aunty's face, focusing on her mouth. She said:

'I awoke to find myself on Hao Dashou's brick bed, dressed in men's clothes. With both hands he handed me a bowl of mung bean soup, the simple fragrance of which cleared my head. I was sweating after a single bowlful, and was suddenly aware of how much I hurt and how hot my skin felt. But that cold, slimy feeling that had made me scream was already fading. I had itchy, painful blisters all over my body, I spiked a fever, and I was delirious. But I had passed an ordeal by drinking Hao Dashou's mung bean soup; I'd shed a layer of skin, and my bones had begun to ache. I'd heard a legend about rebirth, and I knew I'd become a new person. When I regained my health, I said to Hao Dashou: "Big Brother, let's get married."'

On the Occasion of Our Fourth Divorce Anniversary

Lana Bastašić

Maybe it was the woman's voice and the way she asked us. The room so banal, the table too long and holding only a piece of paper and a silent cellphone, the clock seven minutes late and her question as pointless as the ashtray in front of her. *What would you like to list as the reason?* We looked at each other. Was it that first year in Prague? First week, first everything, us sitting on the bed fighting, and you said *I think in terms of doing, not being*, with such disdain that I felt the *doing* was something done to my chest. He thinks I'm stupid, I thought. He thinks I'm a savage Balkan girl. He doesn't know I've never read Proust. And all I wanted to do was go out with that British actor and do LSD and peel my twenties off like band-aids. Let my tissue breathe devouring a Big Mac by the communist museum. Give me a purple jungle and the horror of uncovered mirrors. You were already tired. You walked alone and took photos of old circus posters and garbage cans. You weren't writing. And the woman's voice was perhaps already there, echoing back through the abandoned factories and their dead chimneys, only we couldn't hear it. We thought love was a handwritten letter before swallowing cum. *I have never been happier.* But I loved the mini croissants in that place around the corner where we'd talk about Barthelme and the authentic fakeness of Lana Del Rey and our friends' open relationships and how none of them worked. We believed we possessed a fragile little knowledge in our fragile little language, unattainable to anyone else, even Lana Del Rey. We figured it out. We worked. The cheesecake you made for my twenty-eighth birthday, our gorgeous grey cat yawning at our parade, and the "Blue Moon" rule. Perhaps it was the jazz band that couldn't play our song at our wedding? Or the flea-market ring that shattered into pieces when the jeweler tried to fit it to my size? My fingers were too small. Or maybe it was something else. Maybe it was my red shoes. My mother said they'd bring bad luck. What if I click my heels by accident and I'm transported back to Bosnia, I asked you. Don't worry, the real ones were silver. Because you always knew better, knew more. And then someone speaking in Catalan, telling me about us, about marriage, asking questions. I was bored. I clicked my heels in vain. The only word I knew was *sí*. Happy, happy. We bought records that day and a ukulele. Look, I said, the ukulele is called Rochester. I thought of the madwoman in the attic and how badly I wanted to give her a bath and brush her hair when I was fifteen. How I never identified with Jane. She was too quiet, too Jane. You were writing a long book about American postmodernism and couldn't be bothered with three Victorian sisters and ukulele superstitions. Rochester, I thought. It's called Rochester. And the first string broke on our first wedding anniversary but you refused the implication. This would be too much for fiction, I said. We still had three years left and no madwomen in the attic. We never had an attic. The madness was in the kitchen, toasting bread, doing the dishes, looking through the window at the loud green birds thinking—if I jump I would just break a couple of bones, it's not high enough. No one was swallowing anything anymore. My orgasm was a mathematical equation you had solved a million times. I wanted to sleep. I planted an avocado. I bought a sewing machine and made dolls for my nieces. I dyed my hair blue. You weren't writing. You watched me talk in my sleep to someone in the garden, to the avocado perhaps, in a language you never learned. It's too difficult, you said. I wanna do it right, you said. You woke me from sleep paralysis and whispered that it was ok, it was ok, nobody was there, it was just a hallucination. Your mother gave me her therapist's number and I sat in a huge sunlit office overlooking Passeig de Gràcia trying to translate my fears into Spanish. *Padre*, she said. And *madre*. She asked about my dreams and I worried about the subjunctive. Years later a woman in Belgrade would tell me how she ran across a barren field in the middle of the night with a battered face and two small children. You're divorced as well? And I felt embarrassed by all the breakfasts you made and the avocado you watered and the fancy therapist's office with hand-colored tiles in the bathroom. Yes, I'm divorced. I sleepwalked and could no longer touch him. I was my own barren field. But I said nothing. Nothing of my last birthday in your apartment, no cake, no "Blue Moon," because we thought we were set in stone. We became a series of *of courses*. Of course we do. Of course we are. Of course we would. I dyed my hair black and cut it short in our bathroom. I watched it cover the floor like a dark season. You were writing. I walked down Verdi Street with another man and he bought me ice cream and Bergman's *Marriage Scenarios*. I was wet when he hugged me and wet when he said goodbye and I felt my insides dry off like hanged meat as I walked back to your apartment. There was an abandoned stuffed panda bear by the garbage can and I thought how fitting it would be to cry there and then, but I couldn't. I was dry. I took a photo for my Instagram. You were writing. You were playing a game called *Clash of Clans* and you had a whole village to defend. You were texting a young blue-haired waitress. Her dog died and she was sad. You called her pretty. I looked at the heavily filtered photos of her and her dog on Facebook trying to picture you next to them. Wondering if she read Proust and swallowed your cum. I would finish work late and come back by train right around the time when her shift started and would walk to the bar and ask her to pour me a shot of tequila. She had hentai eyes and very thin arms and some nights I thought the weight of the bottle would break her. Her hair made me think of "Blue Moon, I saw you standing alone" and that first week of letters and our long-distance dancing to Spotify. *I can't wait for us to start* in your small handwriting in Xavier de Maistre. She smiled gently when I used the wrong article for tequila and I thought she was a good person. And anyway, it wasn't her face in that room years later when the woman asked the reason. It was my own. It was my mother's. My mother sitting on my bed that day, crying her eyes out because she had just caught her first boyfriend cheating on her. I was seventeen, looking through the window at the boys playing soccer in the schoolyard. They were shouting insults at each other, one of them had a bloody knee. My mother's face turned purple and she could barely catch her breath. His car, she said, his car. She came to me because I had more experience with men. I held her shaking form in my arms, that woman who allowed me to pierce my bellybutton as long as it was a doctor doing it, she was my daughter now. Asshole, I whispered into her thinning brown hair. My fake sunflowers and a Rita Hayworth poster on the wall and the green furniture my father hated because green, he said, was a Muslim color. He's an asshole, I said and caressed her protruding spine. And the boys screamed in the distance. Offside, you motherfuckin' piece of shit! Offside! I could still hear them in the lawyer's room. I no longer wore a bellybutton ring. There was a small hole there now. I liked it better that way. Your skin was intact and clear of tattoos and your parents held hands when we walked in the forest that day. When they kissed I looked away. They made tea and gave me rent money when I left you. When you were little they used a special method to teach you maths. Your mom showed you pictures of colorful dots and you said *dotze, divuit, trenta-sis!* You knew the difference between Chopin and Schubert. Your teacher called you a child prodigy. And here you were divorcing a Bosnian woman who never read Proust and had holes in her skin. It cost us eight hundred euros. Afterwards we sat in a small coffeeshop over two *tallats* and felt robbed of a ritual. Was that it? I needed to slaughter an animal and dance in its blood. I needed to scream at the moon and scratch my hands until they bled and burn my ukulele. I needed to mourn the narrators of our first letters. Instead I moved to a small room in a building full of drug dealers and shared a toilet with four strangers. I started reading *Swann's Way* in English and I thought No. This wouldn't have saved us. These are just words. But I guess we knew that already in Prague, that day on the bridge, when we told the American girl she didn't have to take a photo of us. We don't do photos, we said. We remember.

Loba Lamar's Last Kiss

("Silk Ribbons at My Funeral, Please . . .")

Pedro Lemebel

Translated from Spanish by Gwendolyn Harper

She had street smarts and a genius for her own behind in flaunting that name, that triumph of maritime vaudeville that crowned the dance floor the moment it left the announcer's lips. The brasses blaring out "Mambo No. 8," the bloody wink of the spotlights, the hands clapping her onstage. Those hands slapping her skinny man's ass as it shook to the beat of the tambourine.

She went by Loba Lamar, the Sea Lioness, maybe for the wet grime of her dark skin, for the olive algae of her pelt that the sailors wrung out every night. But Loba Lamar was more than that: a teardrop of black lamé, the trampled embers of a travesti Africa, a dark glimmer among the harbor lights. She used to trip on the stairs as she retraced her path up the hill to her seedy rented room, tumbling onto the steps amid peals of drunken laughter and the sharp smell of belladonna. It was hard to keep upright at that hour, after having mamboed through the night in those unmistakable stilettos. After weathering the seasickness of AIDS, clouding it over by mistaking the sea for the sky, which splashed a vertigo of stars against the waves. In those moments, Loba believed that it had all finished oh so quickly, oh so painlessly, oh so suddenly, that an AIDS death was just a missed step on the dance floor, a path of sparks over the Caribbean like a passage to another world. A moon in the water, caught in tropical currents, beyond the epidemic's reach. But morning always found her there just the same, leaping from star to star. Her missed step was not death, more like a pale return to her destitute life as an unsung loca.

Lobita never understood what being a carrier meant, which was lucky, or AIDS would have taken her straight down on its depressive toboggan. But Loba didn't have much of a head for connecting her own positive result with the drama of disease. She thought everything was fine, there was no convincing her that this check mark was an eviction notice. And though she turned and turned the report card between her fingers, the arithmetic of converting plus to minus didn't enter her head, and her little bird brain never solved the math problem, never drew those little boxes that help you add and subtract. Loba was always a hopeless loca, rubbish at her studies and bullied at school. A plus could no less subtract than a minus could ever add up, and up yours with those numbers and to hell with life. And if I won a prize, she said, this paper isn't going to convince me.

We never saw Loba sad, but a dark cloud bloomed in her yerba maté that day. She folded the sheet and took a deep breath, inhaling the room's stale air. She gulped and sighed until the stench overwhelmed the gravity of the news. Then she walked to the window and opened it, looking out over the rusting seaside roofs. She took a lock of her hair, faded by cheap dye, and yanked it out, making a sound like ripping paper. She watched it flash copper in a ray of sunlight reflected by the glass. Then she opened her hand, letting the strands float into the feathered breeze that cushioned the afternoon.

La Lobita never let emaciation ruin her looks. As she yellowed, she added rouge; the bigger her bags, the bigger her smoky eyes. She never let herself go, not even in those final months, when she was a string of a body, her cheeks stuck to the bone, her scalp shining through a downy fuzz of hair. Even then she looked bronzed by the sun, "though my heart is in winter," a line she tirelessly repeated in her variety show, when fatigue no longer let her dance.

For us, the locas who shared her room, Loba had made a pact with the devil. How has she lasted so long? How does she still look pretty with those scabs falling off like petals? How, how, how? No AZT, just spunk and her own pulsing heart, and boy did her stubborn ass resist. It was the sun, the good weather, the heat. She withstood the whole summer like a cherry, the whole fall which was warm, and only as winter arrived, as the harbor rain began to drizzle its numbing brine, only then did she show symptoms of goodbye. She fell onto her cot and never got up again. And so the agonies began.

Lobita never wanted to go back to the doctor after that first exam. He's in bed with the gravedigger, she said. She couldn't stand those health centers either, which she thought looked like leper concentration camps. Like in *Ben-Hur*, the only movie she'd ever seen in her entire life. She remembered perfectly that part when Charlie Heston goes looking for his mother and sister in the leper colony. And they both hide, not wanting the boy to see them like that, stripped of skin, their flesh falling off in chunks. Because they had been so beautiful, gorgeous, real nice-looking, though never nearly as nice as Loba, who spent whole nights delirious, recounting the movie. Burning with fever, she cursed the Roman galleys together with Ben-Hur. And she made everyone who was perched on her cot row along with her, threatening to drown herself as the hot waves of her temperature made her shout, Attention, whores of the oar! Onward, maracas of mambo!

We took shifts caring for her, washing her bum like a baby. We were her nannies, her nurses, her cooks, a troop of slaves she bossed around with her Cleopatra airs. We were so patient with her, we would count to twenty, twenty breaths to stop ourselves from wringing her neck. If she'd only shut up and let us sleep a little. At least an hour, during all those insomniac nights on her deathbed. Her demented condition of moribund queen, refusing to kick the bucket and wanting every little thing, every eccentric whim satisfied. One midnight, in the rainy depths of winter, she wanted fresh peaches. And like idiots we left the house in the downpour, all of us wetter than pelicans, rummaging for change as we searched the deserted streets, waking up every shopkeeper in the port, going up and down the hills until we found a can of the damned fruit. And when we returned, shaking ourselves dry like dogs, la Loba chucked the can at our heads because her craving had come and gone. Now she wanted tangerine ice cream. Tangerine ice cream? Can't you want something else, honey? They don't make tangerine ice cream in Chile, Lobita, understand. But she insisted that it had to be tangerine, threatening to die right then and there if she couldn't smell that spring fruit's bittersweet perfume. And in the middle of June, frostbitten with cold, the locas turned around and went out again, braving the elements until they found a slick-eyed Argentine who, after hearing them wail the dying mamacita tango, agreed to sell them a cone. But even then Lobita couldn't sleep, now fixated on the pink flesh of a summertime melon. Ay! sighed the faggot over the sweetness of a cantaloupe, as if she feared not living to see January. As if she couldn't leave this world with that craving still drying her mouth. Because in hell there are no peaches, or tangerines, or melons. And that much heat makes you thirsty.

Ay! Slaves of Egypt, bring me melons, grapes, and papayas, raved the poor thing, waking the whole boardinghouse with the cries of her queenly pregnancy. As if the disease's holocaust had become a gestation of grief, swapping life for death, birth pangs for the throes of agony. The deranged Loba transformed AIDS into a promise of life, imagining that what she carried was a child incubated in her anus by her lost love's fatal semen. That prince of Judea, Ben-Hur, who had planted the fruit in the Roman galleys one night and then left at dawn, leaving her pregnant in a sinking ship.

Night after night we heard her call him, as we tried to placate Loba's parturient cravings. Because then she insisted we make clothes and a cradle for this prince she was bringing into the world. She set us all to knitting little sweaters and hats and vests and booties for her baby. She made us sing lullabies, rocking her as we fanned her with feathers, as if we truly were the slaves of an expectant Nefertiti. At some moment or another she had managed to cast us in her movie, so convincingly acted that, drained by exhaustion, we, too, came to believe in the coming delivery. So all the locas kept getting up in the freezing cold, sneezing, listening to her psych-ward fantasies, her final dalliances, her little voice strangled by coughing fits, more muffled each day but still shrieking orders. Until one afternoon, still haughty, she opened her mouth like a hippopotamus on the Nile and no sound came out. She was struck dumb in her pharaonic command. And there we sat, waiting, covering the mirrors so that Loba wouldn't look at herself again. Begging, praying, pleading for that airplane from nowhere to arrive soon. Mopping her sweat, saying Ave Marias and reciting rosaries like background music. All of us there, paler and shakier than Lobita herself, awaiting the minute, the second, in which this loca would sigh her last breath and our prayers could cease. The whole holy night spent watching her face, which to tell the truth looked more gorgeous than ever. Her silk skin, like a black tiger lily, rippled with light in that abyss. Her swan neck of dark pearl drooped like a ribbon. Then a cold breeze blew through the window, as if someone had opened a tomb. La Loba tried to say something, call someone, modulate a scream out of those tensed lips. She opened her rolling eyes, trying to snatch one last photo postcard from life. We watched how she flapped, desperate not to be swallowed by the shadow. We felt an icy touch that left us stiff, unable to do anything, unable to look away from Lobita, her jaw wide open but unable to let out a scream. We stood there like idiots, shocked by the dark corridor of her mouth, open like a black hole, like a cesspit in which we could just glimpse her prattling tongue. Her bottomless mouth paralyzed in the immense "AH" of a silent opera. Her marvelous mouth unchained like the entrance to a tunnel, like a sewer drain that had carried Lobita into the foul waters of that whirling, sinister eddy. And only then did we react, only then did we run to the edge of that ditch, shouting down, Don't die, Lobita darling. Don't leave us, beautiful. Sobbing, still horrified by her mouth, we stuck our hands into that darkness, trying to grab her by the hair as she fell. All of us struggling to reach her, to drag her back into the living. We grabbed her hands, rubbed her feet, shook her, embraced her, covered her in kisses, sissies crying in unison, sissies laughing neurotically, sissies bringing her water, pushing her, not knowing what to do or what to serve our guest, Señora Death, who was calling at such a disagreeable hour.

And we saw our friend depart on that river of weeping, on that trusty diseased glider carrying her open-mouthed to heaven. She can't go like that, the poor thing, said the locas, already calmer. She can't get stuck with her trap open like a hungry frog, herself so divine, so careful with every gesture and pose. She should always be remembered as a diva. Something must be done. Quick, close her mouth with a scarf before it stiffens. One long enough to wrap around her chin and knot on top of her head. Not yellow, stupid, what a depressing color. Not polka dots either, she'd look like a cartoon, and Lobita would never have worn that. Green? Worse, she hated the cops. Sky blue? Nuh-uh, she's no premature baby. What about that turquoise chiffon with gold thread, yes that same one you're hiding you faggot piece of shit with your friend here dead. This looks fabulous on her yes and wraps all the way around her jaw and there's even enough for a bow. Don't knot it on her forehead, for the love of God, the ends look like rabbit ears and turn her into Bugs Bunny, the poor dear. And don't put the knot under her chin either, as if she were Heidi or some Russian babushka. Better on the side, near her ear, like how Lola Flores wore it, back when they called her the Pharaohess, Lobita thought the world of her. A nice, tight knot, even if it crushes her cheek, leave her jaw shut for an hour at least, until it sets and hardens. So for an hour the locas busied themselves bathing the corpse in enough milk and starch for a Babylonian queen. They smeared her with boiling wax, leaving her hairless and slicker than a nun's tit, while someone else gave her a manicure, gluing on little mollusk shells like fake nails, and another sawed off her calluses and bunions, scaling off the calcified grime of her feet. Because you, dearie, were like Christ, who walked across the sea without touching water. Gordita, you were never all that black, you just roly-polied in the dirt, too lazy to wash with soap, always applying rouge and perfume over the muck, said the locas, scrubbing Lobita with chlorine. While they were waxing her eyebrows and curling her lashes with a heated spoon, the dead queen began to go stiff. So they untied the knot mooring her face to do her makeup and discovered with glee that the scarf had closed her mouth as tight as a crypt. But just when the locas touched her cheek, Loba's lips opened into the macabre smile of rigor mortis. Ay no, shouted one of the queens, she can't go looking like that, with a vampire grin. Something must be done! Bring hot towels to soften her up. Make them practically boiling, the girl can't feel a damn thing. But the heat from the rags made a nerve spasm and her jaw dropped again, her lips opening into a cackle. Looks like our girl is having a laugh at our expense, growled la Tora, the Bull, a burly loca who'd been a wrestler when she was younger. Leave her to me. And we kept quiet because an angry Tora is a serious thing. We meekly reminded her to do it with love. Remember, she's quite frail, amiga. Don't worry, said la Tora, snorting, she's not going to beat me. We watched her disappear before coming back sheathed in her lucha libre attire, with her scarlet cape and devil mask that had earned her the nickname Lucifer, The Un-fallen Angel, The Invincible Flame. After warming up with a few jumps and a couple of shark attacks, la Tora asked us to clap for her. And in the midst of that Andalusian bullring hullabaloo, her face turned suddenly serious and she cut off the cheers with a shh of silence so she could concentrate. Not even a fly buzzed as she knelt at the foot of the bed and ritually crossed herself, as she would before entering the ring. And with a leap she was on the cadaver, pummeling it with knuckle-bruisers. *Paf, paf,* the sound of punches filled the room until Loba's face looked like mashed potatoes. Then la Tora lifted her hammy fist and, with her thumb and index finger, squeezed Lobita's cheeks together hard until her lips whistled into a rose. Suck your molars, dearie, suck your molars like Marilyn Monroe, la Tora said, not moving her hand. She kept those cheeks pressed between her pincers for almost an hour, waiting until Loba's flesh returned to its mournful rigidity. Only then did she let go, and we could see the marvelous result of her necrophiliac handiwork. There we stood, hearts in our hands, all of us teary-eyed as we gazed at la Loba, who threw us a kiss with her puckered smacker. We should cover up the bruises, someone said, reaching for her Angel Face powder. But why bother, when pink and lilac go so well together?

The Free Radio

Salman Rushdie

We all knew nothing good would happen to him while the thief's widow had her claws dug into his flesh, but the boy was an innocent, a real donkey's child, you can't teach such people.

That boy could have had a good life. God had blessed him with God's own looks, and his father had gone to the grave for him, but didn't he leave the boy a brand-new first-class cycle rickshaw with plastic covered seats and all? So: looks he had, his own trade he had, there would have been a good wife in time, he should just have taken out some years to save some rupees; but no, he must fall for a thief's widow before the hairs had time to come out on his chin, before his milk-teeth had split, one might say.

We felt bad for him, but who listens to the wisdom of the old today?

I say: who listens?

Exactly; nobody, certainly not a stone-head like Ramani the rickshaw-wallah. But I blame the widow. I saw it happen, you know, I saw most of it until I couldn't stand any more. I sat under this very banyan, smoking this selfsame hookah, and not much escaped my notice.

And at one time I tried to save him from his fate, but it was no go . . .

The widow was certainly attractive, no point denying, in a sort of hard vicious way she was all right, but it is her mentality that was rotten. Ten years older than Ramani she must have been, five children alive and two dead, what that thief did besides robbing and making babies God only knows, but he left her not one new paisa, so of course she would be interested in Ramani. I'm not saying a rickshaw-wallah makes much in this town but two mouthfuls are better to eat than wind. And not many people will look twice at the widow of a good-for-nothing.

THEY MET RIGHT HERE.

One day Ramani rode into town without a passenger, but grinning as usual as if someone had given him a ten-chip tip, singing some playback music from the radio, his hair greased like for a wedding. He was not such a fool that he didn't know how the girls watched him all the time and passed remarks about his long and well-muscled legs.

The thief's widow had gone to the bania shop to buy some three grains of dal and I won't say where the money came from, but people saw men at night near her rutputty shack, even the bania himself they were telling me but I personally will not comment.

She had all her five brats with her and then and there, cool as a fan, she called out: '*Hey! Rickshaaa!*' Loud, you know, like a truly cheap type. Showing us she can afford to ride in rickshaws, as if anyone was interested. Her children must have gone hungry to pay for the ride but in my opinion it was an investment for her, because must-be she had decided already to put her hooks into Ramani. So they all poured into the rickshaw and he took her away, and with the five kiddies as well as the widow there was quite a weight, so he was puffing hard, and the veins were standing out on his legs, and I thought, careful, my son, or you will have this burden to pull for all of your life.

But after that Ramani and the thief's widow were seen everywhere, shamelessly, in public places, and I was glad his mother was dead because if she had lived to see this her face would have fallen off from shame.

. . .

Sometimes in those days Ramani came into this street in the evenings to meet some friends, and they thought they were very smart because they would go into the backroom of the Irani's canteen and drink illegal liquor, only of course everybody knew, but who would do anything, if boys ruin their lives let their relations worry.

I was sad to see Ramani fall into this bad company. His parents were known to me when alive. But when I told Ramani to keep away from those hot-shots he grinned like a sheep and said I was wrong, nothing bad was taking place.

Let it go, I thought.

I knew those cronies of his. They all wore the armbands of the new Youth Movement. This was the time of the State of Emergency, and these friends were not peaceful persons, there were stories of beatings-up, so I sat quiet under my tree. Ramani wore no armband but he went with them because they impressed him, the fool.

These armband youths were always flattering Ramani. Such a handsome chap, they told him, compared to you Shashi Kapoor and Amitabh are like lepers only, you should go to Bombay and be put in the motion pictures.

They flattered him with dreams because they knew they could take money from him at cards and he would buy them drink while they did it, though he was no richer than they. So now Ramani's head became filled with these movie dreams, because there was nothing else inside to take up any space, and this is another reason why I blame the widow woman, because she had more years and should have had more sense. In two ticks she could have made him forget all about it, but no, I heard her telling him one day for all to hear, 'Truly you have the looks of Lord Krishna himself, except you are not blue all over.' In the street! So all would know they were lovers! From that day on I was sure a disaster would happen.

. . .

THE NEXT TIME THE THIEF's widow came into the street to visit the bania shop I decided to act. Not for my own sake but for the boy's dead parents I risked being shamed by a . . . no, I will not call her the name, she is elsewhere now and they will know what she is like.

'Thief's widow!' I called out.

She stopped dead, jerking her face in an ugly way, as if I had hit her with a whip.

'Come here and speak,' I told her.

Now she could not refuse because I am not without importance in the town and maybe she calculated that if people saw us talking they would stop ignoring her when she passed, so she came as I knew she would.

'I have to say this thing only,' I told her with dignity. 'Ramani the rickshaw boy is dear to me, and you must find some person of your own age, or, better still, go to the widows' ashrams in Benares and spend the rest of your life there in holy prayer, thanking God that widow-burning is now illegal.'

So at this point she tried to shame me by screaming out and calling me curses and saying that I was a poisonous old man who should have died years ago, and then she said, 'Let me tell you, mister teacher sahib *retired*, that your Ramani has asked to marry me and I have said no, because I wish no more children, and he is a young man and should have his own. So tell that to the whole world and stop your cobra poison.'

FOR A TIME AFTER THAT I closed my eyes to this affair of Ramani and the thief's widow, because I had done all I could and there were many other things in the town to interest a person like myself. For instance, the local health officer had brought a big white caravan into the street and was given permission to park it out of the way under the banyan tree; and every night men were taken into this van for a while and things were done to them.

I did not care to be in the vicinity at these times, because the youths with armbands were always in attendance, so I took my hookah and sat in another place. I heard rumours of what was happening in the caravan but I closed my ears.

But it was while this caravan, which smelled of ether, was in town that the extent of the widow's wickedness became plain; because at this time Ramani suddenly began to talk about his new fantasy, telling everyone he could find that very shortly he was to receive a highly special and personalised gift from the Central Government in Delhi itself, and this gift was to be a brand-new first-class battery-operated transistor radio.

Now then: we had always believed that our Ramani was a little soft in the head, with his notions of being a film star and what all; so most of us just nodded tolerantly and said, 'Yes, Ram, that is nice for you,' and, 'What a fine, generous Government it is that gives radios to persons who are so keen on popular music.'

But Ramani insisted it was true, and seemed happier than at any time in his life, a happiness which could not be explained simply by the supposed imminence of the transistor.

Soon after the dream-radio was first mentioned, Ramani and the thief's widow were married, and then I understood everything. I did not attend the nuptials—it was a poor affair by all accounts—but not long afterwards I spoke to Ram when he came past the banyan with an empty rickshaw one day.

He came to sit by me and I asked, 'My child, did you go to the caravan? What have you let them do to you?'

'Don't worry,' he replied. 'Everything is tremendously wonderful. I am in love, teacher sahib, and I have made it possible for me to marry my woman.'

I confess I became angry; indeed, I almost wept as I realised that Ramani had gone voluntarily to subject himself to a humiliation which was being forced upon the other men who were taken to the caravan. I reproved him bitterly. 'My idiot child, you have let that woman deprive you of your manhood!'

'It is not so bad,' Ram said, meaning the *nasbandi*. 'It does not stop love-making or anything, excuse me, teacher sahib, for speaking of such a thing. It stops babies only and my woman did not want children any more, so now all is hundred per cent OK. Also it is in national interest,' he pointed out. 'And soon the free radio will arrive.'

'The free radio,' I repeated.

'Yes, remember, teacher sahib,' Ram said confidentially, 'some years back, in my kiddie days, when Laxman the tailor had this operation? In no time the radio came and from all over town people gathered to listen to it. It is how the Government says thank you. It will be excellent to have.'

'Go away, get away from me,' I cried out in despair, and did not have the heart to tell him what everyone else in the country already knew, which was that the free radio scheme was a dead duck, long gone, long forgotten. It had been over—*funtoosh!*—for years.

AFTER THESE EVENTS the thief's widow, who was now Ram's wife, did not come into town very often, no doubt being too ashamed of what she had made him do, but Ramani worked longer hours than ever before, and every time he saw any of the dozens of people he'd told about the radio he would put one hand up to his ear as if he were already holding the blasted machine in it, and he would mimic broadcasts with a certain energetic skill.

'*Yé Akashvani hai*,' he announced to the streets. 'This is All-India Radio. Here is the news. A Government spokesman today announced that Ramani rickshaw-wallah's radio was on its way and would be delivered at any moment. And now some playback music.' After which he would sing songs by Asha Bhosle or Lata Mangeshkar in a high, ridiculous falsetto.

Ram always had the rare quality of total belief in his dreams, and there were times when his faith in the imaginary radio almost took us in, so that we half-believed it was really on its way, or even that it was already there, cupped invisibly against his ear as he rode his rickshaw around the streets of the town. We began to expect to hear Ramani, around a corner or at the far end of a lane, ringing his bell and yelling cheerfully:

'All-India Radio! This is All-India Radio!'

TIME PASSED. Ram continued to carry the invisible radio around town. One year passed. Still his caricatures of the radio channel filled the air in the streets. But when I saw him now, there was a new thing in his face, a strained thing, as if he were having to make a phenomenal effort, which was much more tiring than driving a rickshaw, more tiring even than pulling a rickshaw containing a thief's widow and her five living children and the ghosts of two dead ones; as if all the energy of his young body was being poured into that fictional space between his ear and his hand, and he was trying to bring the radio into existence by a mighty, and possibly fatal, act of will.

I felt most helpless, I can tell you, because I had divined that Ram had poured into the idea of the radio all his worries and regrets about what he had done, and that if the dream were to die he would be forced to face the full gravity of his crime against his own body, to understand that the thief's widow had turned him, before she married him, into a thief of a stupid and terrible kind, because she had made him rob himself.

And then the white caravan came back to its place under the banyan tree and I knew there was nothing to be done, because Ram would certainly come to get his gift.

HE DID NOT COME for one day, then for two, and I learned afterwards that he had not wished to seem greedy; he didn't want the health officer to think he was desperate for the radio. Besides, he was half-hoping they would come over and give it to him at his place, perhaps with some kind of small, formal presentation ceremony. A fool is a fool and there is no accounting for his notions.

On the third day he came. Ringing his bicycle-bell and imitating weather forecasts, ear cupped as usual, he arrived at the caravan. And in the rickshaw behind him sat the thief's widow, the witch, who had not been able to resist coming along to watch her companion's destruction.

It did not take very long.

Ram went into the caravan gaily, waving at his armbanded cronies who were guarding it against the anger of the people and I am told—for I had left the scene to spare myself the pain—that his hair was well-oiled and his clothes were freshly starched. The thief's widow did not move from the rickshaw, but sat there with a black sari pulled over her head, clutching at her children as if they were straws.

After a short time there were sounds of disagreement inside the caravan, and then louder noises still, and finally the youths in armbands went in to see what was becoming, and soon after that Ram was frog-marched out by his drinking-chums, and his hair-grease was smudged onto his face and there was blood coming from his mouth. His hand was no longer cupped by his ear.

And still—they tell me—the thief's black widow did not move from her place in the rickshaw, although they dumped her husband in the dust.

Yes, I know, I'm an old man, my ideas are wrinkled with age, and these days they tell me sterilisation and God knows what is necessary, and maybe I'm wrong to blame the widow as well—why not? Maybe all the views of the old can be discounted now, and if that's so, let it be. But I'm telling this story and I haven't finished yet.

Some days after the incident at the caravan I saw Ramani selling his rickshaw to the old Muslim crook who runs the bicycle-repair shop.

When he saw me watching, Ram came to me and said, 'Goodbye, teacher sahib, I am off to Bombay, where I will become a bigger film star than Shashi Kapoor or Amitabh Bachchan even.'

'"*I* am off," you say?' I asked him. 'Are you perhaps travelling alone?'

He stiffened. The thief's widow had already taught him not to be humble in the presence of elders.

'My wife and children will come also,' he said. It was the last time we spoke. They left that same day on the down train.

After some months had passed I got his first letter, which was not written by himself, of course, since in spite of all my long-ago efforts he barely knew how to write. He had paid a professional letter-writer, which must have cost him many rupees, because everything in life costs money and in Bombay it costs twice as much. Don't ask me why he wrote to me, but he did. I have the letters and can give you proof positive, so maybe there are some uses for old people still, or maybe he knew I was the only one who would be interested in his news.

Anyhow: the letters were full of his new career, they told me how he'd been discovered at once, a big studio had given him a test, now they were grooming him for stardom, he spent his days at the Sun'n'Sand Hotel at Juhu beach in the company of top lady artistes, he was buying a big house at Pali Hill, built in the split-level mode and incorporating the latest security equipment to protect him from the movie fans, the thief's widow was well and happy and getting fat, and life was filled with light and success and no-questions-asked alcohol.

They were wonderful letters, brimming with confidence, but whenever I read them, and sometimes I read them still, I remember the expression which came over his face in the days just before he learned the truth about his radio, and the huge mad energy which he had poured into the act of conjuring reality, by an act of magnificent faith, out of the hot thin air between his cupped hand and his ear.

The Wounded Man

Abdellah Taïa

Translated from French by Frank Stock

We had broken our fast about two hours ago. It was getting dark. Et Hay Salam was unusually calm. It was as if all the inhabitants of this working-class neighborhood in Salé had suddenly moved to the other side of the Bou Regreg River, not far from the beach in Rabat, everybody who lives here, except for my family. The place was deserted. It made you think that something extraordinary was about to happen, something that would drastically change the entire country, disrupt the land and the people still on it. A huge thunderstorm that would bring hope, rain and a successful harvest. Or else the Apocalypse: the end of the world, starting right now.

My mother, M'Barka, was sound asleep.

Ramadan was an exhausting month for her. Even though fasting made her very tired, on a daily basis and all by herself, she had to prepare rounds of sweets, crêpes and, of course, *harira*, a soup she always loved very tart with lots of tomatoes and lemon juice. In the past, my sisters were happy to help her make every day of this holy month a spiritual and gastronomic celebration, a never-ending ceremony. Now the house was empty. Three floors with nobody living there. Everyone had gone off somewhere, somewhere far away, some other city, some other country, left for another world, to live there among strangers, people I'd never know and never really accept. The only ones left in the house were my mother, my younger brother, Mustapha, whom we almost never saw, and me. M'Barka was afraid to be alone now, quite often afraid, and time and again she'd repeat herself by telling me how solitude is a slow and dolorous poison. That always made me sad, very sad. I never managed to completely share her suffering. On the other hand, I felt like crying every time I heard her talk like that. Every day, she would beg me not to tarry in the city once my classes ended at Rabat University, plead with me to come home early, before it got dark, beg me to catch the early bus and get home fast so the house seemed full again, so I could keep her company, help her get through her everyday tasks, cheer her up just by being there, put some life back in her, share a warm moment, make us feel like a family again before night fell.

At night, just when it came time for us to separate again, she'd never want me to retire to my bedroom. She'd want me to stay there beside her until she had fallen asleep. Sleep was death. And since my father's brutal disappearance one year ago, she suffered from bouts of fear and panic attacks. That's when she'd cling to me. She used to sleep in the living room, where the television was king. She didn't like that "apparatus," as she called it, but it wound up being the companion who got her through the day, this machine that emitted sounds, voices that somewhat reassured her, though not all the time.

Thanks to the price of satellite dishes coming down, we had just started to pick up the French channels, the ones that really interested me. When I could get it, I really liked watching Arte. That channel made me think of myself as someone important: this intellectual and with-it student who was interested in things that people around him found boring or hard to understand. I was proud. I acted proud, like I was one of a kind.

That's the part I was playing that night, after I devoured a good amount of the delicious Ramadan food my mother made. I turned on the television. There was this movie on Arte. I missed the beginning. Locked in the bathroom of some train station, Jean-Hugues Anglade was crying his eyes out. Obviously, he felt abandoned too. He was battling something as well, maybe solitude. I was instantly moved by him, by the actor and by the character he portrayed. Thanks to my knowledge of movies, it only took me about a minute to recognize that film, one I'd never seen before. It was "The Wounded Man" by Patrice Chéreau. A French film from 1983. A cult film. Something off-limits.

My mother was sound asleep. And right there on the screen, they were showing this movie that no one in Morocco could do anything about, whether that meant stopping it entirely or interrupting it to give a lesson in religious morality to this young hero who lived beyond the rules, wore his hair a little too long, and loved other men. This hero who was in love with one particular man.

I was faced with a dilemma. Faced with desire. Ready to watch that movie right to the end. Watch it with my stomach knotted with fear. Constantly on the look out. My mother, asleep in back of me, could wake up at any moment and catch me in the act. Then she'd know my secret, my one big secret, know about my other life, the object of my desire. She'd make a big deal out of it. The whole thing would be a scandal. I'd be so ashamed, I wouldn't know what to do, what to say to her.

My stomach hurt. I ate too much when we broke our fast and couldn't digest it all. I was aroused by the level of desire that permeated the film, that had taken over Jean-Hugues Anglade and the other characters. It was the only thing they lived for, the only thing that kept them alive: sex, love and the danger that went with them. They'd feel attracted to someone, approach him, try to pick him up, flatter him to no end, pay for him, play with his head, rape him, toss him aside, kill him little by little. I was fascinated, hypnotized by what I was seeing. And I wanted to live like one of those characters, to be just like them. Outside the law. I wanted to love just like they did. Love another man. Just one. Alone. Illicitly. I wanted to touch myself. Stroke myself. Lick myself. Bite myself. I wanted to go right up to the toughest one and give him everything I had.

My stomach was heaving. My sex was getting hard. And I didn't know what to do because I was still afraid in spite of the level of desire the television beamed right at me, this urge that overwhelmed me and soon drove me almost crazy.

Now my mother was snoring. Regular exhalations, loud snoring one minute, quiet snoring the next. But once or twice she stopped. I changed the channel immediately. I couldn't help taking this cessation as a sign that she was returning to consciousness, about to wake up and catch me watching this banned movie. Somewhat reassured after waiting an endless minute and turning towards her to make sure her eyes were completely shut and she was still miles away from me and all those images, I went back to watching "The Wounded Man" and his story. And suddenly my desire became uncontrollable and my fear came to the forefront.

Jean-Hugues Anglade was in love with this tall, handsome guy I seem to remember was dark. A little like Gérard Depardieu in the early '80s. This virile, sensitive, hard-edged, merciless man. A king. A dictator. A pimp.

Anglade fell for him the minute he saw him. And from that moment on, life revolved around this man who made him forget everybody else. No one else would ever matter as much as he did. Almost from day one, he gave up everything, his former life, his family, just to chase after this guy. He'd turn up on the street, in train stations, in parking lots, trail after him, pursue him, clumsily try to seduce him, anything to have a minute of his time, a minute of his body. To have him love him. And it never happened. Anglade lived on passion alone. The kind of passion that could only be heartbreaking and tragic.

Patrice Chéreau's film, in the same tumultuous and brutal way it took hold of me that night and has remained forever in my mind, is extreme in the way it depicts the exacerbation of romantic feelings, extreme in the way it reveals how sex dominates the body. This film comes complete with slaps to the face, quarrels, pursuits, every kind of trafficking, tears, orgies, blood, sperm, down and dirty moments, obsessions and death. It shows the never-ending slide of a young man with blood on his hands, a man doomed from the start, toward this crime he commits for love.

I forgot his first name. He was the one I identified with. In love and frustrated, just like him. Ready to give up everything for some wild dream, some rock of a man, some emotion rarer than hen's teeth, some exceptional human being. And constantly afraid. Constantly in hopeless pursuit of the only person I desire. The man I love. The man the Americans call "The One."

One man and one man only. Someone older than me so I could learn something from him, relive parts of the past with him, become this couple people wouldn't recognize. A spiritual leader, a master, a baker, a man of God who prays five times a day, an enlightened man, a parent, an uncle, a cousin . . .

The film played out in front of me, and lodged its force, its hopelessness and its religion in back of my eyes, in back of my mind. Without even knowing it, I had become a believer, someone prone to indulge in this lifestyle on a regular basis, someone adept at perceiving, at wandering about, at banging into bodies, at exploding with joy before I went crazy, even beyond crazy. What was forbidden stood right there in front of me, touching my scrawny and suddenly emboldened body. And what was forbidden stood right in back of me too.

My sex kept getting harder and harder, my heart even more confounded. My eyes were turning red. I was both happy and sad. Fired up and chilled to the bone, as if some gust of northern air, some blast from Tangier had passed over me. At one point, I wanted to wake my mother up and get her to look at these images, get her even more involved in this movie that moved and, for that matter, totally overwhelmed her well-mannered son. Wanted to move in towards her, snuggle up to her, find room on her lap, lift her hand to my stomach, feel her breath on my back, on my neck, recognize her smell in my nose and against my skin. Wanted to go back to where I began, the first door, the first opening that brought me into this world, that let me find life and light. And there, back in the place where it all started, back at my original threshold, I'd hollow out a space, a depression and sit there crying while I watched this wounded man, this young man, this brother disoriented by love's searing intensity, sit there crying, crying over him and right along with him. Wanted to gently move my mouth across his eyes, slowly run my tongue across each one until I finally drank the slightly salty water that flowed from them and ran down his cheeks and across his skin.

I knew just what he was going through. I dreamed about it. Fantasized about it. I stopped thinking. Couldn't think anymore. My eyes hurt, my thighs hurt, my knees hurt, my sex hurt.

I snapped out of it. The wounded man was still walking the Way of the Cross that all lovers walk. That's where this hero would fulfill his destiny, right here in front of us, here in this house that had no father, here in our almost empty living room, here in the privacy of our lives, so filled with silence and obscurity.

I used to think I was sophisticated, but, as I watched Patrice Chéreau's movie, I realized for the first time what an inexperienced movie fan I really was since I watched all movies the same way I always did. And by that I mean, the way I watched them back when my childhood years were ending and, still programmed by others, the religion of Indian films and Chinese karate movies became part of my life forever. I started to rediscover myself. I guzzled images in dark and public theaters, sitting there with prostitutes and thugs. And those images delivered me from the shackles of my homeland, linked me to an art form that little by little gave me a reason to live, a way to see above and beyond things. I could leave the world, go beyond its gravity, see my own nakedness, then return to fight my battles.

I was in the heat of battle. In full revolt. Just days away from Ramadan's holiest night.

Suddenly my mother's music stopped. Not a sound came from her mouth, no wheezing, no humming, not a single breath. Was it apnea? Was she dead, beyond all fear, no longer afraid, gone off to join my father? Was she awake now? Was she sitting there with me watching "The Wounded Man"? Would she figure out what these strange scenes meant, these pictures from another world, these images from hell? Was she suddenly going to jump up and start yelling at me, yelling in that voice she always used when things turned ugly, start pulling my hair, punishing me, pinching me, cursing me out? Would she try to castrate me right then and there?

With my heart in my throat, I turned to face her. Her eyes were open but she was staring at the ceiling. She was dreaming. She was still entangled in the sequence of images that sprang up in this dream that only she cultivated. Somewhat at ease, I changed the channel and asked her, in a quiet voice brimming with respect, if there was anything she needed. Her response was immediate, as if she had been preparing it for a long time, had fallen asleep thinking of it. "I'd love a glass of water, honey!" I ran to the kitchen to get her one. She was very thirsty, had just returned from some long voyage. She wanted another one. "I will die, child, if I don't have another one . . . Oh, my sweet son, may God . . ." She didn't have to ask me twice. I almost ran back to the kitchen, already happy that she would pray for me, remember me in prayers that were always the same, prayers that pictured heaven as someplace real and not some fictitious abode.

Her thirst quenched, M'Barka went back to her sleep, back to tending her dreams. But right before closing her eyes again, she gave me this blessing that absolutely bowled me over and still does: "My son, you need to watch, watch what you want on television . . . I will not get upset . . . Watch what you want . . ."

I turned the sound down and waited for my mother to start snoring again before I went back to watching "The Wounded Man," finally catching up with the film's wounded hero. By now, he had completely run out of patience, was tired of love that cruised a one-way street, tired of humiliation, tired of aimless wandering and all that time, crazed with love, crazed. He was almost at the point where his path to crime would end, the moment, that single and final moment, when he'd have his way with the other man, finally possess the object of his desire. Only death and that hit-man could give meaning, purpose and structure to this young man's tragic story, to his sublime love.

Naked, pressed against the man he loved, he was strangling him with his bare hands, snuffing him out while he made love to him. That's how he gave him everything he had: his body, his heart, his mind, his skin, his blood, his breath. He gave up his life by taking the life of the man who, right up to the end, refused to unite with him in that great religion of feelings and shared embraces.

It was tragic.

Love, like life, which at certain miraculous moments burns with light and intensity, is a tragedy. I knew that, knew it intuitively. I was twenty years old. "The Wounded Man" taught me that, taught it to me once and for all. I had been warned. The choice was mine. Would I give up? Never.

At the end of the movie, the credits flashed in front of my eyes. The name Hervé Guibert came up. He was the guy who wrote the script along with Patrice Chéreau. I had forgotten about him. This movie, this story, they were his too. Part of his life. The way he lived. A lifestyle I discovered and came to love when I read his books. He'd been dead for four or five years now. Tears started running down my cheeks. Finally. But, why was I crying? Who was I crying over? I didn't exactly know what to say, couldn't really answer my own question. Was it for Hervé Guibert, this man I knew inside and out after reading all of his books? Was it for the hero who in the course of that movie turned into a criminal, a brother, a friend, turned into me? Was it for my father who left too soon, who never got to see my life become a book, a story put into writing? Was it for life itself, life, that when you come right down to it, is sad and terribly lonely despite what happiness Ramadan brings?

Even today, I still don't know. Even today, I still cry when I think of what actually happened back then, think about how the movie ended, think about Guibert, think about myself . . . and think about my mother who cried out in silence. And I cry for all of us.

The next day, I woke up very late. I only had one thing in mind. I was in a big rush to find my favorite cousin, Chouaïb, the cousin I was sort of in love with. I ran off to find him, seduce him, corrupt him. I hurried off to hang all over him, talk him into breaking the fast before sunset, breaking it by letting both of us talk about sex. Then we'd climb that hill in Bettana, his neighborhood, and from up there, right next to the old cemetery, we'd be able to see the opposite shore of the Bou Regreg River, see Rabat, the Hassan Tower, the Kasbah built by the Oudayas, the public beach where poor people swam. Both of us would smoke a little hash. Then I'd put my head on his thighs. And in that state of silence and contemplation, I'd tell him all about the movie last night and gently, but directly, invite him to sin, to transgress.

To deliberately sin.

God would be watching us.

We'd do it anyway. Right through to the end. Right down to the sea. Right up into the sky.

Unlucky, one day I'd be unlucky in love, just like "The Wounded Man." In the meantime, Chouaïb, this cousin with a moustache, this bad boy with a body big enough to wrap around mine, has a place in my heart and that's how I drag him off to the movies almost every day, then sit there under the bright lights, my eyes completely shut.

Forty-Eight Steps

Paxima Mojavezi

Translated from Persian by Sara Khalili

I come home and I don't let on that I'm late. I come home and like a good mother I prepare dinner, set the table, feed them, wash the dishes, put the children to bed, and sit on the sofa with the man who is my housemate. I look at him. He is my children's father, with salt-and-pepper hair and a haggard face. I never got to know him, never figured out who he is. I look at his tired hands covered with cuts, at his lips that have turned dark from all the cigarettes he smokes, and at his weary eyes that remain fixed on the television screen.

I want to forget today; every moment of it. I close my eyes. I lean my head back against the wall. I know he is not looking at me. I know he doesn't care what I am thinking about. We both know this indifference well. I have nothing to say to him. Our conversations have been reduced to hellos and good-byes; except some nights when I hear his whisper close to my ear and that too sounds unfamiliar. Without a word, I get up, pass by him and go to the bedroom. I lie down on the bed. I close my eyes. I want to forget today, but I can't, not a single moment of it . . .

A fine snow is falling and the air is foggy. Like every weekday, I've come to the office, but I don't have the energy to work. My hands ache. I need to rest. I have no patience for this desk and this workplace. I find an excuse to take the day off and go back home. But instead of home, I arrive at a faraway café. A café whose name I don't even know. It's old and empty. There is no one here except the old woman serving coffee. I sit at one of the tables next to the window. I'm cold. I shiver. I wring my hands and order a coffee. Waiting for it to be prepared, I think about how my children have grown. The scent of coffee wafts through the café. I massage my hands. The joints are so swollen! I can no longer take off my wedding ring. I'm getting old; I'm not the way I used to be. I hear the delicate clinking of a coffee cup against a saucer. I look outside. The snowflakes are hurling themselves to the ground more briskly. They seem happy that the earth is turning white. But I'm cold. I'm not wearing warm clothes. I'm dressed in an old worn-out cardigan that will quickly get wet in this snow. The old thickset woman comes toward me. There is no smile on her lips and her disheveled silver hair has escaped her pink headscarf. She puts the cup of coffee in front of me and returns to her place behind the counter. The steam rising from the cup warms me. It's a pleasant feeling that—

The café door opens. A man walks in. From behind the counter, with a familiar smile, the old woman says hello in Armenian—"*Barev.*" The man nods. He walks past me and stops a few tables away. I can't see his face in the dim light. He takes off his coat, shakes off the snow and puts it on the chair next to him. He sits down. Without asking, the old woman gets busy brewing. The scent of coffee wafts through the café. My hands ache. I massage them. The man lights a cigarette. It smells so familiar. I take a sip of coffee. My gaze turns to the street and then to the man who has faded away in cigarette smoke. I rest my forehead on the table. I want to end it all; the ache in my hands, the exhaustion, the loneliness. But there is no end to any of it. I raise my head. The man has finished his coffee. He looks at me. I don't see his face, just the glint in his eyes. He puts money for the coffee on the table, takes his coat from the chair next to him and puts it on. He slowly walks past me. He opens the café door and steps onto the snow-covered ground. He stops. He turns back. He looks at me. Should I have gotten up? I get up. I put money for the coffee on the table. I don't care about the old woman's curious looks. I open the café door. I walk out onto the snowy street and toward the man. He sets off, a few steps ahead of me. I follow him. It's an empty street with four alleys. He turns onto the second one, a dark narrow alley. He walks toward the building at the far end. He takes a key out of his pocket. The old door opens with a groan. He steps aside. I walk in first.

He says, "Top floor."

What a strange voice, or perhaps what a familiar one. We climb up forty-eight steps. A door with faded paint that was once blue is in front of me. And now . . . he opens the door. The blue flames of the heater cast the only light in the room. He turns on a lamp. Books are the first things that catch my eyes. On the floor, on the table, even on the bentwood chairs there are stacks of books. There's an ashtray full of cigarette butts, and a few sheets of ink-stained paper are scattered on the floor.

I look at him. He says nothing. His eyes quiver like a pair of black marbles. He walks over to the only other room in his home. I follow him. Other than a bed and a pink floor lamp, the room is crowded with books, papers, photographs, and magazines. I take off my faded cardigan. He looks at me. I look at him. Have I never seen him before? No, he is not a stranger. It seems he is my man who has come from distant years. He has black hair and a fresh young face, hands that are slender and full of vigor, red lips that tremble, and bright captivating eyes that gaze at my face. I must be young; intense passion, a scorching energy, ripples in me. I want all the ice inside me to melt. I want him to take me in his arms, he does, I grow warm, I no longer shiver . . .

It was past ten o'clock when I left that apartment and walked down those forty-eight steps. The darkness of night led me from that deserted narrow alley toward my home.

I come home and I don't let on that I'm late. I close my eyes and I try to . . . I try to forget today.

Magnifical

Linnea Axelsson

Translated from Swedish by Saskia Vogel

A mother does not give her life to the child
that is called her own. No, she only tends
to the fresh seed that in her has been sown.
And the one who sows gives life. The mother is
but a stranger who offers shelter to the plant . . .

—AISKYLOS

to forget caresses
and pain
is no less than to give one's life.

—ANNA AKHMATOVA

The Evening

The boy and I used to make love in the car, we'd lock up Ma's house and drive into the woods and climb into the back seat where I'd get on top of him, it wasn't exactly great but it was arousing. After a party when I was seventeen years old I'd bobbed my head in his lap on our way home at dawn, and when I finally straightened up and leaned back in the seat the pink sky and the lonely road and the woods and the peaceful power I felt had merged into an eternity, which I truly used to believe in. I could still remember the sensation of the boy's skin, his constant sniffles, because he almost always had a bit of a cold. The way his hands flitted as he shook those three big rings of his, forever sliding along his finger, back into place. His fingers had moved with a special rhythm across the keyboard as he typed; it reached all the way into my body. An explosive clatter, followed by a distinct pause, very precise, as if his hands were thinking, then the clattering again. I remembered how at the funeral I'd wanted to reach across the pew in front of me and stick my hand in his cousin's brown hair.

We left the bistro. My friend was holding me by the waist and I could tell she was excited and tired and I was sure that she was drunk. For a brief period maybe a decade ago, I'd taken to laughing her laugh. A laugh that was more ladylike, at times softer, which facilitated an ease when in company, as if being warm were simple and natural. We came to a square where people were passing by or standing around talking to each other, and she grabbed hold of my hand and stopped and pulled me onto an empty bench. I felt someone sniffing my fingers, and when I turned around I saw a German Shepherd with a big smiling pinched-clay face, it gave my hand a quick and thorough inspection before continuing down the street, together with a woman in a long coat. We each lit a cigarette. For a long while we sat in silence on the bench, keeping ourselves at a remove from it all. The wine had gone to my head, to the front of my face, my jaws, and my bite. The yearning for more even though I didn't want more. Have you had a chance to think about it, my friend asked out of the blue, about the thing with the baby. Since we talked about it last, I mean. As if more than a year hadn't managed to pass since that time, as if she hadn't been copiously drunk that time. I remembered her rushing to order a bottle of Côtes du Rhône, probably because she knew she'd get to drink most of it herself. There'd been a long exposition about their plan for how we could do it, even though it wasn't legal. Or was it legal, but might still be difficult for them to take custody of the child. We *have* thought of everything, she said and sucked on her cigarette. No need for you to worry, we'd arrange everything for you, nothing will go wrong. It turns out I've inherited some money, so we can pay you now. If you want to birth our child for us.

And I wasn't prepared for this, and I felt myself smiling very widely, almost like she was. And I said, what?, inheritance, good for you. Yeah, it's not a lot of money, she said, I mean, we're not rich, but we can pay you well for doing it, if you want to help us.

I remembered the body brushing against my belly, the way it turned, treaded. And the uterus rising up hardening, stretched out like a dome. Kneading pulses that come and go, until the hips begin to howl. And then the sudden twinge. When the head grinds against the pubic bone, scraping, like chalk.

I was drawn into her smile. It was no longer possible to tell whether I was inebriated or sad. Out in the darkness, the Eiffel Tower's searchlight moved across the sky. It disappeared behind the buildings, down into the silent river. I still remembered certain nights in that house, when I'd wander over to Ma's bed. The smell of smoked meat and the damp mess of our sheets, skin sticky where our nightclothes had ridden up, while the sky slowly turned blood red and yellow. How I might awaken to sudden coolth, Ma having long since slipped to the floor and curled herself around the dog. Only buy colored towels, maybe blue or green, she'd instructed me when I was young. White terrycloth ends up going grey in the wash. It was my last year of high school. I'd brought home blue glass bowls and blue placemats and a pasta spoon and salad servers in blue plastic, which I then stored in the closet in anticipation of the boy and I moving in together. I guess I was afraid they wouldn't still be in the shops half-a-year later. It had been so hot that whole summer, a heat we weren't used to, that kept us awake at night. We went into the kitchen and made sandwiches, and the butter immediately went soft. Drops of salt sweating out of the glossy surface. We ate in silence standing up, not actually hungry. Ma plodded off in her light blue nightgown in search of a cool place, and I lingered at the kitchen counter, looking at dishes with leftover sausage and chunks of roast potato and fried onions glistening in the night sun, a pale pink gleam through the windows that seemed to be moving and alive, but really it was just the midges dancing. I followed the whirling particles in the light that reached all the way to the porcelain horses and dolls in dusty woolen outfits on the sideboard, and I opened the pantry and started sorting out old baking mixes and grains that were years out of date, while waiting to feel tired.

Come on, my friend said, at least think about it, okay? Then we'll talk some more tomorrow. And she stood up and I got up, too. We dropped our cigarettes and walked on side by side. Soon the dark brick Swedish Church building would come into view. I'd traveled in to the city a few times with the girl to visit, once on an evening several years ago to show her the St. Lucy's Day "train", as the procession was called back home. I tried to explain what we'd be seeing, but she had still been disappointed, when there was no actual train. Just the white-clad throng of children of various ages, from the school somewhere on the upper floors. Hardly any outside noise had leaked in that night, through the fine muntin bar windows. An almost white-haired boy had calmly stepped forward and read verses that brought tears to my eyes, perhaps because so much time had passed since I'd heard someone utter such old Swedish words. A mother had slid down from the pew where she'd been sitting beside her husband, she took a seat on the floor, in the aisle between the pews, and spread her legs like an enclosure around a child who looked to be about a year old. The father was tall and young, with a sparse patchy beard that was either unkempt or had never really filled in. He looked at her disapprovingly, but she'd only be sitting there for a minute or so before giving up, it wasn't working. The child crawled away and I bent over to touch the stone floor, which was hard and cold. The woman had risen from the floor, she was walking out with the child and the father sat alone for a short while, before he too slipped out and disappeared, through the high doors that had felt so strangely weightless when I pulled them open on our way in. Do we get buns after, the girl had whispered, and I'd replied, yes, we get buns.

We walked past the arches with the locked wrought-iron gates. The inner courtyard was dark in front of the church and the well and the steep steps. I'd forgotten that there was ivy growing around the windows but now it hung there black and brittle almost shriveled in its winter coat. My friend turned the corner and I stopped mid-step. Come on, she called to me, just come, just come with me, and I followed her across the street to the sidewalk on the other side. Knitted sweaters that looked to have been plant-dyed were on display in a shop window, there were a few small lipstick cases embroidered with flowers nearest the window and I knew they had a small mirror under the flap because my mother used to have a similar case, she'd had the case but never a lipstick. I could picture her, carefully scraping off the ashes against the sole of her shoe and returning the cigarette to its pack, if she'd only smoked half. Penny-wise, that's what I'd always thought. Much later I realized it was because we were in the woods, and there weren't any waste baskets. At the next junction right next to a lit-up alley, I stopped and said we should start walking back. Where do you think you're going? my friend asked, and I said, aren't we going home? No, you're not going home, she laughed, and entered the alley. I said, aren't I? No, you're not going home, here it is, look. She nodded towards a hotel. Here it is, she said again, I thought I'd give you a night at a hotel as a present. And I said, but you already paid for the meal.

The shame that took my voice away when I tried to use my tongue and mouth to spell my name for the woman across the counter. Shame because my friend had given me something so expensive, and which I'd surely fail to appreciate. I stood alone in the room, trying to discern the city's movements across the earth. This building must have ossified. Dust and cold. The plaster from aging facades that was trampled into the sand in the parks, carried around the streets, catching in car tires and the soles of shoes and animal paws. The trees that cracked the asphalt with their writhing roots. I'd actually been disappointed when the woman downstairs handed over a regular key, and not a keycard, like they did seven years ago, at the hotel in Normandy.

Once upon a time a long time ago somewhere very close to this alley I'd been crying on the phone behind an ancient stone portico leading to a park that spanned several blocks trying to persuade Ma to fly down to keep me company and take care of me until the evil thoughts loosed themselves from all the others and disappeared, harmless and silent as shadow beings.

I warmed up and took off my jacket and scarf. I kicked off my shoes and stretched out on the bed, pulling off my sweater and tank top and then my jeans and socks in one and the same writhing supine motion. The stomach, the grey-white panties. The curve of thigh. My gnarled feet. Searching for every answer, every sign. The pale pink silk of my flat nipples. After one of the first times we made love, my husband had tried to pluck a long translucent strand of hair from one of my nipples, then had embraced me laughing when he discovered it was stuck. I got up from the bed and went into the bathroom. In the early days after the girl's birth, urine fell out of me. It was as if there was no elasticity left, no musculature. A hot fragrant mist dispersing my already dissolved pelvis. Trickling softly onto the white enamel. Woven with thick streaks of blood. A testament to the child that had grown inside and then pushed its way out of my body's depths. To the breath and pulse of life and its cessation and its death as long as I wanted this. As long as I was still able. Until the last fish-shimmering pearls left their meandering passages and channels. And the negative space of the ovaries would spread like little blown-out grottos. Emptied and expired. Shining with moisture and pink. Like the desolate shuck where the sea remains only in the smell of salt. A murmuring whisper. I tore off a piece of paper and dried myself and went back into the room and stretched out on the bed once more and looked at the dark window.

I searched my body for the boy's arms. His lips, which had been full and pink, with a blue undertone. The downy strands that would only sprout out from the skin of his upper lip several days after he'd shaved. Surely because he hadn't had a particularly hairy body, but also because he was so young. If my husband licked me some hours after he shaved off his beard, it might cut me. He could shave in the morning, and by one o'clock he'd have a dark shadow on his cheeks and around his mouth.

I pulled my handbag onto the bed. I could picture him stretched out on the sofa in the dark holding his phone, letting it ring, because I still wasn't home, because I hadn't called earlier. Hi, I said, well, we finished a while ago. How was it? he asked, and I said, you know, we had a good time, is she asleep. Yes, she's asleep, of course she's asleep, he replied. And I said, hey, I probably should've called you right away, but, I'm going to be staying at a hotel tonight, she thought I needed to rest up. And he said, what, at a hotel? Footsteps out in the corridor could be heard, the room next door being unlocked and someone walking into it. Someone with a dainty body who immediately washed their hands.

After I hung up, I felt the tears come. I held the phone up in front of my face, searching through the names. The last call I made before this one to my husband was to my mother, it was always Ma's number and my husband's number or our girl's number, sometimes my friend's. Each trace had been so important in the beginning, right after the boy had died. I'd been given a better phone as a hand-me-down, and I realized too late that I had thrown away his number along with my old phone. I lay there staring for a long time, staring at the window and the phone. I didn't have to search my memory for the right numbers. I hadn't forgotten them.

It rang several times. Then I heard a shift in the sound. A room opening up far away. His mother's room, where she'd sit in front of the TV, the wine-red sofa and the coffee cup in her hand, I could feel myself standing there. Remote controls in a row, the painting with the bear and the lynx, next to the diploma from the king, by the dining room table with its runner. And a little further in, the room with the desk, and the bed that was no longer there. The narrow bed with half-worn-away stickers on the headboard, where the boy had tied my wrists with a kimono sash before he started to help himself into me with his free hand, as I lay listening for his mother's footsteps.

I recognized her voice. It had barely aged. I was so scared that I started shaking. I heard his mother say, oh my, it's you. Yes, it's me, I said, how's it going. And she said, oh, I can't complain. I said, well, I thought I'd give you a call, it's been so long, and I'm at a hotel. I never usually stay in hotels, but, it was a gift, so now I'm lying here, alone. How's the dog, I asked, you do have a dog now. And she said, sure, we've got a dog. Say, are you still living in Paris, she asked, remembering after a while. And I told her that I did still live here, that I had my girl too, she was ten years old now. And she said, yes, right, good for you. Yes, I said, it is good, and she's so big now, kind. My voice broke. The girl's growing body that had slipped out of me like a fish. The slap of her slender tail. Those wonderful heart-shaped shoulder blades. Which I was barely allowed to touch anymore. It was really her, the boy's mother. All at once I realized that not for a moment had I understood the extent of her pain.

I'm sorry, I said, I don't know why I wanted to call. It's been so long, tonight ended up being such a strange one over here. And then, I suddenly came to think of him. I miss him.

The Day

When I woke up in the room in the darkness and silence, the boy was sitting on the edge of the bed. I cried out and threw myself forward, trying to wave away his phantom, but instead of air what I felt was warm and firm, and I withdrew my hand. The boy raised his face. I couldn't tell if he was sad or just earnest or solemn or tired. His eyes were larger and sadder, marked by what they'd seen, and he was both tinged with something aged and frightening and different to how I remembered him, and exactly the same nineteen-year-old boy as when he disappeared. Death had changed him. I reached out and gently and tentatively touched his shoulder. It *is* you, I said, of course I can see that it's you. My God, you're so young. My breasts stuck to my belly, soft from breastfeeding, and I pulled up the sheet. I looked at his body and it was clear and firm, like a living thing. Is it you, I whispered, not daring to take my eyes off him. Dear you, dear love. I sobbed and stroked his arms, I cried and clung to his neck, which was soft and warm, but a barren, mute warmth. Well, go on, say something, I said, straightening up and trying to meet his eyes. Say something, can't you speak.

A fox or birds called from the alley in the morning haze, and the boy turned towards the sound. As if on cue, he straightened his back and he rose slowly and tentatively until he was on his feet, and he stood perfectly still for a while, listening. Silently, and with evident effort, he took a step across the floor. Trembling I got up and the sheet slipped off me and then the blanket, which came to rest in a heap between us, and I stood with both my arms around the boy and held him by the waist and steadied him. Come, I said, come and sit back down, come on, let's have a seat. The boy did not answer. Hey, I said, you have to talk to me. He looked like he was about to collapse, and I pulled him onto the bed. I felt his forearm against my naked thighs. The curve of his stomach against my fingers. His small shiny pink fingernails. I sat with our hands in my lap. My mind went blank. There was a faint buzzing, it buzzed and buzzed, and then it stopped. After a moment the buzzing started up again. I both understood the sound and did not. I shoved my hand under the pillow and retrieved my phone. I saw that my husband had called a couple of times, as had my friend.

The girl's voice almost always made me speak in a much lighter, softer tone. She asked me to describe the room where I'd slept in detail, then I had to promise that she would get to come with me the next time I stayed in a hotel. I promise, I said. Look, tell Dad that I'm just going to go for a walk through the city, then I'll come right home. Tell him, well, to figure something out for lunch. I think there are pizzas in the freezer.

When she was seven or eight years old, the girl would still call out for me if she woke up in the night. She never came wandering into our bed like other people's children did, I was the one who had to go to her. She would call for me in the dark, and I'd come. I needed it for myself, too. I needed to be brought back to sleep by my child. Made safe by her resting body and sweaty hairline. Her chest, where the lungs were breathing. The little buttocks. Her warm mouth.

Only one time, my mother once told me, did her sister have to babysit. You were maybe six months old, she said, and I wanted to go see *Jaws* at the movies with a friend. Now why did I have to do that, when I had a little baby at home.

My girl had still been small at the time of Ma's visit. She must have been no more than three because she hadn't started school yet. I let her nap in the middle of the day even though she should have outgrown it, and this made it hard to put her to bed at night. We usually watched children's television with the volume on high. Eventually the girl would be so exhausted by the blaring shows that kept coming and coming in a boundless loop that she'd fall asleep on the sofa. I switched off the TV and drew the blanket over her body and went out to the bedroom to turn on the computer my husband had bought from a friend, the procedure each time was as slow and as unsettling. But after a drawn-out process of several steps, with the same obligatory wait for the programs to launch and the various windows to open and the modem to dial up, I'd arrive at the site. The women no longer moaned in that Nineties way they used to. In the way I still couldn't help but do, because that's how I'd learned it once, when I started having sex.

Afterwards, once I'd carefully wiped away each trace from the computer's memory, I felt like a coward. I wanted us to be watching together but it had gone too far, I had been hiding myself from my husband for too long to suddenly say what I desired. The unexpected thing was that when I told him a few years later that what I liked most at the time was talking dirty and being caressed, it wasn't at all the case that he didn't think it sounded sexy or like no fun for him.

The boy was still sitting quietly on the edge of the bed. I reluctantly got up again, and I clamped the sheet under my arms and dragged it behind me across the floor and went into the bathroom and steadied myself on the sink for a moment, it looked like stone but the marbling was no more than brown paint poured into some lighter mass. I was afraid the boy would disappear if I wasn't there, and with the door open I watched him sitting there in the hazy light, silent and still, looking out the window, while I peed.

I walked back through the room, and this couldn't be me walking back nor the boy sitting there on the bed. I sat down next to him, ran my finger across his face, along his eyebrows, his nose. That all this was gone, had gone to waste. For nothing. It feels strange talking to you, I said, without you answering, do you know why you're here. The boy stared at the window and the daylight filtering through the grimy panes, without a word. You see me, don't you, I asked. Have you been able to see me this whole time. His chest was not moved by any breath. At the same time, it was as if he himself were wind, having taken shape as weightlessly and silently as the air itself. Carefully I touched his sweater, which was very thin, its color as indeterminate as those altered eyes. Rust-pink earth-grey tones. Like raw silk worn smooth. What do you want, I asked, go on, answer me. I can see that you understand what I'm saying.

Then the boy lifted his gaze and turned it to me. A distance and dreadful stillness echoed from his face. At the same time, it was as if his body, when last I'd seen it had been attentively dressed before being put in safe-keeping amidst the scent of wood and the great oblivion of the coffin that was to be sealed, was slowly and with great hesitation approaching the space that my questions had prepared for it. No sound came. Only an expression of despair on his face, as if something right behind or inside him were pushing him to act and pushing him again, to no effect other than that I soon could feel myself sitting there and quietly weeping. Dear you, dear love, I said, stop it, just stop. And he stopped at once and looked away.

The stories kept breaking apart, as they'd already done upon the boy's death. The world that my maternal grandfather had conjured up. Him teaching me to pour a little coffee back onto the earth after borrowing a place to rest, to set out the bones after a meal in the woods to encourage new life. That the dead were still here as long as I remembered them. None of it had been true. When the boy died, he was gone. I sensed him nowhere. He hadn't transmuted into anything. A light that had simply faded away. But don't push him now. Just touch him. Keep looking at him. Now that he's here again.

After a while, I glanced at the clock and I got out of bed. I looked silently at the boy who was still sitting there as enigmatic and solitary in his nature, like a mermaid washed up from the sea. I walked around the bed and found my clothes on the floor where I'd peeled them off the previous night. My lips were stiff because I was freezing and I was dehydrated and hungover and I didn't understand what kind of world this was anymore.

When I came out of the bathroom, the boy had gone up to the window and he was standing there in the light of the awakening day and he turned around and looked at me. I put on my jacket and shoes and wrapped the scarf around my neck. I opened the door and saw that the boy was following me. We moved through the corridor and I made no comment, just walked on, down the carpeted steps. I could remember the boy's bluish heels against the floor as he slipped out of my room, naked in the moonlight. Ma and Auntie and my cousin had long since fallen asleep, and he'd come back almost immediately, with the blanket from the couch wrapped around his hips. Someone's knocking at the door, he'd whispered, and I whispered, what, now. And we put on some clothes and walked through the dark hall toward the front door's textured windowpane and the silhouettes in bold relief there, in the glow of the porch light, the one that Ma always turned off when she went to bed and that Auntie and I would switch back on. It was the old couple who lived a ways into the woods. They were wasted and chipper and looked incredibly tired, and I did as I had been taught and said, come on in, are you hungry. Would you like some coffee. When I got down to the hotel lobby, I stopped. No one was at the reception desk and I hurried over and dropped off the key. I didn't know what to do, if I could just leave. Or would they think I was staying on and having my friend pay for more nights. I headed for the glass doors and waved the boy over. His young face. Broad and fine and inscrutable. Those strangely gray-shimmering clothes. Which looked as if dipped in stone.

Carefully he stepped out onto the pavement. His body at my side was soundless and light. Not because he lacked heft, but because he moved with great caution. As if he were walking on glass or were himself made of glass. He looked around and blinked in the light of the grayish sky. Hazy and mild and winter shouldn't be mild. Winter is cold and clear and the dead do not walk the earth they become earth. Several bicycles had been left in a rack across the street. I saw a magpie draw up behind them, it was hopping oddly on its short legs and I thought it might be hurt, but then it took flight and sailed sharply up the side of a grime-white building and disappeared above the sooty rooftops.

Somewhere out there was the lake. The lower lake where the dead reside. The one that Grandpa told me about. It spreads through the earth, below the lake among the living. And maybe it was more than something he'd said to soothe a child. To leave an opening behind him.

He died one Sunday. Ma had pushed me aside and whispered that I shouldn't stand there staring at him, one shouldn't stare in that calculating way at a person who is old and sick. I never quite figured out how to keep him company on his deathbed in the nursing home, the air of which filled with conversation and low moans, now and again during the morning and day as we sat there, Ma and my aunt and I, and it was raining. The psalms of the aged in the sitting room could be heard through the walls and the shut door. Ma had also begun to hum, intoning in that surging way our tribe typically sings, but low enough so that no words could be made out. As if the song came from the other side of a forest. She reached out to brush away a lock of white hair. Just that brief and tender gesture.

In the afternoon I was taken to a long table to paint on silk with the old people. I suppose I have to do something, my aunt had moaned from behind her high belly, where my cousin was curled around herself in her secret water, and a nurse suggested that Auntie take a break, maybe do something with her hands. You're coming too, aren't you, girlie, Ma asked, tossing Auntie a pleading glance. Her eyes were eerie, but not as faded and brackish as Grandpa's, extinguished on the pillow, behind those quivering lilac eyelids.

My aunt's patience would last for ten minutes. She put down the brush and handed over the frame with the smooth fabric on which she had only made a few fine blue lines. They looked weak, contained the same weakness as the hands that moved uneasily between her upset face and sweater and hair and the face and the sweater again. Tugging at the fabric where it had slid into the roll between the curve of her belly and her resting breasts. Fingering the underside of her chin. The skin of her elbows. A few moments later, Grandpa was dead, and Ma announced her intention to stay the night. One of the nurses in the room, the one who'd just come on shift and was looking gravely at the blanket she'd been straightening, turned to my mother. I'm not sure it would be appropriate, she said, for you to sleep in here, I mean. I saw my mother staring at her. What do you mean *not appropriate*, she said, I've been sleeping by his side all week. You mean I can't do it anymore, just because he's dead.

The three of us, along with the women who worked at the nursing home, had seen sign after sign leave his body and slip away. Like the wind lifting grain after grain of sand from a dune until the beach is as smooth as before it was stirred. And he was in agony and went still and he was gone. It was a slow exit. When the boy's mother called and woke me up on the night of the accident, she wasn't crying ordinary tears. It sounded like something large crying out. The same sound that came from me in those last minutes of birthing my girl. When with a few long contractions, I pushed her out of me, with incomparable relief.

My husband and I had watched a film about breathing that my cousin had sent. A midwife was explaining in Swedish how some women let out a kind of bellowing sound in the final phase of childbirth. Almost like an animal, she said. But it's better to try and direct that power inwards downwards and not unleash it. It was the phrase to which I reacted: almost like an animal. And for days after the delivery, I felt shame, along with power and hubris.

We wandered slowly north. I watched the boy as he moved, a being who no longer belonged here, whose vital organs at the last moment had been donated, sewn into another person. Chest tacked, hollowed out. Thick purplish blue stitches. We walked down the street. An old woman drew near with three small children for whom she was probably caring, I felt uncertain and relieved when none of them seemed to notice him. After a while we came to a long rectangular opening in the ground covered by a grate, on which a man had lain down to rest with two open beer cans by his head, and his straw-colored locks were fanned out and moving with the hot air that puffed up from the darkness from time to time. A pigeon swooped in from behind over our heads and I took the boy's hand and didn't let it go. We passed a grocery store. I watched the boy observe a woman leaning against a pillar and smoking, how she blew out the smoke so that it looked like a pleasure.

For a long time there was a flock of ravens that would keep to the roof across my street. I'd liked one of them in particular. The one that always flew up and planted itself right by the chimney, and proceeded to frantically peck drifts of white dusty mortar out with its beak, from a hole it had made there. Those were still the days when seagulls were never heard in town. There were pigeons and the jet-black ravens and blackbirds in the twilight outside the window in the small kitchen facing the courtyard, as I stood washing the grease off a skillet I'd inherited from my husband's mother.

I thought of the Seine winding its way between the quays a short distance from here, was its movement as slack as I remembered. Pale green strands of hair that flowed billowing by under the bridges, parting around the island and gliding away, disappearing toward the sea. I could never tell if the river was beige or green or gray, I'd never been able to learn how to perceive its color, but my husband loved the river. He used to like traveling into the city when he didn't have to work, reaching these streets and following them to the water where we'd walk and talk. Or he'd want to find a bench for a rest in the sunshine if it was summer. A shrill beeping could be heard and a garbage truck came backing out of an alley, at the same time as there was the roar of two men in green emptying a container of glass across the street. The boy did not react to these sounds. He'd spotted an ancient person laboring along ahead of us, a lone man with a crutch. His back was so bent he was almost doubled over and his grayish-yellow hair was so dirty and tangled that I could hardly bear to look at it, because it reminded me of the boy.

What would I say to my friend about her baby. That she was hopeless. That she was romantic. That I shouldn't say no to money.

The joy that would wash through my body when the girl was four, when she was six. The smile that broke out on her bare face when she caught sight of me, as the teacher led the class out of the school building, and she'd come running toward me. That incessant playing, which she was still doing at the age of seven, how it later stopped. How desirable it had been to be allowed to touch her wrinkled little bottom, and how at some later point I wasn't allowed to anymore. All her lifetimes, variably revealing themselves in her growing body, and her voice deepening. To deny my friend that existence. The three microscopic chicken pox scars on the girl's face, which only I could see, because I didn't know I was supposed to care for the scabs and apply salve as they healed.

I tried to explain the color of the river to the boy, that it felt so different. It's roily and kind of dirty white, I said, almost like dishwater, like when they pour water into that aniseed liqueur. The boy looked at me and nodded, it was as if he could hear what I was saying, as if we were talking to each other, and I felt myself burst into tears. I noticed that a child standing beside one of the trees that was streaming with light and twisting itself out of the earth along the street was watching me anxiously. A woman was walking around near the child, talking on the phone, the child was wearing a patterned little bag over her belly, the kind you could buy from the merchants down on the river banks and in the big open squares around a fountain. Ma had bought one of those little bags when she came to visit us ten years before, when she wanted to meet the girl. Well, I have to see her sometime, don't I, she'd said.

Darkness had fallen, and I stood by myself in the still-oppressive late summer heat, doing the dishes in the kitchen, listening to the fading sound of Ma struggling down the stairs as she made her way to the small courtyard, and the garbage cans hose broom and lone lemon tree, to smoke. Then she carved pieces off a large slab of meat she'd brought with her and stored in our freezer. She would take those slabs of meat out of the freezer and let them thaw a while, slice off thin strips for a big stew, and if there was enough meat left on the bone for another meal, she'd stick it in the bag again and put it in the freezer. Christ, it's cold, she said, shaking the hand that had been holding the meat. She looked around the kitchen, which was so small that she had unconsciously shrugged up her shoulders the first time she walked in, and she reached for the oven glove I'd use to take trays out of the oven, then changed her mind and grabbed the rag hanging over the faucet instead, and she put the rag on the half-thawed piece of meat and used it to grab hold.

We had talked about how nowadays I liked the feeling of hot water on my hands and found it relaxing to stand there alone in silence taking care of the kitchen, and how the dishes and the kitchen were something I'd previously tried to avoid at all costs. I'd had to push myself to ask Ma to wash her hands before picking up the newborn baby after she'd had a cigarette. Ma quietly stepped up to the kitchen counter, she plunged her hands into the dishwater and shook them off over the floor and wiped them on her pants, before she took the girl from my husband who had been carrying her around the room, to keep her happy.

Ma and I had snuck out to buy a present for my aunt. We were looking at trays depicting a cat sitting at the foot of a narrow staircase, there were coasters with the same motif. Knowing that the fridge was fully stocked made me feel safe, and for a moment it was as if the incomparable calm a sleeping baby emanates reached all the way to where Ma and I were, far away from the girl and her father. In the end we couldn't make a decision, and we turned around and set our course for home in order to buy some tobacco for my aunt, from the café on the corner of our street. You can ask for me, can't you, Ma had said, ask for an exciting kind. I'd only recently started speaking a little French. The man behind the counter had grown tired of our waffling and returned to his newspaper. Excuse me, I said, which tobacco is the most popular. Ma took her wallet out of her handbag, which she had been anxiously moving from shoulder to shoulder for the full past hour. According to her, I had insisted that my newborn cousin sleep in my room after she and Auntie were discharged from the hospital. It had just been her and a little girl, no father. As it was in Ma's and my constellation.

When we got back with the tobacco, the girl was whimpering anxiously. Ma thought she might be tired. She tried to put her down in the stroller that we had made room for right behind the front door, we had carried away the hall furniture and had taken to throwing our jackets on the sofa when we came in, but as soon as Ma put her down in the stroller the girl began to scream. I wouldn't want to lie in that black hole either, Ma said. Children want color. Gray and white and black won't cut it. And as she slipped behind me, down the narrow hall to the toilet and bedroom, I caught a lingering whiff of fire smoke and forest that awakened something forgotten, or perhaps only tucked away, inside me. Slitting open membranes. Long silvery white strands of fur sticking to the blood on my fingers. My hand reading the position of the steak.

There were evenings when I came back from the girl and her bedroom as from a world that still smelled of sea and sweetness, of the amniotic fluid that had enveloped her. The water that had allowed her to grow. The preservative viscous plug, its membranes having at some unpredictable hidden moment broken into an orifice that burned its way into my abdomen, from where she had twisted her way out. The pain of dry childbirth. Like that of dry intercourse. The moisture that opens the world. I had come out into the room where the TV was on but muted. Something embarrassing must have been going on in the film because I saw my husband take off his glasses, as he always did when something on the TV embarrassed him. He took them off and rubbed his forehead and shook his head and closed his eyes, then he raised his face and put them back on, when he thought the embarrassing part was over. I asked after Ma. I walked around the couch and squeezed myself between the armrest and my husband, and I heard Ma say, I'm here, and I discovered her in the dark on the floor stretched out on her side, supporting her head in one hand. How'd bedtime go, she asked, and I said, yeah, it was alright, it just took a while. And we drank hot coffee in the heat and we planned what we were going to eat in the coming days, and we talked about the girl. The wolf fur on her ears. The down that ran along her forehead and back. Sparse translucent eyelashes, long as spider legs, that bent if she blinked hard, they had a tiny point of light at the very end of each tip, as if plucked from a larger light, and fastened around her hazy eyes, which might still be able to see the world she'd just come from, the one where there was no language, but which she nonetheless must have experienced. World. Water. Warmth. Movement. Muffled sounds on the drum. Probing hands pressing into her body as they searched for her contours.

Later on, when they'd thickened and darkened, I'd envy the girl's eyelashes. She got them from me, my husband would say, they're not like yours, stubby bristles. He liked to sneak up behind me and smell my hair, run his nose over the brown birthmark that stuck out like a little button on the back of my neck. You've got a lot of birthmarks there, my mother had observed one night when I was a teenager, and she was eyeing me from the other end of the couch. I thought only men had that.

I squeezed the boy's slender hand, it felt lifeless and cool but cool in and of itself and not from cold, as if his re-entry to the world had swept away the chill that usually clung to the rugged old buildings in January. I would have wanted to be able to feel a mark somewhere on his skin, how someone had held him by the wrist and led him to where he was going, helped him across the river. If indeed it was a river.

On the windiest days, the large parks were kept locked. Once the girl and I had gotten lost around here. We'd suddenly ended up in an open space from which rose a sooty old temple with enormous stained columns in front of lines of freezing people that were winding their way towards its maw, while the sun sat in silence behind the cloud cover, drenching the earth with its blind light, just continuing to stir up life. What kind of place is this, Mama, she'd asked, staring at the temple and the people. And I replied, I don't know, some important old building.

There had never been a father. There were memories of someone carrying me on their shoulders one autumn in time. We are both looking ahead, at the same gravel road, and the house at its end. The small house that Grandpa had been so proud to be able to build, one of the first in our tribe to have been permitted to live in a house. The forest growing silently around it all. Careful hands around my shins. There were memories of another man, his long hair brushing across my body. There were memories of someone with frost in their beard. A damp knitted glove, and me sitting in an embrace, Ma laughing. There were memories without explanation or context, and there was a word so empty that it had in a few stifling moments taken up all the space. A word whose spirit and incarnation I'd never really experienced and often had not known to feel the loss of. My father.

Perhaps it had only been about a single happy or unhappy night. Perhaps he had never held me. Perhaps he didn't even know that I had come into being. Perhaps my fatherlessness was the clothing Ma had needed to put on in order to preserve her shell. To be able to occasionally remove from everyone's sight these objects of so much hassle and discord, namely she and her sister.

Do you remember the lake, I asked the boy, running my fingers across the back of his hand that was reaching across the chasm between us, and whether it was out of fear or motion that he clung so tightly to me I could not tell from where I was, and held on to him as tightly. I thought I saw him nod again, without looking at me this time, as if the memory hurt him. Of course you do, I said, I just, well, imagine if you were still here. We might have been there now, up at the lake. Only everything would have been different.

One night the girl had come to me in the kitchen. One of many kitchen evenings in a row, as I was stirring a stew, each of the evenings equally filled in that exhausting, eventually relieving, way by the day that had preceded them. Day added to day with its particular events, different but run through with the same spirit, through the being that was me, where everything flowed together so that time could no longer be felt was not real, and so neither was it particularly surprising for something with roots in a different end of time to suddenly emerge and settle in nearby. I was thinking I might indulge myself and run the long hot program on the dishwasher, when the girl came in, and showed me an old photograph that she must have found among my things. I wiped my hands. I said, now where have you been rooting around. Is that you, she asked, holding up the picture, and before I could answer she said, what are we having. And I said, stew, chicken stew, with cream and thyme, grapes. She turned down the corners of her mouth and did the same quick pouting gesture with her lips that my husband would do, and might mean not bad, or there you go, or simply, okay, or oh. I didn't have control of the specific muscles in my face needed to do that myself, but the girl could perform those facial gestures that her father often made, they could move their ears by willpower alone, their hair too, they both had such muscular scalps.

In the photo, I can be seen from a distance. A huddled figure in dark pink and green surrounded by fells and water. I'm wearing boots and am hugging my legs. I'm sitting on a rock at the very top of a mountain. Opening up behind me are the valley and the lake at the bottom of the ten-kilometer-wide depression between the fells, which rise up again on the other side, unfolding green and gray against the sky, unchanging in their stone-garb of slopes and ravines, snow-white at their peaks. The brimful lake, uppermost in a chain of lakes in the river that had been dammed, in spite of our tribe's many protests. The once wandering waters.

I confirmed that it was me. The girl asked where it was and I said it was up by the lake, by your grandmother's cabin there, that we used to go to when I was little, my maternal grandmother and grandfather's place. Auntie and I had gotten it into our heads that we were going to climb that mountain. It was so funny, I said, when we came back down, a few hours later, we met an older man from the village, he also moved up to the camp by the lake in the summer. We told him what we had done, and we asked him if he had ever been up that mountain, and he said, no, and thought about it a while. No, he said, I've never had any business up there. I stopped talking and smiled and looked at the girl. It was clear that she hadn't caught the joke in the old man's reply. The attitude toward life and the cartography it laid bare. Which had also been our way of life, really. Ma's and Auntie's and mine. And how we'd ended up not feeling bound by those ways.

The girl had nodded and backed down the corridor between her room and the main room, into which, after a few years with her, my husband and I had dragged our bed. The kitchen and bathroom one after the other along one side of the corridor, with windows facing the inner courtyard. She was still holding up that picture in front of her face and heading to her room, walking backwards blindly yet habitually, used to moving around in the cramped apartment where her body had grown up, a certain bounce in her step, as if in response to a constant underlying song, the song that had been inside her until she turned nine and began to move quite like a teenager, a controlled woman-child, at times antsy and unruly perhaps, but no longer singing unguarded. I watched her walk away, and a shameful feeling rose up in me, how I was inspired by her body because it was so delicate and slim, and she waved and shut her door in that gentle way of hers, I never knew if it was because she liked being careful or was afraid of making noise.

Auntie and I had walked wearily back towards Ma's cabin. It was only Ma who'd inherited it, after Grandma followed soon thereafter by Grandpa had died. Auntie could build her own cabin if she wanted to, on a hill a little higher up that had once been given to her as a gift, by Grandma's sister. Something she and Ma after the old people had died had confirmed that everyone in the community was in agreement on, so that no one could later object. Tender trampled grass. A rust-stained washing-up sink against the back wall of the cabin. The smell of wet earth. We saw that Ma had leaned the broom against the front door and Auntie stopped and swore. What's this, she's left, what happened now then. Auntie looked at the clock. So she must have taken the tourist boat. She shook her head. Do you know what happened. There was a bit of a quarrel yesterday, I said, about, well, where you were. And Auntie interrupted me and said she was going to have a little rest, and stepped onto the little stoop that was no more than a pallet that had been left where it was once put as a quick fix. She leaned the broom back against the wall and went into the cabin. I called out, wait, and took off the backpack with the bread and some of the meat we had dried in the spring, and I ran over and handed it to her. We had planned to eat it on the mountain, if we managed to get to the top. But once we had, we found that we were standing on a large open patch of grass, surrounded by rocks and larger boulders, seemingly strewn here and there. We simply looked around. And we stretched out on the grass and lay still a long time, without speaking to each other. We didn't make a fire, although we had collected some branches from a good spot further down, where there had been twigs and small birch trees and old birch bark cover. We drank no coffee. Just felt the mountain pulsing under us. I remembered lying there and imagining a mirror-figure in the earth, her back against my back, the soles of her feet against mine as I moved beneath the sun, and she came forth like a fixture in the earth's darkness where I would one day go. A girl like me, but of different stuff.

The boy stumbled and his hand slipped from mine as if it had been no more than a handful of fine sand, and I swung around and stopped and I felt my heart break and then expand in my chest as soon as I saw that he was still there. A door opened in the building in front of us and a man came out with an old dog that kept its head low, moving as if its hips ached. It was wearing some kind of choke collar made of chain, but not attached to a leash. It padded calmly on and sniffed me and it sniffed the boy. The owner gave a short whistle and shouted, come on, come, he said, leave her be, and he walked off in the other direction, under the sheltering trees. The boy had bent forward a little, as if to greet or pat the dog, and he looked on as it lumbered into the withered avenue and disappeared with feeble bounds.

I could see the lake before me. The fells and the slopes. More beautiful than I had ever seen them in real life. I have a girl, I said, looking at the boy. You know, with another man. He didn't react. Made no particular expression. No sign of jealousy. And why would he. She wants a dog so badly, I said, and I followed the boy's gaze to the red lights that had changed and the cars that came rushing by. Sometimes she lies there crying, she wants a pet so badly, and I tell her that dogs don't want to live in the city, they don't want to live in such a small apartment. I explain that we can't afford a dog, that we wouldn't be able to go away anymore, not because we usually go anywhere. It just feels so harsh, I said, because, well, I know it would do her good, and I could just as well live that way. We could have lived out in the woods somewhere, and had animals, that would have been, or if you and I would have been the ones to have a child. But then it wouldn't have been her, of course, I said. Someone else would have arrived.

My husband and I had lain as if in a cave, the girl between us. We turned off all the lights in the hospital room and closed the windows. We slumbered and woke to a rhythm that came only from her sleep and her cries and also from the boundless need to look at her, to feel that warm skin, simply to awaken there with her, outside of time, to be fully absorbed in the existence and care that she had brought with her.

That's the truth, I said to the boy. It's the beauty and magnitude of the gift that makes me feel I can't pass it on to my friend. And with this he was gone, in a shift of wind filled with the silence of all the years I hadn't heard his mother's voice, leaving me as alone with everything that was tangled up with growth and loss and origins as I had always been.

An Ambitious Good-Hearted Leftist

Adania Shibli

Translated from Arabic by Christopher Stone

The United Transport Company stands alone on a square kilometer of land in the heart of Jerusalem. It is bound on the west by street number 1, which falls on the line that divided the city into East and West Jerusalem in 1948. To the east are the Garden Tomb and Schmidt's girls school. To its south is the Jerusalem Hotel, and to the north lies Damascus Gate, which leads into the old city. Here one usually finds large and small white buses with green lines on their sides on which is written, "The United, Jerusalem-," then the name of the area where that particular bus is headed. In the eastern part of the bus station sits a small building with a lounge for bus drivers and an office where the company's founder and majority shareholder usually sits. "Ra'ed al-Tawil," as he is called on official documents, is the eldest son of Umm Ra'ed and Abu Ra'ed al-Tawil. While only his wife and a few family members call him Ra'ed, everyone else calls the company's founder Abu Arab.

In the early nineties Abu Arab fell in love with a girl from Jaffa, a beautiful girl, except perhaps for her prominent jaw. This girl, however, did not reciprocate Abu Arab's feelings, which naturally saddened him. He first met her on one of the trips from Jerusalem to the Sea of Galilee that leftist students used to take in the small bus that he rented out and always drove for just such occasions. Abu Arab had bought the bus to support the family after his release from prison. His mother had sold all of her gold jewelry so he could buy it. Abu Arab had been a "security prisoner" for two years because the Israeli authorities suspected him of being a member of the Popular Front for the Liberation of Palestine. His father had preceded him to prison on the same accusation, then another brother, then the next, and then the next. When, one night, the Israeli army raided their house in one of Jerusalem's overcrowded neighborhoods and asked Umm Ra'ed about the whereabouts of the remaining brother, who was twelve, she beat the soldiers to the room where this brother was sleeping and started kicking him while shouting, "Get up, Mr. George Habash, get up!" At that moment the head of the military unit intervened and saved him from her. Yet later, the investigator resumed the kicking with such intensity that that brother confessed to having thrown stones at a military patrol. His classmate, however, never confessed, a fact that has left his soul deeply scarred.

The bus project turned out to be a success. Soon after buying the first bus, Abu Arab was able to get another one for his brother for when he got out of prison. The brother drove workers, whereas Abu Arab continued to drive university students and sometimes journalists or artists, something he really enjoyed. Even though, after prison, Abu Arab had given up completely on the idea of finishing high school, he still felt sad about it. And perhaps this sadness increased when he realized that the college girl from Jaffa did not like him, and that perhaps no left-wing college or cultured girl would like him, because he had not finished high school and was just a bus driver. Eventually, however, the women of the family met and decided to introduce him to another girl, a cousin named Abla, who just happened to look a lot like the first girl. The two immediately fell in love, though perhaps Abla loved him a bit more. Abu Arab, in turn, introduced her to his intellectual and artist friends. She was shy with them at first, but his close friends soon got to know her intimate and gentle side. Also at the beginning, because of Abla's family's reservations, Abu Arab was not able to meet with Abla alone, something he so much longed to. Instead, Abla's grandmother, the family's supreme authority figure, always had to chaperone them. Thus the grandmother also met Abu Arab's university and intellectual friends, who were able to soften her up and convince her to leave Abla and Abu Arab alone by themselves. Her only condition was that they tell no one. Therefore I ask the reader to keep this fact a secret, even though the grandmother died a few years ago, and now Abla and Abu Arab are married and have seven children, six girls and a boy.

The first child is Kamilya. Abu Arab named her after his friend Kamilya Jubran, the lead singer at that time of the group Sabreen, of which Abu Arab was a huge fan. Kamilya is a beautiful girl who studies at the Rosary School and Abu Arab can't wait for the day she goes off to university and he sees her standing at the Qalandia checkpoint on her way from Birzeit University back to Jerusalem. As for the second daughter, Karmel, her name was chosen on the way to the maternity hospital in Talbiyya, on the road that divides East and West Jerusalem. Everyone liked the fact that she was named after a Palestinian mountain and that the name began with the letter "K" like Kamilya's. Abla and Abu Arab, however, knew that they couldn't keep up this pattern of names starting with the letter "K," for as soon as they had a boy, they were going to name him Farid after Abu Arab's father. Truth is, they dropped the "K" names after Karmel's birth, which was an extremely difficult one. While giving birth Abla began to beat Abu Arab and to scream, "It's all your fault!" It saddened Abu Arab, who held onto her hand, to see Abla in so much pain, which he was helpless to stop. That day they thought they might not have more children. But luckily the following births were easier. Karmel is a beautiful and smart girl who studies all the time. As for Farid, he's a gentle and intelligent boy who loves his six sisters a lot, perhaps with the exception of Aya, who is a year older than he. She's also not so fond of him. This might be due to the fact that Farid is a highly sensitive child who feels gratitude towards those who love him, whereas Aya couldn't care less about that and seems, rather, to be completely consumed by her curiosity towards the world. The other three are still small. The oldest of them speaks somewhat slowly, giving each and every letter its phonetic due. This could be because of a fall she had from the second floor two years ago. The ambulance took forever to come, as usually happens in the case of Palestinian injuries. That day, Abla felt a great hatred for the whole world, including herself and to some extent Abu Arab, since it had never occurred to him to encourage her to get a driver's license. The time she spent waiting for the ambulance was among the most painful in her life, more painful even than giving birth to Karmel. However, it's a good thing that Abla didn't have a driver's license at the time, for she was hardly able to stand on two feet that day.

It wasn't a problem for the family that the little one spoke somewhat slowly. They gave her all the time she needed, especially since Aya's rapid-fire speech, which really annoyed Farid, saved them so much time. The two smallest ones still cannot talk. They are fraternal twins, but if one did not know they were siblings, one would never guess that they were even from the same city.

Abu Arab and Abla's ambitions were not limited to expanding the world's population, but also expanding their own company. And, generally, the number of buses they owned grew with the number of children they had, until they eventually possessed five small buses. Then Abu Arab suddenly thought about selling them, along with a small plot of land the family owned in Bethlehem, all for the sake of a new project. But his efforts to convince his parents, and especially his siblings, failed initially. According to them and to many of his friends and acquaintances, it was a completely crazy idea. Still, Abu Arab was not to be deterred. He decided to carry out the plan on his own. He sold his share of what the family agreed was his after years of tireless work, which came to two small buses. Then he sold all of Abla's gold without telling anyone (and I ask the reader again to please keep this information a secret). Abla not only loved Abu Arab, but also believed in him. Objectively, though, the idea, which was to buy the Ramallah-Jerusalem bus line itself, seemed like something only a crazy person would support.

The line was owned by the Ramallah Bus Company, which had remained in operation until the beginning of the 1990s, when its buses stopped running and the company disappeared completely. Before that, its service had been limited to running two old and run-down buses that no one dared ride except for those who had both no money and all the time in the world.

It was, then, only a few senior citizens who used the Ramallah-Jerusalem buses, and occasionally students who couldn't pass up the chance to procrastinate between home and school. But this wasn't the main problem. The main problem was that even fifteen years ago, these buses were run-down. Now they were more like worthless archeological ruins. The second problem was that there was no longer a direct road between Ramallah and Jerusalem that buses could use even if they were able to make the trip in the first place. The road had been divided into several sections in years past, what with checkpoints and the Wall. So now everyone, including the senior citizens and schoolkids, definitely preferred the shared taxis that were quite fast. Quite fast, that is, when they were actually moving, which gave the rider the sense, even if illusory, that they were moving at the fastest possible speed after however many hours of waiting at the checkpoints.

Last but not least, the idea was also crazy because Abu Arab did not possess a license to drive large buses. Rather, neither he nor any of his brothers ever would. According to Israeli transportation law, former "security prisoners" were barred from obtaining the license needed to drive large buses. In short, he and Abla threw all of their hard-earned savings into something that no longer existed, and, most probably, could not exist in the future. But Abu Arab looked at the situation differently. While all of this was true, Abu Arab could see beyond the present circumstances. For him, the success of any project depended on the possibility of the creation of different circumstances in the first place.

So, Abu Arab started down this path all by himself, spending long hours in the garage where the buses had been lying like sick cows, trying to fix what could be fixed. He repainted the buses and reupholstered their seats. After several months of work, the two buses began running again. One of them ran from Ramallah to the Qalandia checkpoint and the other from the Qalandia checkpoint to Jerusalem, even though their signs said that they went from Jerusalem to Ramallah. The phrase "Jerusalem to Ramallah" was like words on a gravestone, a reminder of a life that no longer existed. In any case, at least now a route that had been dead for a long time had come back to life, even if a limited and partial life. These two buses slowly got more and more attention from riders, and not only because they had been refurbished or because they saved riders something on transportation costs, which had become exorbitant thanks to the breaking up of the road to and from Jerusalem into small segments, but also because people believed that the drivers of the small buses were a pack of thieves, drug dealers, sexual harassers, and even collaborators. And even though no one scrutinized these claims very closely, the drivers' behavior did nothing to help their reputation. Thus the popularity of the Ramallah-Jerusalem buses rose every day, especially since the buses left at scheduled times and not just when they filled up. Their popularity rose not just among the passengers, but also the drivers, who respected Abu Arab as the lawful owner of the route which many of them currently used unlawfully.

One day Abu Arab, who as already mentioned in the title, was an ambitious good-hearted leftist, called for a meeting of all of these drivers. His suggestion was as follows: as a bus owner he, like them, wanted to ensure his and his customers' safety and well-being. This required that they unite and work together. Like everyone knew, he was the owner of the Jerusalem-Ramallah route, but that was beside the point. What he was suggesting was that the owners of all the buses that used this route join his company, which would be called, instead of the Jerusalem-Ramallah line, the United Transport Company. As the sole owner, founder, and investor in the company, he would hold fifty-one percent of the shares, dividing the rest among the drivers who joined the company, which they could do without investing any money. All they had to do was join with their buses, buses that would remain their property, not the property of the company. The company would simply be an umbrella bringing together all of the bus drivers and owners to ensure and protect their rights, as well as the rights of the passengers, especially in the face of the Israeli authorities, who were constantly harassing the drivers of small buses. All the bus owners had to do was provide accident insurance for their passengers and adhere to the ticket system so as to be able to pay the taxes levied by the Israeli authorities. They would also have to make sure that all drivers wore the same uniform so that it would be easy for the passengers to identify them, and agree to standardizing the colors and signage used on the buses in line with the logo of the company of which they would now be shareholders.

The number of members of the company increased day after day until all of the bus lines leading to Jerusalem had joined in, a situation the passengers were very much in support of. And finally, Abu Arab's family came around to the project.

Obviously, Abu Arab still cannot drive any of the large buses that he owns or that fall under the umbrella of his company. But at least he owns two cars. One, an old jeep, he drives when he goes on long trips with his entire family. The second is nothing special, something he uses to take the kids to school every morning on his way to the office, where he remains until late at night, making sure that any problems connected to the company are on their way to being solved.

Islands

Aleksandar Hemon

1

We got up at dawn, ignored the yolky sun, loaded our navy-blue Austin with suitcases, and then drove straight to the coast, stopping only on the verge of Sarajevo, so I could pee. I sang communist songs the entire journey: songs about mournful mothers looking through graves for their dead sons; songs about the revolution, steaming and steely, like a locomotive; songs about striking miners burying their dead comrades. By the time we got to the coast, I had almost lost my voice.

2

We waited for the ship on a long stone pier, which burnt the soles of my feet, as soon as I took off my sandals. The air was sweltering, saturated with sea-ozone, exhaustion, and the smell of coconut sun-lotion, coming from the German tourists, already red and shellacked, lined up for a photo at the end of the pier. We saw the thin stocking of smoke on the horizon-thread, then the ship itself, getting bigger, slightly slanted sideways, like a child's drawing. I had a round straw hat with all the seven dwarfs painted on it. It threw a short, dappled shadow over my face. I had to raise my head to look at the grown-ups. Otherwise, I would look at their gnarled knees, the spreading sweat stains on their shirts and sagging wrinkles of fat on their thighs. One of the Germans, an old, bony man, got down on his knees and then puked over the pier edge. The vomit hit the surface and then dispersed in different directions, like children running away to hide from the seeker. Under the wave-throbbing ochre and maroon island of vomit, a school of aluminum fish gathered and nibbled it peevishly.

3

The ship was decrepit, with peeling steel stairs and thin leaves of rust that could cut your fingers on the handrails. The staircase wound upwards like a twisted towel. "Welcome," said an unshaven man, in a T-shirt picturing a boat with a smoke-snake wobbling on the waves, and, above it, the sun with a U-smile and the umlaut of eyes. We sat on the upper board and the ship leapt over humble waves, panting and belching. We passed a line of little islands, akin to car wrecks by the road, and I would ask my parents, "Is this Mljet?" and they would say, "No." From behind one of the islands, shaven by a wildfire, a gust of waylaying wind attacked us, snatched the straw hat off my head and tossed it into the sea. I watched the hat teetering away, my hair pressed against my skull, like a helmet, and I understood that I would never, ever see it again. I wished to go back in time and hold on to my hat before the surreptitious whirlwind would hit me in the face again. The ship sped away from the hat, and the hat was transformed into a distant beige stain on the snot-green sea. I began crying and sobbed myself to sleep. When I woke up, the ship was docked and the island was Mljet.

4

Uncle Julius impressed a stern, moist kiss on my cheek—the corner of his mouth touched the corner of my mouth, leaving a dot of spit above my lip. But his lips were soft, like slugs, as if there was nothing behind to support them. As we walked away from the pier, he told us that he forgot his teeth at home, and then, so as to prove that he was telling us the truth, he grinned at me, showing me his pink gums with cinnabar scars. He reeked of pine cologne, but a whiff redolent of rot and decay escaped his insides and penetrated the cologne cloud. I hid my face in my mother's skirt. I heard his snorting chuckle. "Can we please go back home!" I cried.

5

We walked up a sinuous road exuding heat. Uncle Julius's sandals clattered in a tranquilizing rhythm and I felt sleepy. There was a dense, verdureless thicket alongside the road. Uncle Julius told us that there used to be so many poisonous snakes on Mljet that people used to walk in tall rubber boots all the time, even at home, and snake bites were as common as mosquito bites. Everybody used to know how to slice off the bitten piece of flesh in a split second, before the venom could spread. Snakes killed chickens and dogs. Once, he said, a snake was attracted by the scent of milk, so it curled up on a sleeping baby. And then someone heard of the mongoose, how it kills snakes with joy, and they sent a man to Africa and he brought a brood of mongooses and they let them loose on the island. There were so many snakes that it was like a paradise for them. You could walk for miles and hear nothing but the hissing of snakes and the shrieks of mongooses and the bustle and rustle in the thicket. But then mongooses killed all the snakes and bred so much that the island became too small for them. Chickens started disappearing, cats also, there were rumors of rabid mongooses and some even talked about monster mongooses that were the result of paradisiacal inbreeding. Now they were trying to figure out how to get rid of mongooses. "So that's how it is," he said, "it's all one pest after another, like revolutions. Life is nothing if not a succession of evils," he said, and then stopped and took a pebble out of his left sandal. He showed the puny, gray pebble to us, as if holding unquestionable evidence that he was right.

6

He opened the gate and we walked through a small, orderly garden with stout tomato stalks, like sentries, alongside the path. His wife stood in the courtyard, her face like a loaf of bread with a small tubby potato in the middle, arms akimbo, her calves full of bruises and blood vessels on the verge of bursting, ankles swollen. She was barefoot, her big toes were crooked, taking a sudden turn, as if backing away in disgust from each other. She enveloped my head with her palms, twisted my head upwards, and then put her mouth over my mouth, leaving a thick layer of warm saliva, which I hastily wiped off with my shoulder. Aunt Lyudmila was her name.

7

I clambered, dragging a bag full of plastic beach toys, after my sprightly parents, up a concrete staircase on the side of the house, with sharp stair edges and pots of unconcerned flowers, like servants with candles, on the banister side.

8

The room was fragrant with lavender, mosquito-spray poison, and clean, freshly ironed bedsheets. There was an aerial picture of a winding island

(Mljet, it said in the lower right corner) and a picture of Comrade Tito, smiling, black-and-white, on the opposite wall. Below the window, the floor was dotted with mosquitoes—with a large green-glittering fly or a bee here and there—still stricken by the surprise. When I moved toward them, the wisp caused by my motion made them ripple away from me, as if retreating, wary of another surprise.

9

I lay on the bed, listening to the billowing-curtain flaps, looking at the picture of Mljet. There were two oblong lakes, touching each other, at the top end of the picture-island, and on one of those lakes there was an island.

10

I woke up and the night was rife with the cicada hum, perpetual as if it were the hum of the island engine. They were all sitting outside, around the table underneath the shroud of vine twisting up the lattice. There was a long-necked carafe, full of black wine, in the center of the table, like an axis. Uncle Julius was talking and they all laughed. He would bulge his eyes, lean forward, he would thrust his fist forward, then open it, and the hand would have the index finger pointed at the space between my mother and his wife, and then the hand would retract back into the fist, but the finger would reappear, tapping its tip against the table, as if telegraphing a message. He would then stop talking and withdraw back into the starting position, and he would just watch them as they were laughing.

11

Uncle Julius spoke: "We brought beekeeping to Bosnia. Before the Ukrainians came, the natives kept their bees in mud-and-straw hives and when they wanted the honey they would just kill them all with sulfur. My grandfather had fifty beehives three years after coming to Bosnia. Before he died, he was sick for a long time. And the day he died, he asked to be taken to the bees and they took him there. He sat by the hives for hours, and wept and wept, and wept out a sea of tears, and then they put him back into his bed and an hour later he died."

"What did he die of?" Aunt Lyudmila asked.

"Dysentery. People used to die of that all the time. They'd just shit themselves to death."

12

I went down the stairs and declared my thirst. Aunt Lyudmila walked over to the dark corner on my right-hand side, turned on the light ablaze, and there was a concrete box with a large square wooden lid. She took off the lid and grabbed a tin cup and shoved her arm into the square. I went to the water tank (for that's what it really was) and peeked over. I saw a white slug, as big as my father's thumb, on the opposite wall. I could not tell whether it was moving upward or it was just frozen by our sudden presence. The dew on its back twinkled, it looked like a severed tongue. I glanced at Aunt Lyudmila, but she didn't seem to have noticed anything. She offered me the cup, but I shook my head and refused to drink the water which, besides, appeared turbid.

So they brought me a slice of cold watermelon and I drowsily masticated it. "Look at yourself," Uncle Julius said. "You don't want to drink the water! What would you do if you were so thirsty that you were nearly crazy and having one thought only—water, water!—and there's no water? How old are you?" "Nine," my mother said.

13

Uncle Julius told us that when he was in the Arkhangelsk camp, Stalin and his parliament devised a law that said if you were repeatedly late for school or missed several days with no excuse, you would get six months to three years in a camp. So, suddenly, in 1943, the camp was full of children, only a little bit older than me—twelve, fifteen years old. They didn't know what to do in the camp, so the criminals took the nicest-looking to their quarters and fed them and, you know (no, I didn't), abused them. So they were there. They died like flies, because it was cold, and they lost their warm clothing, they didn't know how to preserve or protect the scarce food and water they were allotted. Only the ones that had protectors were able to survive. And there was a boy named Vanyka: gaunt, about twelve, blond, blue eyes. He survived by filching food from the weaker ones, by lending himself to different protectors and bribing guards. Once—I think he drank some vodka with the criminals—he started shouting: "Thank you, Vozhd, for my happy childhood!" At the top of his lungs: "Thank you, Stalin, for my happy childhood!" And they beat him with gun butts and took him away.

14

"Don't torture the boy with these stories. He won't be able to sleep ever again."

"No, let him hear, he should know."

15

Then they sent Uncle Julius to a different camp, and then to another one, and he didn't even know how much time or how many camps he passed through, and he found himself in Siberia. One spring, his job was to dig big graves in the thawing ground, take the dead to the grave on a large cart, and then stuff them into the grave. Fifty per grave was the prescribed amount. Sometimes he had to stamp on the top of the graveload to get more space and meet the plan. He had big, big boots. One day they told him that there was a dead man in solitary confinement, so he pushed his cart there and put the corpse on the cart, and as he was pushing, the corpse moaned: “Let me die! Let me die!” I was so scared I almost died, I fell down and he kept moaning: “Let me die! I don’t want to live!” So I pushed the cart behind the barrack and I leaned over him. He was emaciated and had no teeth and one of his ears was missing, but he had blue, blue eyes. It was Vanyka! He looked much older, oh my God! So I gave him a piece of bread that I had saved for the bad days and told him that I remembered him and this is what he told me.

16

They took him away and mauled him for days and did all sorts of things to him. Then they moved him to another camp and he had problems there all the time, because he would speak out again, despite his better judgment. He knew how to steal from the weaker and there were still men who liked him. He won acclaim when he killed a marked person, some Jew, after losing a card game. He killed more. He did bad, bad things and learned how to survive, but he could never keep his snout shut. So they sent him to the island where they kept the worst of the worst. The nearest guard was on the shore fifty kilometers away. They let the inmates rob and kill each other like mad dogs. Once a month the guards would come in, leave the food, and count the corpses and graves and go back to their barracks by the sea. So one day Vanyka and two others killed some other inmates, took their food and clothes, and set out on foot towards the shore. It was a very, very cold winter—pines would crack like matches every day—so they thought they could walk over the frozen strait, if they avoided the guards. But they got lost and ran out of food and Vanyka and one of the other two agreed by exchanging glances to kill the third one. And they did and they ate his flesh, and they walked and walked and walked. Then Vanyka killed the other one and ate him. But the guards with dogs tracked him down and caught him and he ended up in solitary confinement here and he didn't know how long he had been there. All he wanted was to die and he'd smash his head against the walls and he'd try to choke himself with his tongue. He refused to eat, but they'd force him, if only to make him live longer and suffer more. "Let me die!" he cried and cried.

17

Uncle Julius was reticent and no one dared to say anything. But I asked: "So what happened to him?"

"He was killed," he said, making a motion with his hand, as if thrusting me aside, out of his sight.

18

I woke up and didn't know where I was or who I was, but then I saw the photo of Mljet and I recognized it. I got up, out of my non-being, and stepped into the inchoate day. It was purblindingly bright, but I could hear the din of the distant beach: bashful whisper of waves, echoes of sourceless music, warbling of boat motors, shrieks of children, syncopated splashing of oars. Bees levitated over the staircase flowers and I passed them cautiously. There was breakfast on the table in the net-like shadow of the vines: a plate with smoldering, soggy eggs, a cup with a stream of steam rushing upwards, and seven slices of bread, on a mirroring steel tray, leaning on each other like fallen dominoes. There was no one around, apart from shadows stretching on the courtyard stone pavement. I sat down and stirred my white coffee. There was a dead bee in the whirl and it kept revolving on its back, slower and slower, until it came to a reluctant stop.

19

After breakfast, we would go down a dirt path resembling a long burrow in the shrub. I'd carry my blue and white Nivea inflatable ball and sometimes I would inadvertently drop it and it would bounce, ahead of us, in slow motion. I'd hear bustle in the thicket—a snake, perhaps. But then there would be more bustle and I'd imagine a mongoose killing the snake, the whole bloody battle, the writhing snake entangled with the mongoose trying to bite off its head, just the way I saw on TV, on *Survival.* I'd wait for my parents, for I didn't know what sort of feeling a fierce mongoose would have toward a curious boy—would it, perhaps, want to bite his head off?

20

We'd get to the gravel beach, near the dam dividing the two lakes. I'd have to sit on the towel for a while before I would be allowed to swim. On the left, there would usually be an old man, his skin puckered here and there, a spy novel over his face, white hair meekly bristling on his chest, his belly nearly imperceptibly ascending and descending, with a large metallic-green fly on the brim of his navel. On our right, two symmetrical old men, with straw hats, in baggy trunks, would play chess in serene silence, with their doughy breasts overlooking the board. There were three children a little farther away. They would sit on the towel, gathered around a woman, probably their mother, who would distribute tomatoes and slices of bread with a layer of sallow spread on them. The children would all simultaneously bite into their slices and their tomatoes, and then chew vigorously. The tomato slime would drip down their chins, they would be seemingly unperturbed, but when they were done eating, the mother would wipe their recalcitrant faces with a stained white rag.

21

Finally, my parents would tell me I could swim and I'd totter over the painful gravel and enter the shallows. I would see throbbing jellyfish floating by. The rocks at the bottom were covered with slimy, slippery lichen. I'd hesitantly dive and the shock of coldness would make me feel present in my own body—I'd be clearly aware of my ends, I'd be aware that my skin was the border between the world and me. Then I'd stand up, the quivering lake up to my nipples, and I'd wave to my parents and they'd shout: "Five more minutes!"

22

Sometimes I'd see fish in pellucid water, gliding along the bottom. Once I saw a school of fish that looked like miniature swordfish, with silver bellies and pointed needle noses. They were all moving as one and then they stopped before me, and hundreds of little wide-open eyes stared at me in dreadful surprise. Then I blinked and they flitted away.

23

We walked up the path as the sun was setting. Everything attained a brazen shade and, now and then, there would be a thin gilded beam, which managed to break through the shrub and olive trees, like a spear, sticking out of the ground. Cicadas were revving and the warmth of the ground enhanced the fragrance of dry pine needles on the path. I entered the stretch of the path that had been in the shadow of the tall pines for a while, and the sudden coolness made me conscious of how hot my shoulders felt. I pressed my thumb firmly against my shoulder and, when I lifted it, a pallid blot appeared, then it slowly shrank, back into the ruddiness.

24

There was a man holding a German shepherd on a leash, much of which was coiled around his hand. The shepherd was attempting to jump at a mongoose backed against a short ruin of a stone wall. As the dog's jaw snapped a breath away from the mongoose's snout, the man would pull the dog back. The mongoose's hair bristled up, and it grinned to show its teeth, appearing dangerous, but I knew it was just madly scared. The eyes had a red glow, akin to the glow that people who glanced at the flashlight have on bad color photos. The dog was growling and barking and I saw the pink and brown gums and the bloodthirst saliva running down the sides of the jaw. Then the man let the dog go and there was, for just a moment, hissing and wheezing, growling and shrieking. The man pulled the dog back and the mongoose lay on its back, showing its teeth in a useless scowl, the paws spread, as if showing it was harmless now, and the eyes were wide open, the irises stretched to the edge of the pupils, flabbergasted. There was a hole in its chest—the dog seemed to have bitten off a part of it—and I saw the heart, like a tiny tomato, pulsating, as if hiccuping, slower and slower, with slightly longer moments between the throbs, and it simply stopped.

25

We walked through the dusk. My sandals were full of pine needles and I would have to stop to take them out. Thousands of fireflies floated in the shrubs, lighting and vanishing, as if they were hidden fairy photographers with flashlights, taking our snapshots. "Are you hungry?" my mother asked.

26

We would sit under the cloak of vines, with a rotund jar of limpid honey and a plate of pickles. Uncle Julius would dip a pickle into the honey and several bees would peel themselves off the jar and hover above the table. I would dip my finger and try to get it to my lips before the thinning thread of honey would drip on my naked thighs, but I would never make it.

Sometimes, around lunchtime, Uncle Julius would take me to his apiary. He would put on a white overall and a white hat with a veil falling down on his chest, so he looked like a bride. He would light a torn rag and order me to hold it, so as to repel the bees. He would tell me to be absolutely silent and not to move and not to blink. I'd peek from behind his back, my hand with the smoldering rag protruded. He would take the lid off a beehive, carefully, as if he were afraid of awakening the island, and the buzz would rise like a cloud of dust and hover around us. He would scrape off the wax between the frames and then take them out, one by one, and show them to me. I'd see the molasses of bees fidgeting. "They work all the time," he'd whisper. "They never stop." I'd be frightened by the possibility of being stung, even though he told me that the bees would not attack me if I pretended not to exist. The fear would swell, and the more I'd think about it, the more unbearable the unease would be. Eventually, I'd break down and run back to the house, get on the stairs, from where I'd see him, remote, immobile, apart from the slow, wise motions of his apt hands. I'd watch him, as if he were projected on a screen of olive trees and isles of beehives, then he'd turn to me and I could discern a peculiar, tranquil smile behind the veil.

27

Mother and Father were sitting at the stern, with their feet in tepid bilge water, Uncle Julius was rowing, and I was sitting at the prow, my feet dangling overboard. The surface of the lake would ascend with an inconspicuous wave and my feet would delve into the coolness of menthol-green water. With the adagio of oars, creaking and splashing, we glissaded towards the lake island. There was a dun-colored stone building, with small drawn-in windows, and an array of crooked olive trees in front of it. Uncle Julius steered the scow toward a puny desolate pier. I slipped stepping out, but Uncle Julius grabbed my hand and I hung for a moment over the throbbing lake with a sodden loaf of bread and an ardently smiling woman on a magazine page stuck to the surface, like an ice floe.

28

"These lakes," Uncle Julius said, "used to be a pirate haven in the sixteenth century. They'd hoard the loot and bring hostages here and kill them and torture them—in this very building—if they didn't get the ransom. They say that this place is still haunted by the ghosts of three children they hung on meat hooks because their parents didn't pay the ransom. Then this was a nunnery and some people used to believe that even the nuns were not nuns but witches. Then it was a German prison. And now, mind you, it's a hotel, but there are hardly any tourists ever."

29

We walked into the sonorous chill of a large stone-walled hall. There was a reception desk, but nobody behind it, and a smiling Tito picture over the numbered cubbyhole shelf. Then we walked through a long tunnel and then through a low door, so everyone but me had to bow their heads, then we were in a cubicle-like windowless room ("This used to be a nun cell," Uncle Julius whispered), then we entered the eatery (they had to bend their knees and bow their heads, as if genuflecting, again) with long wooden tables and, on them, two parallel rows of plates and utensils. We sat there waiting for the waiter. There was a popsicle-yellow lizard, as big as a new pencil, on the stone wall behind Uncle Julius's back. It looked at us with an unblinking marble eye, apparently perplexed, and then it scurried upwards, towards an obscure window.

30

This was what Uncle Julius told us:

"When I was a young student in Moscow, in the thirties, I saw the oldest man in the world. I was in a biology class, it was in a gigantic amphitheater, hundreds of rows, thousands of students. They brought in an old man who couldn't walk, so two comrades carried him and he had his arms over their shoulders. His feet were dangling between them, but he was all curled up like a baby. They said he was a hundred and fifty-eight years old and from somewhere in the Caucasus. They put him sideways on the desk and he started crying like a baby, so they gave him a stuffed toy—a cat, I think, but I can't be certain, because I was sitting all the way up in one of the last aisles. I was looking at him as if through the wrong side of a telescope. And the teacher told us that the old man cried all the time, ate only liquid foods, and couldn't bear being separated from his favorite toy. The teacher said that he slept a lot, didn't know his name, and had no memories. He could say only a couple of words, like water, poo-poo, and such. I figured out then that life is a circle, you get back right where you started if you get to be a hundred and fifty-eight years old. It's like a dog chasing its own tail, all is for naught. We live and live, and in the end we're just like this boy"—he pointed at me—"knowing nothing, remembering nothing. You might as well stop living now, my son. You might just as well stop, for nothing will change."

31

When I woke up, after a night of unsettling dreams, the suitcases were agape and my parents were packing them with wrinkled underwear and shirts. Uncle Julius came up with a jar of honey as big as my head and gave it to my father. He looked at the photo of Mljet and then put the tip of his finger at the point in the upper-right corner, near the twin lakes, which looked like gazing eyes. "We are here," he said.

32

The sun had not risen yet from behind the hill, so there were no shadows and everything looked muffled, as if under a sheet of fine gauze. We walked down the narrow road and the asphalt was cold and moist. We passed a man carrying a cluster of dead fish, with the hooks in their carmine gills. He said "Good morning!" and smiled.

We waited at the pier. A shabby boat, with paint falling off and *Pirate* written in pale letters on the bow, was heading, coughing, towards the open sea. A man with an anchor tattooed on his right arm was standing at the rudder. He had a torn red and black flannel shirt, black soccer shorts, and no shoes—his feet bloated and filthy. He was looking straight ahead towards the ferry that was coming into the harbor. The ferry slowed down to the point of hesitant floating, and then it dropped down its entrance door, like a castle bridge, with a harsh peal. It was a different ship than the ship we had come on, but the same man with the hobbling-boat shirt said "Welcome!" again, and smiled, as if recognizing us.

We passed the same islands. They were like heavy molded loaves of bread, dropped behind a gigantic ship. On one of the islands, and we passed it close-by, there was a herd of goats. They looked at us mildly confounded, and then, one by one, lost interest and returned to grazing. A man with a camera, probably a German tourist, took a picture of the goats, and then gave the camera to his speckle-faced, blue-eyed son.

The boy pointed the camera towards the sun, but the man jokingly admonished him, turning him, and the camera, towards us, while we grinned at him, helpless.

33

It took us only four hours to get home from the coast and I slept all the time, oblivious to the heat, until we reached Sarajevo. When we got home, the shriveled plants and flowers were in the midst of the setting-sun orange spill. All the plants had withered, because the neighbor who was supposed to water them died of a sudden heart attack. The cat, having not been fed for more than a week, was emaciated and nearly mad with hunger. I would call her, but she wouldn't come to me; she would just look at me with irreversible hatred.

Offside

Cristina Rivera Garza

Translated from Spanish by Sarah Booker

I would soon run out of gas, so when the battered sign appeared announcing a gas station ahead, I smiled. Ten kilometers. My agitated breath fogged up the windshield, but my hands, protected by thick wool gloves, were able to clear enough space to see the gray band of highway. An arrow in black.

Here.

The desolation of the gas station didn't surprise me so much as the scrawny face of the man on the other side of the dark counter, staring out at snowflakes whimsically floating through the air. His attitude made me pause before the window to watch the winter landscape, caught in the strange calm. For a moment I forgot my old car was there, immobile and waiting for the precious liquid. Forgot the cold. Forgot I had a long way left to go. It wasn't until a gust of wind rose, spinning a rusted weathervane, that I came back to reality.

. . .

"**Gasoline**," I murmured, too timidly, placing a handful of coins on the counter.

The man looked at the coins first and then at my face without any change of expression. He didn't seem to understand what was happening. I repeated the word and pointed to my car. In response, he emitted a series of unintelligible grunts and then went back to watching the snow with the same concentration as before. If I hadn't been so bewildered by his response, I might have found something pleasing in the way his gaze reached out to meet the snow. Something childlike. Something in perpetual levitation. Perhaps I noticed it. Perhaps I understood it. I cannot otherwise explain why I left that room so meekly and why I started walking toward the center of that town. One kilometer. A black-colored arrow.

Here.

As soon as I entered the restaurant, I knew I was hungry. The smells were unrecognizable, but my stomach gurgled in anticipation of being filled. I sat down at one of the many free tables and immediately asked for the menu. The waitress who stopped at my side seemed annoyed by my request. She looked at me for what seemed a long time, then, without saying a word, handed me two loose sheets of paper. But I couldn't decipher them, as hard as I tried.

"I'm sorry. I don't understand anything," I said. And she, who didn't seem to understand me either, headed toward the kitchen. Out came a tall, disheveled man who enunciated a wavering greeting as he dried his hands on his white apron.

"Foreign?" he asked. Blue eyes. Open eyes. Eyes that knew things.

I answered immediately that yes, I was indeed *foreign*. The word, a bit anachronistic, pleased me a great deal in that moment. I truly liked it.

When he sat down at the table and started talking in the hesitating, slow way of someone not perfectly in control of the language, I realized this was the first true conversation I'd held in days. Before: hands on the wheel. Before: the interminable highway. Before: the humming of the engine. Before: the wide, white, terrible, winter silence. Before: nowhere.

"You won't be able to leave with this storm," he said, pointing outside, concerned. "Come," he added almost immediately, without waiting for an answer.

The sunlight had faded—I reconsidered too late. I was also slow to notice how quickly the footprints leading from the restaurant to the narrow door of his house vanished. Two-hundred meters. No arrow in the color black. Here.

I slept many hours. Perhaps twenty-three. Maybe thirty-one. The first thing I saw when I woke up was the face of the man from the restaurant whose eyes gleamed at the word "foreign."

"Your car," he told me with a remorseful gesture. "Your car is gone."

The news didn't scare me. I neither asked how it had happened nor did I get upset. Instead, I remained silent. I closed my eyes again. I stretched under the white sheets. I flexed each of my toes. I assume the time passed. I opened my eyes again, observed him. Only then could I confirm, with a strange serenity, that the winter landscape on the other side of the window was the same.

That's how I met him. And that's how I agreed to stay. A black arrow. Here.

I soon learned the winter wasn't fleeting in this place. The snow kept falling, sometimes lightly, sometimes tumultuously, but always white. Always. The cold limited my excursions and, on the rare occasions I accompanied him to the restaurant, my poor handling of their language made me awkward. I preferred to sit in front of the fire, looking out the window, letting time pass. I came to understand why the man at the gas station was so silent. Had I been able, I would have liked to talk to him. Talk for a long time. Talk about the hypnosis the falling snow provokes. In what I imagined was summertime in some other part of the world, the man from the restaurant and I had our first son. Two autumns later, the second was born. I accepted both with equal strength, with equal affection. In the moment of their birth, I insisted on placing their bloody bodies on my chest. Here. A red arrow. That warmth. When they were old enough to speak, I taught them my language.

"That's how I learned," their father said, accidentally interrupting one of our morning sessions. "My mother was a foreigner," he added, as if I already knew. Then he placed the tips of his fingers on my chin, which I took to mean he approved of my teaching.

Soon after, he started taking the children out without any notice, without any indication of where they were going. He asked only that I bundle them up and make a basket with provisions, canteens filled with water. Then they would abruptly disappear only to reappear, days later, days that felt like entire weeks to me, with their cheeks reddened, their hair dirty, their legs covered in bruises, their faces crisscrossed with scratches. Once, one of them, the smaller one, came home missing a tooth.

I would hardly recognize them when they returned. They looked like another woman's children. They looked, in fact, like they didn't come from any woman. Their faces had that unintelligible and furious air of the nomads who, from time to time, would occupy the central plaza without anyone being able to do anything about it. They came, sold their leather goods, their iron tools, their seeds, and they left. There was something wild in their bright eyes, something determined in the way they picked up objects or breathed in the afternoon air. There was something powerful. Something like an echo. I moved among my own children as if they were strangers. As if they were the Nomads. When they ate around the fire, the boys would throw their arms in the air, screaming, bursting into laughter. I envied them that. Their gestures. The gleam in their faces. The sudden happiness. They only fell silent if they heard my footsteps or sensed, as they often did, that I was crouched behind the kitchen door, listening. If I suddenly appeared with a steaming pot of soup or with hot bread in my hands, they would change the tone of their voices. To talk about me they would use that universal term: "Ma." I, in such moments, only called them "the boys."

From the beginning I tried to learn where they went, what they did there, why they returned. I thought of questions I would later ask in intimate moments, such as before bed, when I'd bundle them up under eiderdown comforters, or during our language classes, when I knew no one else was listening to or understood us. Most of the time I settled for discreetly spying on them, watching them out of the corner of my eye as they played on the patio, or walking at the same speed when they accompanied me to the market to buy vegetables. Nothing worked. They were as hermetic as their father. Their silence was like the snow: sometimes constant, sometimes flexible, but always white. Always falling like a subtle curtain between us. Always separating us.

A lot of time had passed when I tried to get information from the man at the gas station. I was out of my mind. I went to the gas station during one of their absences, one afternoon right before the storm began. I stood in front of him like the first time and, defeated once again by his concentrated attitude, I watched the falling snow in absolute silence by his side. The thin yellow light behind the flakes made me think that surely, in some other part of the world, it was winter once again.

"You're never going to accept it, are you?" the man asked me softly; a warm voice, in fact. When I realized I understood him, I sank into a sudden sadness, and my stupor kept me from saying anything in response.

"You should give up," he added, unbothered by my silence, and without lifting his deep, gray eyes from the window's surface. "Why would you want to know?"

I was going to say that I had the right to know, that I wanted to know them, that they were part of my family. Mine. Of my body. I was going to say so many things, but I only managed to open my mouth. The condensation made me think that the world was nothing more than a great, steamed-up windshield, and this thought provoked in me a silent fit of tears.

"Look," the man said, pointing to a white hill barely visible through one of the window's corners. "Look," he insisted.

I dried my tears and looked. I saw it. I saw it all. I blew my nose and looked at him, holding my breath: he was the same, composed and comfortable behind the counter. He was a strange man, but he no longer scared me. I swung open the door of his business, passed the immobile weathervane and, without thinking about it, without making any decision, leapt onto the mountain he had forced me to see. When I was able to remove enough snow, I opened my car door and got in. It felt like a museum where you aren't allowed to touch anything. I leaned my forehead against the steering wheel out of pure instinct. And out of pure instinct I tried to see something through the windshield.

An Unlucky Man

Samanta Schweblin

Translated from Spanish by Megan McDowell

The day I turned eight, my sister—who absolutely always had to be the center of attention—swallowed an entire cup of bleach. Abi was three. First she smiled, maybe in disgust, then her face crumpled in a frightened grimace of pain. When Mom saw the empty cup hanging from Abi's hand, she turned as white as my sister.

"Abi-my-god," was all Mom said. "Abi-my-god," and it took her a few more seconds before she sprang into action.

She shook Abi by the shoulders, but my sister didn't respond. She yelled, but Abi still didn't react. She ran to the phone and called Dad, and when she came running back Abi was still standing there, the cup just dangling from her hand. Mom grabbed the cup and threw it into the sink. She opened the fridge, took out the milk, and poured a glass. She stood looking at the glass, then looked at Abi, then back at the glass, and finally dropped the glass into the sink as well. Dad worked very close by and got home quickly, but Mom still had time to do the whole show with the glass of milk again before he pulled up in the car and started honking the horn and yelling.

Mom lit out of the house like lightning with Abi clutched to her chest. The front door, the gate, and the car doors were all flung open. There was more horn honking, and Mom, who was already sitting in the car, started to cry. Dad had to shout at me twice before I understood that I was the one who was supposed to close the door.

We drove the first ten blocks in less time than it had taken me to close the car door and fasten my seatbelt. But when we got to the main avenue, the traffic was practically at a standstill. Dad honked the horn and shouted out the window, "We have to get to the hospital! We have to get to the hospital!" The cars around us maneuvered and miraculously let us pass, but a couple cars ahead we had to start the operation all over again. Dad braked, stopped honking, and began to pound his head against the steering wheel. I had never seen him do such a thing. There was a moment of silence, and then he sat up and looked at me in the rearview mirror. He turned around and said to me:

"Take off your underpants."

I was wearing my school uniform. All my underwear was white, but I wasn't exactly thinking about that just then, and I couldn't understand Dad's request. I pressed my hands into the seat to support myself better. I looked at Mom and she shouted:

"Take off your damned underpants!"

I took them off. Dad grabbed them out of my hands. He rolled down the window, went back to honking the horn, and started waving my underpants out the window. He raised them high while he yelled and kept honking, and it seemed like everyone on the avenue turned around to look at them. My underpants were small, but they were also very white. An ambulance a block behind us turned on its siren, caught up with us quickly, and started clearing a path. Dad kept on waving the underpants until we reached the hospital.

He parked the car by the ambulances and they jumped out. Without waiting, Mom took Abi and ran straight into the hospital. I wasn't sure whether I should get out or not: I didn't have any underpants on, and I looked around to see where Dad had left them, but they weren't on the seat or in his hand, which was already slamming his car door behind him.

"Come on, come on," said Dad.

He opened my door and helped me out, then locked the car. He gave my shoulder a few pats as we walked into the emergency room. Mom came out of a doorway at the back and signaled to us. I was relieved to see she was talking again, giving explanations to the nurses.

"Stay here," said Dad, and he pointed to some orange chairs on the other side of the main waiting area.

I sat. Dad went into the consulting room with Mom and I waited for a while. I don't know how long, but it felt long. I pressed my knees together tightly and thought about everything that had happened so quickly, and about the possibility that any of the kids from school had seen the whole display with my underpants. When I sat up straight, my jumper rode up and my bare bottom touched part of the plastic seat. Sometimes the nurse came in or out of the consulting room and I could hear my parents arguing. At one point I craned my neck and caught a glimpse of Abi squirming restlessly on one of the cots, and I knew that, at least today, she wasn't going to die. And I still had to wait.

Then a man came and sat down next to me. I don't know where he came from; I hadn't noticed him before.

"How's it going?" he asked.

I thought about saying "Very well," which is what Mom always said if someone asked her that, even if she'd just told me and Abi that we were driving her insane.

"Okay," I said.

"Are you waiting for someone?"

I thought about it. I wasn't really waiting for anyone; at least, it wasn't what I wanted to be doing right then. So I shook my head, and he said:

"Why are you sitting in the waiting room, then?"

I understood it was a great contradiction. He opened a small bag he had on his lap and rummaged around in it, unhurried. Then he took a pink slip of paper from his wallet.

"Here it is. I knew I had it somewhere."

The paper was printed with the number 92.

"It's good for an ice cream cone. My treat," he said.

I told him no. You shouldn't accept things from strangers.

"But it's free, I won it."

"No." I looked straight ahead and we sat in silence.

"Suit yourself," he said, without getting angry.

He took a magazine from his bag and started to fill in a crossword puzzle. The door to the consulting room opened again and I heard Dad say, "I will not condone such nonsense." I remember because that's Dad's clincher for ending almost any argument, but the man didn't seem to hear it.

"It's my birthday," I said.

It's my birthday, I repeated to myself. What should I do?

The man held the pen to mark a box on the puzzle and looked at me in surprise. I nodded without looking at him, aware that I had his attention again.

"But . . ." he said, and he closed the magazine. "Sometimes I just don't understand women. If it's your birthday, what are you doing in a hospital waiting room?"

He was an observant man. I straightened up again in my seat and I saw that, even then, I only came up to his shoulders. He smiled and I smoothed my hair. And then I said:

"I'm not wearing any underpants."

I don't know why I said it. It's just that it was my birthday and I wasn't wearing underpants, and I couldn't stop thinking about those circumstances. He was still looking at me. Maybe he was startled or offended, and I understood that, though it hadn't been my intention, there was something vulgar about what I had just said.

"But it's your birthday," he said.

I nodded.

"It's not fair. A person can't just go around without underpants when it's their birthday."

"I know," I said emphatically, because now I understood to what extent Abi's misbehavior had been a personal affront to me.

He sat for a moment without saying anything. Then he glanced toward the big windows that looked out onto the parking lot.

"I know where to get you some underpants," he said.

"Where?"

"Problem solved." He stowed his things and stood up.

I hesitated. Precisely because I wasn't wearing underpants, but also because I didn't know if he was telling the truth. He looked toward the front desk and waved one hand at the attendants.

"We'll be right back," he said, and pointed to me. "It's her birthday." And then I thought, *Oh please dear Jesus, don't let him say anything about my underpants*, but he didn't: he opened the door and winked at me, and then I knew I could trust him.

We went out to the parking lot. Standing, I came up to just above his waist. Dad's car was still next to the ambulances, and a policeman was circling it, annoyed. I kept looking over at the policeman, and he watched us walk away. The breeze wrapped around my legs and rose, making a tent out of my uniform skirt. I had to hold it down while I walked, keeping my legs awkwardly close together.

He turned around to see if I was following him, and he saw me fighting with my jumper.

"We'd better stick close to the wall."

"I want to know where we're going."

"Don't get persnickety with me now, darling."

We crossed the avenue and went into a shopping center. It was an uninviting place, and I was pretty sure Mom didn't go there. We walked to the back where there was a big clothing store, a truly huge one that I don't think Mom had ever set foot in, either. Before we went in he said, "Don't get lost," and gave me his hand, which was cold and very soft. He waved to the cashiers the same way he'd waved to the desk attendants when we left the hospital, but I didn't see anyone respond. We walked down the aisles. In addition to dresses, pants, and shirts, there were work clothes: hard hats, yellow overalls like the ones trash collectors wear, smocks for cleaning ladies, plastic boots, and even some tools. I wondered if he bought his clothes there and if he would use any of those things in his job, and then I also wondered what his name was.

"Here we are," he said.

We were surrounded by tables of underwear for men and women. If I reached out my hand I could touch a large bin full of giant underpants, bigger than any I'd seen before, and they were only three pesos each. With one of those pairs of underpants, they could have made three for someone of my size.

"Not those," he said. "Here." And he led me a little farther to a section with smaller sizes.

"Just look at all the underpants they have . . . Which pair shall you choose, my lady?"

I looked around a little. Almost all of them were white or pink. I pointed to a white pair, one of the few that didn't have a bow on them.

"These," I said. "But I can't pay for them."

He came a little closer and said into my ear:

"That doesn't matter."

"Are you the owner?"

"No. It's your birthday."

I smiled.

"But we have to find better ones. We need to be sure."

"Okay, darling," I ventured.

"Don't say 'darling,'" he said, "or I'll get persnickety." And he imitated me holding down my skirt in the parking lot.

He made me laugh. When he finished clowning around he held out two closed fists in front of me, and he stayed just like that until I understood; I touched the right one. He opened it: empty.

"You can still choose the other one."

I touched the other one. It took me a moment to realize it was a pair of underpants, because I had never seen black ones before. And they were for girls because they had white hearts on them, so small they looked like dots, and Hello Kitty's face was on the front, right where there was usually that bow Mom and I don't like at all.

"You'll have to try them on," he said.

I held the underpants to my chest. He gave me his hand again and we went toward the changing rooms, which looked empty. We peered inside. He said he didn't know if he could go in with me, because they were for women only. He said I would have to go alone. It was logical because, unless it's someone you know very well, it's not good for people to see you in your underpants. But I was afraid of going into the dressing room alone. Or of something worse: coming out and finding no one there.

"What's your name?" I asked.

"I can't tell you that."

"Why not?

He knelt down. Then he was almost my height, or maybe I was a couple inches taller.

"Because I'm cursed."

"Cursed? What's cursed?"

"A woman who hates me said that the next time I say my name, I'm going to die."

I thought it might be another joke, but he said it very seriously.

"You could write it down for me."

"Write it down?"

"If you wrote it you wouldn't say it, you'd be writing it. And if I know your name I can call for you and I won't be so scared to go into the dressing room alone."

"But we can't be sure. What if this woman thinks writing my name is the same as saying it? What if for her, saying it means informing someone else, letting my name out into the world in any way?"

"But how would she know?"

"People don't trust me, and I'm the unluckiest man in the world."

"I don't believe you, there's no way to know that."

"I know what I'm talking about."

Together, we looked at the underpants in my hands. I thought that my parents might be finished by now.

"But it's my birthday," I said.

And maybe I did it on purpose. At the time I felt like I did: my eyes filled with tears. Then he hugged me. It was a very fast movement; he crossed his arms behind my back and squeezed me so tight my face pressed into his chest. Then he let me go, took out his magazine and pen, and wrote something on the right edge of the cover. Then he tore it off and folded it three times before handing it to me.

"Don't read it," he said, and he stood up and pushed me gently toward the dressing room.

I passed four empty cubicles. Before gathering my courage and entering the fifth, I put the paper into my jumper pocket and turned to look at him, and we smiled at each other.

I tried on the underpants. They were perfect. I lifted up my skirt so I could see just how good they looked. They were so, so very perfect. They fit incredibly well, and because they were black, Dad would never ask me for them so he could wave them out the window behind the ambulance. And even if he did, I wouldn't be so embarrassed if my classmates saw. "Just look at the underpants that girl has," they'd all think. "Now those are some perfect underpants."

I realized I couldn't take them off now. And I realized something else: they didn't have a security tag. They had a little mark where the tag would usually go, but there was no alarm. I stood a moment longer looking at myself in the mirror, and then I couldn't stand it anymore and I took out the little paper, opened it, and read it.

I came out of the dressing room and he wasn't where I had left him, but just a little farther away, next to the bathing suits. He looked at me, and when he saw I wasn't carrying the underpants he winked, and then I was the one who took his hand. This time he clasped mine tighter and I was fine with that; together, we walked toward the exit.

I trusted that he knew what he was doing, that a cursed man who had the world's worst luck knew how to do these things. We passed the line of registers at the main entrance. One of the security guards glanced at us and adjusted his belt. He would surely think my nameless man was my dad, and I felt proud.

We passed the sensors at the exit and went into the mall, and we kept walking in silence all the way back to the avenue. That was when I saw Abi, alone, in the middle of the hospital parking lot. And I saw Mom, on our side of the street, looking around frantically. Dad was also coming toward us from the parking lot. He was following fast behind the policeman who'd been looking at our car before, and who was now pointing at us. Everything happened very fast. Dad saw us, yelled my name, and a few seconds later that policeman and two others who came out of nowhere were already on top of us. The unlucky man let go of me, but my hand hung there reaching out toward him for a few seconds. They surrounded him and shoved him roughly. They asked what he was doing, and they asked his name, but he didn't answer. Mom hugged me and checked me over from head to toe. She had my white underpants dangling from her right hand. Then, patting me all over, she noticed I was wearing a different pair. She lifted my skirt in a single movement: it was such a rude and vulgar thing to do, right there in front of everyone, that I jerked away and had to take a few steps backward to keep from falling down. The unlucky man looked at me and I looked at him. When Mom saw the black underpants she screamed, "Son of a bitch, son of a bitch," and Dad lunged at him and tried to punch him. The cops moved to separate them.

I fished for the paper in my pocket. I put it in my mouth, and as I swallowed it I repeated his name in silence, several times, so I would never forget it.

About the Contributors

Rabih Alameddine is the author of nine books, including the novels *An Unnecessary Woman* and *The True True Story of Raja the Gullible (and His Mother)*, which won the 2025 National Book Award. His books have been translated into more than twenty languages. His most recent awards include the 2019 Dos Passos Prize, the 2021 Lannan Literary Award for Fiction, and the 2022 PEN/Faulkner Award for Fiction.

Tahmima Anam is a novelist and anthropologist, and the author of the Bengal Trilogy. She is the recipient of a Commonwealth Writers' Prize and an O. Henry Award and has been named one of *Granta*'s Best Young British Novelists. She was a contributing opinion writer for *The New York Times* and was recently elected as a fellow of the Royal Society of Literature. Born in Dhaka, Bangladesh, she now lives in London, England.

Linnea Axelsson is a Sámi-Swedish writer, born in the province of North Bothnia in Sweden. In 2009, she earned a PhD in art history from Umeå University. In 2018, she was awarded the August Prize for *Ædnan*, which was also a finalist for the 2024 National Book Award for Translated Literature. She lives in Stockholm, Sweden.

Lana Bastašić is a Yugoslav-born writer. Her debut novel, *Catch the Rabbit*, won the 2020 European Union Prize for Literature. She lives in Italy.

Eric M. B. Becker is a writer, an editor, and a literary translator from Portuguese. He has earned fellowships and residencies from the National Endowment for the Arts, Fulbright, PEN America, and the Louis Armstrong House Museum. He was a finalist for the 2021 PEN Translation Prize and received an honorable mention for the Modern Language Association's Aldo and Jeanne

Scaglione Prize for Translation of a Literary Work. Becker is the cofounder of the transatlantic Pessoa Festival, and the former digital director and senior editor of *Words Without Borders*. His work has appeared in *The New York Times*, *Foreign Affairs*, *Freeman's*, and other publications.

Carol Bensimon is a Brazilian author based in Mendocino, California. She received the Jabuti Award, the most prestigious literary prize in Brazil, for her novel *O Clube dos Jardineiros de Fumaça*. Her novels *We All Loved Cowboys* and *Diorama* have been published in English.

Sarah Booker is a teacher and literary translator. Her translations include novels by Mónica Ojeda, Cristina Rivera Garza, and Gabriela Ponce. She is also an associate editor with *Southwest Review*.

Can Xue is the pseudonym of celebrated experimental writer Deng Xiaohua, born in 1953 in the city of Changsha, China. She is the author of *Vertical Motion*, *Frontier*, *Barefoot Doctor*, and *Five Spice Street*, among other books.

Ted Chiang is an American science fiction writer. His work has won four Nebula awards, four Hugo awards, six Locus awards, and the PEN/Malamud Award. His novella "Story of Your Life" was the basis for the film *Arrival*. His most recent short story collection, *Exhalation*, was listed as one of the Top Ten Books of 2019 by *The New York Times*, and included in President Barack Obama's 2019 reading list. In 2023, he was named one of *Time* magazine's 100 Most Influential People in AI.

Mia Couto, born in Beira, Mozambique, in 1955, is one of the most prominent writers in Portuguese-speaking Africa. After studying medicine and biology in Maputo, Mozambique, he worked as a journalist and headed several Mozambican national newspapers and magazines. Couto has been awarded numerous literary prizes, including the 2014 Neustadt International Prize for Literature, the Camões Prize (the most prestigious Portuguese-language award), the Prémio Vergílio Ferreira, the Prémio União Latina de Literaturas Românicas, and the FIL Literary Award in Romance Languages. He lives in Maputo, where he works as a biologist.

Edwidge Danticat is the author of numerous books, including *The Art of Death*, a National Book Critics Circle Award finalist; *Claire of the Sea Light*, a *New York Times* Notable Book of 2013; *Brother, I'm Dying*, a National Book Critics Circle Award winner and National Book Award finalist; *The Dew Breaker*, a PEN/Faulkner Award for Fiction finalist and winner of the inaugural Story Prize; *The Farming of Bones*, an American Book Award winner; *Breath, Eyes, Memory*, an Oprah's Book Club Pick; and *Krik? Krak!*, also a National Book Award finalist. She was the winner of the 2018 Neustadt International Prize for Literature and the recipient of a MacArthur Fellowship. Her latest book is *We're Alone*, which was a finalist for the National Book Critics Circle Award.

Diao Dou was born in 1960 in Shenyang, Liaoning Province, China. Since graduating from the Beijing Broadcasting Institute in 1983, he has worked as a journalist and latterly as a literary editor. Although his first book was a collection of poetry, he is best known as an author of novels and short stories. He is the author of numerous novels and story collections. In 2003, he was awarded the ninth annual Zhuang Zhongwen Prize for Literature. His first appearance in English was the collection *Points of Origin*.

Kari Dickson is an award-winning literary translator from Norwegian. Her work includes crime fiction, literary fiction, children's books, theater, and nonfiction. She has worked with the University of Edinburgh and British Centre for Literary Translation as a tutor and mentor, and served on the committee of the Translators Association (UK).

Mariana Enriquez is a writer based in Buenos Aires, Argentina. In English, she has published the novel *Our Share of Night* and three story collections, *A Sunny Place for Shady People*, *Things We Lost in the Fire*, and *The Dangers of Smoking in Bed*, which was a finalist for the International Booker Prize, the Kirkus Prize, the Ray Bradbury Prize for Science Fiction, Fantasy & Speculative Fiction, and the Los Angeles Times Book Prize.

Nona Fernández has published a variety of books, including the novels *Space Invaders* (2013), a finalist for the National Book Award, and *Chilean Electric* (2015). The novel *La Dimensión Desconocida* (2016), a finalist for the National Book Award, was endowed with the Sor Juana Inés de la Cruz Prize, granted by the Guadalajara Book Fair. Her authorial work has been acknowledged as a pivotal framework to understand the recent historical memory of her country; a window to the active process of memory regarding the critical years of the dictatorship that continue to shape Chile's current reality.

Beth Fowler has been a translator since 2009, working from Portuguese and Spanish to English. She won the Harvill Secker Young Translators' Prize in 2010. Her published translations include novels by Iosi Havilio, Marcela Serrano, Carol Bensimon, and Carmen Sereno. She lives in the west of Scotland.

Karen Gernant and Chen Zeping collaborated on translations of Chinese literary fiction from the late 1990s until Professor Chen's death in 2022. Their book-length translations of Can Xue's works include *Blue Light in the Sky*, *Five Spice Street*, *Vertical Motion*, *Frontier*, *I Live in the Slums* (longlisted for the International Booker Prize and for the National Translation Award in Prose from the American Literary Translators Association), *Purple Perilla*, *Barefoot Doctor*, and *Mother River*. Their publications also include works by Zhang Kangkang, Zhang Yihe, and Alai. Karen Gernant is professor emerita of Chinese history at Southern Oregon University. She was a recipient of Fujian Province's Friendship Award in 1999, its inaugural year. Chen Zeping, who was professor emeritus at Fujian Normal University, was highly regarded in his field of Chinese linguistics, publishing numerous books and articles, as well as receiving several prestigious research grants.

Howard Goldblatt, a Guggenheim Fellow and former academic, translates literature from China and Taiwan, most notably the novels of Nobel Prize laureate Mo Yan. Singly and with his cotranslator, Sylvia Li-chun Lin, he has introduced nearly a hundred literary works to English-language readers, garnering several awards for translated fiction.

Katharine Halls is an Arabic-to-English translator from Cardiff, Wales. Her translation of Ahmed Naji's prison memoir *Rotten Evidence* was awarded the Saif Ghobash Banipal Prize for Arabic Literary Translation and was a finalist for the National Book Critics Circle Award. Her work has appeared in *AGNI*, *The Kenyon Review*, *The Believer*, *McSweeney's*, *The Common*, *Mousse*, *Frieze*, and elsewhere.

Han Kang was born in 1970 in South Korea. She is the author of *The Vegetarian*, winner of the International Booker Prize, as well as *Human Acts*, *The White Book*, *Greek Lessons*, and *We Do Not Part*. In 2024, she was awarded the Nobel Prize in Literature.

Gwendolyn Harper is a writer and a translator of Latin American literature. She won the National Book Critics Circle's Gregg Barrios Book in Translation Prize, a National Endowment for the Arts fellowship, and a Work in Progress grant from the Robert B. Silvers Foundation for her translation of the Chilean writer Pedro Lemebel's *crónicas*.

Aleksandar Hemon was born and raised in Sarajevo, Bosnia and Herzegovina, and now lives and teaches in Princeton, New Jersey. He has written fiction, nonfiction, poetry, and screenplays. He has produced music and videos, and performs as a DJ occasionally.

Mieko Kawakami was born in Osaka, Japan. She is the author of the international bestseller *Breasts and Eggs*, a *New York Times* Notable Book of 2020, and *Heaven*, a finalist for the 2022 International Booker Prize. Her third novel, *All the Lovers in the Night*, was a finalist for the 2023 National Book Critics Circle Award. Her latest novel, *Sisters in Yellow*, will be published in English in 2026. Kawakami's books have been translated into over forty languages.

Sara Khalili is an award-winning editor and translator of contemporary Iranian literature. Her translations include *Seasons of Purgatory*, *Moon Brow*, and *Censoring an Iranian Love Story* by Shahriar Mandanipour, and *The Pomegranate Lady and Her Sons* by Goli Taraghi. Her short story translations have appeared in *AGNI*, *The Kenyon Review*, *The Virginia Quarterly Review*, *EPOCH*, *Granta*, and *Words Without Borders*, among others.

Jamaica Kincaid was born in St. John's, Antigua. Her books include *At the Bottom of the River*, *Annie John*, *Lucy*, *The Autobiography of My Mother*, *My Brother*, *Mr. Potter*, *See Now Then*, *Among Flowers*, *My Garden (Book)*, *Putting Myself Together: Writing 1974–*, and, with Kara Walker, *An Encyclopedia of Gardening for Colored Children*. She is professor emerita at Harvard University and lives in Vermont, where she is a Comedian to The Plants.

Eka Kurniawan was born in Tasikmalaya, Indonesia, in 1975. He studied philosophy at Gadjah Mada University, Yogyakarta, Indonesia. He has published several novels, including *Beauty Is a Wound* and *Man Tiger*, as well as short stories. His novels have been published in a number of languages, including English.

Pedro Lemebel (1952–2015) is considered one of the most important queer writers of twentieth-century Latin America and was also an activist and a performance artist. Born in Santiago, Chile, he became a renowned voice of Latin American counterculture during the Pinochet dictatorship and its aftermath, receiving Chile's José Donoso Prize, Germany's Anna Seghers-Preis, and a Guggenheim Fellowship. He is best known for his *crónicas* and one novel, *My Tender Matador*, which has been translated into more than a dozen languages and was adapted in 2020 into a critically acclaimed film by the Chilean director Rodrigo Sepúlveda.

Antonia Lloyd-Jones has translated works by many of Poland's leading contemporary novelists and reportage authors, as well as biographies, essays, crime fiction, poetry and children's books. Her translation of *Drive Your Plow Over* *the Bones of the Dead* by the 2018 Nobel Prize laureate Olga Tokarczuk was shortlisted for the 2019 Man Booker Prize. For ten years she was a mentor for the National Centre for Writing's Emerging Translators Mentorship Programme, and she is a former cochair of the Translators Association (UK).

Melanie Mauthner is a writer, translator, and former academic who lives in London. A Hawthornden Fellow, she won the French Voices Grand Prize in 2013 for her translation of Scholastique Mukasonga's novel *Our Lady of the Nile*. Her haibun (a Japanese form that combines prose and haiku) about learning Russian have been published in *East–West Review: The Journal of the Great Britain–Russia Society*.

Megan McDowell's translations have won the National Book Award for Translated Literature, the English PEN award, the Premio Valle-Inclán, and two O. Henry Awards, and have been nominated for the International Booker Prize (four times) and the Kirkus Prize. She is from Richmond, Kentucky, and lives between Santiago, Chile, and Barcelona, Spain.

Mo Yan (literally "don't speak") is the pen name of Guan Moye. Born in 1955 to a peasant family in Shandong Province, China, he is the author of ten novels, including *Frog* and *Red Sorghum*, which was made into a feature film; dozens of novellas; and hundreds of short stories. Mo Yan is the winner of the 2012 Nobel Prize in Literature and the 2009 Newman Prize for Chinese Literature.

Paxima Mojavezi, born in Tehran, Iran, in 1978, is an Iranian American author and journalist with a PhD in the sociology of literature. She has published four collections of short stories and two nonfiction books. She currently lives in the United States, where she continues her literary and journalistic work.

Scholastique Mukasonga was born in Rwanda in 1956. She settled in France in 1992, only two years before the brutal genocide of the Tutsi swept through Rwanda. Her groundbreaking books include the debut novel *Our Lady of the Nile*; *Cockroaches*; *Igifu*; and the National Book Award–nominated *The Barefoot Woman*, expertly translated by Jordan Stump. In 2021, she won the Simone de Beauvoir Prize for Women's Freedom.

Haruki Murakami was born in Kyoto, Japan, in 1949 and now lives near Tokyo. His work has been translated into more than fifty languages, and one of the most recent of his many international honors is the Cino Del Duca World Prize, whose previous recipients include Jorge Luis Borges, Ismail Kadare, Mario Vargas Llosa, and Joyce Carol Oates.

Marie NDiaye was born in Pithiviers, France. She is the author of many novels, including *Rosie Carpe*, winner of the Prix Femina, and *Three Strong Women*, winner of the Prix Goncourt. *Vengeance Is Mine* was a finalist for the National Book Critics Circle Award. Her most recently translated novel is *The Witch*. She lives in Paris, France.

Zanta Nkumane is a Swazi writer and journalist. He was the 2022–23 UEA Booker Prize Foundation Scholar as an MA student in creative writing at the University of East Anglia. He is an editor at *Translator Mag*.

Idra Novey is the author of the novel *Take What You Need*, which was a *New York Times* Notable Book of 2023 and a finalist for the Joyce Carol Oates Prize. Her earlier novel *Ways to Disappear* was a finalist for the Los Angeles Times Art Seidenbaum Award for First Fiction. She has published several collections of poems and translated the work of numerous authors, including Clarice Lispector, Manoel de Barros, and Garous Abdolmalekian.

Brendan O'Kane spent a decade in Beijing, China, working mostly as a freelance translator and the cohost of the Mandarin-learning podcast *Popup Chinese*. He lives in Philadelphia, Pennsylvania.

Gunnhild Øyehaug is the author of thirteen books, including *Evil Flowers*, *Present Tense Machine*, *Knots*, and *Wait, Blink*. Her latest novel in Norwegian, *Here Comes the Sun*, was published in 2024, and in 2025 her *Collected Stories* appeared. Øyehaug lives in Bergen, Norway, where she teaches creative writing.

Cristina Rivera Garza is the award-winning author of *The Taiga Syndrome*, *The Iliac Crest*, and *Death Takes Me*, among many other books. Her memoir, *Liliana's Invincible Summer*, won a Pulitzer Prize and was a finalist for the National Book Award. A recipient of the MacArthur Fellowship and the Sor Juana Inés de la Cruz Prize, Rivera Garza is the Hugh Roy and Lillie Cranz Cullen Distinguished Chair and director of the PhD program in creative writing in Spanish at the University of Houston.

Jay Rubin is well known for his translations of Haruki Murakami's works. He received his PhD in Japanese literature from the University of Chicago and is the Professor of Japanese Literature Emeritus at Harvard University.

Salman Rushdie is the bestselling author of twenty-three books, including *Midnight's Children*, for which he won the Booker Prize and the Best of the Booker. His most recent book is *The Eleventh Hour: A Quintet of Stories*. His previous book, *Knife: Meditations After an Attempted Murder*, was a finalist for the 2024 National Book Award for Nonfiction.

Samanta Schweblin won the 2022 National Book Award for Translated Literature for her story collection *Seven Empty Houses*. Her debut novel, *Fever Dream*, was shortlisted for the International Booker Prize, and her novel *Little Eyes* and story collection *Mouthful of Birds* were both longlisted for the same prize. Her latest book is *Good and Evil and Other Stories*. Originally from Buenos Aires, Argentina, Schweblin lives in Berlin, Germany.

Adania Shibli, born in Palestine in 1974, writes novels, plays, short stories, and narrative essays. Her latest novel, *Minor Detail,* was published in the United States in 2020, in a translation by Elisabeth Jacquette, and has been translated into many languages. *Minor Detail* was a finalist for the National Book Award and longlisted for the 2021 International Booker Prize.

Deborah Smith is a British translator of Korean fiction. She ran Tilted Axis Press from 2015 to 2022.

Rawaa Sonbol is a Syrian author of short fiction, theater, and children's literature. She has published three short-story collections: *The Tongue Hunter* (2017), which received the Sharjah Award for Arab Creativity; *The Green Dragon's Wife and Other Colorful Stories* (2019); and most recently *Do, Yek* (2023), which was shortlisted for the 2024 Almultaqa Prize. She lives in Damascus, Syria, where she works as a pharmacist.

Frank Stock was born and schooled in Rhodesia (now Zimbabwe) to parents who were refugees from Germany. In 1964, he left the country to attend university in the United Kingdom and was called to the bar in 1968. He went to Hong Kong in 1978, where from 1986 to 1991 he was solicitor general, and then was appointed to the High Court bench. He retired from full-time judging in 2014.

Christopher Stone is an associate professor of Arabic at Hunter College. He conducts research on Arab popular culture and is the author of *Popular Culture and Nationalism in Lebanon: The Fairouz Rahbani Nation*. He has translated literary texts by Najwan Darwish, Adania Shibli, and Muin Bseiso for publication.

Jordan Stump, a professor at the University of Nebraska–Lincoln, has published some thirty translations of novels from French, including works by Marie Redonnet, Eric Chevillard, Marie NDiaye, and Scholastique Mukasonga. His translation of Claude Simon's *The Jardin des Plantes* (2001) was awarded the French-American Foundation's Annual Translation Prize in 2001, and in 2006 he was named Chevalier de l'Ordre des Arts et des Lettres. In 2020, he was awarded the National Translation Award in Prose from the American Literary Translators Association for NDiaye's *The Cheffe*.

Abdellah Taïa was born in Rabat, Morocco, in 1973, and has written many novels, including *Salvation Army*, which he also made into an award-winning film, and *Infidels*. He lives in Paris, France.

Colm Tóibín is the author of eleven novels, including *The Master* and *Brooklyn*, as well as several books of criticism and three story collections, the latest of which is *The News from Dublin*. He is the Irene and Sidney B. Silverman Professor of the Humanities at Columbia University and was named the 2022–24 Laureate for Irish Fiction by the Arts Council of Ireland. He has been awarded the Bodley Medal, the Würth Prize for European Literature, and the Prix Femina spécial for his body of work.

Olga Tokarczuk has won the Nobel Prize in Literature and the Man Booker International Prize, among many other honors. She is the author of a dozen works of fiction, two collections of essays, and two children's books; her work has been translated into more than fifty languages.

Annie Tucker is a writer and translator of Indonesian literature.

Saskia Vogel is the author of the novel *Permission* (2019) and the deputy editor of the British arts-and-literature biannual *Erotic Review*. She is an award-winning translator of over two dozen Swedish-language books, including Linnea Axelsson's *Ædnan* (2024), a finalist for the National Book Award.

Zoë Wicomb (1948–2025) was a South African writer who lived in Glasgow, Scotland, where she was professor emeritus at the University of Strathclyde. She is the author of *You Can't Get Lost in Cape Town*, *Still Life*, *October*, *The One That Got Away*, and *Playing in the Light*, as well as *David's Story*. She was an inaugural winner of the Windham-Campbell Prize in fiction.

Hitomi Yoshio is the translator of Natsuko Imamura's *This Is Amiko, Do You Copy?* and cotranslator of Mieko Kawakami's *Ashes of Spring* and *Sisters in Yellow*. Her short story translations have appeared in *Granta*, *Freeman's*, *Words Without Borders*, *Monkey*, *World Literature Today*, and *The Penguin Book of Japanese Short Stories*. She received her PhD from Columbia University in New York and is a professor of global Japanese studies at Waseda University in Tokyo, Japan.

Credits

"Super-Frog Saves Tokyo" from *After the Quake: Stories* by Haruki Murakami, translated by Jay Rubin, copyright © 2000 by Harukimurakami Archival Labyrinth. Originally published by Shinchosha Publishing Co., Ltd. English translation copyright © 2002 by Harukimurakami Archival Labyrinth. Used by permission of Alfred A. Knopf, an imprint of the Knopf Doubleday Publishing Group, a division of Penguin Random House LLC. All rights reserved.

"The Illumination of Santiago," an extract from *Chilean Electric* by Nona Fernández, translated by Idra Novey, copyright © 2015 by Alqumia Ediciones and Nona Fernández. Translation copyright © 2015 by Idra Novey. Reproduced by permission of Nona Fernández c/o ampimargini Literary Agency and Idra Novey.

"Apples" by Gunnhild Øyehaug, translated by Kari Dickson, extract copyright © Gunnhild Øyehaug. Translation copyright © Kari Dickson. Reproduced by permission of Gunnhild Øyehaug c/o Rogers, Coleridge & White Ltd., 20 Powis Mews, London W11 1JN and Kari Dickson.

"My Sad Dead" from *A Sunny Place for Shady People: Stories* by Mariana Enriquez, translated by Megan McDowell, copyright © 2024 by Mariana Enriquez. English translation copyright © 2024 by Megan McDowell. Used by permission of Hogarth, an imprint of Random House, a division of Penguin Random House LLC. All rights reserved.

"War of the Clowns" from *Rain and Other Stories* by Mia Couto, in a translation by Eric M. B. Becker, copyright © 1994 by Mia Couto. Translation copyright © 2019 by Eric M. B. Becker. Reprinted by permission of Biblioasis.

"One Minus One" from *The Empty Family: Stories* by Colm Tóibín, copyright © 2010, 2011 by Colm Tóibín. Reprinted with the permission of Penguin Books Limited and Scribner, an imprint of Simon & Schuster LLC. All rights reserved.

"The Flower Garden" by Mieko Kawakami, translated by Hitomi Yoshio. Reproduced by permission of Mieko Kawakami, c/o Creative Artists Agency and Hitomi Yoshio.

"Night Women" from *Krik? Krak!* by Edwidge Danticat, copyright © 1991, 1995 by Edwidge Danticat. Reprinted by permission of Soho Press, Inc. All rights reserved.

"The July War" by Rabih Alameddine was first published in *The Paris Review*. Reprinted by permission of Rabih Alameddine and Aragi Inc. All rights reserved.

"Cattle Praise Song" by Scholastique Mukasonga, translated by Melanie Mauthner, copyright © 2010 by Editorial Gallimard. English language translation © 2018 by Melanie Mauthner. Printed by permission of the publisher, Archipelago Books.

"Garments" by Tahmima Anam, copyright © 2016 by Tahmima Anam, first published in *Freeman's*. Used by permission of The Wylie Agency LLC.

"Rotten Stench" from *Kitchen Curse* by Eka Kurniawan, translated by Annie Tucker. Reproduced by permission of Verso Books UK.

"Amira Who Knows" by Rawaa Sonbol, translated by Katharine Halls, copyright © 2023 by Rawaa Sonbol. English translation copyright © 2024 by Katharine Halls. This story was originally published in Arabic in the collection *Do, Yek* (Mamdouh Adwan Publishing House, 2023). Reprinted by permission of Rawaa Sonbol and Katharine Halls.

"Petite Mort" by Zanta Nkumane, reproduced by permission of the author.

"Girl" from *At the Bottom of the River* by Jamaica Kincaid. Copyright © 1978, 1979, 1981, 1982, 1983 by Jamaica Kincaid, used by permission of The Wylie Agency LLC.

"The Fruit of My Woman" by Han Kang, translated by Deborah Smith, extract copyright © Han Kang. Translation copyright © Deborah Smith. Reproduced by permission of the author c/o Rogers, Coleridge & White Ltd., 20 Powis Mews, London W11 1JN and Deborah Smith.

"Vertical Motion" from *Vertical Motion* by Can Xue, translated by Karen Gernant and Chen Zeping, copyright © 2011 by Can Xue. Translation copyright © 2011 by Karen Gernant and Chen Zeping. *Vertical Motion* is published by Open Letter Books at the University of Rochester. Reprinted by permission of Open Letter Books at the University of Rochester.

"You Can't Get Lost in Cape Town" by Zoë Wicomb, copyright © 1987 by Zoë Wicomb. Used by permission of Feminist Press.

"Squatting" from *Points of Origin* by Diao Dou, translated by Brendan O'Kane. Published by Comma Press. Reprinted by permission of Comma Press.

"Sparks" by Carol Bensimon, translated by Beth Fowler. Reproduced by permission of Transit Books.

"Exhalation" by Ted Chiang, copyright © 2008 by Ted Chiang. Reprinted by permission from the author.

"The Ugliest Woman in the World" by Olga Tokarczuk, translated by Antonia Lloyd-Jones, extract copyright © Olga Tokarczuk. Translation copyright © Antonia Lloyd-Jones. Reproduced by permission of Olga Tokarczuk c/o Rogers, Coleridge & White Ltd., 20 Powis Mews, London W11 1JN, and Antonia Lloyd-Jones.

"The Good Denis" from *Le Bon Denis* by Marie NDiaye, translated by Jordan Stump, copyright © 2025 by Mercure de France. Translation copyright © 2025 by Jordan Stump. Reprinted by permission of Mercure de France.

"Frogs," an excerpt from *Frog: A Novel* by Mo Yan, translated by Howard Goldblatt, copyright © 2009 by Mo Yan. English translation copyright © 2014 by Penguin (Beijing) Ltd. Used by permission of Viking Books, an imprint of Penguin Publishing Group, a division of Penguin Random House LLC. All rights reserved.

"On the Occasion of Our Fourth Divorce Anniversary" by Lana Bastašić. Reprinted by permission of the author.

"Loba Lamar's Last Kiss" from *A Last Supper of Queer Apostles: Selected Essays* by Pedro Lemebel, translated by Gwendolyn Harper, *La esquina es mi corazón* copyright © 1995 by Pedro Lembel. *Loco afán: Crónicas de sidario* copyright © 1996, 2020 by Pedro Lembel. *Poco hombre* copyright © 2013 by Pedro Lemebel. English translation copyright © 2024 by Gwendolyn Harper. Used by permission of Pushkin Press and Penguin Classics, an imprint of Penguin Publishing Group, a division of Penguin Random House LLC. All rights reserved.

"The Free Radio" from *East, West: Stories* by Salman Rushdie, copyright © 1994 by Salman Rushdie. Used by permission of The Wylie Agency LLC and Pantheon Books, an imprint of the Knopf Doubleday Publishing Group, a division of Penguin Random House LLC. All rights reserved.

"The Wounded Man" by Abdellah Taïa, translated by Frank Stock. Reprinted by permission of Abdellah Taïa.

"Forty-Eight Steps" by Paxima Mojavezi, translated by Sara Khalili. Reprinted by permission of Paxima Mojavezi and Sara Khalili.

Excerpt from *Magnificat* by Linnea Axelsson, translated by Saskia Vogel. Reprinted by permission of First Edition MGMT and Saskia Vogel.

"An Ambitious Good-Hearted Leftist" by Adania Shibli, translated by Christopher Stone, copyright © Adania Shibli. Translation copyright © Christopher Stone. Reproduced by permission of Adania Shibli c/o Rogers, Coleridge & White Ltd., 20 Powis Mews, London W11 1JN and Christopher Stone.

"Islands" from *The Question of Bruno* by Aleksandar Hemon, copyright © 2000 by Aleksandar Hemon. Published in the UK by Picador, a division of Macmillan Publishers International Limited. Reproduced by permission of Macmillan Publishers International and Nan A. Talese, an imprint of the Knopf Doubleday Publishing Group, a division of Penguin Random House LLC. All rights reserved.

"Offside" from *New and Selected Stories* by Cristina Rivera Garza, translated by Sarah Booker, copyright © Cristina Rivera Garza. English translation copyright © 2022 by Sarah Booker. Used by permission of The Wylie Agency LLC and Sarah Booker.

"An Unlucky Man" from *Seven Empty Houses* by Samanta Schweblin, translated by Megan McDowell, copyright © 2015 by Samanta Schweblin. English translation copyright © 2022 by Megan McDowell. Used by permission of Oneworld Publications Ltd. and Penguin Books, an imprint of Penguin Publishing Group, a division of Penguin Random House LLC. All rights reserved.